BECOMING *Mary*

BY

AMY STREET

Published in the United Kingdom 2015 by Amy Street

EBook ISBN: 978-0-9932799-1-1

Paperback ISBN: 978-0-9932799-0-4

Part One: The Visit to Pemberley

◆

My Uncle Philips had been at the point of death for so many months, that I could not understand why Mama was so shocked by the tidings that he had died at last. When the express came from Meryton that evening, her wailing could be heard all over the house. Kitty came into the music room where I was playing the piano.

"Mary! Stop that dreadful noise and come into the parlour!" she said. "Do you not realise that Uncle Philips has died?"

"Of course I do!"

"Well then, I would have thought that even you would have had more consideration than to carry on playing. Come through at once and help with Mama!"

I did not understand why she was so vexed; I had deliberately chosen a piece in a minor key to provide a fitting accompaniment.

"I am helping!" I said. "'Whoever sings songs to a heavy heart is like one who takes off a garment on a cold day'." I was not precisely sure what this meant but I had memorised a number of suitable quotations in preparation for my uncle's death.

"Don't be ridiculous! You are making it worse! Now stop talking nonsense and come into the parlour to comfort Mama!"

Mama was laid upon the sofa, alternately wiping and fanning her face with her handkerchief, emitting sobs and groans. Papa was by the fireplace, his expression one of boredom and impatience.

"Ah, Mary," he said, "I have bad news. Your Uncle Philips has died, and your mother is distraught. But now that you are here, I am sure you will be a great comfort. No doubt you have any number of epigrams concerning loss and the afterlife at your disposal?"

"I do," I replied, pleased to be able to oblige. "'The sting of death is sin, and the power of sin is the law'." As my uncle had been an attorney this seemed apt.

Papa stared at me, then sighed. "You must excuse me," he said. "I will leave you. A man is never much use in these situations. Mary, Kitty, take care of your mother."

With this he returned to his library. Kitty and I stood apart while Mama continued to sob.

"My poor sister!" she cried. "How she will feel this! Such a dreadful shock to us all!"

"But he has been ill these past six months, Mama, and we have expected him to die all week," I said reasonably.

"Oh, you have no sensibility, Mary!" Mama snapped. "I must go to your aunt, but I am too overset. No, I must go at once. Kitty, ring for Hill and ask her to pack whatever should be needful."

"You will not go tonight, Mama?" Kitty said. "Shall we not send a message, and then you can go in the morning?"

"No, no, of course not, for who should help lay out your uncle's body but myself? Do not be forever questioning me, Kitty! I have enough to distress me without that."

Kitty rang the bell and then threw herself down onto a chair.

"Don't just stand there, Mary!" my mother said. "Speak to your father and tell him I shall need the carriage immediately."

I went to do her bidding. Papa was not pleased to be interrupted in his library. He was reading a periodical and sipping port, and wearily obeyed my mother's command. When I returned to the parlour Kitty was alone.

"I suppose I shall not be able to go to Pemberley after all this summer," she said crossly. "No doubt Mama will need me."

"I do not see why," I said. "I am sure I can be just as much of a comfort to her as you."

Kitty laughed. "You? I hardly think so! No, depend upon it; I shall be trapped here all summer, with nobody to keep me company now that Maria Lucas is flirting with John Summerton. How bored I shall be, with nothing but death and funerals to talk of!"

"Perhaps if you embarked on a course of study as I do, you would not be so bored!"

"No, I thank you! I would rather die of boredom than become a bore myself!"

"There is nothing boring about having a well-informed mind!" I retorted.

"As you do not have a well-informed mind, you cannot pronounce on the matter."

"I know more than you!"

"But what do you know of any use? Nobody is interested in your sayings or your piano playing. Papa thinks you are just as silly as me, despite all your book-learning. You cannot sew; last time you tried, you cut through Mama's best tablecloth! And you know nothing of housekeeping or entertaining."

"At least I do not flirt!"

"Please, dear sister, promise me you will never attempt to do so! I could not bear the mortification of seeing you try."

This was going the way of all my conversations with Kitty, so I went to my chamber. I heard the carriage draw up outside the house, and soon Mama was gone and all was quiet.

We heard very little from her over the next few days. Papa went to the funeral and brought news that my mother was looking after my aunt, who was prostrated with grief. Kitty was impatient to hear from our sister Elizabeth at Pemberley, and drove me mad with her fretting. Every day she asked our father if there had been a letter from Elizabeth, but it was not until some two weeks had passed since Uncle Philips's death that a letter came.

"Well, Kitty," my father said at breakfast, "you have had your wish. Your sister has invited you to Pemberley again this summer. Why she should desire your company I cannot imagine, but I do not complain, and at least if you embarrass yourself while you are there, I shall not have to witness it. Still, I am hopeful to be spared any further blows to our family's reputation, as I gather there is no militia stationed in the area at this time."

Kitty ignored the greater part of this speech and clapped her hands.

"Thank goodness! I am going to Pemberley! I shall not have to spend the summer with only Mary for company. Oh, how happy I shall be!"

"Defer your transports for a moment, Kitty; your sister Mary is to accompany you."

"What?" we both said, equally horrified.

"Perhaps I did not express myself clearly enough. Mrs Darcy requests the pleasure of your company, Mary, as well as Kitty's. You have not yet been to Pemberley, I believe."

"But I do not wish to go, Papa!"

"Please do not let her go, Papa!" Kitty cried. "She will ruin everything."

"This does not show sisterly devotion, Kitty."

"I care nothing for that! Mary would much rather stay at Longbourn, would not you, Mary?"

"Indeed I would!" I said, for once in agreement with my sister. "I do not have to go, do I, Papa?"

"I am afraid so, Mary. Your mother will be staying with your aunt Philips for some time now, and she wrote particularly to Elizabeth begging her to ask you. It is a most flattering invitation, you should be grateful."

"But Lizzy does not want me! And I should be much happier at Longbourn!"

"And I should be much happier to have Longbourn to myself for a few weeks!" Papa said, standing up. "You will leave on Saturday week. Mr Darcy is to send a servant to meet you at Hertford, and I suppose we could spare our carriage to take you that far."

He left the room, signalling that there was nothing more to be said on the matter.

"Oh! It is too infuriating!" Kitty cried, with tears starting to her eyes. "I do not want you to come to Pemberley, it is all spoiled now. You will destroy everything! And do not think to be friends with Georgiana Darcy! She is *my* particular friend and she will not be interested in you."

"I have no wish to be friends with her! I have no wish to go to Pemberley! I would much prefer to stay with Mama and be of assistance to her."

"You might as well come, for all the help you would be to Mama! Oh, it is so vexing! And no doubt you will be playing the piano forever and mooning about the library. All my pleasure is destroyed!"

"You need not think I will get in your way. It is just as irksome to me as to you. I have no desire to be with you all summer, or with Lizzy."

"Well, she does not want you either. She only invites you under duress."

It was true: Lizzy had never invited me before, and I did not see why I should go now. I was sure Mama would prefer me to attend to her in her grief: surely a mother would need her daughter at this time, and I was her eldest daughter now that Jane and Elizabeth were both married, so it was my place to be with our mother. And I knew that Elizabeth did not really want me. My sisters did not value me. They took no notice of me when I tried to correct them, even though I had studied many texts relating to the proper conduct of young ladies. And now I was to be sent to Pemberley to be ignored and mocked, once again to be overlooked and unappreciated. Well, there was nothing for it. I must obey my parents and accept my fate with Christian resignation.

◆

"Dearest Mama,
This is the first opportunity I have had of writing to you since we left Longbourn, and I trust you and my father are in good health, and that my aunt is not too troublesome in her grief. Mr Darcy is not here but Lizzy says I can get a frank for this from his steward. As you can see we are safe

arrived at Pemberley, and I have been put in the Chinese room which is so called because of the wallpaper, which is green and decorated with birds and flowers in the Chinese style, according to my sister. It is very large, as is the whole of Pemberley. I asked Elizabeth how she could live in such a house, but she just laughed and made out that the housekeeper had taught her how to go on. I would not be surprised if this were true, as I remember you saying that you thought Lizzy was overly familiar with her servants and that no good could come of it.

Our journey passed without incident. Mr Darcy's carriage was very comfortable but it was most extravagant of Lizzy to send a groom as well as the driver to accompany us. However, it is not for me to criticise. Of course I would not have minded travelling post, as I am not one to complain about a little discomfort.

Another time, Mama, I wish you would speak to Kitty. I do not know why she must face forward and take up a whole seat in the carriage, while I must face backwards which she knows makes me carriage-sick. And if she writes to you to say that I snored when we stayed at the inn at R___, then she is lying, because how could I have snored when I was awake all night listening to the noise she was making herself? When I finally did drop off it was only for a moment or two before the maid came to light the fire.

Derbyshire, I confess, is everything that I have heard it to be. I would have enjoyed my first views more if Kitty had not pointed out every landmark and village with an anecdote and other unnecessary displays of knowledge. I suppose that she is so unused to having any knowledge at all to display in my company that she must use her rare opportunities. You will be relieved to know that I informed her that is unbecoming in a young lady to be constantly boasting about her friendship with elevated people such as Georgiana Darcy. Fortunately, Georgiana has gone away to her aunt, Lady Catherine, for three weeks, otherwise I would have had to tolerate Kitty's raptures, which are tedious. As it is, everyone praises Georgiana Darcy to the skies. I am told that she would like to play piano duets with me when she returns from Rosings, but I am sure I will not be able to keep up with such a paragon. I do think too much praise of a young woman's talents will make her conceited. I certainly would not expect such constant admiration, or wish for it. I told Eliza that I am still practising, and she said that Georgiana has offered me the use of her pianoforte, and looked at me in a way that I did not understand. Perhaps she was warning me not to be in the way. I shall take advantage of Georgiana's absence to practise, and I also intend to recommence my studies when I have found the library here, which is supposed to be so fine.

You asked me particularly for news of little William Darcy. I am pleased to report that he is quite well, only somewhat quiet. Elizabeth brought him to meet us when we arrived, and he clung to her skirts and would not speak. Lizzy says he is shy, but if she indulges his shyness by cuddling him and letting him bury his head in her shoulder, how is he to learn to go on in society? After all, he is two years old now.

I am afraid that Lizzy does not look her best. Her hair was not well-dressed, and she seemed to think that having just come from bidding farewell to Mr Darcy, who has escorted his sister to Kent, was excuse enough for her lack of care for her appearance. I would have thought that with the multitude of servants she can afford to employ now that she is mistress of Pemberley, one of them might have dressed her hair for her before she came to greet her sisters. Still, she is in good health, and I suppose that is more important than anything. I will write again soon.

With all my affection to you and Papa, Your daughter Mary."

Once I had finished my letter, the day was spent in rest after our journey. I had brought some improving books with me, and was happy to read in my bedchamber. On the second morning, Elizabeth received a letter from Mr Darcy to say that he would return later that day. I thought that she looked particularly at me when she told us the news.

"What is the matter, Lizzy?" I asked. "Is all well with Mr Darcy?"

"Yes, of course. He says he has met with Colonel Fitzwilliam who will be coming to visit us soon. The colonel often comes here in the summer months."

"I remember Colonel Fitzwilliam from your wedding!" said Kitty. "He is quite a handsome man."

"He is certainly a very agreeable man, and always a pleasant addition to our family party."

"Shall you give a ball while we are here, Lizzy? You always do, and it would be a dreadful shame if you didn't."

BECOMING MARY • 7

"I think we shall. We have had a ball here every summer since I married. Now you put me in mind of it, Kitty, I think we should decide on a date. I will talk to Mr Darcy about it when he returns. I must speak to Mrs Reynolds about the matter of bedrooms."

She stood up to go, then turned to me. "Mary, you have not tried Georgiana's piano yet. Do go after you've had breakfast. I will instruct Thomas to open it up for you."

"Thank you, Lizzy, I shall."

"If there is to be a ball," said Kitty after Lizzy had left us, "then I must think about a dress. I have worn the same dress for the last two assemblies in Meryton, and it is time I had something new. We shall go to Lambton and look in the drapers there for material. Let us ask Lizzy when we might have the carriage."

"You may go, but I do not need a new dress. My blue dress will do perfectly well."

Kitty snorted. "No it won't, Mary! It is well enough for Meryton but it will not do for a ball at Pemberley. "

"You know I do not care for such things."

"Well, you should care for them! You will never be a beauty but you could certainly make more of yourself - you might even look passably pretty if you but made an effort."

"Thank you for the compliment, Kitty! But a woman has no need to be even passably pretty unless she is trying to attract the attention of a man with a view to marriage, and as you know, I have no such ambition."

"You only say that because you know you never *could* attract the attention of a man! You would rather pretend you do not want a man."

"I assure you it is no pretence," I said calmly. "The life of the mind is where my interest lies. That, and bearing Mama company when I am needed."

"But you do not want to be an old maid! When the Collinses inherit Longbourn and you are turned out of our home, will you want to live alone? Fifty pounds will not go very far, you know."

"I am sure I shall manage very well. And my sisters will not wholly cast me off, I believe."

"Well, *I* should not want to be hanging off my sisters all my life. And nor should you."

"We can never agree on this subject, Kitty."

"At least buy some new trimming and furbish up the dress a little! It would be shameful to appear so countrified and unfashionable as you normally do. I will do it for you myself if you will not."

"If you insist, Kitty, I give you leave. I am no seamstress anyway."

Kitty leant back in her chair with a sigh. "At last! A glimmer of sense!"

"I think I have quite enough sense for both of us, I thank you."

Kitty went off to the nursery to play with William, and I, as instructed by Lizzy, went up to the room where the piano was. It was in a large drawing-room of great grandeur and elegance, very different from our own cosy morning-room at Longbourn. I knew Mama would have said that it would be very cold in winter, despite the enormous fireplace.

The instrument was open and for a while I simply looked at it, admiring the gleaming dark wood of the casing, stroking the carved music stand and the creamy ivory keys, not yellow or cracked like our piano at home. I tried a few notes: the sound was sweet and true, no ugly twangs or broken strings. No wonder Georgiana's playing was so admired with such a piano at her disposal! Even the stool was something out of the ordinary, more of a bench than a stool, big enough for two and upholstered in a silver damask that matched the fittings in the rest of the room.

I opened the piano stool and found a pile of music. There were pieces by Handel, Telemann, Mozart and Haydn and some Italian composers whose names I did not know. Near the top of the pile was a piano duet by Mozart: this must be the one Lizzy had meant that Georgiana would like to play with me. I took it out, thinking it would be as well to have a look at it; I knew I was Georgiana's equal, but I did not want her to have too much of a start on me.

I started playing the upper part and was surprised at how difficult it was. Perhaps it was the unfamiliar keyboard but my fingers were particularly clumsy and awkward – I was sure the keys were a different size to our old-fashioned instrument. I tried one of my old pieces from memory, but even this did not flow well. It must be that the travelling and the few days without playing had made me stiff and rusty.

The next piece I found was an aria from one of Handel's operas with many trills and difficult passages, but it did not go too high or too low and I thought if I were to learn it, it would make a great impression. I started singing, playing the tune at the same time. Certain vulgar and insulting comments made by my younger sisters about my singing came unbidden to my mind, something about a cow mooing to be milked, but I knew better than to take any notice of them. Next I tried an aria by Gluck. I had sung it before at a party in Hertfordshire, and it was a particular favourite of mine. I remembered that my performance had been much praised by Lady Lucas.

◆

I was so involved in what I was doing that I was surprised when the door opened. I stopped abruptly and stood up. A man came into the room. He was tall and slender, with untidy black hair, thick dark brows and exceedingly dark eyes. He had rather strong features, but I thought he was not an ill-looking man. His clothes were plain except for a small gold pin that held his neckcloth in place.

"I beg your pardon," he said, bowing slightly, "I did not mean to interrupt, but I heard the sound of singing and came to see who it was."

"Who are you?" I asked, surprised into bluntness.

"My name is Signor Antonio Moretti. I have just arrived at Pemberley with Mr Darcy. We have driven down from London."

"Oh! With Mr Darcy! I did not know he was returned to Pemberley so soon! Are you – are you come for a visit?"

"Yes, I am to stay for the summer, for two or three months perhaps."

"I see." I did not see at all, but I did not know what to say. He had a most penetrating gaze: his eyes seemed to bore into me expecting a response, and it disconcerted me.

"Moretti!" I attempted at last, "Is that – is that an Italian name? Your voice does not sound Italian."

"Yes, it is confusing, is it not! I was born here and have lived in England all my life, so it is not so very surprising that I sound English. My grandparents came to live in London many years ago."

After a moment he added, "I am guessing that you must be Miss Mary Bennet. Mrs Darcy has told me that you are the musician of the family."

"Yes, that is correct," I said, seeing no need for modesty or pretence.

"Well, how do you do. I am a musician also, that is my work in London, at the opera mostly."

I thought it was strange that the Darcys should invite a musician to stay at Pemberley as a guest. Perhaps he was here to provide entertainment, but if that was so, why would he have travelled with Mr Darcy, and be wandering freely around the house instead of being confined to the servants' quarters?

"What do you do at the opera?" I asked politely. "Are you a singer?"

"I am a pianist like yourself," he replied, coming over to the piano and starting to leaf through the pile of music I had placed on the stand. "I teach the singers and sometimes I conduct the performances, or play violin in the orchestra when I am not needed to conduct."

I was secretly impressed, but I did not want to show it. No doubt he already thought he was rather fine, with his Italian name and his violin playing.

"I have often been told by our neighbour in Hertfordshire, Sir William Lucas, that I could have done very well as an opera singer," I said, "but my mama would not permit it."

He smiled. "I hope you will do me the honour of letting me hear you sing."

"Very likely. I am usually called upon to sing and play for the entertainment of the company."

He picked up the Mozart piano duet. "Have you been playing this? Would you like to try it?"

I jumped. "What, now?"

"Yes, now, why not?"

I did not know how to answer him. Nobody – certainly no man – had ever suggested such a thing to me. I was sure it was not proper.

"I have not practised it!" I said.

His eyes were glinting. "Nor have I, but that will make it all the more amusing."

"Sir," I said breathlessly, "I – I am not accustomed to duets, or playing at sight."

There was a pause. His expression became more serious as he looked at me searchingly.

"Very well," he said after a few moments, "perhaps at a later date, when you have had a chance to practise, we might give it a try."

I nodded. I was glad he did not press me. I did not think I would play with him. After all, he was a professional musician, and although I did not doubt my ability, he would probably despise anyone who was not of his world. He continued leafing through the music, until he came to the Handel aria I had been trying.

"I thought I heard you singing Handel earlier," he said. "You are fond of Handel?"

"Yes, I am fond of Handel," I said. It was unusual for me to be asked my opinion, but since he wished to know, I carried on. "Some people say he is old-fashioned, but I do not think one should be swayed by the excitement of the new, when it may be just a passing fad, and when it has not stood the test of time. Handel's music has great gravity and depth."

Signor Moretti bowed his head to me. "You are, I perceive, a woman of taste. That is, you agree with me."

This surprised a laugh out of me. "You are very sure of your own opinion!"

He smiled. "Only as much as anyone. After all, who else's opinion could I be sure of? But Miss Bennet, have you heard any of the new operas that are currently taking London by storm? Rossini's operas are very popular, and even a purist such as yourself may find them rather attractive and enjoyable. They are very comic, too. I believe he may become the most popular composer of the our century, just as Handel was of the last."

I had never heard of Rossini. "You must forgive me, Signor Moretti," I said stiffly, "but I am afraid I am rather faithful in my tastes and opinions. I do not give them up on a whim. I have been taught that the most sublime and interesting compositions are those which convey sentiments that are elevated and virtuous."

"Oh, I quite agree with you," he replied, "But listen to this!" and he sat beside me at the piano and started to play and sing.

At first I could hardly pay attention to the music, as I was surprised to be suddenly sitting on the piano bench with him. I had not hitherto been so close to a man as he sang, and his voice vibrated through me in a most peculiar way. The song was in Italian, rather slow but with a simple melody that flowed. Signor Moretti's voice was not strong, though it was true and pleasant on the ear. After a few moments, I stopped thinking about anything and found myself falling into a reverie. Abruptly he stopped and turned his head, startling me.

"Well? What is your opinion?"

I did not know what to say. I was somewhat dazed, and again he had surprised me by wishing to know my opinion.

"It is very pretty," I said. "Is it an Italian folk song?"

"No, it is by Giordani, from one of his operas. It is not as difficult as Rossini, or the Handel that you were playing earlier, but it is, as you say, very pretty. Would you like to learn it? I can send to London for the music and it would be here directly."

"I?"

He nodded. "I could play the piano part, then you could concentrate on the singing."

"I do not know if I wish to learn it. And anyway, I am perfectly capable of accompanying myself," I said.

"No doubt, but it does make it easier to improve if you are only concentrating on one element of the music at a time."

I wondered why he thought I needed to improve my performance, and was about to ask him, when the door opened, and Elizabeth came in, followed by Mr Darcy. Signor Moretti and I both stood quickly, as though caught out, although there was nothing improper in what we had been doing, so I did not know why I should act guilty.

I had forgotten how very tall and imposing Mr Darcy was. I had not seen him since Lizzy's wedding: although Lizzy had visited us at Longbourn since their marriage, Mr Darcy had not. He did not look as grave as I remembered him, but he was as strikingly handsome. I curtsied, and Mr Darcy bowed politely, and then came forward to shake my hand.

"How do you do, Mary. And I see you have already met Signor Moretti," he said. "I hope you are settling in to Pemberley."

"Yes, thank you," I replied, feeling shy. "It is so much larger than I am accustomed to, but I am starting to find my way around the house."

"I mean to take Mary and Kitty for a drive tomorrow," Lizzy said, turning to her husband. "If the weather continues to improve, it will be a wonderful time to see the park just as summer gets under way."

"Signor Moretti and I have been talking about music," I said, rather clumsily, still feeling that I should explain our tête-a-tête.

"Oh, good!" Lizzy cried. "I was going to bring him to you, but he has saved me the trouble. Signor Moretti used to be Georgiana's music teacher, you know. He gave her piano and singing lessons until a year or two ago."

"Oh! Is Georgiana to have music lessons when she returns?" I asked, thinking that this might explain the presence of a musician as a guest at Pemberley.

Elizabeth hesitated, then spoke in something of a rush. "No, Mary. We have asked Signor Moretti here because - because we thought *you* might enjoy the benefit of his teaching."

I was completely taken aback, and did not know how to answer. Why would they think that *I* needed teaching? Surely my playing and singing were good enough for any evening party, at Pemberley or at Meryton? I was so shocked I could not reply; there was a blockage of some kind in my throat.

Lizzy spoke again, in an unfamiliar gentle voice that I had not heard before. "You see, Mary, you have always worked so hard at your music by yourself, you have taught yourself everything, and Darcy and I thought you might enjoy the attention of an expert. You are so serious about your music, yet you have rarely had the benefit of a master to help you improve."

"To *improve*?" I said, finding my voice at last, "You think my playing and singing are not - are not proficient?" Now I knew what Signor Moretti had meant when he said I could improve my singing if he played the piano. Of course, he was part of this plot. No doubt he had been trying to soften me up by feigning interest in my playing and my opinions.

Lizzy looked at Mr Darcy and he took up the subject. "Your performance has always been much admired, Mary, but − nobody ever reaches perfection. Elizabeth and I felt that this would be an opportunity that you, perhaps more than anyone, deserved."

I looked from one to the other, to read their countenances. Lizzy smiled encouragingly, Darcy held my gaze impassively and Signor Moretti, after briefly catching my eye, looked out the window beyond me.

"We have surprised you," Darcy said at last.

"Yes, that is my fault," Lizzy added with a sigh. "I had meant to have told you before Signor Moretti arrived, but somehow the moment did not arise. You will need time to consider."

◆

They left me alone, and I sat down on the piano stool with a thump and laid my fingers silently on the keys. My mind felt quite blank and I found that my heart was beating loudly in my chest. A teacher! For me! What did they think he could possibly teach me? I could already play with great dexterity and musical expression and understanding despite what people said. Anything else remaining to be learned I could master myself.

I cast my mind back to the last time there had been anyone to teach us music. Charlotte and Maria had had a governess at Lucas Lodge who taught us to decipher music and play and sing some simple songs. There had been a young man from Meryton who came for a while to teach us piano, but Kitty and Lydia behaved so ill and would not mind him, that he did not stay long, so I had more or less taught myself to play. The others had little interest - Lizzy could sing and play a simple folk song well enough, Jane was tone deaf and Kitty and Lydia only wanted to play silly pieces with two fingers or their knuckles or elbows.

It was not so for me, and I had practised for many hours together. The lack of interest in my family did not deter me and I became noted in the neighbourhood for the complexity and ambition of the pieces I performed.

And now I was to have a teacher! I did not doubt that *Signor Moretti* thought himself something quite out of the common – most likely his Italian heritage would make people think that he was a virtuoso before he had even played a note. I had thought from the start that there was something too forward about his manner, too confident and lacking in propriety.

Now I understood why he had been so friendly towards me! He had been feigning a genuine interest in me as a musician, as though we were equals, when all along he had intended to lord it over me and patronise me by parading his *superior* knowledge. He thought he could just walk in and take charge, as though everyone must give way before him.

Of course he had already taught Georgiana, and everything *she* did was supposedly so perfect. Everyone would think he must be marvellous if he had taught *her*. No, this was not to be! It was in every way an affront to my dedication and talent. I had taught myself from the start, and I would continue. There was no need for any Italian teachers of the pianoforte.

I picked up a sonata from Georgiana's music. It was a popular piece, one that I had performed myself at an evening party at my Aunt Philips's before my uncle died. I remembered there had been much applause and Mama had said that I acquitted myself very well. I started to play and it quickly came back to my fingers. One passage caused me a little difficulty, so I played it over a few times until I could do it, and I felt very satisfied.

Even so, I did not become calm, and my thoughts still returned to the affront that had been dealt to me. How dared Lizzy and Mr Darcy employ a music teacher for me without my consent or even knowledge! Lizzy's behaviour was less surprising: she had never really understood me or been able to comprehend the depths of my musical understanding. She played only to please and entertain others, and did not explore music as I did. Nor did she push herself to get better: once she could manage a few ditties she was content to trot them out when required. I was more surprised at Mr Darcy: I had thought him to be a person of solemn and profound discernment, accustomed to hearing the very best. Probably he let Lizzy persuade him: I had often noted how men would let their wives rule them when they were married. I doubted he knew what he was taking on with Lizzy: he saw only her charm and liveliness of manner; he did not know how officious and self-important she could be. I confess I was disappointed in him.

My spirits began to revive: I must not forget that being pretty and charming were merely superficial qualities, and that I had depths of understanding and virtue that were unknown to my sisters.

That evening, Signor Moretti sat at dinner with us. Kitty and I were on either side of Mr Darcy; Signor Moretti sat next to Kitty. Compared to Mr Darcy, Signor Moretti's features suddenly looked coarse and lumpish. I did not know how I could have thought he was handsome. Now I could see that his nose and eyes were too large, and his complexion was swarthy and his hair somewhat unkempt.

"You will play for us, won't you, Signor Moretti?" Kitty cried. "Lizzy says you are *so* good; she says your fingers simply fly over the keys like Boccherini playing the violin!"

"I think you must mean Paganini, Kitty," I said crushingly. I pitied him for having to tolerate her silly, sycophantic chatter.

"Why would I say Boccherini if I meant Paganini?" she snapped. "Lizzy, you *did* say Boccherini, didn't you?"

Lizzy merely smiled and would not reply.

"And I am sure Signor Moretti would *not* like to play for us," I said. "After all, he is a London musician, why would he deign to play to a set of ordinary country people such as ourselves?"

"I assure you, I am perfectly ordinary," he replied, regarding me steadily.

"It must be prodigiously exciting to teach music to all the grand ladies of London!" Kitty went on, uncrushed. "You go in and out of all the great houses, I'll be bound."

He smiled at her, the same misleading smile he had shown me earlier in the day. "I do teach a great many young ladies."

Lizzy said, "I expect it would be more exciting if they demonstrated a little more talent and interest in music."

He turned towards her. "There are very few Georgianas to be found."

Lizzy nodded towards me. "Perhaps Mary will surprise you."

"I look forward to hearing Miss Bennet play."

I bowed my head in acknowledgement. I did not think it would be proper at the dinner table to say that I had no intention of letting him hear me play.

I said, "Unfortunately, it is too much the way of the world that the young ladies are educated for mere show. Yet they should have an acquaintance with the fine arts, because they enrich beauty and imagination." I had read this in a book, and I thought it would impress Signor Moretti. He should know that I was not some neophyte to be influenced and despised.

"That is a very fine sentiment, Miss Bennet," said Signor Moretti.

"Mary loves to proclaim wise sayings," Kitty said. "If only one could have the faintest idea what she meant!"

I did not lower myself to respond. If Kitty wanted to display herself in her true colours, silly and ignorant as Papa always said, that was up to her.

Signor Moretti ignored her, and said to me, "Of course, an acquaintance with the fine arts, as you describe it, can also lead a young lady to creating her own art. Do you compose music yourself, Miss Bennet?"

I thought it was a ridiculous question and I smiled indulgently. "I? No, I have never attempted to do so. It would be arrogant of me to compose, when there are such people as Mozart and Handel. I could never equal their stature, so what is the point of trying!"

He looked at me quizzically. "It is fortunate that neither Mozart or Handel felt as you do, nor Beethoven, Haydn or any other composer, or we should be lamentably short of repertoire!"

"I did not mean that *nobody* could equal them, only that I myself could not," I explained, "or perhaps any young lady of gentle birth. It would be considered presumptuous to try, I am sure."

"Perhaps, perhaps not. Have you ever tried?"

His expression was blandly enquiring, and I declined to answer him. I was sure that he was trying to provoke me, but I was too accustomed to being mocked by my sisters to rise to his bait.

"Signor Moretti also teaches singing," Lizzy said, stepping into the breach. "And not just to the young ladies of the upper classes."

"You are much in demand at the opera house, I believe," Darcy said.

"Indeed I am," Moretti replied. "These days I am at the King's so much, I am thinking of setting up home in the rehearsal room."

"Are you not needed in London at present?" I asked. "I am surprised you can spare the time to come to the country if you are so much *in demand.*"

"The theatres are closed now for the summer. I did my final performance last week. It was Giulio Cesare – the aria you were singing came from that."

"You are mistaken, Signor Moretti," I said, pleased to be able to correct him. "It was from Julius Caesar, by Handel."

"I beg your pardon, Miss Bennet, it comes naturally to me to pronounce it in the Italian style."

Kitty gave that annoying little snort of laughter that she does whenever she feels she has defeated me in some way. I decided to set her an example by ignoring her and continuing to behave with decorum.

"Have you no wife or family to keep you in London?" Kitty asked, ignoring me in her turn. I saw Darcy and Elizabeth exchange a quick glance, and Signor Moretti's countenance changed abruptly.

"I was married, but my wife died two years ago, with our child," he said quietly.

There was a painful silence.

"Your wife was a singer too, was she not?" Lizzy said.

"Yes. She was a soprano and was beginning to have a career singing in the concert hall."

"I heard her sing in Temple Church once," said Darcy. "She had a voice of great purity. It was a pleasure to listen to her."

Moretti's face took on a slight flush. "Thank you, Mr Darcy. I had forgotten that you had heard her sing."

Lizzy and Darcy exchanged another glance, with some meaning in their eyes that I could not fathom.

Kitty said, "What are some of the grand houses you have played in, Signor Moretti?"

I looked sternly at her. I did not think she should have changed the subject so abruptly from one so solemn to one so frivolous.

"Do you go to the Prince Regent?" she went on.

The servants came to clear away our plates before Kitty could embarrass herself further.

I was dismayed when Lizzy led us to the music-room for our tea.

"I hope you do not expect me to play, Lizzy," I said.

"Not unless you wish to."

"I wish I had not asked Signor Moretti about his wife," Kitty said. "I was mortified! Why did you not warn me, Lizzy?"

"And why did you not warn me that I was to have a music tutor? Or even ask me?"

"Did I do wrong, Mary? If so, I am sorry. Darcy told me to prepare you but I missed the moment, and then when I saw you chatting so comfortably with Moretti, I thought all was well. And we were sure that you of all people would like to have a teacher."

"You certainly need one!" Kitty said, giving that irritating snort of hers

"Kitty, that laugh of yours is extremely unladylike," I said. "You sound like a pig."

"I prefer to sound like a pig than look like one!" Kitty retorted.

♦

It was extremely awkward to me to have Signor Moretti at Pemberley. When the gentlemen joined us after supper, Darcy naturally solicited me to play and sing. I did not want to before Moretti, as he might think that I was reconciled to his becoming my teacher and judge my performance. In the end Lizzy sang and played, and she sang well enough. The song was Robin Adair, a great favourite of hers, and she managed the scotch snap with a certain gusto. Afterwards she sat next to Darcy and I saw him reach for her hand. I had not thought to see Darcy behave so in public. I never saw a married couple touch each other like that when there were other people present; certainly Mama and Papa never had, but then they were always provoking each other. I did not know whether they loved each other at all.

"How did you like the piano, Mary?" Elizabeth asked me, "I think it a fine instrument."

"Indeed it is," I said. "If we had had such a piano at Longbourn we would have been very fortunate."

"What would be a convenient time for us to meet, Miss Bennet? Shall we start on Monday morning?" Moretti asked me.

I was taken by surprise. I had been hoping to arrange quietly with Lizzy that I should not have lessons, but of course I could not be so rude as to reject him in public. "I do not know," I stammered. "Perhaps after breakfast?"

"Oh no, Mary!" Kitty cried. "I have quite decided that we will go to Lambton to buy ribbons and materials on Monday morning. Lizzy has said we can have the carriage."

"In the afternoon then," Moretti said. I did not know what to say, so just nodded.

Later, after we had all supposedly retired to bed I went to Lizzy's bedchamber. I knocked on the door; there was some noise within and then a call to enter. I was taken aback to see Darcy in her room, and without his jacket. It looked most strange, especially as Lizzy was wearing some kind of robe over her night things. Darcy bowed to me and left us through another door. Lizzy was at the dressing table unpinning her hair, which looked sadly untidy.

"Well, Mary, you wish to speak to me?"

"Lizzy, I do not think I – why was Mr Darcy here?"

She looked up at me laughingly. "He is my husband, Mary. And I have not seen him for two or three days."

"Husbands and wives often do not see each for weeks together. I am sure Mama and Papa do not."

"Mama and Papa - they are not the only example to look to. They must have seen each other more often at one time."

"I do not think so. Papa is always in his library."

"But how do you think they had five children, if they were always apart?"

As her meaning sunk in, I gasped. "Lizzy! How can you be so unladylike to mention - I do not wish to consider - "

"No, nor did I at one time. But I am a married woman myself now. These things are not so very strange. Mama and Papa must have loved each other once."

I hardly knew where to look. "I did not come here to talk of that. Lizzy, I am very grateful for your efforts on my behalf in engaging Signor Moretti but I am quite decided that I do not wish for music lessons."

"But Mary, surely you can see how advantageous it will be for you."

"No, I do not see. I have always managed perfectly well by myself hitherto, why should everyone think I suddenly need a teacher?"

"Dearest Mary, of course you have managed by yourself, you have done wonders considering how little education any of us have had. We are all woefully ignorant, as I have discovered since I have been living with a really educated man. But how much better it would be to get the benefit of someone as - someone who earns his living through music, who is in demand by members of the *ton!* Is that not to be valued?"

"I'm sure it may be, for those young ladies who only wish to learn to play like performing monkeys in the salons of Mayfair. But I am not of that kind. I prefer to study music my own way, and not to have to adapt to some ideal of society of how a young lady should play."

"But Signor Moretti is not that kind of teacher. Think of Georgiana! She takes her playing quite as seriously as you do, she is no performing monkey."

"Always Georgiana! Is she the measure by which everything I do must be judged?"

Lizzy sighed. "I do not understand you, Mary."

"No, I have never been understood by anyone in my family. That is how I learned that it was best to rely on myself, and so I do not relish the sudden interference of a teacher."

"Very well, you have made yourself plain. I will tell Signor Moretti tomorrow of your decision."

She turned back to her mirror and I concluded that there was nothing more to be said. But I could not leave it there.

"Lizzy, I know you think I am being churlish, but you should have asked me. I have no wish to offend Signor Moretti."

"Your wishes are quite clear to me, Mary. I only regret that I surprised you."

I took myself off to bed but felt strangely restless. I could not understand myself. I knew I did not want or need to have music lessons with Signor Moretti, but even though he had deceived me with his attention and feigned interest in me, I was still uncomfortable about rejecting his services. Lizzy made me feel as though I was being silly, but she did not understand, nor did she appreciate my ability; she was too frivolous a person herself.

Perhaps it was because I was no longer in my regular and routine life at Longbourn that everything was confusing. I was staying in a house that was so much grander than anything I had ever experienced. I had not started my studies and practice, and I was already missing the quiet contemplation and solitude that I was accustomed to. All these things were difficult and interfered with my peace of mind. There was Kitty – I had already been in her company too much since we had left Longbourn, and without her friend Maria she was more demanding and was her usual cutting and provoking self. Then Lizzy too was different: she had a child now, and a husband, and a great home, and I thought it had made her very superior and overbearing. She thought she could do anything to anybody now as though she were a queen and we were all to be her subjects. I did not know how Darcy could tolerate her. I did not know how I could tolerate her myself, or Kitty. No, the sooner I commenced a regime of study and practice the better.

◆

I was still feeling rattled the next day when Elizabeth told Kitty and me to make ready to go for a drive around the grounds of Pemberley.

"Thank you for my part, Lizzy, but I wish you would rather show me the library. I would much prefer to begin my reading and studying."

"Nonsense, Mary, there will be plenty of time for that. But it is the first really fine day for a week and we must take advantage. I mean to drive you myself."

There would be no arguing so I acquiesced gracefully. But I was dismayed when Kitty came to join us holding William in her arms.

"Oh, please let him come, Lizzy. He told me how much he loves the horses."

"Horses," said William, pointing to the pair of bays that were hitched up to the carriage.

"Of course he can come!" Lizzy cried. "How delightful! But you must hold him tight, Kitty."

Kitty handed William to me as the groom helped her into the carriage. He immediately started to cry and struggle to reach Lizzy.

"Perhaps we shouldn't take him," I said. I could see he was going to spoil the drive.

"He will be better once we start."

Kitty held him then and we began. He stopped crying but he struggled so to reach Lizzy that she was forced to stop the carriage.

"Here, Mary, you take the reins for a moment."

"I? But I cannot drive!"

"It is not hard. They are very well behaved. Darcy bought them specially for me to learn to drive."

She handed me the reins and cried giddy-up. The horses broke into a brisk trot.

"What am I to do, Elizabeth? I do not know how to drive!"

"Just let them go, they know the way."

There was nothing to be done but hold the reins. I heard Kitty laugh in the carriage behind. It was all very well for her, but what if they decided to bolt? Then the carriage might overturn and we should all be killed. Then what would Mama do? And what would Mr Darcy say when he found that I had killed his family? I would be blamed forever and no doubt they would write some unjust epitaph on my gravestone.

It was impossible to enjoy the countryside while all this responsibility was in my hands. Lizzy and Kitty were oblivious, playing with William and pointing at cows and walls and trees and clapping ridiculously every time he said a word. We started down a hill.

"Lizzy! They are going too fast!"

Kitty laughed in her usual inconsiderate way.

"Pull on the reins then, Mary, and they will walk."

I pulled and the horses stopped abruptly.

"Mary!" Kitty shrieked. "Be careful! My reticule! Everything has spilled!"

"I did not know they would stop! I meant to slow them."

"Darcy did say they were beautifully mouthed," Lizzy said unhelpfully.

"You pulled too hard, Mary," Kitty said. "You are so stupid!"

"Then you drive! I shall walk!"

I jumped down from the carriage.

"Mary, don't be silly," said Lizzy, "Kitty could have done no better herself."

"Yes, I could!" Kitty retorted. "I think I know better than to tug on the reins like that! Mr Blakeley said I was a natural driver when he took me out last summer."

I ignored her and started to walk back the way we had come. It would serve them right if the horses ran away with them. I would much rather be by myself anyway and then I could think and admire the prospect without Kitty's chatter or the baby's babbling. Unfortunately the road was somewhat muddy from the recent rain and soon my hem was damp and dirty, but I would prefer anything than stay with Kitty a moment longer. And I was sure we had not driven very far. Every corner must bring me in view of the house.

And yet my trudging seemed to go on forever, and my shoes turned out to be most unsuitable for walking through mud as they kept sinking in and slipping off my feet. How typical of Kitty, and Lizzy too, to drive away and leave me to walk! And why were there so many hills at Pemberley?

When I heard a carriage coming behind me I was relieved, and I wondered how Kitty and Lizzy could have turned around. It was not them, but a gentleman driving an extraordinary carriage with enormous wheels and a small seat perched several feet above the ground. It looked most precarious; nor did I care for his horses, a pair of large, wall-eyed, high-stepping creatures, matching grey in colour. I stepped hurriedly to one side but the driver pulled up, the horses snorting, fretting and tossing their heads impatiently.

"May I be of assistance, ma'am?" the gentleman enquired, in a nasal voice that sounded as though he was suffering from a head cold. "I am come to pay my respects to Mrs Darcy's sisters, and I see by your resemblance that you must be one of them. May I take you up? You cannot wish to walk in all this dirt!"

I looked up at him. His face was curiously babyish and his figure rather portly; he was dressed in a plain brown coat and a clerical neck cloth, but his sober attire was set off by a most unclerical high-crowned straw hat, decorated with an exceptionally large and ornate jewelled buckle. All in all, I did not know what to make of him. Everything about him contradicted everything else; I could not imagine who he might be.

He was, however, smiling at me in a most friendly fashion, even though my surprise must have been evident on my face.

"I beg your pardon, I have been too precipitate. I should perhaps introduce myself. My name is Arthur Speedwell and I am fortunate enough to be the incumbent of the parish of Kympton in the neighbourhood."

"You are the rector?" I asked in astonishment.

He laughed, a loud guffaw that caused his horses to stamp and fidget.

"I know, I know," he exclaimed, "it's the hat, isn't it? My sister warned me about this hat, she said it was quite wrong for a man of the church, but how could I resist? Such a crown! Such a buckle! But the coat – surely the coat is more *comme il faut*? You could not ask for a more sensible coat!"

He paused, seeming to expect a response from me, but I did not know what to say. I had never heard a man talk like this. He seemed to read something in my face because he pressed his fingers to his brow and said, "You are judging me, I know you are judging me! No, no, you are quite right, I am sure you are right, I should have listened to my sister, she is a great connoisseur in matters of dress. Now, are you Miss Mary Bennet or Miss Catherine Bennet? Wait, do not tell me, let me guess. I know this is not the usual form of introduction, Miss Bennet," he went on, "but do, please, forgive me. I'm afraid I have no manners at all, I'm known for it, you see. Everyone says so – Arthur Speedwell – no manners at all. But now that I'm so serious and important, and vicar of this parish and all that sort of thing, I am *trying* to be correct and do things properly."

I was a little flustered by the speed and nature of his speech, but gathered myself for a moment before replying. "Although I believe that the conventions of society are important," I said, "I acknowledge that situations are bound to arise from time to time in which spontaneous introductions will occur without the benefit of the usual forms."

Mr Speedwell clapped his hands. "Oh, how perfect! That is *exactly* what I have always said myself, but never half so elegantly! I see you have thought very deeply about this matter. *That* leads me to the conclusion that you must be Miss Mary Bennet!" He wagged his finger. "Your reputation precedes you, you see. Oh my manners, my manners! What can I be thinking of to be talking to you from this great height!" He jumped out of the carriage with unexpected grace. "You will ride with me back to the house, will you not?"

He was such an odd creature, but I thought he meant well and I did not see any reason to mistrust him.

"Thank you," I said, "if you are sure there is room for me."

He laughed. "I know, I know, I am sadly fat, but there is plenty of room for two. It is easier if I mount first and then reach down to you."

Mr Speedwell stepped into the carriage again and helped me up beside him.

I must have looked rather anxious, because he said, "Now, do not be concerned, Miss Bennet. I faithfully promise not to overturn you. I am a clumsy oaf in many ways, but I've never overturned a carriage yet. And old Simon and Paul here are as quiet as kittens."

Seeing the horses stamping impatiently, I was not sure I believed him. "It is just that I have never ridden in such a tall carriage," I said.

"Oh dear, in the wrong again! I know what you are thinking, you are thinking what is a country clergyman doing with a fashionable phaeton and a pair of Irish thoroughbreds! And you are quite right! I should have taken Eloisa's advice – that's my sister, you know. She said no, she said I must change my ways if I am to gain the respect of my parishioners. She said I must be simple, I must be understated, I must be sober. But I could not give up my greys, and my phaeton! Tell me it was not so very wrong of me, Miss Bennet!"

We drove off as he spoke, thankfully at a sedate pace.

After a while I said, "A choice of horse and carriage is perhaps just as much a question of correct behaviour as other items of dress or manner, and such questions should never be treated frivolously. They may be overlooked by some but without our manners and conventions, society would soon descend into savagery and mayhem."

"I believe you are right, Miss Bennet, I am sure you must be right. Thank goodness you are come amongst us, Miss Bennet, *now* I shall have someone to teach me how to go on!"

His manners were distinctly odd, but if he was willing to take instruction, then that at least showed a proper humility. Despite his peculiar, and even somewhat vulgar, way of talking, he seemed to take the world as seriously as I did, and see things in their proper light.

"Will you stay long at Pemberley?" Mr Speedwell asked.

"Perhaps some two or three months, if our mother does not need us before that."

"How delightful that will be! And I understand you are the musical member of your family? Perhaps we will hear you play and sing while you are here?"

"Are you fond of music?" I asked.

"I like to *listen* to it," he said. "I have been fortunate enough to hear Miss Darcy play and sing on a number of occasions."

Always Miss Darcy!

"I have never heard Miss Darcy play," I said coldly. "Miss Darcy's talents are beyond compare, or so I am always told. I would not want to put myself forward in such august company."

Although I was staring straight ahead as I spoke, I could tell that he turned to look at me. No doubt he was wondering how anyone could dare speak so about Miss Darcy. Well, I was not afraid to say what I thought, in fact I held it as a rule that honesty and forthrightness are qualities to be aspired to at all times. And why should Georgiana Darcy be so admired, when I myself put in hours of practice and hard work and was never so much offered a kind or complimentary word? Some of us had to manage without being the centre of attention: perhaps Georgiana would not be so praised and cosseted if she was one of five sisters.

"Oh, Miss Bennet," cried Mr Speedwell, "never say so! You would not deprive me of the pleasure of hearing you! Tell me you will not! Yes, of course, Georgiana Darcy is an angel, an absolute angel, such singing, such playing, there is nothing to equal her, but I am sure you are just as fine a musician as she is!"

"I do not know," I said. I was still smarting from my treatment by Elizabeth and Signor Moretti.

"Well, Miss Darcy is an accomplished player, to be sure," Mr Speedwell said, more slowly and calmly than he had spoken hitherto, "but it would give us all great pleasure to hear you, Miss Bennet."

I shrugged, and then remembered that Mama has always told me not to shrug. I hoped he had not noticed. Even though his own manners were odd, I would not like him to think I did not know how to behave, or that Longbourn manners were somehow below Pemberley manners.

There were a few moments of silence. Then Mr Speedwell said,

"The lanes are rather muddy for walking today. Would you not drive with your sisters? I passed them as I came in."

"I *was* driving with them but - " I was surprised to find that I was about to tell him the whole sorry tale of Kitty's unkindness, when I thought better of confiding thus about my sister to a stranger. I would not want to show her in such a bad light. "I was driving with them but I decided I would prefer to walk. Two days journey from Hertfordshire has left me confined and carriage-sick."

"You are not feeling sick now, are you?" Mr Speedwell asked anxiously. "I am used to think this is the most comfortable carriage in the whole world, I would hate to think you were feeling unwell in my carriage!"

"I am quite well now, I assure you," I said.

"You know, if you do feel unwell, you must allow me to give you one of my home-made remedies. Everyone says I have no equal for brewing a comforting tea or any number of potations and tonics. I could set you up in an instant. Truly, Miss Bennet, I can make you an infusion of fennel twig tea that will calm any upset stomach. My sister Eloisa quite swears by my concoctions! Oh, *why* didn't I bring any with me today!"

"You are very kind," I said, almost laughing, "but I am perfectly well now. It has quite faded."

At last we rounded the final corner to the house.

"Perhaps you would like to get down here," Mr Speedwell said, "and I will take the carriage round to the stables."

He handed me down and I went into the house to change my dress, realising that I would be expected to receive him and entertain him until Lizzy returned.

◆

There was a knock on my door while I was changing and Elizabeth walked in.

"Mary, Mr Speedwell is here to visit us, will you come down to the drawing room to meet him? I wasn't sure if you knew the way."

"Thank you, Lizzy. Perhaps Judith can show me when she has finished my hair. But I have already met Mr Speedwell, he took me up in his carriage when I was walking home."

"Oh, how kind of him! I am glad you did not have to walk all the way back."

"No thanks to Kitty."

"Kitty is - Mary, perhaps you might try not to take such quick offence at Kitty. She can be nervous and irritable, I know, but she does not mean anything by it."

"I would try to be more patient with her if she would try not to be so ill-tempered. She is always snapping and finding fault. *She* could not have driven any better."

"No. I am sure she could not, but she is of a nervous and volatile disposition and if you could have been a little more tolerant of her ways, there would have been no need for you to walk and miss a lovely drive. And William kept asking about you in the drollest manner. He said, where Auntie Mary gone? If he said it once he said it twenty times."

The maid finished my hair and I stood up. "I'm flattered by William's regard for me. Perhaps if Kitty were a little more like William we would do better together. No doubt you have spoken to her also?"

We began to walk down the stairs. "I certainly shall," Elizabeth said.

I said no more. I doubted that Lizzy would speak to Kitty. Nobody cared that Kitty could be as horrible to me as she pleased, and yet I was always expected to be tolerant and patient. Of course as a Christian it behoved me to forgive her, but what about Kitty and *her* moral character? Why must she always be made allowances for? If she was not corrected she would come to believe that any behaviour of hers would be acceptable. But it was not for me to do it.

Mr Speedwell was reading a book by the fire when we entered. He stood up and came bustling towards us.

"Mrs Darcy! What a pleasure to see you again! You look extremely well, your drive must have agreed with you. I know how much you enjoy to be outdoors in the fresh air."

"Thank you, Mr Speedwell, we did indeed have a lovely drive. And you have met my sister Mary, I believe?"

He bowed towards me. "I have had that pleasure. I am so grateful to you, Mrs Darcy, for allowing me to meet your sisters." He turned to me. "I have so many sisters of my own, you know, and I miss them sorely. The older ones spoiled and indulged me as you may imagine, but my younger sister Eloisa was spoiled by me in her turn, and we were the best of friends, being so much younger than the others. They are all married with households of their own now and scattered across the country, and there is nobody to indulge me any longer. I look forward to meeting your younger sister, Catherine. The more sisters the better, in my estimation! Will she be joining us?"

"She will be down soon," Lizzy said. "Will you take tea, Mr Speedwell?"

"How delightful, the tea here is always so excellent."

I saw Lizzy smile as she turned away to ring the bell; I suppose she thought Mr Speedwell overly fulsome in his enthusiasm. But then perhaps Lizzy did not understand what it might feel like for a dependent cleric in the presence of the great lady that she had now become.

"Have you not met Kitty, Mr Speedwell?" I asked. "She has been visiting at Pemberley before."

"Mr Speedwell has only had the living at Kympton since the new year," Lizzy said. "He was not here when Kitty came last."

"And are you happy in your new position?" I asked.

"Indeed I am," he said, glancing towards Lizzy. "I count myself extremely fortunate in my patronage."

Lizzy laughed. "And extremely fortunate in the hunting to be had in Derbyshire! I believe it was the prospect of being able to ride with the Quorn and the Atherstone that tempted you into accepting the offer of the living!"

Mr Speedwell burst out laughing. I was surprised again at how loud his laugh was, it did not seem appropriate for a man of his profession. "You know me too well, Mrs Darcy! But will we have the pleasure of your company on the hunt next season?"

Elizabeth hesitated and coloured. "I do not know. Mr Darcy would like me to hunt, but at Longbourn, although we could all ride well enough for practical purposes we never had much opportunity to cover the sort of ground that prevails in Derbyshire."

"Oh, I quite understand you, Mrs Darcy!" Mr Speedwell said. "I sometimes shudder to think what mishaps might occur in this rough country!"

Lizzy laughed. "Your anxiety does not appear to interfere with your enjoyment! I do not think you have missed a meeting since you came to Derbyshire!"

Mr Speedwell made a great show of ruefulness and pretend modesty. "And what about you, Miss Bennet?" he said, turning to me. "I know you are an intrepid walker, but does the thought of riding out with the Quorn not appeal to you?"

I smiled. "I do not consider myself to be an intrepid walker. When you met me today it was necessity that found me there." I looked pointedly at Lizzy when I said this, but she ignored me. "My pleasures are of the mind. I prefer to study, read, and work at my music."

"Indeed! I knew you were an intellectual the moment I saw you! I should like to talk with you of your studies. I was a classicist at Oxford, you know. It will be a great pleasure to have someone to talk to of matters of the mind."

I was pleased by the attention, though I did not quite know what to make of him. His manners were so extraordinary, at times wild, at others showing a more calm and reflective side. I decided to reserve judgement, but it was in his favour that he had realised that I was someone who could be turned to for advice and example.

Just then a footman came in with the tea, followed by Kitty. Kitty mantled and simpered as she always did when introduced to a man of marriageable age. It was to Mr Speedwell's credit that he did not appear to mind but was very attentive to her, offering her a seat near the fire and handing her a cup of tea. He even admired her new lace mittens.

"Is Mr Darcy at home?" he asked Elizabeth.

"He has just returned from escorting Georgiana to London, but he is very busy today on the estate."

"Ah yes, Miss Darcy is to visit her aunt, in Kent, I believe."

"Mr Darcy bade me ask you to dine with us this Sunday if you are not engaged."

"How kind. I have no other engagement and if I did, I would cancel it at once! I cannot imagine anything more delightful! I do hope the Miss Bennets will entertain us?"

Kitty laughed in a most unladylike way. "I'm sure *Mary* will be only too pleased to play for you. And Lizzy too, of course, if you are not got too grand to sing in company now, Lizzy."

"Do you not play, Miss Kitty?" Mr Speedwell asked politely.

"No, indeed, how could I learn, for Mary was always on the instrument whenever I wanted it."

I restrained myself from refuting her lie in company, but at least Elizabeth had the decency to intervene.

She laughed, "Kitty, what a story! You never wanted to play the piano in your life, except to bash out some silly doggerel with Lydia."

Kitty did not even have the grace to look ashamed but laughed.

"What about you, Mr Speedwell?" I asked, in order to change the subject. "As a clergyman, you must be able to sing. I would be happy to play for you, if you would grace us with a song"

"I would do my best, Miss Bennet, but Mrs Darcy has heard me sing on a Sunday morning and I am not sure whether she could abide to hear me twice in one day!"

This provoked more laughter from my sisters, and Mr Speedwell joined in heartily with his strange braying laugh. I began to wonder whether he was quite as profound a fellow as a clergyman ought to be. However, a while later, Elizabeth suggested that he and I go to the library together and see what might be of interest there. Out of politeness, I asked Kitty too, but she said she would rather return to the nursery to play with William.

Pemberley's library was, at least on first glance, everything I could hope to see. It was a large room, with shelves going up to the ceiling, crammed with books of all ages, beautifully bound in leather with gilt titles. It was panelled in a dark stained wood, and the floor was richly carpeted. I noticed a globe and also a curious globe of the night sky.

Mr Speedwell looked appreciatively about him. "Where does one begin in such a place? I see Darcy has all the great Romans – see, there are Horace, Tacitus, and Juvenal. Trust him to keep up with his studies! Can I fetch something for you, Miss Bennet? Perhaps the Greek philosophers are more to your taste? Here is something of Plato." He pulled a book from the shelf. "It is in the original Greek."

"I do not read Greek," I said. But I could not leave it at that, I felt I must explain myself; I did not want him to think that I was so ignorant through any fault of my own. "We were not taught. Perhaps if I had had brothers there might have been a tutor who could have taught me too, but everything I have learned I have had to find out for myself."

"Perhaps there will be a translation. But Miss Bennet, you look a trifle discomposed. Is anything the matter? I hope you are not regretting that you cannot read Greek! I am sure you are wise not to make the attempt! When I remember the hours spent at school trying to learn such stuff, I cannot think why one should do so, when there is so much to educate and entertain written in our own language."

I was surprised at him reading my countenance and taking note of what I might be feeling and did not at first know how to reply.

"I think - I think there are so many books, that as you said, I do not know how to begin. Perhaps if there were a history book? I understand that the study of history can be most improving."

"Of course. Look, here is Gibbon."

"Gibbon?"

"Decline and Fall of the Roman Empire. Which volume would you like?"

"Oh! I - that is, I am not sure at present what I will read while I am at Pemberley. I will need time to acquaint myself with the contents of the library and then I will embark on a course of study."

"Very wise. And if you become tired of study, here are some novels – the work of Maria Edgeworth, here is the Monk which will quite chill your blood, and look, the Children of the Abbey."

"I do not read novels."

He turned away from the bookshelves and surveyed me searchingly. "Then perhaps I might persuade you to try while you are here. They can be very entertaining. Eloisa and I used to take turns reading aloud to each other in the evening, and I assure you it was most enjoyable. Eloisa is a remarkable reader, she has a different voice for each character. I was often doubled over with laughing, if I was not beside myself with terror. I am sure you would like it. Perhaps you could read aloud to your sisters of an evening?"

It did not sound like the sort of thing I or my sisters would enjoy doing at all. "I have hitherto concentrated on more improving texts," I said. "Particularly when reading aloud to my sisters."

"That is most commendable. But why not try this one when you have some leisure," and he handed me a book by Ann Radcliffe. "Many consider her too Gothic for our rational times, but there is much to admire and enjoy."

I took the book but I did not know what to make of Mr Speedwell. On the one hand he was recommending novels, wearing flamboyant clothes and riding to hounds, in general behaving nothing like my idea of a clergyman. Then a moment later he proved himself learned and serious, polite and considerate. It was really most curious.

Part Two: The Visit to Church

◆

Elizabeth did not come to church on Sunday, as she was apparently a little indisposed, so Kitty, Signor Moretti and I rode in the chaise with Mr Darcy. It was a fine morning and there was leisure to enjoy the scene while Kitty chatted glibly to Signor Moretti. He was very patient with her, which I thought stood to his credit. I would have corrected her if I had been part of the conversation. Mr Darcy seemed content to ride in thoughtful silence. Occasionally I looked at him and studied his countenance while his attention was elsewhere. He always appeared somewhat grave and serious, but he did have extremely fine features: I thought he was probably the handsomest man I had ever seen. He certainly outshone my other brothers-in-law. Mr Bingley was pleasant looking, though beginning to lose his hair, and Mr Wickham - from what I remembered: we had not seen either him or Lydia since they had moved north - had an air of candour quite out of keeping with his character; but Mr Darcy was truly noble-looking.

He caught my eye and said, "How do you find Pemberley now, Mary? Have you had much chance to see the park?"

"Lizzy did take us for a drive," I replied, "and I am enjoying what I am seeing today." I blushed, thinking that I had just been staring at him, but I soon recovered myself. He could not know my thoughts.

"May and June are particularly good months for the gardens here if you are interested in flowers."

As usual Kitty could not bear to be left out. "I think I am more interested in flowers than Mary. She always has her nose stuck in a book, you can never get her to come outdoors."

"That is not true, Kitty, I often take a turn about the grounds at Longbourn."

"Yes, with a book in front of your face so that you cannot even see where you are going!"

I could see that this conversation was going to degenerate quickly. "Kitty, perhaps you could remember that we are on our way to church, and try to show an appropriate devoutness and poise. I would like to collect my thoughts in preparation."

"You didn't say that when Mr Darcy was talking to you!"

I purposely turned my head away. We were just entering the village of Kympton so there was no prolonged silence.

"Is that the rectory?" Kitty asked, pointing to a pleasant modern house close to the church.

"Yes, it is. My father built it twenty or so years ago," Mr Darcy answered.

"It is very large for one man, I wonder Mr Speedwell does not marry. Mama says that all men must marry eventually."

"I have heard her say so myself, Kitty," said Mr Darcy. "But Mr Speedwell has a great many friends in the neighbourhood and shows no inclination to enter the state of matrimony."

"Perhaps he has not yet met the right woman," I said.

Kitty laughed. "Oh, do you see yourself as the wife of a rector, Mary? I'm sure you could write all his sermons for him."

There was no answer to that, but I was concerned for Kitty that she should show herself up before Mr Darcy and Signor Moretti.

Mr Speedwell's singing was indeed very bad. He cleared his throat a great many times before he began, and the organist pointedly played his starting note again. Unfortunately Mr Speedwell began on a note quite other, which meant that the rest of the chant was rather high. This made further difficulties for the congregation when it came to the responses, and the singing lacked conviction. When we sang the hymns it was not much better. Mr Jackson on the organ had very little sense of timing, nor did he play the correct notes. One man, a burly fellow who looked like a farmer took it upon himself to lead the congregation's singing, but as this involved breaking away from what Mr Jackson was doing, it was difficult to know which to follow. Mr Darcy joined in with the farmer so I thought I would too. Signor Moretti gave up altogether and merely watched the proceedings with an unreadable expression on his face. Kitty, of course, embarrassed herself and all of us by succumbing to uncontrollable giggles, including that ridiculous snort of hers. I wondered at her lack of regard for Mr Darcy's position as principal landowner of the area, a personage whom all the other churchgoers looked to for example and precept. I felt for him extremely.

Mr Speedwell's sermon somewhat compensated for his lack of expertise as a singer. Although the timbre of his voice itself was not pleasing, it was delivered with great ease of manner, even occasionally with a theatrical panache, and for once most people were engaged, not falling asleep or gazing out of the window with blank expressions. I thought his point about the casting of the first stone was well made, but the sermon on the whole was perhaps a little short as sermons go. As we left I mentioned this to him.

"Too short, Miss Bennet? Is that a fault or something to be praised?"

I answered, "I am aware that for many people listening to a sermon is too onerous a task, but perhaps it is still the duty of a clergyman to try and instil some knowledge of scripture."

He smiled. "But perhaps just a little at a time? Any medicine goes down better in small doses."

I was prepared to discuss with him further but there were others coming out of the church now, and I thought we could continue later when he came to dine.

When we returned to Pemberley Kitty decided that she did not like her bonnet and so started tearing it to bits to make it up again with new ribbons. Lizzy was somewhere outdoors with William. I went to the library. I needed time there alone to accustom myself to the range of books that was there so that I could begin to study. I liked to find a book that I could respect and then make extracts of the parts of the book, which I thought were worthy of further thought. I took down the copy of Plato that Mr Speedwell had opened the other day. I wondered what it might be like to learn Greek, but I did not know how I could begin, unless there was a Greek primer on the shelves somewhere. It would be helpful if there were a system for storing the books so that I might know where to look. The door opened and Mr Darcy came in.

"Mr Darcy! I am sorry, I hope -"

"Pray do not concern yourself, Mary, I am just come here to consult a map of the park with a view to moving a boundary wall on one of the farms. Please continue exploring. Unless I can help you to find something particular?"

"I thank you, no. Unless -"

"Yes?"

"Unless you had a Greek primer?"

"You would like to learn Greek?"

"It is merely an idea."

Mr Darcy stared at the shelves for a moment. "If such a thing is still in existence, it is more likely to be in the schoolroom, left over from my own boyhood. I do not think Georgiana ever learned Greek."

I thought it might be very satisfying to know something that Georgiana Darcy did not. "It was Mr Speedwell who put me in mind of it," I said, "when he found this Plato. We had no such volumes at Longbourn. He also showed me a novel and said he thought I might enjoy it. But I have been told that novels are unsuitable for young ladies."

"I have heard so too, but I think that is a view that is somewhat old fashioned. There are many novels quite worth your while to read, and very entertaining."

"Have *you* read novels, Mr Darcy?" I asked in astonishment.

He smiled, "Certainly I have. And enjoyed them too. It was your sister who suggested I might broaden my diet of literature to include fiction."

How typical of Lizzy to think that she knows best about what other people should do.

"Have you read this one, The Italian? Mr Speedwell thought I might enjoy it."

I took it from the shelf and handed it to Mr Darcy.

"No," he replied. "See, the pages have not yet been cut."

He went to a desk and found a paper knife and began cutting the pages.

"Here, you can read the first few chapters now. And you know where the knife is kept for future use."

There was a moment's silence. I did not know what to say now. Then Mr Darcy said hesitantly,

"Mary, Elizabeth tells me that you have made up your mind not to take lessons from Signor Moretti."

"That is true," I said, feeling awkward. I wished Lizzy had not discussed it with Mr Darcy. "I – I would prefer not to talk about it any further. I made my reasons clear to Lizzy."

"Yes, I understand that you do not wish for a teacher now, having taught yourself for so long."

I looked up at him. "I wish Lizzy had asked me."

"Yes, we were both at fault. We thought you would welcome it and so did not ask you beforehand. We should not have assumed."

"But - but Signor Moretti is more than just Georgiana's teacher. You said he would be your guest even if he did not teach me."

"Yes, we are indebted to him for his dedication to Georgiana. His presence and kindness helped her through some difficult times."

I could not imagine what difficult times Georgiana could have had.

"We feel we are returning the favour by inviting him here for the summer. His spirits have never been high since his wife and child died, and during the summer he often has less employment. However, he has agreed to play at Lizzy's ball and will be bringing a party of his fellow musicians to perform for us. That will give him something to work for. A man often needs occupation when he has grief to bear."

I nodded, and a line I had read during church fortuitously occurred to me. "In the bible it says, 'For in much grief is much wisdom: and he that increaseth knowledge increaseth sorrow'."

I was unsure whether I had got the words in quite the right order, but Mr Darcy said nothing.

◆

At dinner that evening there were other guests apart from Mr Speedwell. Lizzy had invited a local landowner, Squire Carding and his wife. He was the gentleman from the church who had sung very loudly during the hymns. Despite wearing evening clothes, including a frilled shirt, he still looked more like a farmer than a squire, with a very red nose and roughened skin, and extraordinarily large and reddened hands. I could not help noticing them and thinking that *he* would not be able to play piano. His eyes were staring and his expression choleric. His wife was a very thin person with no bosom to speak of, and an unfortunately pointed nose. He was very loud; she said virtually nothing at all, despite Lizzy's best efforts to draw her out. They had also brought their son, who looked with disdain upon us all and immediately took Kitty's fancy. She made up to him constantly throughout the meal. It seemed his name was Frederick and he had no interests or ambition that could be discovered. When Kitty asked him what he intended to do, he said he liked shooting on his father's estate and nothing more could he be persuaded to say.

Mr Speedwell spoke to me. "I believe you have two other sisters, Miss Bennet?"

"Yes," I answered. "My sister Jane, the eldest, is married to Mr Bingley and they live in Warwickshire about 30 miles from here. And my youngest, Lydia, is married to a soldier, at least he was a soldier, I believe he may have sold out now. And they live in the North."

"In the North?" he said smiling, "I have been used to think of *Derbyshire* as the North. But then I am a Londoner born and bred. Even going to Oxford was like visiting a foreign country."

"What nonsense you talk, Arthur!" Lizzy cried. "You should know, Mary, that Mr Speedwell has travelled to many foreign countries, far more exotic than Oxford."

"Or even Derbyshire?" he said, quizzing her.

"Oh Mr Speedwell, what countries have you visited?" Kitty asked. "I do so long to travel!"

" I have been to France, to Italy, to Germany, and even to Spain."

"Spain!" breathed Kitty. "I should love to go to Spain! Were you set upon by brigands?"

"No, indeed, for I was safe at the embassy in Madrid. Oh, are you disappointed? Would you like to have such an adventure?"

"It would certainly be very romantic!" she replied.

"It would certainly be very uncomfortable!" I said. "You would not really like to be in such danger, Kitty."

"Yes, I should, particularly if it was a very handsome brigand. They say that the Spanish brigands are the handsomest of all."

There was laughter at this, but I thought Kitty sounded excessively silly.

Mr Speedwell disappointed me by joining in with Kitty. "*I* have certainly never seen such handsome brigands anywhere!" he said.

"There are brigands enough in Derbyshire, Darcy!" Squire Carding bellowed in my ear. "Those dashed coal merchants in Lambton are trying to charge me six shillings the ton! They want shooting."

"My dear, your language!" his wife whispered across the table.

"When the new coal mine in Alfreton is fully working you will find the price comes down," said Mr Darcy calmly.

"There was an engineer trying to persuade Papa to mine on his land," said young Mr Carding, surprising both himself and the company by his sudden contribution.

"Dash cheek," said the squire. "I'll see them all hanged first."

"My dear!" again remonstrated his wife.

I wanted to say something about the need for progress but I did not know how to phrase it.

"There is a need for more coal in this industrial age we are living in," said Mr Darcy. "Much as we might wish it, things cannot stay the same for ever."

"That is quite what I was thinking," I said, but I do not think Mr Darcy heard me.

Squire Carding started to turn an alarming colour of scarlet, and Lizzy, seeing it, swiftly changed the conversation.

"Signor Moretti, there are a great many changes in the world of music, are there not? Last month Georgiana was playing a piece by the Austrian composer, Beethoven. It sounded very unusual to my ears."

"Yes, I believe Beethoven has changed the language of music for ever," Signor Moretti replied. "But music must change, has changed indeed over the centuries."

"But I have been used to thinking that we had reached the pinnacle of musical taste and style," I said.

"I believe every age believes itself to have reached a pinnacle of taste and understanding," said Signor Moretti. "Perhaps because those of us with limited powers to create and innovate cannot conceive of what form the changes might take."

I did not know how to reply to this. Nor did anyone else it seemed.

"That's all very well," said Squire Carding, after a moment or two, "But there are a lot of newfangled ideas out there which won't do anyone any good. If these miners have their way, there will be no grazing left for any of us. And what they expect to be paid! It takes my breath away. You wouldn't want them digging up Pemberley, eh, Darcy?"

"I would certainly not wish to spoil Pemberley, and while my farms and land are enough to sustain the estate, there is no need. But times are changing, Squire, and we would all do well to prepare ourselves for that. In these times of unrest and revolution, the sensible man keeps on eye on the current situation."

"Oh, please do not talk of such dreadful things!" moaned Lady Carding. "I cannot bear to think of it."

"Then perhaps this would be a perfect moment for the ladies to retire," said Elizabeth, standing up.

Lizzy begged me to play when we reached the drawing-room, and as there were only ladies present I obliged. I first played the sonata that I had tried before, and was very pleased with my performance. Lady Carding begged me for a song so I obliged with an aria from Medea by Cherubini. Everyone listened most attentively except Kitty who had started embroidering and yawned loudly throughout. I was glad to stop before the gentlemen came in. I did not want to perform for Signor Moretti, and I did not think that either Squire Carding or his son would have much appreciation of music. Lizzy was requested to sing and again sang something rather simple, but it was well received, by the gentlemen especially.

On Monday morning Kitty and I went to the small town of Lambton where there were a number of shops. I did not want to go. I had letters to write, to Mama and to Maria Lucas, but Kitty insisted and I had said I would. I did not expect to take much pleasure from the trip.

The town was busy, with many people on the street with baskets and the shops bustling with customers. We went first to the drapers to look at materials as Kitty was determined to have a new dress for the ball. Elizabeth had an account in the shop and had told us that we might both buy whatever fabric we pleased. Kitty was wildly excited by the prospect and meant to take full advantage of Lizzy's -

that is to say, Mr Darcy's - generosity. I had decided that I would allow Kitty to choose me some new ribbons but that was all.

The draper's was a well-kept shop, with a surprisingly large array of bolts of cloth to choose from. Kitty had soon struck up a conversation with the lady who presided there, who she knew from before, and I wandered around, idly fingering the materials, trying not to become impatient but endeavouring to remain in a state of serene resignation. I had spent time in shops with Kitty before and there was no hurrying her. She took an age to decide anything, and went back and forth between items before she could make a choice.

"Mary, come and advise me!" she called.

I obeyed because that was the simplest thing to do.

"What did you think of these? This for the underdress, and this laid over?"

She showed me a muslin of the palest yellow, and a diaphanous fabric of a similar hue, sprigged with tiny flowers.

"It is very pretty," I said, knowing that that was what Kitty would wish to hear. Though in fact it was very pretty, even I could see that.

Kitty laughed triumphantly. "Then *you* shall have a dress from it!"

"I? No, indeed, Kitty, I have no need for a new dress."

"That is your opinion, Mary, which nobody shares."

"My blue dress is very serviceable and will do well for whatever occasion arises while we are at Pemberley."

"There you are quite wrong, Mary. Your blue dress will not do for anything at all. It is many years behind the mode and it does not become you."

The shop lady joined in. "No indeed, Miss, if I may venture to suggest, your sister is quite correct and blue is not at all the colour for you. With your colouring, yellow or pink would be extremely flattering."

"There! You see?" Kitty crowed.

"Pink? I do not wear pink."

"No, you always want blue so you can masquerade as a bluestocking. I am so insistent on this, Mary, that I will even offer to make up the dress myself."

"There! What a fine offer!" said the shop lady. "And the lady such a fine seamstress!"

I wondered how she knew Kitty was a fine seamstress. I supposed Kitty had been boasting.

"You see, Mary, everyone is against you. You cannot refuse me. And Lizzy pressed me very hard to buy something for you to have a new dress, she knew you would try to refuse."

I did not think it proper that Kitty should talk about Lizzy thus in a shop. I thought it would be best to end the conversation as quickly as possible, before the shopkeeper thought we were both as wild and hoydenish as each other.

"Very well," I said, "thank you, Kitty. I accept your offer."

"I knew you would not resist for long! Now let us go next door to the haberdashers and buy gold braid. I long to make a pelisse a la Hussar!"

◆

I was not sure from my conversation with Mr Darcy whether he intended to inform Signor Moretti of my determination not to have lessons, but I thought it would be impolite to leave him waiting by the pianoforte. Accordingly I went up there in the afternoon. Nobody was there and I felt some relief.

I had become curious about the composer Beethoven that Lizzy had mentioned. Papa was able to afford so little sheet music that we had rarely bought anything new. I often copied music from the Lucases, but they had nothing out of the common, and none of our acquaintance in Meryton or nearby was particularly serious or interested. In Georgiana's piano stool I found copies of a number of Beethoven's sonatas. One of them looked as though it had not yet been used and I thought that would be the one I should try.

The beginning said "*Grave*" which I knew meant solemn and slow. It began very loudly with a chord and then went immediately quiet, followed by a silence. The second phrase came abruptly with an equally loud and shocking chord. My curiosity was instantly roused and I sat down and began to play.

It really was very different from anything I had played before, more dramatic and striking, and exceedingly difficult. My hands were not big enough to play all the notes in some of the chords, and I played many wrong notes because I did not notice the number of flats in the key signature. When it moved into the allegro there was a notation that I did not understand so I sketched through that part. But then it was followed by a section in which the right hand was required to cross back and forth over the left at great speed, with trills and extra flats and sharps. How could anyone be expected to play such music?

I was so engrossed in puzzling my way through the piece that I did not notice Signor Moretti come in for some time. I did not know how long he had been standing there. I stopped playing immediately.

"Pray continue," he said, "I see you are trying out the *Pathétique*."

I looked at the music and noticed the title for the first time. "*Pathétique?* That is like the English, 'pathetic', I assume, full of feeling, of pathos?"

"Yes I think it must be," he said, coming to stand at my shoulder.

"It certainly describes the opening passage," I said. "I do not know anything else that is so startling and dramatic."

He nodded, staring intently at the music. "Sometimes I think it is Beethoven's wish to shock us all out of our complacency."

"I did not know we were so complacent," I said, rather nettled.

"One does not, I believe," he murmured.

I was thoughtful for a moment. "I do not imagine that there are many young ladies who could master this style of music."

"No, Beethoven does not really write for amateurs. He writes what he wishes to write."

"Then perhaps he will not be rich and successful, if he does not try to please others."

"Actually, he is extremely successful, I know that he has many patrons who admire his music greatly, and so he is free to write exactly as he wishes. He is fortunate: many artists are ignored and reviled in their lifetime. Even Mozart did not receive the patronage he should have and was more appreciated after his death than in his last years."

"I did not know that. You seem to have made a study of it."

He hesitated. "I am interested in the lives and fortunes of my fellow musicians. Sometimes it can be inspiring, sometimes a warning or a lesson."

"Do you compose music also?" I asked.

"Yes, I have written some music, but performing and teaching are what I mostly do. I have never written anything to equal these sonatas."

I said, "Perhaps that is a good thing if your music is unlike these, because your music might be able to be played. Miss Darcy could manage to play Beethoven, I suppose."

"Yes, perhaps, but she has never learned this particular one. She was learning Beethoven's first piano sonata: this, you see, is his eighth."

At this moment a plan formed in my mind: *I* would learn the *Pathétique* sonata! I would learn it by the time of the Pemberley ball, and would astonish the company with my superior performance. Georgiana herself might be surprised to hear me. I became lost in thought as I imagined my triumph, the attention and the applause I should garner. Then I glanced up and saw that Signor Moretti was looking at me with a curious expression on his face that I did not know how to understand. His eyebrows were frowning but his face did not look severe, rather it was softened, and I suddenly felt that his eyes saw into my mind and he could read my thoughts. I turned away quickly. I realised that I had been talking to him about music for some minutes without even noticing it, when in fact my intention was to tell him that I did not require a teacher. Now he would think that we were to proceed as the Darcys had planned. I decided to speak immediately before this went any further.

"Signor Moretti, I have enjoyed our conversation but I should inform you that I do not need a teacher. I have always taught myself to play and a teacher might interfere with my methods."

He looked thoughtful. "I understand you perfectly. It can be extremely confusing to have a new person come in and unsettle a method which is working well." He paused, then continued. "But if, while you are studying this sonata you come across any problems to which you do not have the answer, you may come to me for help at any time."

I doubted whether I would need to do that, but I thanked him all the same. But then it occurred to me that I did not know how to play the left hand in the allegro. It was a strange way of writing that I had never seen before.

"Perhaps, before you go," I said, "you could tell me what this means." I pointed at the relevant bar.

"Ah yes, that is a reduction - it is a quick way of telling you to repeat the octaves from the bar before so that the copyist or the printer does not have to write out the same notes again and again."

"Oh, I see." I tried the first few bars of the left hand. "Yes, that makes sense."

I saw him looking frowningly at my hand as I played, as though he were about to say something, and unexpectedly I felt extremely upset.

"Signor Moretti, I do not wish -" and I ran out of the room, nearly colliding with Georgiana's harp as I went.

I went to my bedchamber and threw myself down on the enormous canopy bed, tears starting from my eyes. I did not know why I should be so upset. I was accustomed to slights and insults and I never cried then, so why should an insignificant conversation with an insignificant teacher of music bring me to this condition?

I wished I had never come to Pemberley! I had been much more content at home with Mama, with nobody to bother me or have schemes about me which were supposedly for my benefit but in fact made me exceedingly uncomfortable and put out. I did not like to have anyone observing me or trying to tell me things.

It was all Lizzy's doing! Why must she be so interfering? What gave her the right to tell me that I needed piano lessons, when out of all the Bennet girls I was well known for my proficiency on the instrument and my wide-ranging repertoire? She had become so puffed up with her own importance she thought she could order the lives of others as she pleased. I was sure that Mr Darcy would never have come up with such a scheme. He was a truly gentleman-like man, with dignity and consideration for the feelings of others.

I started to recover myself. I would not let Elizabeth upset me with her high-handed ways. And I would show her. I would show them all. The Beethoven sonata *was* very difficult, but I knew I could manage it if I practised hard and *that* I would do. There would be no need for teachers: I would learn it myself and perform at the ball. Perhaps just the first movement, but it was impressive enough to stand on its own.

◆

When I was feeling better I went to the library to write a letter to Jane. I knew she would sympathize with me. As I finished Mr Darcy came in and greeted me with a bow. When he saw I was writing a letter he offered to frank it for me.

"Thank you," I said. "It is for Jane."

"She will be pleased to have your congratulations. It was not a particularly easy birth."

I had forgotten that Jane had just had another child.

"If you are in the mood for writing, Elizabeth is doing the invitations for our ball and would no doubt be glad of your help."

I thought he wanted to be rid of me so I curtsied and left.

Elizabeth and Kitty were in a little parlour that looked out across the lawns to the wooded groves of the park. Lizzy was industriously writing, while Kitty lolled on a sofa, fanning herself with a piece of paper.

"Have you come to help, Mary? Kitty, as you see, is quite exhausted."

"Well, it is so tiresome writing the names of hundreds of people one has never heard of and then having to do it again just because they have been spelt wrong. My wrist is aching."

"I am happy to help," I said calmly, hoping to shame Kitty by my example.

"Mary," Kitty called, "there is to be an assembly on Thursday next, at a place called Amberfield. We are all to go. Lizzy says they do the waltz there."

"The waltz?" I said. "You surely do not imagine that is of interest to me."

Kitty snorted. "No, for you have two left feet. I tell you merely to warn you so that you should not dance. Anyway, Mr Speedwell is to come and teach us. Lizzy says he is a very fine dancer."

"A dancer!" I exclaimed. "That is unusual for a clergyman, is it not, Lizzy? *And* he rides to hounds!"

"He is not *terribly* pious or austere, it is true, but for all that he is a kind and good man, very attentive to the poor of his parish."

I was surprised to hear it. I had been starting to think he was merely a frivolous sort.

"And he and Darcy were good friends at Oxford," Lizzy continued. "I believe Arthur did Darcy a service at some time."

"Well, *I* like him," Kitty said, "even if you do not approve, Mary. Perhaps it is because of all his sisters, but I have never met a man who understands a woman's concerns as he does. He told me where I might purchase some swansdown to trim that old cloak of mine. Of course, he is not precisely handsome, certainly not as handsome as Mr Carding or Signor Moretti - "

"Signor Moretti!" I gasped. "You cannot mean it, Kitty. He is not handsome, he is far too gloomy and morose."

Kitty stretched out her foot to look at her slipper. "I think he looks brooding and romantic and extremely handsome."

"He is definitely not a handsome man," I said. "He is too tall and thin."

"But his shoulders are broad, and he has a firm chin."

"Kitty! Mary! Enough! This is most improper talking. Poor Signor Moretti, to be dissected like a side of beef in a butchers."

"At least you must admit Mr Carding is handsome, Mary."

"I cannot deny it. But he is excessively dull and stupid, with nothing to say."

"He is rather a shy young man, and much in awe of his father," said Lizzy. "You might find him more agreeable and forthcoming in different company. I am sure he will be at the assembly in Amberfield. I know he is very fond of a dance."

"Is he?" I said scathingly. "I thought he was only interested in shooting on his father's estate!"

"He won't ask *you* to dance, Mary, you can be sure of that. Especially if you wear that fright of a blue dress. Lizzy, tell Mary she must not wear that dress any more. She can wear one of mine, I will take it in for her at the bosom." At this Kitty burst into fits of laughter. I did not find her conversation either funny or proper, and I thought the best course was to ignore it.

After a moment, Lizzy said, "It may be best if you wear something a little more elegant and a la mode, Mary. Much as I deprecate her manners, Kitty is right when she says that the blue dress is past its best. Will you let Kitty lend you one of hers? The white stripe muslin would be very suitable."

"Not the one with the little rosebuds!" I pleaded.

"Don't talk about my dress with such disdain, Mary! I wouldn't lend you that dress if you asked me. Anyway it is spotted muslin, not striped. The striped one has a rope trim, so you had better take care of it. *I* shall wear the rosebud dress, though I mean to change them for some violet sprigs that I bought in Lambton."

"And what shall you wear, Lizzy?" I asked, more out of politeness than interest.

"I have a silk dress of pale pink that Mr Darcy bought for me in London last season."

"Silk!" sighed Kitty. "Oh Lizzy, how much I should like a silk dress!"

"Then you had better marry a rich man!" I snapped.

After all, the dancing lesson was not so very bad. I would have preferred to play the piano for the dancers, but Lizzy insisted on playing, saying she knew very well how to waltz and did not that day have the inclination for all the twirling and spinning required. It still struck me as odd that a clergyman should play the part of dancing teacher. I could not imagine our cousin Mr Collins doing such a thing, but Mr Speedwell was so flamboyant as he demonstrated the steps to us. The oddest part of all was to be held in the arms of a man. Mr Speedwell did not seem to feel any awkwardness, merely telling me where to put my hands and how to place my feet, but it was extremely strange.

Dancing in steps of three was also difficult to comprehend. It meant starting each group of three with a different foot, which was very confusing.

"Mary, you are so clumsy!" Kitty laughed, as she witnessed me stepping on Mr Speedwell's toes for the fourth or fifth time.

I blushed. "I'm afraid I am."

"Nonsense! You are doing very well, you have nearly got it. And you let me lead, which is more than I can say for your sister. Come, we will try again. My sisters used to tell me that I was the clumsiest creature in nature, and made me practise again and again until I learned the steps. Being the only brother, you see, meant I was much in demand, and I had to learn willy-nilly, they would not let me rest until I had mastered it. And then I in my turn taught my youngest sister Eloisa, and she became a very fine dancer, so I know I can do the same for you. You are very much of a size with her. A few repetitions and you will be dancing as well as anyone."

I felt as though I would never learn to waltz. If it was not for Kitty constantly mocking me I would have walked out of the lesson, but my pride was up and I would not be bested by her.

Mr Speedwell had just taken Kitty for another try when Mr Darcy came in. He smiled when he saw what we were doing.

"Come, Darcy," said Mr Speedwell, "your arrival is most felicitous. Miss Bennet is without a partner and needs your help."

I looked away. I did not wish Mr Darcy to feel that he must dance with me, and one thing I remembered about him was that he was not an enthusiastic dancer. But then I felt my hand taken, and he was bowing over it.

"Will you do me the honour, Miss Bennet?"

If my cheeks were not already fiery red from embarrassment and exertion I would have blushed anew.

"I am not yet very adept," I said. "Perhaps you should dance with Elizabeth and I will play the piano."

"That rather defeats the purpose of having a dancing lesson, Mary," said Lizzy from the piano.

"I am not as graceful a dancer as Mr Speedwell," said Mr Darcy solemnly, "but I believe I know the steps."

I thought it would be ungracious now to refuse, so I stepped forward and allowed Mr Darcy to place my hand on his shoulder. When his hand encircled my waist I felt the heat of it through my muslin dress. It was most peculiar.

Dancing with Mr Darcy was very different from Mr Speedwell. He was taller and I had to reach up to his shoulder, whereas Mr Speedwell was a more comfortable height for me. He had said he was not graceful, but it appeared to me that he danced effortlessly, and to my surprise I found that I was starting to keep in step with him.

"Mary, look up!" Kitty called as she spun past me.

I had been staring at our feet and I knew I was not supposed to, so made an effort to look at Mr Darcy's face. It was not easy. He was so very handsome, and he held my gaze without awkwardness.

"You are an experienced waltzer, Mr Darcy."

"I confess I am."

"I thought you did not like to dance."

He glanced at Lizzy. "I have grown more reconciled to the amusement in recent years. But Mary, perhaps you are not aware that you are talking and dancing at the same time. That is quite an achievement for one afternoon's lesson."

I was a little breathless by now, so did not reply. But I lost my step and ended up coming adrift.

Lizzy stopped playing. "I think that is enough for today."

Mr Darcy went to the piano. "You have not tired yourself I hope, Elizabeth," he said in an under-voice.

She smiled up at him. "No indeed, I am very well. But my sisters are hot, and Mr Speedwell has given nobly of his time and energy. I will ring for the refreshments to be brought up. Will you stay for a moment, Darcy?"

"Alas, I cannot. I should not have stayed as long as I have. I said I would meet with my bailiff at three and it is past that now. I do not want to keep him waiting."

He kissed Lizzy's hand and left the room.

Kitty flopped onto a chair. "I do not see why Mr Darcy is worried about keeping a mere bailiff waiting. If I were as rich and important as Mr Darcy I would do what I like."

"Kitty," I admonished her, "there is more to rank and responsibility than just the power to indulge your whim. A good landowner treats his tenants and employees with respect and consideration."

Lizzy laughed, I did not know why. "You are quite right, Mary. With high birth comes great burdens. Now, if Mr Speedwell can spare us the time we may be able to have another lesson before Thursday."

◆

Our visit to Pemberley was not turning out as I had expected. Apart from the dancing lessons, there were preparations to be made for the ball, visits to be received and paid with other great families in the neighbourhood. I barely had time to pursue my studies and piano practice. I had to stand for what felt like hours while Kitty measured and pinned the dress she was altering for me.

"Mary, you have so little bosom I do not know how I am going to make this dress fit you. Do you not have a better corset?"

"No, I do not, Kitty! And do not offer to lend me one. I cannot wear your undergarments as well as your dress."

"Do not disturb yourself on that account, Mary. My corset would not fit you, we would have to crunch up some muslin and stuff it. Perhaps we should do that anyway."

"No, that you will not!"

"It's only a jest, Mary. And stand still, unless you want a pin in your shoulder! We shall just have to lace you very tight. "

I sighed. I hated to be tightly laced.

"I know you do not like to be laced tight, Mary, but Lizzy and I are determined that we shall improve your appearance."

"Lizzy and you! Have you been plotting together about me?"

She stood back and surveyed her work. "Of course we have not been plotting! We have merely been discussing your wardrobe and your hair, and we are both resolved that you must improve. You are not so bad looking, you know, with properly fitting clothes, and colours that become you - not blue, whatever you may think. And Judith the maid can do hair wonderfully well. She is to do both of ours for the assembly."

"I do not like you and Lizzy to be discussing me."

Kitty pulled out a pin and stretched the dress hard across my chest.

"Of course we discuss you! Everyone talks about everyone, you must know that! Why, Lizzy and I were talking about Jane, and about Lydia too only yesterday."

I was distracted from my grievance for a moment. "Is there news of Lydia?"

"Only that she is writing to Lizzy for more money and Lizzy does not know what to do. Darcy does not like to give them money."

"Did Lizzy tell you that?" I asked, surprised that Elizabeth would talk so loosely to Kitty about her husband.

"Oh no, but Mama has often said so. You must have heard her whenever she gets a complaining letter from Lydia, she is always reproaching Mr Darcy for not being more generous towards Lydia and Wickham."

"I think Mr Darcy is quite correct not to give money to Lydia and Wickham. How will they ever learn economy and good management if they never have to do without? Ouch, Kitty, be careful!"

"But the Darcys have so much, why should they not help their sister who is living in poverty?"

"I do not believe Lydia is living in poverty! She will be spending beyond her income, and so will Wickham, unless he has forsworn his gambling habits."

"I don't think Wickham *can* forswear anything. Nor Lydia. There! It is done, and I think it will fit you very well. You might as well keep it now, Mary, I won't be able to restore it to my size once it's altered for you."

I decided to delay my studies until after the assembly. I wanted to spend time practising the piano. There were not many weeks now till the Pemberley ball, and also Georgiana would be returning soon, and would no doubt want the piano for herself. There was another piano in one of the smaller drawing rooms, Georgiana's old one, and I could practise on that if necessary but I wanted to take advantage of having the good instrument to myself.

The Beethoven was, I soon found, extremely taxing. The fast octave pattern in the left hand that went on for so many bars made my wrist and fingers ache and I had to rest often and practise the right hand alone. I did not understand some of the rhythms, but as they were bravura passages I did not think it mattered too much if I played them exactly in time. I was coming to admire the piece very much, and I could understand why Beethoven might be so popular. It was very exciting and did indeed live up to its name and was full of pathos. I was sure I could convey the drama of it very well, though there would be one or two passages that might be difficult. The section which required the player to cross hands put severe demands on my capacity to play accurately, but I was sure that over the next weeks it would come.

I was just having a look at the slow movement in order to give my hands and mind a rest, when the door opened and Signor Moretti came in.

"I heard you playing, Miss Bennet, I wondered if I might listen."

"No!" I blurted without thinking. "I beg your pardon, Signor Moretti, but I am merely practising and I would not like to have an audience for that."

"I understand." He hesitated. "I could not help noticing certain notes that you played in the slow introduction."

"Certain notes?"

"I wonder if you have always understood when the sharps and flats recur through the bar."

I looked at the first few bars and saw that I had missed them, which was perhaps why some of the harmonies sounded so odd.

"Yes, I see," I said. "Thank you."

I waited without speaking, hoping that he would take the hint and go. He did not, but instead wandered around the piano to look over my shoulder at the music.

"How are you finding the left hand octave ostinato? I remember it being fiendishly difficult."

"It is difficult to keep repeating the same thing over and over again," I said, "but I am sure I will master it in the end."

"I am sure you will," he agreed in a mild voice. "My hand used to ache at first."

I was tempted to ask him about that phrase, 'at first'. It made it sound as though he had found a way of making the passage easier. But I knew what he was trying to do: he was trying to draw me in by degrees so that without realising it I would end up having a lesson involuntarily. No doubt Elizabeth had instructed him to behave so, thinking to win me over. Well, they should not succeed. I was not to be so easily beguiled.

"My hand aches too, but I am sure with enough repetition my fingers will become stronger. That is how I have always practised, and it has stood me in good stead."

He frowned and chewed on his lower lip. He looked as though he wished to say something so I waited, sighing a little.

"No doubt you are quite right, Miss Bennet," he said finally. "I will leave you."

He bowed and wandered out of the room. It was some moments before I felt able to play again.

Another dancing lesson took place the day before the assembly. Now that I had danced with Mr Darcy, I felt much more confident and was able to do better with Mr Speedwell. Even Kitty was moved to compliment me.

"Well, Mary, I have never seen you dance so well. Imagine Lydia's surprise if she saw you!"

"I would prefer not to think of anything so uninteresting."

Mr Speedwell laughed. "I take it you have some differences of opinion with your youngest sister."

"I do not mean to be disloyal or speak ill of a sister – "

"Yes, you do!" interrupted Kitty.

I ignored her. "But Lydia and I could never be together without disagreeing. She is all frivolity."

"And you are all sobriety and sternness!"

I replied to Kitty with difficulty as Mr Speedwell was still turning me round the room, and Lizzy playing the piano. "Life is serious, Kitty. Remember: 'What is your life? It is even a vapour, that appeareth for a little time and then vanisheth away'."

"Very good, Miss Bennet!" declared Mr Speedwell.

"All the more reason to have fun while it lasts!" Kitty retorted.

"Touché, I think you'll find," said Mr Speedwell under his breath to me.

"All the more reason to do good works and prepare for the afterlife!" I snapped.

Mr Speedwell laughed. "A hit!"

Lizzy stopped playing abruptly. "You know, I think today's lesson has gone on for long enough."

Mr Speedwell looked rather shamefaced for a moment, but then I saw that his eyes were glinting with mischief.

"I do beg your pardon, Mrs Darcy, I felt so much as though I was at home amongst my own sisters, that I am afraid I have been infected by their high spirits," he said with false meekness.

Lizzy laughed. "I think you have quite enough high spirits of your own, Arthur."

Part Three: The Assembly in Amberfield

◆

By Thursday I was quite sure that I did not want to go to the assembly. I wanted to practise the Beethoven, and not give a whole day over to preparations for a dance in a place I did not know amongst people who I had either never met or who were the merest acquaintances. But as usual my wishes were not consulted. When ever my sisters wished to go on outings of pleasure, they always got their way, and it would never be worth my while to argue, as I would simply be overruled. Mama always took their side: I suppose she thought we should meet marriageable men. Well, that had worked for Jane, Elizabeth and Lydia, but not for Kitty and me. I did not think I would ever marry, but I knew Kitty was determined, and was not particular about who she pursued. Tonight she was mostly excited about young Mr Carding, even though she confessed herself that he was rather dull company. But that did not weigh with her: any passably well-looking young man had a good chance of catching her interest.

Judith did seem to know what she was doing with my hair. I usually wore it simply, pulled back into a bun, and let my fringe fall as it may. But she made an elaborate braid to wrap round the bun, and insisted on making tiny curls out of all the hair around my face. I thought it looked most peculiar and felt that I was unlike myself. Kitty came in shortly afterwards. Her hair had been curled and piled on the top of her head, with a wide bandeau in the same violet-sprigged fabric as her dress.

She had put more violets on her slippers, and when she saw me looking, said: "Yes, well, I had some violets left and my slippers were so dull and worn. I think I have brightened them up considerably, do not you, Mary?"

Judith said, which saved me the trouble of answering, "You look all of a piece, Miss Kitty, everything about you matches with everything else."

"I think I do look rather fine. I hope Mr Carding will admire me and ask me to dance."

"You are not truly interested in him, surely, Kitty? He is so very taciturn."

"I do not require him to speak, only to dance." She looked at me critically. "You look very nice, Mary, considering."

"Considering what?"

"Considering the raw materials that Judith has to work with."

I rolled my eyes. "Can you never make a compliment, Kitty, without a sting in its tail?"

"I do not know," she laughed unrepentantly. "I will attempt it one day. My dress fits you very well now. And you do not look quite so flat-chested as you do normally. Everyone will want to dance with you tonight, Mary, and you will have me to thank."

"You know I do not really care for dancing."

"That is because usually nobody asks you and you have to sit out watching your sisters dance. I prophecy tonight that unless there is a great shortage of men, which Lizzy says there is not in Amberfield, you will be asked to dance every dance."

I suppose I did look quite nice, now that my fringe was curled around my face. It was less severe, and my eyes were more visible. They looked surprisingly bigger than usual, though being grey they would never be particularly remarkable. The rest of my face struck me as neither pretty nor plain. Certainly I had always been told that I would never be as pretty as my sisters, but with my new hairstyle I did not think I was so very plain. My mouth looked somewhat frowning and discontented, I noticed. I could possibly smile more, but I did not like to simper and smirk and flirt like Kitty and Lydia always did, and anyway I had a crooked tooth, which showed if I smiled too widely.

We put on our cloaks and our long gloves and went down to await Lizzy, Mr Darcy and Signor Moretti. They soon came down. The two gentlemen were dressed in knee breeches and black coats. Signor Moretti's coat looked rather shiny and worn next to Mr Darcy's, which fitted him extremely well. I suppose he would have his coats made to order by a tailor, whereas Signor Moretti would have to make do with whatever might be found to fit him.

Lizzy's dress was a very pretty and unusual pink. She had lovely new pink slippers with silver rosettes, and there was lace around the neck of her dress. She wore a long string of pearls, which I supposed were real, and two combs with pearls in her hair. For once her hair was tidy, with thick ringlets tumbling out of a bun and clustering round her neck.

"You do not wear a cap, Lizzy," I said, "even though you are a married lady."

She looked up at Mr Darcy with laughing eyes. "I confess I do not care for a cap. Is it very wrong of me, Mary?"

"Of course not," I said politely. I wondered why she should ask my opinion. The wife of Mr Darcy of Pemberley could surely do as she pleased.

We arrived at Amberfield after a short drive that took us through Kympton. Our carriage drew up at the vicarage, and in a few moments Mr Speedwell came out and joined us. He was not in clerical clothes, but wearing a coat of broad green and white stripes, a diamond pin caught in an out-sized ruffle, and a waistcoat embroidered with silver threads. His hat was tipped at a rakish angle, and all in all he did not conform in the least to my notion of a man of the church. He squashed in between Lizzy and me, emitting a squeal and then laughing loudly at our confined situation. We did not have to suffer for long, but soon arrived at Amberfield. There were a great many people arriving, and as we went in we saw the room was very full. I looked for Squire Carding and his family as the only faces we might recognise but they were not to be seen amongst the throng of people. Beside me, Kitty could barely contain her excitement at being at an Assembly amongst strangers. I meanwhile steeled myself for a very tedious evening.

We had no sooner stowed our cloaks than the band struck up for a country dance. Mr Darcy led Elizabeth onto the floor and I saw how the company made way for them to go to the top of the dance. I would have been happy to watch, but Mr Speedwell bowed before me, and simply took my hand and led me onto the floor without waiting for my acceptance. Kitty I saw being introduced to an odd-looking man with large ears, and was soon in the dance, further down. It was a dance we often danced at the assemblies in Meryton, so I managed quite easily. Mr Speedwell had a little smile on his face the whole time, as though enjoying some private joke.

At last I said, "Why do you smile so?"

"With the pleasure of dancing with you, of course!" he replied with great aplomb.

I frowned. "That cannot be so. It is mere flattery."

He looked affronted, but still smiled. "But it is not flattery! Flattery implies an exaggeration of the truth, and it is no exaggeration to say that I have great pleasure in dancing with you. And when I see the envious looks I am getting from all the beaux and young bucks of Amberfield, my pleasure is doubled!"

"Now you go too far."

The dance took us apart for a moment, and I found myself circling with Mr Darcy. When I looked up into his face, he smiled at me and I smiled back, forgetting my unfortunate snaggle tooth for a moment. I was quite sure that at that moment, it would be the watching *ladies* who would be envious of my good fortune.

Mr Speedwell was back beside me, and we waited for our turn to go up the line. "Miss Bennet," he said, "If you are not sought after for every dance, I will be very much surprised. I am willing to stake a large sum on it."

"You are a very strange clergyman," I said. "I would suspect that your bishop would frown on you for gambling."

He gave a shout of laughter so loud that a number of people turned their heads to look at us, making me wish to melt into the ground.

"Oh, Miss Bennet, you are such a cordial! I rely on you to keep me to the straight and narrow."

"If that is what you wish, may I point out to you that you should step with your left foot first?"

"I thank you," he said, with that same mocking smile.

"Are you never in earnest?" I asked, still trying to understand this strange creature.

"Of course I am, but never when dancing."

◆

After a light supper I danced more, and then the last with Signor Moretti. It did not go well. It was a boulanger and neither of us knew all the steps. There was no opportunity for conversation as we were both watching the other dancers in trying to keep up with the dance. Whenever we joined hands his were rather clammy, or perhaps worse still, it was mine that were clammy. Certainly by this point of the evening, it was uncomfortably hot in the assembly room and most of the dancers had red and glowing faces. Signor Moretti's face remained sepulchrally pale. I thought he lost the rhythm of the music quite often, which surprised me considering he was a musician himself, and was accustomed to conducting, which must have meant being able to keep time.

Between steps he apologised to me. "I am afraid I am not a very adept dancer."

I said, "But neither of us know the dance, it is hardly surprising."

I confess I had been also looking around for Mr Darcy. He was dancing with Elizabeth as was only to be expected. He looked very graceful and in command of himself and I wished I had been dancing with him. I saw Kitty with Mr Speedwell romping around the floor. All in all, Mr Speedwell was not proving to be quite what I would expect from a clergyman. He was certainly nothing like as reverent as our cousin Mr Collins, who thought just as he should on all matters of propriety and correct behaviour. There was something loose about Mr Speedwell: I wondered if he should have gone into a different profession from the church, he seemed more fitted for the law or the military or some such.

I was very glad when the assembly ended and we could return to Pemberley. We were all very hot in the carriage and Kitty became tedious as she recounted every dance she had danced.

"And you know, Mr Carding was quite talkative. He told me all about the horses he is breeding for his father, racehorses and another kind with very strong legs for pulling the plough."

"How interesting," I muttered below my breath.

Kitty was immediately up in arms. "It would not be interesting to *you*, Mary, because you can only think about books and music and history and other things of no use to anyone. But someone has to plough the fields and get food to everyone."

"Surely one needs food for the mind as well as the body," said Signor Moretti.

"Man cannot live by bread alone," intoned Mr Speedwell, in what I considered to be a falsely pious voice. Everyone laughed, except Kitty and me.

"Well, Mary would have us starve to death!" Kitty retorted. "You cannot eat books."

"I never said you could! Don't be so ridiculous, Kitty, and don't put words into my mouth that I did not say."

Kitty flopped back on the seat, her face flushed and angry. "You think I am just foolish, Mary, but if it wasn't for me, you would have been wearing your old blue dress tonight, and spent the entire evening sitting amongst the matrons and dowagers as you usually do."

I felt tears starting behind my eyes. Of course I was grateful to Kitty for altering her dress for me to wear, but my sisters always made me feel silly and unimportant. Kitty thought that *she* was not getting due recognition for her talents, but she had no understanding of what *I* had had to endure at the hands of my sisters, my mother and even my father over the years. She had never had the mortification of being the plainest and least interesting of five sisters, and when I did excel at music or in my studies, I would be mocked by my younger sisters, dismissed by the elder, and ignored by my parents.

There was silence in the carriage. Kitty and I were too upset to speak, and everyone else too embarrassed. Finally Mr Speedwell broke the spell.

"I must say, that there is nothing so apt as a family row to bring an enjoyable evening to a perfect close. I now feel that I am quite at home." He said it with such an air of studied pomposity that Kitty snorted with laughter, and I almost smiled myself. Elizabeth and Darcy exchanged a look, and even Signor Moretti creased slightly around his eyes.

The next day both Kitty and Lizzy stayed in bed late to recover from the exertions of the assembly, but I had too much to do and was pleased to have some solitude to practice the piano. I worked for two hours but was unsure about my progress. Some sections I could manage, but the ache in my left hand after the long octave passage was impossible to overcome. My mind kept returning to Signor Moretti and his enigmatic phrase, "at first". Had he really found a way to conquer the difficulty of that octave pattern?

I went to the library where I thought I had seen Czerny's treatise on piano technique. When I entered I saw Lizzy sitting on a small settee with a man who looked faintly familiar. He was wearing a military jacket and breeches, and I thought at first it might be Wickham, but quickly realised my mistake. He and Lizzy were sitting with their heads close together, and they both started when they heard the door close behind me.

"Mary!" cried Lizzy. "Come and meet Darcy's cousin, Colonel Fitzwilliam. Rowland, this is my sister, Mary. I believe the last time you met would have been my wedding."

He bowed. "I remember you very well, ma'am, but I do not expect you to remember me."

I said, "I thought your face was familiar but I could not think from where. Your regimentals reminded me of my brother-in-law, George Wickham. I do not know if you have met him, he was not at Lizzy's wedding."

"I do know George Wickham very well: he grew up here at Pemberley and I was a frequent visitor here myself during my childhood."

"Oh yes, I had forgotten that Wickham grew up here. Are you come for a long stay?"

He looked towards Lizzy and there appeared to be some awkwardness between them.

"I do not know at present. I have leave from my regiment, but I am not sure of what duration."

"You know you can stay at Pemberley as long as you like, Rowland," said Lizzy, with unusual warmth in her voice.

"Thank you, Mrs Darcy, you are too good," and he kissed her hand. I was surprised to see Lizzy colour and I looked from one to the other in consternation. Suddenly I wondered what they could have been conferring about so intently when I came in, and why they should jump apart so guiltily. Had they feared that the intruder to the library was Mr Darcy himself? If so, what could they have to hide? And yet Colonel Fitzwilliam seemed a very gentleman-like man, with a friendly and open countenance. He was not someone I would naturally suspect of wrong-doing. But of course that meant nothing: consider how Wickham had deceived us all with his appearance. I did not know what to think.

"I have come to find a book about piano technique that I saw here the other day," I said uncomfortably.

"We were just about to go in search of Darcy," said Lizzy. "I think he is ridden over to Westcott Farm. He may be back and in the estate office by now. Shall we go?"

Colonel Fitzwilliam bowed to me, took Lizzy's arm and they left the library. I started to look through the shelves for my book but my eyes were not seeing the books properly. I felt strangely agitated.

◆

Mr Darcy was very pleased to see Colonel Fitzwilliam, and the conversation was lively at the dinner table. I had rarely seen Mr Darcy so relaxed in public; it was odd to see him smiling and laughing when he was usually so grave. Elizabeth watched her husband and his cousin chatting together and said little. She too was happy and at ease, and the half-formed suspicions in my mind started to seem ridiculous. Kitty was in a more benevolent mood towards me and we were able to remain tolerably polite to one another. She spoke mostly to Signor Moretti which I was pleased about, because he looked particularly pale and mournful.

When the gentlemen joined us after dinner I took a cup of tea to Signor Moretti and then sat beside him. I was worried that it was my fault he was looking so morose, because I had refused to take lessons from him. Once I had sat down I did not know what to say.

"Do you play at backgammon?" I finally blurted out, spotting the game on a shelf under a table.

"Why, yes, I do. Would you like a game?"

We sat at a table normally used for whist or other card games, and started to play. I was not very proficient; I barely knew the rules and had to be reminded. It soon turned out that Signor Moretti had a keen judgement of the game: of course the dice were in his favour, but he did make the better decision more often than I would, and he quickly beat me three games in succession.

"I am not very good, it appears," I said.

He looked at me in that thoughtful, slightly frowning way he had. "You have not played very much, I think."

"No, not much. My younger sisters used to play, but everything they did became silly or a quarrel and I did not want to join in. And my older sisters, Mrs Darcy and Mrs Bingley, were always together."

Suddenly, as I spoke I was surprised to feel a pain in my chest, an ache as though I were hungry or ill, and yet I knew I was neither.

"Miss Bennet? You look - troubled."

"Perhaps - I do not know."

I did not know what I was feeling. But for some reason speaking of my sisters and their friendships with each other had created a pain. My mind was strangely cloudy and full, and I shook my head hoping to clear it.

"Often - " he spoke hesitantly, and gazed into nowhere for a moment before continuing, "Often the life of the keen student, whether it is of music or history or some other subject, can be a lonely one."

"Lonely? I - I do not think - "

I stopped speaking. I could not understand why he would think I would be lonely. One was never alone at Longbourn; in fact, trying to get a moment's peace and quiet had been the aim of most of my days. Kitty and Lydia were everywhere, noisily laughing and arguing, my mother's voice could be heard all over the house. Even now with just Kitty and me at home, there still was little enough time to be alone, with Mama having constant need of our company, either to alleviate her headaches or to accompany her on visits to neighbourhood families or to help entertain callers.

I did not like him thinking that I was lonely. It sounded rather feeble, as though he thought of me as some tragic waif-like creature, as though I had not chosen my solitude.

"I was not lonely!" I declared. "I was very content with my own company, I assure you!"

My voice sounded considerably more cross than I had intended, but Signor Moretti did not seem to mind, only nodded in that grave way he had. I felt unaccountably annoyed.

"Perhaps it is *you* who feels lonely, Signor Moretti!" I said triumphantly.

He nodded again. "You are quite correct, Miss Bennet, I am often lonely."

I was surprised at his answer and was silent for a moment. "How can you say so? You are always busy playing music or teaching. You must be surrounded by people all the time!"

"This is true, but at all those times I am working. It is not the same as having somebody who is just for you."

I was discomfited and looked away. He was talking of his wife and the baby who had died.

"I am sorry," I stammered, "I had not thought - I had forgot - of course, your wife -"

"Thank you, Miss Bennet."

We were silent for a moment. Both of us held a backgammon piece in our hands and were turning it over and over in our fingers in a similar way. My throat was strangely constricted and I felt sorry for Signor Moretti.

"Was your wife - was she very beautiful?"

He looked quickly up at me and smiled. I saw that even his face could be changed by a smile. He said, "I think perhaps not everyone would call her so. She did not answer to the conventional model of female beauty; she was too small and inclined to be plump as many singers are. But her spirit, her character was such that she could light up a room merely by walking into it. At least, that was how it seemed to me."

"How did you meet her?"

"She came to me for singing lessons. She had already started to sing in public concerts, but she was untaught, everything she could do she had taught herself.."

"What was her family?"

"She was a foundling." He said this almost with pride though I knew that most people would be ashamed to be a foundling. "She was left at the Foundling hospital in Coram Fields as an infant, and grew up there. Her talent for singing was soon discovered, and she was adopted by a musical family as companion to their daughter. But she always knew she would have to earn her own living. When I met her, her benefactor's daughter had recently become engaged, and Isabella urgently needed to find a way to support herself."

I thought to myself that she had been fortunate to meet Signor Moretti, and make him fall in love with her. She had probably enticed him into marriage.

"Were you able to help with her singing problems?" I asked, more out of politeness than interest.

"I was. We worked together for a time, but after a few lessons I felt that she needed a singing teacher with more knowledge than me, so I sent her to my aunt, who had been a great opera singer in her youth."

"Oh!"

Kitty wandered over to our table with some cards.

"What are you talking of so intently?" she asked. "Flirting again, Mary?"

I blushed furiously. Why did Kitty have to ruin everything? For the first time I had been able to have a reasonable conversation with Signor Moretti and she had to poke fun and defile it.

"I was telling Miss Bennet of my aunt who was once an opera singer," said Signor Moretti. I looked quickly at him and he caught my eye. He was signalling to me that our conversation had been for us alone, not be shared with my sister.

"Shall we play at cards?" Kitty asked. Without waiting for an answer she called for Colonel Fitzwilliam to come and join us, which he obediently did. Kitty decided that we were to play vingt-et-un as if we were at a gambling house, and we could use the backgammon pieces to bet with. I did not really know the rules and so I quickly lost all my pieces, causing Kitty great delight. She amassed a great number of pieces, but I soon saw that the gentlemen were deliberately betting when they were bound to lose so that Kitty could win. I began to be bored.

"Will you not play some music for us, Miss Bennet?" said Colonel Fitzwilliam as the game came to an end.

"Yes, why not, Mary?" cried Kitty. "You have hardly played for us at all since we came to Pemberley. It is not like you to be so modest."

"I do not care to play at the moment," I said.

"You mean you do not care to play before Signor Moretti," she said, with great significance.

This annoyed me. "No, indeed. Signor Moretti has heard me practise a number of times. I do not mind playing before Signor Moretti," I said.

"Then perhaps you will do us the honour," he said, with that measured, sombre kindness that was beginning to become familiar to me.

"Yes, do play, Miss Bennet," said the Colonel.

"Perhaps Lizzy would like to play?" I said.

"No, I thank you, Mary," Lizzy said. "Without Georgiana here I am called on far too often as it is. Please play."

Despite what I had said to Kitty I really did not like to play in front of Signor Moretti. I knew he would always be comparing me to Georgiana, and now that I knew more about his wife I would certainly not be singing. But there was nothing for it so I played a piece by Gluck, an arrangement of an aria from *Orfeo*. I was surprised when Signor Moretti stood up without warning in the middle of my performance and left the room. I stopped playing abruptly.

Elizabeth stood up too. "What has happened to Signor Moretti?" she asked.

"I expect it was your playing, Mary," Kitty said, "you've driven him out of the room."

"No, I do not think it was," said Lizzy seriously, as though it might have been the case. "At least - what were you playing Mary?"

"It was from *Orfeo*, it was one of the songs, it was called *'Che faro senza Euridice'*."

"What does *that* mean?" Kitty asked.

Mr Darcy said, "I think it means, 'What shall I do without Euridice'."

Lizzy's hand flew to her mouth. "Oh no, poor man. It must have reminded him of his wife."

"She has been dead two years," I said, disbelieving.

Mr Darcy said quietly, "A love like that comes but once in a lifetime."

◆

York, May, 18__

So, my dear Mary, you are at Pemberley at last! I suppose you will find it prodigiously boring. There is never anything to do in the country. Wickham and I are much happier now that we are moved to York, where there is much more society. Of course things are rather difficult with Wickham in prison, as I am sure Lizzy has told you. If it was not for the kindness of Mr and Mrs Blackstone I do not know how the children and I would get on. Mary, could you talk to Lizzy and Darcy and solicit them on our behalf? I would ask Jane but she has just had another child and Mama is sure that Lizzy could well spare two hundred pounds or so to help us. My darling Wickham is determined to work hard to assist Mr Blackstone in his business venture when he comes out of prison and as soon as his debts are paid all will be well. I know you cannot be so hard-hearted to refuse: think of your niece little Philomela, she misses her papa so very much. Give my love to Kitty and ask her to speak to Lizzy also.

Lydia Wickham

Warwickshire, May, 18___

My dearest Mary, it was so lovely to receive your letter from Pemberley and quite set my mind at rest to know that you and Kitty had arrived safely. The letter was given to me only a week after I was brought to bed of your nephew, Henry Thaddeus Bingley. You will be pleased to hear he is a fine stout fellow even though it took him a very long time to be born, much longer than his brother and sister, which surprised me as I had thought it might be a little easier this time. I have been greatly exhausted so you must forgive me for not replying sooner. I wanted to keep little Henry with me and not send him out to nurse as I did Sophia and Charles, so I have been much occupied, but you will be pleased to know that he is becoming quite fat and I am very happy to be with him so much. Mr Bingley of course is very pleased with him but I think he might have liked another girl, as he adores Sophia so much. Not that he does not love little Charlie too, indeed who could not so charming as he is, but I think he was surprised at how it would be to have a daughter. My sister-in-law Caroline is here on a visit at present with her husband Sir John Loftus but I do not see them much as I keep to my chamber. Still I do not repine: much as I value Sir John, I do not feel that his loud voice would be very comfortable for little Henry. I am sure that at his home in Leicestershire where he is master of the hunt a loud voice will be a very useful thing, but in the nursery it is rather out of place. Kitty has written to me nearly every day and tells me that you are both very busy at Pemberley. I was so happy to hear of your success at the assembly and how pretty you looked. No doubt between you both you will have all the young men of Derbyshire in a flurry.

But my dearest sister, I know you will forgive me if I mention a subject which is perhaps a little difficult for you. When Lizzy told me that she had engaged the services of Signor Moretti on your behalf I was not sure that she had done the right thing, I thought that you might be unwilling to learn from someone you neither knew, nor were familiar with his reputation. Of course I would not press you, but I have met Signor Moretti and he has always proved a most thoughtful and kind man. When he has suffered so much, with the loss of his wife and baby, would it not, my dear Mary, be an act of kindness on your part to give him some occupation and let him help you with your piano? It is not

that I think you stand in dire need of instruction - you have always worked so hard and Charles and I have always said how much we enjoy and admire your playing - but of course nobody reaches a state of perfection with nothing more to learn. You would be both improving yourself, and helping a man who deserves our compassion. He is too proud to press you himself, and I know his self-respect will be affected if he feels he is not repaying the Darcys for their care and kindness. I have also heard from some of Charles's London friends the Blanchards who live in Hill Street that he is highly thought of throughout society as a teacher. I am sure I could rely on you not to let him know that there was any element of pity or doing him a favour involved. And while I am thinking of favours, I know Lydia and Wickham are very short of money at the moment, I believe Wickham to be in debtors' prison though I think Mr Bingley is trying to keep the knowledge from me while I am still in my confinement. He did not know that Mama has already written to me to beg me to send Lydia money. I have sent them some of my own money but it is very little, but I think at present Lizzy should not be troubled by Lydia's misfortunes. I know Darcy does not wish to be forever getting them out of debt and it might cause a rift between Darcy and Elizabeth if too much pressure is brought to bear on her. Charles and I have quite given up hoping to be paid back the last draft he sent them, but I hope that when Wickham gets out of prison he really does mean to reform his ways and settle down with the Blackstones. I cannot believe a man who Lydia loves so much could be so irresponsible, I am sure that this time he will make a success. Here is Nurse with little Henry, I wish you could see him Mary; everyone thinks he looks just like Papa. I do not see that, to me he is the image of his father. Henry sends you his love as do I and to my sisters and brother.
Jane Bingley.

Hertfordshire
May 18__
So Mary you are quite settled at Pemberley now and barely a thought for your father and me back at Longbourn I expect. Well so it always is, not that I complain although I am back and forth to Meryton every day to be with your Aunt Philips so much that I don't know if I'm coming or

going. Your Aunt is very ill: she has taken the loss very badly, cries every day and has used up all my smelling salts and her own, and does not know how she will go on without your uncle. Not that she is short of money for he has left her very well provided for: in *her* case there is no entail or children to be worried about, and so I tell her when she laments for ever about being all alone in the world. There is nothing so wonderful about having children I tell her, they are nothing but expense and worry and then they go off and leave you with never a second thought and hardly a letter through the post except little short things with the barest details of their occupations. She should be grateful she has not had children with their ingratitude and lack of consideration. But there I am not one to complain about my lot and that would certainly be wrong at this time of your aunt's grief, even if her grief does seem to be going on a long time. Your father is very well except for a headache, which plagues him at most inconvenient times of day. Whenever I want a word with him what should happen but he has a headache and must have peace and quiet in his library. I expect you have heard that Maria Lucas is engaged to be married at last: I thought Lady Lucas should never get her off, so plain as she is. Lady Lucas and I have often commiserated about the difficulties of having plain daughters, though of course she has *two* plain daughters. That silly boy of theirs has got himself into trouble and sent down from Oxford for some prank or other, but Sir William never reprimands him but treats it all as a high joke. We dined last week with the Ashtons, the Gouldings and the Harpers at Netherfield. It is the first time we have been invited to Netherfield since the Harpers moved there and even though the pork was not well cooked it made me quite melancholy for the days when Jane and Mr Bingley were living there. Alas that it was not taken by a single gentleman as I begin to despair about you and Kitty. At least you will not be homeless when I am turned out of Longbourn by the Collinses, but I hope you are taking advantage of being at Pemberley and not turning your nose up at any eligible young men in the neighbourhood. You will never be really happy Mary unless you have a husband and children, as long as they treat you with more consideration than I have been treated. And another matter, I wish you would drop a hint to Lizzy about Lydia's troubles. I know Darcy does not care for Wickham but surely he does not wish Lydia and her dear children to suffer for Wickham's misdoings. I rely on you to help your sister, Mary, and I send you a mother's fondest love.

◆

I was practising for an hour or two when Lizzy came in with little William in her arms.

"Mary, will you come for a turn about the gardens with William and me? It is such a beautiful morning and we would be glad of your company."

"Where is Kitty?" I asked crossly. I did not want to be interrupted.

"Kitty is gone to the kitchen to learn to make a comfit."

"Why would she take such an idea into her head?"

Lizzy smiled. "She is determined to learn to be a good housekeeper, or perhaps it is to tempt the palate of Squire Carding's son with sweet things. Now do come, Mary, you have hardly seen William since you have been here."

There was no help for it, so I followed them out to walk about the gardens.

It was a beautiful day, the sort of day that May can afford, when everything was fresh and green and slightly sparkling. William ran ahead of us on the gravel path, tripped and fell, roared and had to be comforted. Conversation was impossible until he could be put down again.

"I wonder the nursery maid does not accompany us," I said.

"Sometimes I like to have William all to myself," Lizzy replied.

"Does Mr Darcy not mind?"

Lizzy looked at me. "Why should he mind?"

I shrugged, and then remembered I was not supposed to shrug. "I did not think grand ladies such as yourself were supposed to bring up your own children. Will William not become spoilt if he thinks he can have his mama whenever he wants?"

"I do not think so, Mary. A little boy needs his mama, and he is not with me all the time, you know."

We walked on in silence for a while, occasionally admiring the beautifully kept gardens, trees, shrubs and flowers carefully arranged. It created a peaceful atmosphere of order and good husbandry.

I did not intend to speak of Lydia, even though her letter and my mother's letter were still sounding in my head. I did not see why

Lydia should get more help to rescue her and her profligate husband, when he was known to be an inveterate gambler, they both spent more than their income and neither had any notion of housekeeping. They would never learn economy and sense if they were for ever being rescued from every predicament they fell into. Anyway, the Blackstones, whoever they might be, had taken the Wickhams under their wing, so they were hardly going to starve. Lydia had an uncanny ability to find shelter and friends, however irresponsibly she behaved.

I was surprised to see Colonel Fitzwilliam appear, walking towards us from a different path. William immediately went dancing towards him with his arms outstretched, a foolish way for a child of two to run and having its inevitable result that he fell again. The colonel scooped him up and the child was so surprised that he stopped crying immediately, and started to pull at his rescuer's neckcloth.

"Don't let him spoil your neckcloth, Rowland!" Lizzy called laughing, as we caught up.

"Too late!" smiled Colonel Fitzwilliam. "Hours of effort gone to waste!"

"Nonsensical man! You have never spent hours on a neckcloth in your life."

"Oh, Miss Bennet, how can you let your sister give me such a bad character? You will think I have no care for my appearance at all!"

"I should respect you more if you did not," I said.

"Will you walk with us, Rowland?" Lizzy asked.

"That would be my pleasure," he answered, and with a swift movement he lifted William into the air and placed him on his shoulders. William squealed with delight and immediately buried his hands in the colonel's hair, sending Lizzy into more laughter.

"You will be a scarecrow by the time my son has finished with you."

"If William can turn me into a scarecrow, I dread to think what Darcy will do to me!"

It was meant to be a humorous comment, but both he and Lizzy were suddenly silent as though he had said something of great importance and meaning. I looked from one to the other in perplexity but they hardly seemed aware of my existence. All my suspicions immediately returned with double intensity. There could be no doubt in my mind that there existed between my sister and the colonel an understanding, an understanding from which Mr Darcy was excluded.

I did not comprehend how Elizabeth could have fallen into such lack of decorum or sense of her proper place. How could she behave in such an unbecoming way? Nay, how could she treat her husband so, and how could she favour a man like the colonel, agreeable as he was, above a man of Mr Darcy's station and character? I did not know what was between them, I did not want to let my imagination run away, although after the conversation Lizzy and I had had in her bedroom the other night, anything might be possible. But to risk the marriage and the life that she had gained - for what? What could Fitzwilliam possibly offer to Lizzy that Darcy could not equal or surpass?

We continued to walk along the garden paths, finding ourselves in the kitchen garden, where fruit trees were in blossom and most beds were showing green shoots. Our path took us past the forcing houses, but I could not see in because the windows were steamed up. A gardener and his boy tipped their hats to us and Lizzy exchanged a word or two with them. Other than that none of us spoke. I supposed Lizzy and Colonel Fitzwilliam were wishing me away so that they could continue discussing their secrets, but I was determined to stay with them and put paid to any such notions they might have. I owed it to Mr Darcy for his kindness to me, and however undeserving she was proving herself to be, to my sister to protect her good name and save her from her worst self. The colonel I saw in a new light: his agreeable manners and countenance now counted for nothing, compared to his treacherous character. I was shocked and dismayed, and hardly knew how to contain myself.

Later, Kitty and I were sewing together in the little parlour while Lizzy was resting.

"What think you of Colonel Fitzwilliam?" I asked Kitty.

"Oh Mary, you are not setting up another flirt, are you? How many men must you have to satisfy you?"

"Don't be ridiculous, Kitty. I do not flirt, as you well know. I only ask because I cannot make out his character. He seems an agreeable man, and yet I am not sure."

"Why do you doubt him, Mary? Everyone at Pemberley is so fond of him; he is welcomed here like a brother. Georgiana speaks so warmly of him. As to what I think of him, I never think of him from one moment to the next. He hardly ever wears his regimentals and he is shockingly old, even older than Mr Darcy, I think. There, does that answer you?"

Nothing could answer the suspicions that were raging in my mind, but I had to be content with what Kitty offered me.

I had been more affected than I intended to be by Jane's pleas regarding Signor Moretti. I decided that perhaps it would be the gracious thing to do to allow him to teach me, even if just the once. As Jane said, I would be doing him a kindness.

There was no need to hesitate, so the next time I encountered him, I said that I would be pleased to have a lesson from him, since he was at Pemberley for that purpose.

His expression was somewhat surprised, but he acquiesced politely.

"What time would be convenient for you?" he asked.

"Why not immediately, if you are not otherwise occupied?"

"Very well."

We went to the music room, and Signor Moretti began leafing through some of Georgiana's music.

I said, "As you know, I am working on Beethoven's *Pathétique* sonata. I intend to perform the first movement at the ball next month."

He looked up. "I see. That is very – ambitious."

"Yes, I think it is, but I am not afraid. I am sure I will be able to learn it before the ball. I thought we might use these lessons to improve it."

He came round to the piano and looked thoughtfully at the music.

"I think – I think it might be better if you were to leave the Beethoven on one side at present."

"What! Why?" I asked warily.

"Well..." he paused. "How have your lessons been in the past?"

I did not understand why he was asking this. "I have never had any lessons. There was a governess at our neighbours' house, and she started us off – Lizzy and me, that is – but after that, I taught myself."

"I see," he replied in his slow and quiet way. "So you have never worked on your technique, or been guided by anyone?"

I bridled. "I have read books about keyboard technique and applied them."

"That is most admirable. Unfortunately, there is no substitute for a teacher, for someone who can observe your playing and help to correct it."

I thought this an arrogant assumption; clearly he was trying to assert his own importance. I could understand why a man in his position might need to do this, and I did not want to crush him, so I spoke tactfully. "Of course, that is true of some people but not all. Perhaps you have not yet met anyone who has the devotion and the determination to learn at the level that I do. I know you work in the homes of very fine young ladies, who may perhaps be exceedingly spoilt and expect everything handed to them on a plate, to be told how to go on by others. I myself think it is quite possible to learn from books and from one's own practice and exploration, if you have the dedication and the intelligence."

"I am sure you are right, but since I am here, perhaps you will allow me to make some suggestions. I may be able to help you."

"Certainly," I said. "After all, you did help me decipher the notation that I had not come across before. There may be other things for you to show me in the piece."

"Thank you. My first suggestion is that if you are going to perform at the ball, you consider this sonata by Haydn as an alternative to the Beethoven. I think you will enjoy playing it, and it is slightly less demanding than the *Pathétique,* so you would have more chance of mastering it in the time available."

"Haydn!"

"It is a very attractive piece. May I play it for you?"

"If you wish."

He sat at the keyboard and started to play. It was indeed very attractive, full of vitality, and I was happy to concede that he played very well, with great vigour and accuracy. I suspected that he set such a fast tempo in order to impress me, just the sort of disguised boasting that I deplored. He looked up at me as he came to the end.

"What do you think, Miss Bennet?"

"It is a very nice piece, but I do not think it would get such a reaction as the Beethoven. I think you underestimate my abilities, Signor Moretti. I am accustomed to performing works of great length and complexity; people would be surprised to hear me play such a frippery piece as that."

He raised his eyebrows. "Beethoven himself greatly respects the music of Haydn. In fact, Haydn taught him for a number of years. It may sound light-hearted, yet there is great spirit and originality within his music."

"I do not disagree with you. I am only saying that it does not compare to the Beethoven for grandeur and drama and emotion. It would not have such an impact."

He was silent for a moment, as though he was struggling with some thought.

"Indeed," he said finally. "Very well. Let us look at the beginning of the Beethoven, and see what can be improved."

I sat down and played the first phrase, the sequence of minor chords.

"Shall we pause a moment and consider that phrase?" Signor Moretti said.

I stopped playing, irritated to be interrupted so quickly.

"Try it again, and endeavour to strike all the notes of each chord at the same time. At present, your fingers are going down at different times."

I played again. This time I could hear what he meant. I tried again, but I could not make all the notes sound simultaneously.

"I think there is something wrong with this piano," I said. "I do not have this problem at home. Perhaps some of the keys are loose and do not respond properly."

"Try the right hand alone," he said. I did so. I thought it sounded neater.

"That is better, but the contrast between loud and soft is very important here. Also, do you notice the dotted rhythm? The short note should be shorter, and that is a B natural, not B flat at the end of the phrase. Just try the right thumb alone."

I did what he asked, but I did not like it. I was starting to feel stupid. He was treating me like a child who knew nothing about music.

"You are very particular," I said.

"Yes, I am."

"It is very laudable, I'm sure, but in my opinion, if you break the music up too much, you risk destroying all spontaneity, and you will not convey the excitement of it."

"I understand what you are saying, Miss Bennet, but it is only by attending to the detail of the music during practice that you can fully convey its meaning and depth of expression. Only then can you have the freedom to be spontaneous."

"I think you and I cannot agree about this. I have my own views on music, and you have yours. I suspected this might be the case, and I think it best if we do not continue."

He looked shocked, but I would not be moved, even though my heart was beating rather fast. Eventually he said, "As you wish," and left the room.

I felt a little shaken and unable to do anything for just a moment or two, but gradually my composure returned, and I congratulated myself that I had at once satisfied Mr Darcy's request, and proved to my own satisfaction that I had been right all along. I would be much better off sticking to my tried and tested methods of working by myself. Haydn, indeed! He would see how he was mistaken when I astounded the company at the Pemberley Ball with my superior performance of the Beethoven.

However, it was more difficult than I had anticipated to attend to my piano practice. I was interrupted again and again, there was always some activity or other to be done, visits to be paid, William to be taken on outings and Mr Speedwell came to give us another waltzing lesson. Kitty had been disappointed that there was no waltzing at the Amberfield assembly but I was glad of it: I would have been obliged to dance and I did not think I had mastered it properly.

Lizzy played for us again, and Kitty and I danced with Mr Speedwell and Signor Moretti. It was quite awkward at first with Signor Moretti, as I had not spoken to him since our lesson, but the concentration required for the dance soon overcame other considerations. I thought Signor Moretti was improving as I was, and we were beginning to dance in time to the music and manage to change direction. Mr Darcy had driven to a nearby estate to talk with another landowner, but quite soon Colonel Fitzwilliam came to join us.

Kitty laughed breathlessly. "Look at this, Mary, for once more gentlemen than ladies. It is never like this at Longbourn. My sisters and I usually dance with each other."

When that dance had ended, Signor Moretti went to the piano and spoke quietly to Lizzy. After a brief argument, she stood up and he took her place.

"Are you going to dance now, Lizzy?" Kitty asked. "Oh dear, there ends my enjoyment of being outnumbered. Well, I shall sit this one out, I am so hot I can barely breathe!"

"Come along, Miss Bennet," said Mr Speedwell. "You and I shall show these two the way, even though they are fresh and we are almost spent."

This was not what I wanted to happen, but there was nothing for it, and Colonel Fitzwilliam bowed to Lizzy and took her easily into his arms for the dance. Signor Moretti began to play and we were off. I tried to keep an eye on Lizzy and the colonel, but it was hard to do anything but concentrate on my own steps and harder still to see anything when I was twirling round the room.

"Mary, what are you doing?" Kitty called. "You are not minding the dance."

It was hopeless. There was nothing I could do about Lizzy. I could see that she and the colonel were dancing very well together, that was all. I might as well think about myself. Certainly Mr Speedwell was a very fine dancer, it was practically impossible to dance ill with him, he knew just how to direct me without seeming to. For a few moments I gave myself over to the pleasure of dancing.

But then the door opened and Mr Darcy appeared. He stood and watched us dance, with a slight smile on his face. I saw him with pity.

He had no suspicion that there was anything untoward between his wife and his cousin; indeed why should he, I could barely believe it myself.

◆

Mr Speedwell stayed for supper and he and I had some conversation.

"Your dancing has improved - I declare, you have been hiding your light under a bushel all this time. I was going to say by leaps and bounds but I could not bear to see your disgust at such an appalling play on words."

As usual, I did not know how to respond to his banter. Lizzy would have known, but I did not have the art.

"And what about your study of Greek?" he asked. "How has that progressed?"

"Not as well as I would have liked. I have been very busy with my music, and then there is always so much to do at Pemberley, I have not had as much time to myself as I expected."

"That is a pity. I was hoping we could have a conversation in Greek by this time."

I looked at him wonderingly. "Can you really speak Greek?"

"A very tiny soupçon - we are not usually called upon actually to *speak* these ancient languages, just to read and understand them a little."

"I would have thought that you might need to understand Greek to read the ancient Christian texts."

"Indeed I would, if I were to do anything so fantastic."

"You do not read the bible?"

He smiled a touch ruefully. "Not as often as I should – and certainly not in Greek."

I did not approve of his levity.

"You are not very devout, Mr Speedwell."

"You are quite right, Miss Bennet, though - I wonder -"

He turned to Elizabeth who was sitting on his other side. "Mrs Darcy, would it be quite proper of me to take your sister on a tour of B__ when I next visit some of the schools and manufactories there? She has challenged my fitness to be a clergyman and I am on my mettle."

I was surprised by his offer, and I did not think I would like it. I had seen poor people before and they were not very interesting. They tended to be dirty, odorous and ill-mannered.

"I should think it would be acceptable," said Lizzy, "if Kitty or a groom was to accompany you."

Kitty overheard and cried out, "'Kitty or a groom'! *That* is no great compliment to me. What are you talking of?"

"Mr Speedwell has invited Mary to visit B___ with him, to see some of the work he does with the poor there," Lizzy replied. "Perhaps you would like to go with them?"

"Oh no, thank you, I see quite enough poor people every day in Meryton. They are rough and rude."

Even though Kitty was only saying aloud what I myself had thought, it brought out a stubbornness in me and I said, "I should like very much to go with you, Mr Speedwell. Perhaps we could take a basket of nourishing items from Pemberley's kitchens with us. And some improving literature. I could prepare a pamphlet."

He smiled. "What a splendid idea! I am sure a nourishing basket would be most acceptable to the poor of B___. And I would heartily endorse your idea of a pamphlet, but most of the adults cannot read, and those of the children who are able to attend school are well provided for in respect of their moral education."

Our trip was to be in two days. I spent as much time as I could the next day practising the piano and was pleased with my progress. The octave passage still caused me pain, but I found that if I varied the speed occasionally I could get through it. When it came to the cross hands passage I found that was more playable at a slower speed. I did not think it mattered too much to change the speed, as nobody was likely to know how the piece went. The slow introduction was also causing me difficulties, but if I left out certain notes of the chord I could get some flow, and the rushing ornamental scales could be managed, again a little slower than written.

I had found a book by Clementi with some instructions for piano technique, which I was following exactly. It meant keeping my wrist rigid and avoiding all unnecessary motion. It did make my arms ache but I knew that meant it would be doing me good.

Mr Speedwell came to collect me shortly after breakfast on the day of our visit to B____. He was wearing an extravagant and unsuitable white driving coat with at least seven capes, and although I was relieved to see that we would not be travelling in the curricle, I was rather shocked that he had yet another carriage; an extremely smart blue chaise drawn by a pair of lively looking grey horses with one of Mr Darcy's grooms mounted up behind. Colonel Fitzwilliam came out to admire.

"What did you pay for those, Speedwell?" he called, patting the neck of one of them.

"Less than they were worth, you can be sure of that," Mr Speedwell answered. He jumped down at this point to help me in. I looked at him disapprovingly. Surely it was not right of a man of the church to be pressing for bargains and cheating gullible people out of their due. I said as much to him as we drove away.

"You think me a very poor sort of clergyman, Miss Bennet," he said, with an exaggerated air of contrition.

I was not diverted by his play-acting. "I do not understand your morality. How can you be pious and devout, and yet lead a life like any country gentleman, as you clearly do?"

"I do not know how, but you are quite correct, that *is* what I do. Might it not be possible to do both? Are they mutually exclusive?"

"If you are constantly seeking pleasure and gratification, how can that serve God?"

He shook his head. "Do you think worshipping God must be all denial and mortification of the flesh?"

"'Blest are the pure in heart, for they shall see God'."

"Ye-es, the Beatitudes, Matthew, chapter 5, verse 8. But what does it mean to be pure in heart? Does it mean to be always solemn, always doing without?"

I was impressed despite myself at his easy knowledge of the bible. "But surely for a clergyman the appearance of goodness is important, to set an example."

"You are very tenacious of your point, Miss Bennet, but I am not disheartened: remember, I have six sisters so I too will pursue my point to the death! So, I would argue with you on two counts: first, who is to say that owning fine horses, giving waltzing lessons and riding to hounds does *not* give an appearance of goodness? And second, to outquote you: again Matthew, chapter 23, verse - verse 27 I think, or it may be 28: 'Even so you outwardly appear righteous unto men, within you are full of hypocrisy and iniquity'. Is not false goodness, false piety which conceals uncharitable thoughts more iniquitous than my modest venality?"

I could not help laughing. "You are so very clever, Mr Speedwell. I cannot match you for quotations. At least, perhaps I could, if I had time to prepare."

He smiled and said, "I must take care never to warn you of the subject matter of an intended dispute. You might vanquish me and then I would be quite cast down. I did not know that you liked to debate."

I was silent for a minute or two. "I did not know either. At home - my family are not interested in such matters."

"Then I must take the place of a sister and debate with you."

As we crested a hill, the town of B__ became visible. It was very unlike Amberfield where we had attended the assembly. That had been a large and prosperous country town, with the usual businesses and houses, not so very different from Meryton or Hertford. My first sight of B__ encompassed an enormous set of buildings clustered together, two monstrous chimneys and a number of large and gaunt warehouses, surrounded by tight rows of houses.

"What is that?" I asked breathlessly.

Mr Speedwell followed my gaze. "That, my dear Miss Bennet, is Allington's New Mill. I am sure you have heard of Benjamin Allington?" I shook my head. "He is one of the chiefest industrialists of Derbyshire. He built this mill; he built half the town to house all the workers that he needs. There are schools, churches and chapels, even parks for the workers to use."

"I have never seen anything like it," I said.

"Impressive, is it not?"

"And what do you do in B__?" I asked.

"I visit certain of the families, perhaps where the father is absent or cannot work, and help to get charity for the mothers, so that the children can go to school and not to have to go to work too young. We shall take your basket to a family that I know well, and then we shall have some refreshment in the Allington Arms. I have bespoken a private room for us there, and there will be a maid to lend us propriety."

This was all very strange and new. To come to such a town, and in the company of Mr Speedwell, a gentleman unlike any I had ever met, to dine with him. I did not know how to comprehend it, and for much of the rest of the day I felt as though I was existing in some sort of dream.

We dismounted at the inn, leaving the coach and horses with the groom.

"It is not far to the house of the Heely family, I see you have stout shoes for walking."

"The streets are very quiet. Where are all the people?"

"I imagine they are at work in the mill. Let us hope we have gone by the time the whistle blows for the end of the working day."

We turned off the main street into a side street, where the houses were older, and generally lower and dirtier. Mr Speedwell knocked at the door of one of them and it was opened by a tiny and well-scrubbed boy, who looked barely bigger than William Darcy.

"Eh, Mum, it's the vicar man! And a lady!" he called into the hovel. I guessed he must be older than he looked as he spoke much better than William.

"Hello! Mrs Heely!" Mr Speedwell called. "Tis only Mr Speedwell."

A thin, hard-faced woman came to the door, a small girl behind her clutching her skirt. "Eh, it's you is it, Mr Speedwell. I might have known when I saw that coat of yours. I thought when he said vicar it was that one from the chapel. He won't leave us alone that one, for ever preachifying and driving all sensible folks mad with his sermons and his pamphlets that none of us can make head nor tail of, not even our Joe though he has got his letters now."

Mr Speedwell caught my eye briefly during this speech. "No, no pamphlets, Mrs Heely, but may I introduce Miss Bennet from Pemberley, who wanted to bring a basket of food for you."

"That's very kind of you, Miss." She looked at me shrewdly, then back to Mr Speedwell. "So you're courting at last are you, vicar? About time, too. She's not so pretty but she'll make you a sensible wife enough by the looks of her. Sam, take the basket from the lady. "

Mr Speedwell roared with laughter. "I don't think Miss Bennet will thank you for your matchmaking, Mrs Heely. I am sure she could do very much better for herself."

I blushed to the roots of my hair. I was not accustomed to being spoken of in this way, and I did not know what to think of Mr Speedwell for his easy manners.

"There now, we've embarrassed the lady. Eh lass, don't you get het up over our funning. But you could do worse than the vicar here. Some might say he's not the marrying kind, but he's a decent man for all his joking ways. And at least he don't bore you to death with morality which I can't abide and don't need, for we're good folk here."

"No, indeed," I stammered, "I mean, yes - I..."

"There now, come in and take tea with us. Margaret, that kettle's been hissing these last ten minutes."

Part Four: The Visit to the Heely Family

◆

The little girl took my hand and drew me into the house. Her hand was grubby and I would have preferred not to touch her for fear of catching something but it would have been rude to pull away so I let her take me to a wooden bench, where Mr Speedwell and I sat side by side, while Mrs Heely busied herself making tea. Mr Speedwell removed his enormous white coat, to reveal an oddly cut riding jacket over a highly embroidered waistcoat and his usual bloated and intricately knotted neckcloth. I wondered what the Heely family would make of his extravagant style of dress.

"Will you have some food, Miss? Mr S?" she asked, with a familiarity that shocked me.

"Thank you, no, Mrs H, for Miss Bennet and I are to take luncheon at the Allington Arms later. But a cup of tea would be extremely welcome."

I was surprised to see that the china was of a decent quality, not dissimilar to our second best service at Longbourn, and the cups were very clean. Margaret and Samuel brought our drinks to us, carrying them with great concentration.

"And where is Joseph?" Mr Speedwell asked. "At school, I hope."

"Not today," Mrs Heely replied gruffly. "They needed extra hands over at Allington's and well, we need the money."

"The drink again?" Mr Speedwell said sympathetically.

"When is it anything else? Heely gets paid end of week, and if I don't catch him to get the money out of his hand, then he'll have drunk it away by nightfall. He don't mean to, just once he starts he forgets everything and can't stop. And it's bad for Joe, as he loves his schooling. They've got a grand teacher over there now, as doesn't beat them for the smallest thing, and he's learned all his letters, he can cipher, you should hear him tell his times tables. He's got Meg and Sam copying him now"

"I should very much like to hear him. I hope he will be here next time I visit. Will you give him my best wishes, and tell him I am pleased to hear that he is being such a credit to his mother?"

"That I will, Mr S."

While they spoke I gazed around the little cottage. It was a small dark room with a cooking range and a little bed, as well as the table and the benches where we were sitting. It was very clean and orderly and there were signs that tasks had been interrupted by our visit: a tub of wet clothes, a broom with a pile of crumbs next to it. I had been in poor people's homes in the country, but this place was particularly bare of possessions. Yet Mrs Heely had a cheerful energetic manner as though she was not bowed down by her deprivation.

"And the little ones look well?" Mr Speedwell was saying.

"Yes, they are well. As long as I don't start increasing again, that's all I hope for."

There seemed to be no inhibitions on what was a proper subject of conversation. I did not like to say anything about it, but I felt uncomfortable in front of Mr Speedwell. I tried to change the subject.

"You keep a very nice home here, Mrs Heely," I said, remembering the kind of thing Mama would say when we went on similar visits around Meryton.

Mrs Heely was not particularly grateful for my compliment. "We may be poor, Miss, but we don't live like animals."

Mr Speedwell said hastily, "I am sure Miss Bennet intended no slight on your home, Mrs H. And after all, compared to some - "

I did not know why he should be apologising for me, I had said nothing wrong. But even so, she was barely mollified. "Aye, that's true enough. But perhaps the young lady has come here with improving ideas like them others that come sauntering into our homes, telling us how to live."

"Indeed no, Mrs H. Miss Bennet is from the South near London, and she has not visited one of our new manufacturing towns. I told her that she could not do better than to meet the Heely family."

"Yes, well, we're people with our own values, and we don't take kindly to being told how to live our lives. I should like to see some of those grand ladies keep their little ones fed and their houses clean on the money I have to manage on, that I should."

"Quite right, Mrs Heely," Mr Speedwell said, laughing. "There is nothing easier than to tell other people how to live their lives, while having no understanding of their different situations."

I thought this was a reproof to me and my wish to bring a pamphlet for the edification of our hostess, and I tightened my lips. Mrs Heely noticed and said,

"There, now look what we've done, we've gone and upset the lady. Don't you worry about me, miss, no offence taken, I'm sure. But if you'd had to put up with the lectures and moralising that those fine ladies bring here, and nothing that can actually help or put food in my children's bellies, well then, you wouldn't blame me for being a bit quick to fly off the handle."

"No, indeed!" I said stiffly. I was increasingly confused and upset by this conversation. I had never heard talk like it, such familiarity between a man of the church and a poor cottager such as this was outside my experience or belief. I could no sooner imagine our dear rector at Longbourn speaking in this way with a woman of this class, or indeed Mr Collins doing so, than I could imagine either of them flying to the moon. I could not understand why Mr Speedwell tolerated such disrespect and plain speaking. And he seemed to expect me to be equally tolerant.

We took our leave soon after and returned in an awkward silence to the Allington Arms, where I was pleased to see some refreshments had been laid out on a little table in a back room. As we sat down, I said to Mr Speedwell:

"Why do you permit her to speak to you so?"

"Permit? I do not think I have much say in the matter."

"You do. By continuing to visit her and not reprimanding her, you give countenance to her behaviour."

"You think I should perhaps be more quelling?"

"She is not your equal in birth or education. It is overturning the proper order of things."

He said quietly, "I think the order of things may be overturning without my assistance. It is very different in a town like B___, Miss Bennet, to what you have been used to in Hertfordshire. The times are changing in such places, and the people change with them. My sole wish is to be of assistance to a family in dire need, a family who are trying their best to survive and are certainly, you must admit, a deserving case."

He spoke so reasonably, but I still felt upset. "And when she took offence at what I said, you did not defend me, but instead you *apologised* for me! All I said was that she had a nice home! There is nothing wrong in that, it was what Mama would have said."

He wrinkled his brow and looked at me in consternation. To my complete chagrin, I felt tears beginning to form in my eyes.

"My dear Mary, whatever is the matter?" he said, his voice warm and full of concern. This was too much. To have him become suddenly kind, and to hear him use my first name disconcerted me. I turned my head away; I did not want him to see. I was conscious of the maid's presence in the room: Mr Speedwell seemed to read my thoughts and dismissed her.

"Now do talk to me, and tell me what is troubling you. My sister Eloisa always told me that I am a very good listener."

I tried to restrain myself, but I could not help it, the words burst out of me. "Everything I do is wrong! Wherever I go I say the wrong thing, I am always on my own, nobody thinks as I do even though I always endeavour to think correctly. It was not like this before I came to Pemberley! Now everyone is trying to make me change, to think differently. I was brought up to believe that there was right and wrong, that everyone has their place, that the stability of our society depends on everyone knowing their place, yet I come here and I do not understand - I do not understand how you, a clergyman, can talk like - like an *equal* to people such as that, should even take *her* side against *me*, a person of your own class. I have never met anyone like you."

He said quietly, "You may not intend it as such, but I will take that as a compliment."

"And you are making it into a joke, as you do about everything," I said resentfully.

"I am treating you disgracefully," he said, with the hint of a laugh in his voice, and to my astonishment he reached across the table and took my hand in his. I snatched it away at once.

There was a pause for a moment or two as neither of us said anything. Finally Mr Speedwell spoke.

"Perhaps if I could try and explain, Mary. I know my behaviour is unfamiliar to you, and might appear unusual."

"I did not give you permission to use my name," I said in a small voice.

"No. No, you did not. I beg your pardon, it just slipped out quite easily, perhaps because I have mostly seen you in the company of your sisters, and you remind me so much of my own sister. It comes naturally to me to be informal with you. I shall now recover myself and treat you with due respect."

"You are doing it again! You are making fun of me!"

He said, laughing helplessly, "Indeed, I am not! I am sorry, Mar - Miss Bennet, I do wish to speak seriously to you, and I will try to be sensible. Will you forgive me and allow me to explain myself and my behaviour, which seems to you so incredible?"

"Very well."

"And will you perhaps partake of these extremely appealing delicacies which the Allington Arms has been so good as to provide us with, to give you the necessary sustenance to survive my exceedingly tedious perorations?"

Now I could not help but laugh.

"You might also find my handkerchief of assistance?"

"Thank you."

I wiped away my tears.

"Now, you have pointed out to me on a number of occasions that I strike you as someone singularly lacking in the correct attributes for a priest of the Church of England. Well, I do not quarrel with that. I was a friend of Darcy's at Oxford, and having to choose a profession, found myself slightly at a loss. When the living became available, Darcy suggested I might like to try it. I am not precisely a religious man in the way that some men are, but I am not *irreligious*, and I thought that a small parish in a congenial part of the country such as this might suit me very well. Not all the duties of a parish priest are as amenable to me as others – I am not at ease with sermon-giving as you so rightly commented, and my singing has been likened to the cry of a particularly unhappy sheep - but I do have a feeling for the poor around me, and though I have not the means to be such a philanthropist as Darcy, I can do some good."

"I understand that," I said, a little impatiently perhaps, "but I still do not understand why you are so disrespectful of the laws of society as regards class distinctions."

He became thoughtful. "Although I have never suffered material deprivation such as Mrs Heely and her like have to endure, I find in myself a sympathy for her lot: a man such as I knows to some degree what it is to be on the edge of society." I could not imagine how he might mean, but I said nothing. He continued: "And - well, I suppose I have a respect for her courage and spirit. You yourself saw what degradation and difficulty she must contend with."

"But surely God has ordained that it should be so?" I said.

"Who am I to argue with the doctrine of predestination?" he replied, the glint starting to return to his eye. "I only know that God has also ordained it our duty to relieve suffering where we can."

"But - the poor you have always with you?"

Now he laughed out loud. "Ah well, if we are going to play quotations, I think you will find I will come out the better. What about 'The Lord raiseth up the poor out of the dust to set them among princes'? Book of Joshua, chapter one."

I was stumped for a moment, then I said, "I think you will find it is in the Book of Samuel."

"Samuel? No, indeed! Is it? We shall see when we return to Pemberley. I am sure there is a concordance in the library. Very well, let battle commence! And eating too."

We drove back to Pemberley in great accord; Mr Speedwell had shown me his more serious side, and despite his strange appearance, his seeming addiction to display of all kinds, his unconventional approach to the church, he was a man of principle it seemed.

I went to find Elizabeth to tell her of my return. The butler told me she was in her little parlour, and as I approached it I heard voices, women and noisy children. One woman's voice was louder and more strident than all the others. My heart sank at the sound. I opened the door, sure by now of what I was about to see: my youngest sister, Lydia, lolling on a sofa, evidently very much with child, and with three whining unhappy children climbing all over the furniture and creating mayhem.

"Mary!" she cried. "How charming you look - though I would not wear such a dress for anything. I am come for a visit as you see. Now shall we not all be merry together?"

◆

"You don't look very pleased to see me!" Lydia said. "Have I interrupted one of your flirtations? Kitty says you do nothing but flirt with the piano teacher all day long. I'm surprised at you, Mary. Get off!" This last was addressed to one of her children who was attempting to clamber up her legs. Abashed, the child sat down and started to wail. I did not know if it was a girl or a boy, or what sex any of the children were, as I had purposely refused to hear anything about Lydia's children, and they were all dressed in identical frocks and pantaloons, rather worn and grey.

"Lizzy, I have had enough of the children now, can we call your nursery maid to take them away?"

"My nursery maid is not expecting to look after three more children as well as William," Lizzy said, and I could see that she was already exasperated with Lydia and her children. "I wonder that you did not bring your own nurse."

"Oh la, we had to turn her off when Wickham went into prison. It has been so dreadful, I have had to look after the children myself all day long. It is not enjoyable, I can assure you. They are forever wanting things and eating things and wetting themselves. If I had known what horrid things they were I should never have had any, and I certainly wouldn't have started another! Though how one is supposed to prevent it I have no idea. How comes it that you have only one, Lizzy? Do you know the secret? Loathsome creatures! Look at them now!"

Even I, who had no sympathy for children, could find it in myself to feel sorry for Lydia's brood. They were a forlorn sight. Two of them were on the floor, one of them crying loudly, the other, the eldest of the three with an expression of blank resignation on its face as it sucked its thumb with great ferocity, and the third still trying to scale Lydia's leg as though she were a tree.

Lizzy rang the bell and said, "I will speak to Mrs Reynolds and see if there is a maid who can be spared from the kitchen or upstairs to help Mrs Knowles and Hannah in the nursery. But you must help too, Lydia, you cannot just leave them amongst strangers."

"Oh, don't be so particular, Lizzy. I leave them amongst strangers all the time. How am I to attend parties and assemblies otherwise?"

Kitty said querulously, "Lydia, can't you make that little one be quiet? My head is aching with her crying."

Lydia tapped the littlest one's head with her fan. "Oh do be quiet, Theodosia." Theodosia merely cried even louder.

"Here," said Lizzy in frustration, and she picked up the crying child and gave her a bobbin to hold. Gradually the child's sobs turned into gulps and then long shuddering breaths as the bobbin caught her interest. The thumb-sucking one stared at Lizzy, while the climbing one was given a push by Lydia, fell to the floor with a thump and then took over crying duties from Theodosia. A footman came in.

"Thomas, would you ask Mrs Reynolds to come?" The footman bowed and left. "Lydia, for goodness sake take the child on your lap, you cannot simply leave him howling on the floor like that."

"Oh, very well," snapped Lydia, scooping up the child and putting him beside her on the sofa, "but this is Philomela, and it never makes the least bit of difference what you do, she cries until she stops quite of her own accord. I have long given up trying to console her; it does no good and only spoils her. She simply expects to be held all the time."

"You do not like being a mother," I said.

"Oh, it is the greatest bore imaginable! Of course I am devoted to them, but it is so much better when one does not have to look after them oneself. When they are clean and the nurse has dressed them, I like them very well, but they are such dirty, sticky creatures and they put their hands on one's clothes and leave marks. Horatio is the most sensible of all: as you can see he simply sits there sucking his thumb and making no noise. I am very fond of him. Wickham is simply infatuated with Horatio, isn't he, Horatio?"

Horatio tore his eyes away from Lizzy and the baby to stare at his mother, but as his thumb remained in his mouth, there was no reply to Lydia's question.

Mrs Reynolds came in and looked around, rather shocked.

"Mrs Reynolds, my sister's children will need to be looked after in the nursery. Is there someone who could help Mrs Knowles? It will be too much for Hannah alone."

"Mrs Knowles has a niece in Kympton if her mother can spare her. I think that would be best."

"That is an excellent notion. Please engage anyone who you think will be needed."

"Excuse me, Madam, Cook would like to know how long Mrs Wickham will be staying."

"We do not know at present. Tell Cook to prepare whatever is needful. Is Mr Darcy returned?"

"Yes, ma'am, I believe he has gone to change out of his riding clothes."

"Thank you, Mrs Reynolds."

Mrs Reynolds curtsied and went out.

"She is still as straight-laced as ever," Lydia said rudely. "She was not very friendly to Wickham last time he was here."

"Lydia, you will mind your tongue while you are here, or your visit will be of extremely short duration," Lizzy said sternly. "I will not suffer my servants to be mistreated at your hands."

"Oh, listen to you, Lizzy. You are quite the grand lady now, with your servants and your durations. Do not be concerned, I shall certainly not demean myself by *mistreating* your servants, as you would have it. But there is no need for you to grudge us a visit. It will not inconvenience you in a place this size, and this was Wickham's home at one time before Darcy turned him out, you know."

"And it most improper of you to refer to that matter. I would beg you never to mention it again."

"Oh, very well, very well, but you know you are far too nice about such things. It is all over and done with and in the past."

"All the more reason not to speak of it," Elizabeth replied, still in the stern voice that was strange to hear from her. "Now please take your children up to the nursery. Kitty will show you the way."

A blessed silence fell as Lydia, Kitty and the children left the room. Lizzy was breathing fast and I could tell she was keeping her temper in check with difficulty.

"Well, Mary, so ends all our peace. Oh, I would not have had this happen for anything! Darcy will dislike it so very much. And Georgiana returns in a week's time. Lydia must be gone by then."

"Does Georgiana dislike her too?"

"No, no, it is - oh dear, I must speak to Darcy and warn him."

"You did not know she was coming?"

"No, we had heard nothing from her, only a letter from Mama asking us to send money for 'dear Wickham'. She bowled up this afternoon as cool as you please in a hired chaise which I had to pay for, as she hadn't a penny, and there was nothing for it, I could not turn her away. It is so like Lydia, to get herself into such straits and then expect to find help wherever she goes. I am only glad she did not go to the Bingleys: most likely she could not afford to travel that far."

I was about to answer when the door opened and Mr Darcy appeared, his face like stone. Lizzy went straight to him and I think would have stepped into his arms were it not for my being there. She put out her hands to him.

"My darling, I am so sorry. I had no idea she would be coming, she simply arrived with her children, there was nothing I could do."

"Do not be distressed, Elizabeth, it could not be helped." He appeared to remember my presence, turned to me and said, "I beg your pardon, my manners have gone begging. Good evening, Mary, I hope you had a pleasant and interesting day with Mr Speedwell."

I curtsied. "Indeed I did, thank you, Mr Darcy." How like him to think of me, even with all this going on and Lizzy in such a state.

"I would like to hear more of it, but perhaps another time," he replied.

"Yes, Mary," Lizzy added. "How horrid for you to have to come back from your outing to all this. I know you are not fond of Lydia. And now Mr Darcy and I have much to discuss. We will see you at dinner."

I nodded and went out, just catching their next words. "Oh Darcy!" Lizzy cried, and his response, a muffled, "Come now, all will be well. We must discuss this like sensible human beings and we will find a way through it."

I smiled to myself. Darcy was a man of such sense and resource, no doubt he could manage Lydia's visit - and hopefully despatch her somewhere else as quickly as possible.

As I left the room I almost walked into Colonel Fitzwilliam.

"Good evening, Miss Bennet. Is Mrs Darcy within?"

"Yes, she is but she is talking to Mr Darcy about a matter of some importance and they do not wish to be disturbed."

"Oh, Darcy's in there, is he?" Colonel Fitzwilliam looked a little uncomfortable. "I suppose that means he knows that Mrs Wickham is here."

"Yes, he does."

We stood where we were for a few minutes. I was determined to face him out and keep him away from Lizzy and Darcy. He hesitated and could not seem to decide what to do.

I said, "I am sure Mr Darcy will be able to deal with the situation perfectly well."

"The situation?"

"Mrs Wickham's sudden appearance with all her children. I know he does not care for Wickham or for Lydia."

He looked at me strangely. "You know that, do you? Yes, quite right, quite right, he don't care for Wickham at all. The man's a thoroughly bad lot. Well, well, I shall go change for dinner. Time is getting on."

He bowed and walked away. I watched him until I was sure he had gone upstairs. His manners were becoming stranger and more disjointed. I did not understand him at all.

◆

Elizabeth was right: with the arrival of Lydia our peace was destroyed. We sat down eight for dinner that evening, as Mr Speedwell had stayed at Mr Darcy's invitation, but with Lydia there it felt more like eighteen. She came down late, wearing an extraordinary gown that would have been more suitable in a ballroom: it was orange satin of a brilliant hue with a deep plunging neckline, a double ruff round the hem, and an overdress of silver gauze with a long train. She looked very peculiar with her large pregnant belly. She had bangles round her arms and on her head a turban with an orange-dyed ostrich feather, somewhat drooping and aged. At least she was not wearing gloves at the dinner table.

"How do you like my dress, Kitty?" she crowed. "You could not make anything so fine, I think. I had it copied from a French magazine."

Kitty did not appear to have anything to say, but merely stared at the dress. I could not tell if it was envy or mortification that Lydia should look so dazzling, or some other emotion.

Finally Kitty said, "Did you know there is a tear at the back of the sleeve?"

"No, is there?" Lydia twisted round to try and look. "Oh, bother that stupid maid."

"If you ask Judith she will stitch it for you tonight," Lizzy said.

"She should have noticed when she was dressing me!" Lydia exclaimed.

"Lydia, you have not met our guests, Signor Moretti, Georgiana's music teacher, and Mr Speedwell, who is the rector of Kympton."

Lydia put her hand out to be kissed, and curtsied in an exaggerated fashion. "Kympton? Just think, that is the living Wickham might have had. But then, he and I would never have met! And I do not think the church would have suited him. He was much better off in the militia. Oh, Mr Darcy, how do you do? What a fine table, Lizzy! That silver epergne is very like something Wickham and I had before we had to sell it. You cannot imagine how inconvenient it is to have to sell everything. Still, when we moved to the Blackstones we did not have many possessions to bring, so that was a good thing in the end, as their house is not very large and we had to put the children somewhere."

"What is Mr Blackstone's business?" Mr Darcy asked.

"Lord, I don't know. Something to do with canals or roads or some such thing that nobody can understand."

"Let us hope that Mr Wickham understands it," I said, "if they are to go into business together."

"Yes well, that will come about if only Wickham can be released from prison!" She looked pointedly at Lizzy, who held her gaze, her own face expressionless. "I do not know why they should put Wickham in prison all of a sudden. It was such a very little debt too, not more than five or six hundred pounds. For some people that is less than they would spend on a horse. We have often owed as much, if not more, and there has been no talk of prisons. I think someone had a grudge against my dear Wickham: it is often so, I believe, with someone so handsome and charming, and so much admired wherever he goes. There is always a spiteful person -" here she scowled at Mr Darcy, "- who will want to ruin the lives of others who they perceive as more successful."

Lizzy turned to me and said loudly, "Mary, you and Mr Speedwell have been visiting in B__ today. What were your impressions of the town? We would so much like to hear."

"Mary, you secretive person! You are quite changed!" Lydia cried. "First the music teacher, now the rector! Mama will get the shock of her life if you come back from Pemberley married! Out for the day with the vicar! What a goer you are!" She laughed, and Kitty laughed with her: it was as though we were back at Longbourn and nothing had changed. I felt sickened and embarrassed, ashamed to have such a sister. I glanced anxiously at Mr Speedwell to see how he was reacting but his face was calm, even amused. Signor Moretti's face was wholly impassive. I could not now answer Lizzy's question, and anyway, I did not want to expose myself to more of Lydia's ridicule.

There was a silence for a moment or two, when everyone was at a loss. Then Mr Darcy said, "Speedwell, the colonel was admiring those greys of yours. How are they working out?"

"They are a very fine pair, with a good action. I think Miss Bennet had a very comfortable drive today. And no, Colonel Fitzwilliam, they are not for sale!"

The colonel laughed. "I understood that you drove a hard bargain to get them. I would not like to do business with you, no doubt you would fleece me without ceremony."

"Well, you know, we poor men of the church!" This was directed at Mr Darcy, and the mischievous spark in Mr Speedwell's eye made everyone laugh.

"I don't know why you should say so!" said Lydia. "Wickham said the living was worth more than a thousand a year. That would have suited us very well, you know."

Lizzy tightened her lips and tried to frown Lydia down. If we had indeed been back at Longbourn she could and would have reprimanded Lydia, but it was not possible with all these visitors, and anyway, Lydia was a married lady now, and should know how to behave with propriety.

The rest of the meal proceeded in a similar fashion. Ordinary conversations were attempted but were soon interrupted or overruled by Lydia's brash and unsuitable comments. It was a relief when Lizzy rose for the ladies to retire.

I did not go to the drawing room with the others, but instead went down to the library, picking up a branch of candles from a hallway. I could not bear to be with Lydia again, and thought that a few moments to myself might restore the tone of my mind. I picked a book at random from the shelf, a volume of botanical illustrations, and sat in one of the deep leather chairs, turning the pages unthinkingly and barely seeing the carefully executed etchings.

My nerves were jangling and on edge, and even my hands were shaking slightly. I had just been starting to feel that I could relax at Pemberley, that I would not be disturbed or vilified or mocked but could go about my business with impunity. At Longbourn, Kitty and I were thrown much together, and although it was often difficult between us with bickering we had been rubbing along and tolerating each other more or less. With Lydia here, all that would be changed: she and Kitty together had always made my life a misery. I knew that Lydia's attractions would always outweigh mine, and they would join forces against me again. The trouble was that at Pemberley I could not feel quite as indifferent as I had been used to. Apparently I had become accustomed to being treated with a degree of deference and consideration and so I was no longer prepared for Lydia's attacks. This must be why I was feeling so tremulous.

The door opened and somebody came in. I sat up in my chair and tried to look calm and collected. It was Mr Darcy.

"Mary!" he exclaimed. "I did not know you were here. Are you well?"

"Yes, I am quite well. I wanted - I could not -"

"I expect you wanted some peace and quiet."

I smiled at him gratefully. "I am not used to Lydia's company any longer. It is very - different at Longbourn now without her."

Mr Darcy took a seat at a table next to me. "Yes, I can well believe it. And the conversation at dinner was such that we did not have an opportunity to hear your impressions of B__. It is a fascinating place, is it not?"

"Oh! Yes, yes it was fascinating. It was unlike any other place I have been. I did not know that such places could exist. And the family Mr Speedwell took me to were...were most unusual."

"The Heelys?"

"You know them also?"

"I put them in Speedwell's way. I have some connection with the school there and I had come across young Joseph Heely as a promising boy."

"Mrs Heely is very - she is not very respectful."

Mr Darcy smiled. "No, she is not."

I looked at him wonderingly. "You do not mind?"

"There are different kinds of pride, Mary, and there are times when to be too conscious of one's rank must make one insufferable."

"But - rank is rank! These are not matters of whim."

"No indeed, and I would not suffer impertinence or disrespect. But I hope I do not require my rank to be reinforced by humbling people who have their own innate pride."

"No, I see that. She was very proud of her home, even though it is nothing more than a hovel."

"Yes, she is almost as proud of her *hovel* as my aunt, Lady Catherine, is of Rosings!"

I laughed.

"Shall we go upstairs to the sitting room? Elizabeth will be wondering where I have disappeared to."

He stood up and reached down a hand to me. I put my hand into his and let him help me out of the chair.

◆

An invitation had arrived for a dinner at the Cardings, where there was to be dancing and card play, and the invitation had been extended to Lydia, now that her presence at Pemberley was known. I wished we were not going: it meant another day with my hair in curl papers, and more fuss about what to wear.

"You cannot wear my dress again, Mary," Kitty said. "You wore it at dinner with the Cardings when they came here."

"They would not notice," I said.

Lydia was lounging with her feet up on a chair. "In York society no woman would wear the same dress twice amongst the same people. It would be very much frowned upon."

"And I suppose being in a debtor's prison is not frowned upon?"

"Oh Mary, how you do take one up! I am only telling you how things are done in polite society, because I have been about the world, and know so much more than you now. Anyway, there are some very respectable people in debtor's prison, for example, the younger son of the Earl of T__; his family have quite cut him off for spending all his allowance. He and Wickham are good friends now."

"Perhaps I could wear a scarf or a collar," I said to Kitty, trying to ignore Lydia.

"I suppose that might do," Kitty mused.

"Nobody will be looking at you anyway, Mary," said Lydia. "I shall be wearing my new puce gown, it becomes me very well."

"Isn't that a little bold for a simple dinner at the local Squire's manor?" I asked. "You will look overdressed."

Lydia smiled pityingly at me. "I think not. The rest of you will simply look as though you have not made the effort. What shall you wear, Kitty? Not that dress of yours with sprigged roses on it, I hope"

"They are violets now."

"It is so *jeune fille*! You are moving in higher circles now and should try to look more sophisticated, a touch more *décolleté*. I can lend you one of mine, it is pink, oh no, that would clash horribly with my puce. I have one in ivory satin that would do, with a dash of lace and some pearls."

"Mary could wear that," Kitty said. "I have a pale blue muslin that is hardly worn."

Lydia laughed. "Mary cannot wear my dresses, Kitty, she cannot fill them."

They both went into paroxysms of laughter.

"Such hilarity," I murmured. "I will leave you to your conversation. I have better things to do."

I did not have anything better to do, but for some reason I was drawn to go to the library again. Mr Darcy was not there - it was not to be expected at such an hour. I stared at the shelves for a minute or two, thinking about how I was neglecting my studies, remembering my project to learn Greek. I could not understand why I was so much busier at Pemberley than I was at Longbourn. Perhaps because I was practising more, and then there were our waltzing lessons, our visits, but I could not be sure. Something was different at Pemberley, I did not feel quite so in control of my time as I did at Longbourn, I did not feel so settled and sure of myself. I decided to go to my room and write a letter or two. Some solitude, some ordinary activity would do me more good than anything.

As I reached the top of the stairs to the bedroom floor, I saw, down the hall, silhouetted by a window, Lizzy and Colonel Fitzwilliam. She had both his hands encased between hers and was talking to him most earnestly. I backed away and hid behind the wall out of sight. This was getting worse and worse. I could no longer deny the evidence of my own eyes: something untoward was going on between Lizzy and the Colonel.

What was I to do? I could not let Mr Darcy be so deceived. But how could I tell him? What words could I find for something that I could barely allow to become words in my own head? And how could I be the cause of such grief to him? But then I thought, it would not be me causing the grief, but the perpetrators, the betrayers, Lizzy and the Colonel. Yes, it would give Mr Darcy pain to find out what had been going on, but it would be better in the end that he should know. He deserved a better wife than Lizzy, somebody who would value him as he ought to be valued, as a good, kind man. And Lizzy, what a hypocrite she was turning out to be! Talking about her married life with Mr Darcy as though it was so important to her, trying to protect him from the demands of Lydia, acting so contrite, yet all the time carrying on behind his back with his own cousin. How dreadful my sisters were turning out to be! Even Lizzy, who was not afraid to moralise. Mr Speedwell was right, it was worse to be a hypocrite, to pretend to goodness: at least Lydia made no pretence at propriety. Thank heavens for Jane, who could still be relied on for her goodness and honesty. And even Kitty had not strayed, though I could not place great dependence on her moral character.

Lizzy appeared alone at the top of the stairs, and I acted as though I had just arrived there.

"I am going to write to Mama," I said, inwardly marvelling at my appearance of calm. "Shall I send her a message?"

"Give her my love. I shall be writing myself in the next day or two."

She looked a little flustered and ill at ease, but nothing like as guilty as I thought would have been appropriate to her behaviour. Was she so lost to decency that she did not even feel ashamed?

Once I was seated at the escritoire in my room, staring out the window at the rain, my pen sharpened, a notion occurred to me. Even though I would not be able to speak aloud to Mr Darcy, I could write to him. I would not sign the letter, it would be better if he did not know who it was from. I began.

Sir, I wish to inform you that a relationship - no, an improper relationship - exists between your wife and your cousin. I am sorry to cause you pain, but I thought you would wish to know. Yours, a well-wisher.

I disguised my hand by writing in ill-formed capital letters, such as a servant might use, folded the letter, sealed it and addressed it to Mr Darcy, Private. Then I went down towards his bedroom to post it, as that seemed the safest place to leave it.

When I reached Lizzy's door I heard voices within. It sounded like Lizzy and Mr Darcy talking and I wondered what they were doing there in mid-afternoon, and how Lizzy could even look him in the eye when she had just left Colonel Fitzwilliam. I pressed my ear to the door, but could not make out any words, only sounds and murmurings. They seemed occupied, so I quickly ran into Mr Darcy's room and placed the letter under a brush on his dressing table. I had never been in a man's bedroom before and I would have liked to linger and look about me but it would be fatal to be discovered there so I left quickly.

At dinner that night I saw no sign that Mr Darcy had received my letter. His aspect was much as usual, composed and self-contained. Colonel Fitzwilliam and Lizzy however did both appear unlike themselves, a little pale and agitated. I caught Mr Darcy looking at Elizabeth a few times, but his expression was concerned rather than suspicious.

The next day at breakfast I saw Colonel Fitzwilliam. He said good morning to me with his customary friendliness, then added,

"And it is farewell for the present, Miss Bennet. I have had a letter from my general and he dispatches me on an errand to the North."

"Will you return soon?"

"That is my intention."

"But you will miss the dinner at Squire Carding's tonight."

"Yes, I have sent my apologies. I hope you have an enjoyable evening."

This was very mysterious. I did not believe that he had heard from his general. There was something else afoot here. Perhaps Mr Darcy had confronted him and sent him packing? Or Elizabeth had become frightened of discovery and told him to make himself scarce? I could not find out without asking one of the parties concerned, and that of course was impossible.

Perhaps it was not so bad to spend the day getting ready for the party, as it had been raining constantly for two or three days now, and the outdoors looked very dismal. I was quite happy to practice on the pianoforte with my hair in curling papers: I felt no embarrassment when Signor Moretti came upon me in that state. He was more embarrassed than I was, and left the room rather hurriedly.

Lydia came to my room to interfere with Kitty, who was trying to arrange a lace collar to my dress. Lydia was changed into the puce frock she had mentioned. It was a hideous garment, and not at all becoming, nor was her appearance helped by the rouge she had seen fit to apply to her cheeks.

"You look like a clown, Lydia," I said.

"Better than looking like a frump," she retorted. "You can censure my appearance when you are married and have as many flirts as I do. Oh, I forgot," she laughed, "you are now the chief flirt of Pemberley."

"Very amusing, Lydia. Obviously you cannot conceive of the idea that a woman may talk to a man in a rational manner. But of course you cannot, you never spoke in a rational manner in your life."

"Ooh, listen to you! You are turning into quite a wit, Mary. No doubt you will have everyone laughing at you all evening. More than they do already, that is."

To my surprise, Kitty had said nothing throughout this interchange, merely carrying on with her task with tightened lips. I had been waiting every moment for her to join in with Lydia.

"There you are," she said at last. "You were right, Mary, the collar does make it look different."

"A smidgen of rouge would do wonders for your complexion," Lydia said

Kitty answered for me, "Mary does not need rouge, she is getting compliments now for her pale skin."

I looked closely at Kitty to see she if was teasing me, but her expression was perfectly serious.

"Who would say such things?" I asked.

"Oh, I overheard a conversation between Mr Darcy and Signor Moretti. Lizzy said to Darcy did he not think you looked much improved since you had come to Pemberley. He said he did, but still a little pale, and that perhaps you should go outdoors more and not study and practice so much. And Signor Moretti said that alabaster skin such as yours was much admired in London."

"Alabaster?" I said in astonishment. Nobody had ever said such a thing about me before in my life.

"Alabaster!" snorted Lydia. "What a joke! Well, if ghostly pallor is to his taste, I wish him joy of it."

"There is no need to be jealous, Lydia," Kitty said, astonishing me still more. "Nobody is saying Mary is as pretty as you or the rest of us, but she does have *some* attractions, and why should not the gentlemen appreciate them?"

Lydia's mouth dropped open, and she looked as though she was about to speak, when there was a knock at the door. It was Hannah, the nursery-maid.

"Excuse me, Mrs Wickham, Mrs Darcy says please can you come to the nursery as little Horatio is not well and is crying for his Mama."

"Can you not just put him to bed? He is always sickening for something and it never makes the slightest difference if I am there or not."

"Mrs Darcy said most particular that you was to come."

"Oh, very well."

Lydia left us with something of a flounce.

I wondered if Horatio's indisposition would prevent Lydia's accompanying us to the Cardings' but I should have known better. She insisted that there was nothing wrong with him that a bowl of gruel and an early night would not cure, and we set off in good time. The rain was coming down quite hard and I wondered if we were wise to go. Our speed was necessarily slow but we had set off early enough and arrived promptly. I was glad when the journey was over. It was exceedingly crowded, even in Mr Darcy's fine carriage, and Lydia talked incessantly, her conversation punctuated with barbs directed at Lizzy and Darcy, and witticisms directed at me. Although I ignored her as best I could, inevitably her continuing attacks affected me and I was quite shaken up when we arrived. I was all the more touched when Mr Darcy squeezed my hand as he helped me down from the carriage and said quietly,

"Pay no heed to her jibes, Mary. She does not deserve your notice."

I said nothing but looked speakingly into his eyes to convey my gratitude.

◆

The Cardings' home was an old manor, low lying and complicated, with many additions through the years, so that it spread over a vast area. The windows were small, and the interior dark and gothic. There were a number of guests there apart from the Pemberley party, and I saw a good-sized room which had been cleared for dancing. Lydia immediately turned her attention towards young Mr Carding, almost elbowing Kitty out of the way in her eagerness to attach herself to the handsomest young man in the room. I was pleased to see that he was rather shocked by Lydia's forwardness and his eyes seemed to follow Kitty wistfully as she chatted to another young man.

I found Squire Carding by my side offering me a glass of sherry. He smelled to me as though he had been drinking already, and something about the way he lurched towards me unsteadily made me think he might have drunk quite a lot.

"You look to be in very good health tonight, Miss Bennet. We are delighted to have another pretty sister of Mrs Darcy as our guest."

I looked quizzically at him, neither liking nor believing his flattery. I was then shocked and affronted when he chucked me under the chin. "None of that modesty now, none of that. You must know you look pretty as a picture."

"You are too kind. I am not accustomed to such flattery, I do not consider it very truthful."

He looked taken aback. "Eh? Oh, yes, you're the missish one, the bluestocking. Well, I shall introduce you to my friend, Dean Trowbridge, who is visiting us from London. No doubt you will have a deal to talk to each other about."

The Dean was a man in his forties, with a handsome face, if somewhat lined. He was solemn and polite and dressed soberly in black, as befitted a senior clergyman, much more my idea of a man of the church than Mr Speedwell. He took me into dinner and conversed most interestingly of his work at St Paul's Cathedral. Out of the corner of my eye I was watching my sisters. Lydia had abandoned Frederick Carding to Kitty and was very thick with the squire. Kitty was talking with unwonted seriousness with Mr Carding, and I began to wonder if she had more interest in him than I had originally thought. I thought Lizzy was looking a little more sombre than sometimes: with Mr Darcy it was hard to tell - his face gave nothing away and I knew he would not be particularly at ease in this company. I did notice a few tense glances between Lizzy and

Darcy and I began to think that perhaps my letter had begun to take effect.

At one point after the first course had been removed I thought I noticed something touching my leg. I looked at Dean Trowbridge, wondering if he had knocked me by accident. He looked back at me questioningly.

"You were saying, Miss Bennet?" His voice sounded so calm and ordinary that I knew he was unaware that anything had happened.

I said, "I was wondering what sort of work you do with the poor at St Paul's."

"What an interesting question. Is the missionary life something that you have thought of for yourself?"

"I have thought of it, and I think I could do some good."

"I am sure you could do good as a missionary. In my field there is a great need for women to come and share our work."

"What is your field?"

He leaned towards me. "It is hardly a subject for the dinner table."

"Oh!" I thought I knew what he meant.

"But Miss Bennet, I would very much like to discuss this subject more deeply with you. You seem to be a young woman without coyness or affectation with whom a man can talk of important matters such as this."

"Thank you. I hope I am - perhaps there might be a time later in the evening - I believe there is to be dancing - we might be able to find somewhere quiet to talk. As you say, this is not a subject which can be discussed in public."

He nodded a few times, and I thought for a moment that he winked, but I knew I must be mistaken.

My neighbour on the other side, a young friend of Frederick Carding's, then claimed my attention. I thought I felt Dean Trowbridge's hand brush my leg once or twice more, but I took no notice of it. It was not surprising as we were rather crowded round the Squire's table and it meant that we were crushed together somewhat. But it was an odd sensation.

The gentlemen joined the ladies quite quickly after supper, and one of Lady Carding's friends offered to play piano so that "the young people could dance", as she put it. Signor Moretti claimed me straight away for a country dance and I could not well refuse, even though I was quite ready to go and talk with Dean Trowbridge. Part of the reason I wanted to talk to the Dean was to compare his charitable work with what I had witnessed with Mr Speedwell in B__. I felt sure that what Mr Speedwell was doing was not really the proper work of a clergyman, and I hoped that talking to Dean Trowbridge would give me some grounds with which to convince Mr Speedwell of the error of his ways.

Signor Moretti's dancing was getting better and more confident. He swung me round much more vigorously than before - I almost thought he was beginning to have fun. I was quite breathless by the end of it.

"I will get you a drink," he said and went off in search of one. Squire Carding immediately led me into the dance. I would have refused, but he left me no choice. Unfortunately it was a quadrille, which meant I had to endure his hand on my waist. He was gripping me far tighter than was necessary, and because he was the worse for drink he could not keep up with the steps and kept going the wrong way. I nearly laughed when we set-to and he nearly lost his balance. I saw Dean Trowbridge watching from the side of the room with a half smile on his face: I smiled back at him thinking to share the joke but I could not tell if he did or no. For a moment I wished Mr Speedwell had been present to catch my eye.

Lydia was dancing with a young man, despite her pregnant belly. She was not able to be quite as hoydenish as usual but she was still flirting and chatting with him enough. Lizzy and Darcy were not dancing, but were standing side by side. They were not talking to each other and I began to be sure that things were coming to a head between them. I was sorry to see them looking so sober, with no companionable glances, but it was quite Lizzy's own fault, and it was only right that these matters should be known about and put an end to. Kitty was not dancing either, but was sitting down with Mr Carding, again talking very seriously. Then I was dancing another country dance and did not have time to see my sisters.

I was hotter than ever now with the exertion and the number of couples in the room. It was quite airless, with all the windows closed to keep out the driving rain; I looked around for Signor Moretti with my drink. I saw he had been commandeered by Lady Carding and was in polite, bored discussion with her, a drink in each hand. I was about to make my way across to him, when Dean Trowbridge was beside me.

"You look very warm and out of breath," he said. "It would be pleasant to find a cooler spot, would it not, where you can recover from the dance, and we can have our long-postponed conversation. Much as I have enjoyed watching you dance, I confess I have been impatient to be alone with you."

"Oh, yes, indeed," I said, barely attending. "I did want a drink. But I think Signor Moretti -"

"Nothing could be easier," he interrupted firmly. "I know where a drink can be obtained and we can enjoy a comfortable talk, away from all these rackety goings-on."

He took my arm and led me out of the hall. I caught Signor Moretti's eye as I went so that he should know where to find me, as it felt impolite to let him fetch me a drink and then not be there to receive it.

Dean Trowbridge seemed to know his way very well around the Cardings' house, as he led me quite some distance, down winding hallways and round corners and up and down small flights of wooden stairs that connected the ramshackle buildings.

"Are we going all the way to the kitchens?" I asked.

"The kitchens? No, indeed. I know a little room where we can be quite alone and undisturbed, and I have arranged a drink there for you."

◆

The room was a small oak-panelled study, dusty and unused, lit by a single candle on the table. There was indeed a tray with a decanter on it of what looked like brandy. It was very quiet and still in there, so far away from all the company, only the hammering of the rain outside the window. I found myself feeling nervous, though there was no reason that I should.

Dean Trowbridge beckoned me to a chair, sat beside me and poured us both a drink. I tasted it unwillingly.

"Is it brandy?" I asked. "I would have liked water. I am very thirsty."

"Here is some water in a jug, I will mix it for you." I sipped the drink because I was so very thirsty but I did not like it.

"I am very glad to have you to myself, Miss Bennet," said the Dean in his mellifluous voice. "It is impossible for serious and intelligent people such as we to have a proper discussion where there are so many people, such noise and activity."

"Oh yes!" I said. "I do not mind dancing as much as I did, but I much prefer a conversation about serious matters. At home my sisters and friends do not care to talk about such things."

"No, I can see very well that you are cut from a different cloth. I would not wish to speak ill of anyone, but clearly your concerns are at once both higher and more profound than those of most people in society. You inhabit the heights *and* the depths, you see!"

"That is very neatly expressed," I said, rather pleased by the compliment. "I have often wished for more opportunities to talk about important subjects, and am frustrated by the lack."

"Frustrated, yes - I can well imagine. I too am often frustrated. I meet many well-meaning and devout ladies, but it is rare to find someone who brings such an understanding to every topic as you do."

"You were going to tell me about your work," I said.

He looked away. "It is of course not an easy subject to talk about with any gently-reared young lady, even one as elevated as yourself. As I think you have guessed, my work is with the fallen women of London. I try to convince them of the error of their ways, and bring them back into the fold."

I had *not* guessed, and was surprised. "Is it - is it very difficult to persuade them to repent?"

"Oh yes, very difficult. It requires many meetings and long conversations. They know no other life you see, so they are most unwilling to change. They do not know how they will live otherwise."

"Yes - I think I understand."

"But Miss Bennet, you look a little uncomfortable. I am sorry, I did not mean to distress you."

"Oh no, I am not distressed! Only - I had thought I would not be embarrassed by the subject, but I find I am a little. "

He smiled kindly at me. "That is most understandable, most understandable." He then took hold of my hand, and I did not know how to remove it without offending him, as I could tell he was trying to put me at my ease in a fatherly way. I did not want to appear awkward or ill at ease with him. "Even someone so strong minded as yourself will inevitably feel some embarrassment at such a subject," he went on. "Would you like to know more, or shall I return you to your friends to talk of dancing and gowns and the getting of husbands?" he added humorously.

"Oh no, no, that is not what interests me. I am not like them, you know, I do not wish to talk of such frivolous subjects, I think your work is very interesting and I would like to hear more of it. It is - it is pleasant for me to meet someone who takes me seriously."

"I thought you would not be so easily put off," he said. "You are made of sterner stuff than the common run of young ladies -" and without warning he took my hand to his mouth and kissed it. I felt very shy and nervous and my heart beat extremely fast. I knew he was just being kind but I was not used to having my hand kissed, or being alone with a man, however much older than me he was. Men had not generally been interested in talking with me or kissing my hand.

He gave a soft laugh. "How delightfully you blush, Miss Bennet! And what small hands you have! It must make piano playing very difficult."

"Yes - yes, it does." He showed no sign of releasing my hand, but instead was stroking it repetitively with his thumb.

"And I hear you are a very fine musician. I was hoping to hear you play this evening, but the dancing has taken over everything."

It was difficult for me to talk normally when in physical contact with a man like this, but I tried to keep my voice and conversation steady.

"I do work hard at my music," I said, annoyed that my voice sounded so small and shaky.

"You are a very able and talented young lady, just as the Squire told me. Perhaps when you think more seriously about going out into the world and doing good works, you might be interested in working as I do amongst the fallen women."

He took both my wrists now and seemed to be pulling me towards him. "I...do not know," I said. "I think I should go back now, my sisters will be wondering what has become of me."

He pulled harder at my wrists until I was almost slipping off my chair; his voice was still low and persuasive. "Well, you know, Miss Bennet, if you are to understand these women, you must not be prim and prudish, you will estrange them immediately, and then you will not be successful in the Lord's work." He leaned towards me. "You're not going to be coy now, are you, Miss Bennet?"

Now I was sure he was going to kiss me. I tried to pull away but he only tightened his grip and I saw at last that I had been an utter fool, and that he had been flattering me for this one end. I could not get away, his hold was too strong, but I turned my head so that his lips did not meet mine.

This did not seem to displease him. "Oh, so shy! How much you have to learn!"

"Mr Dean, I must go back, they will miss me."

I pulled as hard as I could but I saw that he was very much in earnest now, and I began to be terrified. What was to become of me? I was so ridiculously small compared to him and he could easily overpower me. What a blockhead and simpleton I had been! But how could I have suspected a man of the church? I did not suspect *any* man of having designs on me of this kind, they certainly never had before. He was leaning closer again and I tried to pull back but his hold on me was fast.

"Dean Trowbridge," I began, and then to my great relief there were footsteps, a knock on the door and it opened abruptly. It was Signor Moretti and Elizabeth. I was never more glad to see anyone in my life. I was immediately released and we both stood up, knocking the candle to the floor. I took advantage of the darkness to push my way out and found myself strongly held by Signor Moretti and led quickly down the passage.

"But what about Lizzy?" I said. "You must not leave her with him!"

Signor Moretti chuckled, a sound I had never heard him emit before. "She can deal with the Dean, she is as good as ten men when she is angry. Come, I am taking you back to the dancing, and nobody will know you were even gone."

"Oh, I am such a fool! How did you know? I had no idea he would - that he would be like that."

"No, how could you? I am sure you have never come across a man of his ilk before. When I told Mrs Darcy that you had left the room with him, she knew immediately. His reputation is well-known."

"But I should have understood! I should have realised!" I began to cry and tremble. "I cannot go back in this state. Oh, I feel so stupid!"

"Come, Miss Bennet, do not distress yourself. These things happen all the time and why would you suspect such a man? He is all smoothness and politeness and piety. You could not have known. You are shaking."

Before I could speak he had wrapped his arms around me and held me to his chest. For some reason I did not mind, perhaps because I knew him quite well by now, and I sobbed freely into his coat for some minutes. When my tears subsided I stepped back, and he solemnly handed me a handkerchief.

"There, I think you will feel better in a moment or two. Do not refine too much upon what happened. In my understanding, most young ladies have to cope with a situation of that kind, and it was as well that you beckoned to me before you left the room with him. I thought you wished me to know where you had gone."

"I did, but not for any reason such as that. I did not suspect him of any ill attention."

"Of course not." He led me to a lamp and looked at my face. "You look much better now, nobody will know there is anything the matter."

"Are you sure?"

"Quite sure. And I hear the band striking up for a country dance. If you and I walk straight in and join the line, any remaining redness in your face will soon be mistaken for a sign of exertion."

Signor Moretti was quite right: nobody noticed anything. I caught Lizzy's eye when she returned to the room and smiled gratefully at her. She looked in high spirits, her face breaking into a smile, and I saw her turn to Darcy, perhaps to recount her triumph to him, but he appeared barely to listen or respond to her, and she turned away deflated.

I was greatly relieved when Elizabeth announced that it was time for us to set off. There was no sign of the Dean, and I hoped I would not see him again before we left. The rain still poured down in sheets and we all were quite damp, just walking from the house to the carriage. I felt sorry for Mr Darcy's coachman, and the groom who must walk in front of the carriage with the lantern, and I suspected Mr Darcy was too, as I saw them conferring.

"John Coachman thinks the road may be flooded by all this rain. Perhaps we should not venture out tonight," Mr Darcy said.

"And stay at the Squire's?" I asked, my voice coming out in something of a squeak.

"Kitty would not mind, would you, Kitty?" Lydia said, with meaning.

"Oh hush, Lydia," Elizabeth said. "Must we stay, Darcy? I had so much rather not."

This decided the matter and the carriage set off at a walking pace.

"What a set of people!" Lydia observed. "How dull they all were."

Kitty bridled at this. "I think they are a very good set of people. You danced a great deal anyway."

"What else was I to do, when the conversation was so insipid? And no proper gambling, only penny points. A very poor show, I call it. In York such people would not keep their friends for long, if that is all the entertainment they can offer."

Nobody responded to Lydia. Kitty looked cross and tired, Darcy and Elizabeth were frowning, their heads turned away from each other, Signor Moretti was lost in his own thoughts, though not unpleasantly so. I could not imagine what I myself might look like: I was still very shaken by what had happened and dreaded lest somebody mention the Dean and how much time I had spent with him during the evening. It was just the sort of thing Lydia *would* say; she had a knack of noticing anything that was to do with flirtation. I was still berating myself for my foolishness: how many warnings were there for young ladies of predatory men and the dangers of being alone with a man, and yet I had ignored them all. Worse, they had not even come into my mind: it simply did not occur to me that a man of the cloth and so much older than me would have designs of that kind. And designs on *me*! Perhaps the reason I was so unprepared was because no man had ever shown the slightest interest in me in *that* way; I did not expect it or hope for it.

I must have been frowning to myself, because I looked up and caught Signor Moretti's eye and he smiled ruefully at me, with great understanding. That set my mind down a different track: it surprised me that I had not minded Signor Moretti holding me, nor had I minded crying in his presence. This was odd - partly because I was not given to crying in public, and certainly had never done so with my face buried in a man's coat. I wondered what he thought of me. He had been very kind, without a doubt, but probably he thought I was as idiotic and naive as I thought myself. No doubt he would now have a view of me as the sort of silly female, who could first of all be taken in by the wiles of such a man as the Dean, and then could freely give way to a bout of tears like some weak and feminine heroine of a melodrama. Well, I supposed it did not matter what he thought of me, though it irked me that anyone should make assumptions about me or be mistaken in me.

"Oh, lord!" said Lydia after a while. "Must we go so slow!"

"It is very dark, Lydia, and the roads are extremely muddy," Mr Darcy replied. "You would not wish us to overturn or to come off the road."

"I am sure I do not care! Anything would be better than this snail's pace. And everyone is so dull. We could play I-Spy I suppose but there is nothing to spy. Oh well! Lizzy, what do you think of this match of Kitty's? I think she could do very much better for herself."

"Lydia!" exclaimed Kitty. "What are you talking about? There is no match."

"There very soon will be, if Mr Carding has anything to say about the matter. He was *most* particular in his attentions."

Kitty was about to retort, when the carriage lurched to a stop.

"Oh, now what!" cried Lydia. Mr Darcy opened the door, letting in a shower of rain.

"What news, John?" he shouted.

I could not hear John's reply, but it was not good news.

"The road has flooded further down," Mr Darcy told us. "The river has flooded over the ford as it sometimes does."

"What are we to do?" asked Lizzy. "Can we turn?"

"Not on this narrow part. And John does not think we can go backwards, it is too steep and too muddy. He is going to try and drive through it, it is not too deep, we must hope that the wheels do not get stuck in the mud."

The carriage moved forward again very slowly down the hill, and then levelled out as we approached the bottom of the hill. We were all sitting forward in our seats as though by our postures we could will the carriage to keep going. But it slowed even more, and then with a few judders, ground to a halt.

Part Five: The Dark and Stormy Night

◆

Lydia gave a scream.

"Lord help us!" cried Kitty.

We all sat as though paralysed. Mr Darcy opened the door of the carriage and looked out. I peered over his shoulder. The water did not look deep yet, it was not even up to the level of the carriage, but it looked very dark and fast flowing. There was something terrifying about the rushing water, the dark sky and the blustery wind. The sudden appearance of the coachman and the groom with his lantern wading through the river made me jump.

"What do you think, John?" asked Mr Darcy.

"It's not so bad just yet, but this rain's showing no sign of letting up. It'll only get worse. If everyone got out, we might be able to pull the carriage out of the mud."

"I am sure you are right, John," said Darcy, "and this convinces me yet again that we must get a bridge constructed here. This ford is simply not adequate. But no use talking about that now. Is there any shelter nearby? Somewhere the ladies can wait while we try to remove the carriage?"

John scratched his head. "There's Westcott Farm about quarter of a mile up the road, but they'd be soaked by the time they got there. Might as well wait a few minutes on the bank and see how we do with the carriage."

"Yes, I agree. And I think we must be quick. If the gorge floods higher up, it could sweep all away. With three men I think we can get the ladies to safety without too much trouble, if you hold the lantern, Jackson." Mr Darcy turned to us. "Ladies, wrap up well in your cloaks, but I'm afraid you are all in for a soaking. Lydia first: John and I will take you between us. Moretti, you bring Mary, she's light enough, and then we will come back for you and Kitty, Lizzy." He reached for Lizzy's hand and squeezed it quickly, then jumped out of the carriage into the fast-running water.

He grimaced. "Good god, it is muddy underfoot." He laughed. "Only pray I do not lose my shoes! Here, Lydia, come to the door, put your arm around my shoulder, John and I will make a seat for you."

"Mind you do not drop me in the river!" Lydia said. "I am prodigiously heavy with child, you know."

"Yes, we know, we know! Now come, your hand!"

Lydia was bundled awkwardly out of the carriage, one arm round Darcy's shoulder, the other round John Coachman's, and her legs supported between them. Led by Jackson the groom, they staggered through the stream, Lydia chattering and shrieking instructions to them. I peered around the carriage door, watching their progress anxiously, greatly relieved when they reached the far bank and deposited her under a tree. Signor Moretti climbed out of the carriage and into the water.

"Are you ready, Miss Bennet?"

"I suppose so. Are you sure you can carry me?"

He smiled. "I do not know. I hope so!"

I stumbled awkwardly into his arms, and felt extremely peculiar as he scooped my legs up. The onslaught of the rain on my face overcame all other sensations for a moment.

"Oh my goodness!" I said. "This is terrible!" Signor Moretti struggled and lurched with every step. "Are you sure you will not fall?"

"I shall certainly endeavour not to do so. It is extremely hard-going, however."

The horses were standing passively up to their knees in water. For some reason their calm acceptance of the situation soothed me: if they were calm it could not be so very bad. And then we reached the bank and Signor Moretti lowered me carefully to the ground. I was soaked to the skin and shivering, but whether from cold or excitement or fear, I did not know. The ground was very cold and my dancing slippers were wholly destroyed. Lydia and I huddled close together under the tree. It was a horrible and strange situation, in the dark and the rain. I could barely see what was happening. Darcy and Signor Moretti had plunged back into the water, and John Coachman had gone to the horses' heads. Moments later, Lizzy and Kitty were safely on the ground under the tree with us, and Jackson and the lantern, and the men went back into the water to push the carriage.

I felt singularly useless. Sometimes it was a nuisance to be a woman and not be able to help. Then again, it was probably better to be under the tree than up to my thighs in freezing river water. John Coachman went to the horses' heads while Mr Darcy and Signor Moretti disappeared from sight behind the carriage to push. Even through the noise of the wind and rain we could hear John urging the horses on. Then he called back:

"It's no good, I'll go on the box and drive them that way!"

He scrambled up and cracked the whip. The horses immediately looked more lively and started to strain forward.

"They will never do it!" cried Kitty, clutching randomly at all of us. "What if the river should flood and they all get swept away?"

"Control yourself, Kitty," Elizabeth said. "There is nothing to be gained by hysterics. I am sure the gentlemen are not in any danger."

As if in answer to her words the carriage suddenly lurched forward and the horses, released from their constraint, fairly bounded up the road on the bank next to where we were standing. But in the river, where the carriage had been, there was no sign of Mr Darcy or Signor Moretti.

Kitty screamed, Lydia gripped the tree, and Lizzy and I darted forward towards the water, as though we might be able do something, or at least see something. I stared downstream, thinking I might see their flailing bodies being swept down the river, but in the dark it was hopeless: with the overhanging trees nothing was visible.

"John!" shouted Lizzy. "Mr Darcy has been swept away! John!"

John leapt down from the carriage and came to join us, he too staring at the river. And then, as we watched, two figures rose up from out of the water, still on the ford, not swept away at all. They stood up clumsily, regaining their balance in the fast moving water, and started towards us, their walk slow and ungainly in the mud and water.

Lizzy clutched her chest and cried, "Oh thank god, thank god!" and put out a hand to me. I could hear Kitty behind me start to sob. But somehow in the next moment or two, as the bedraggled figures approached us, Lizzy started to laugh and within a few seconds I found myself laughing too. The rain poured on our heads, our ankles were deep in mud and I had lost a slipper, but the sight of Signor Moretti and Mr Darcy, soaked from head to foot became impossibly funny and Lizzy and I both doubled over. I had never laughed with such abandon, and I thought I would never stop. The next thing that happened was that the two gentlemen started to laugh also. Lizzy and Darcy fell into each other's arms, and while I could not do the same with Signor Moretti - though I nearly did so without thinking - we did look at each other to share the joke.

"How can you laugh?" Kitty called. "They could have been killed!"

"I'm wet!" sobbed Lydia.

Mr Darcy was the first to come to his senses. "Come, we must get you all home before someone catches a chill."

They bundled us into the carriage, but once inside, Lizzy and I started laughing again. The sight, illuminated by the small lantern inside the carriage, of our dishevelled and bemired company was simply too much to bear. Both gentlemen had muddy faces, and their beautifully starched neck cloths and coat collars were utterly limp. As for the ladies, our cloaks clung to our sodden dresses, our carefully curled and dressed hair hung lankly round our ears, and Lydia's rouge was sadly smudged.

Lydia did not appreciate being laughed at, but I had never felt so happy in my life.

"Look at my dress!" she moaned. "I declare it is quite ruined! It is all very well for you to laugh, Mary, in your nasty little muslin frock, but this is pure silk, and Wickham paid more than forty pounds for it - at least he would have if we had settled the account. And now it is quite spoiled."

"I am sorry for your dress, Lydia," Lizzy said, controlling her laughter, "but it could not be helped. We are all in the same pickle."

"Oh no, we are not! *You* can get as many dresses as you please with all your wealth, *you* do not have a husband in prison for debt, because certain people are too unkind and too tight-fisted to help their own sister."

"I expect you can get as many dresses as *you* please, Lydia," I retorted, "if you do not mean to pay for them."

"I am sure Wickham will come about," Lizzy said, and I saw her eyes flicker towards Mr Darcy.

"Well, I do not know how he is to come about if no-one will help us!"

"What about your patron, Mr Blackstone?" Kitty asked.

"He does not have enough funds! He is not swimming in riches, like some." Lydia glared angrily at Darcy who resolutely ignored her.

The conversation, if such it could be called, continued in this vein until Pemberley was reached, which made it even more of a relief to be arrived at last. I had to be carried across the gravel drive once again as I had lost my slipper. It really was most peculiar to be so close to a man: even waltzing with Signor Moretti had not felt so intimate, and my face had never been so close to his before, as he was so very tall compared to me. I dared to look into his eyes at just the moment that he looked into mine and that was more peculiar still. I looked away immediately.

There was a great to-do as soon as we were inside, and maids and footmen were immediately sent running to boil water for baths. Of course there was already a fire lit in my bedroom, and I stood in front of it to dry while Judith wrapped me in a towel and undid my hair.

"Oh, miss, look at the state of you! It's to be hoped you won't catch your death! And what about Mrs Wickham! I wouldn't give a penny for the chances of that baby!"

"Does getting wet commonly affect the unborn child?" I asked. "It must make bathing very difficult."

"Cold *and* wet, though, Miss, that's a different thing altogether."

It was very pleasant to lie in my copper bath and get warm right through and be pampered by Judith. She went down to the scullery to fetch more hot water for me, and I lay back in the bath and closed my eyes, watching the scenes of the day as they passed through my mind. What a day of contrasts! I had narrowly escaped seduction by a hypocritical old man, I had cried into Signor Moretti's chest, I had had such an adventure in the storm, been carried by Signor Moretti, laughed more than I had ever laughed before. I smiled to myself again as I remembered. It had been so very funny; I had never seen anything so funny. I thought for a moment: now that I reflected, I did not think I had ever seen anything funny at all! How strange! And yet Lizzy laughed all the time, and found many things amusing. Though she did not laugh so much now as she used to at Longbourn. Perhaps that was her guilt over betraying Mr Darcy. I realised that Lizzy's treachery had slipped my mind during the drive home. When I thought back over how Lizzy and Darcy were together I could not fathom how things stood between them. One moment they were a couple wholly in accord, affectionate and concerned about each other; the next there was a coldness and distance, a closed look on Mr Darcy's face, an anxious one on Lizzy's. Well, the sooner things were resolved between them the better. I knew I had done right by sending that note to Mr Darcy: he should not be imposed upon.

◆

The only person who seemed to have suffered any ill-effects from our adventure was Kitty, and she had not caught a chill, but was listless and ill-tempered with heavy eyes. Lydia was also ill-tempered, but that was no different to how she had been. She was particularly cross because Mrs Knowles, William Darcy's nurse, had insisted that she take her son Horatio out of the nursery for a while. "For he's a regular spitfire!" she said. This was hard to believe when confronted by the docile little boy who sucked his thumb continually and either sat mutely on the floor, or trailed slowly around after Lydia in a particularly spiritless way. He was not a prepossessing child, having a thatch of blond hair, a thin underfed look and an expression that varied between blankness and discontent.

Horatio was brought down to the ladies' parlour after breakfast, where I was trying to write a letter to Jane. Kitty was sewing, and Lydia lay on a sofa, groaning with boredom every few minutes. Horatio came and stood next to Lydia, still sucking his thumb. I tried to ignore him, just as I was trying to ignore Lydia and her incessant complaining but for some reason it was harder to blot out the silent child from my mind than all Lydia's whining.

Kitty was irritated also. "Lydia, can't you speak to him? He looks very strange just standing there; I am sure you should speak to him or do something with him. Lizzy plays with William when she has him."

"Oh, I'm sure whatever Lizzy does is all very well for her. You talk to him, Kitty. I never know what to say to a child. Look at him, he is not exactly animated or interesting."

"I wonder how animated or interesting you would be if Mama had ignored *you* all the time! Oh, very well, come here, Horatio."

Horatio lifted his eyes at the sound of his name, but made no move towards Kitty.

"Do you not have a toy for him, Lydia?" Kitty asked.

"How should I know? I cannot afford to buy toys with Wickham in prison. Anyway, he is perfectly happy standing there. Otherwise he would be crying."

"Perhaps a walk?" I suggested, as the rain had stopped overnight and it was a pleasant day.

Kitty sighed exaggeratedly and stood up. "I will take him if he will come. You help me, Mary."

"I am writing a letter to Jane," I said.

"Mary," Kitty insisted in a meaning way, "it was your idea. You must come with me."

"Oh, very well."

"Thank god!" said Lydia, "I need a rest. After last night's dramas I am quite exhausted and the baby inside me will not keep still and gives me no peace."

I felt quite disgusted at the thought of the baby inside Lydia moving around, like nothing so much as a fish caught in a drain. It made me glad to get out of the room.

Our spencers were soon fetched and a jacket for the child though rather small for him, and Kitty took his hand and led him outside.

As soon as we were in the garden Kitty said, "I could not bear it another minute! She never stops complaining and the way she neglects her children is intolerable."

I looked at Kitty wonderingly. "I never thought to hear you speak ill of Lydia."

"I am sick of Lydia! I wish she would leave Pemberley. I know Lizzy and Darcy wish it too. If only Georgiana would come back! I think Lizzy had a letter from her this morning. Did she say anything at breakfast?"

"Yes, you are in luck, Georgiana returns tomorrow."

"What a relief. Somebody to talk to at last."

I ignored the slight to myself: I knew how little Kitty valued me, and yet I had thought that she deprecated me less than previously.

"Well, it is not many days to the ball now, Kitty, that should cheer you up."

"Yes, I must finish your dress. Do you mean to play?"

"Yes, I have been practising every day."

Horatio started to whine so Kitty picked him up and carried him for a moment. "You know Georgiana is very good, don't you, Mary?"

"Yes, but I think I will not appear to disadvantage even though she is so good."

"Oh look, there is Colonel Fitzwilliam returned! He must have just arrived, he is still in his riding clothes!"

The colonel was walking through the gardens, having clearly come directly from the stables. It was strange to see his amiable countenance and know that he was a blackguard who had no scruple in betraying his own cousin with his cousin's wife. It was alarming how appearances could be so deceptive. I greeted him coldly.

"Did you complete your errand for your General, Colonel Fitzwilliam?" Kitty asked.

"For my general? Oh, yes, yes, I did, thank you."

I could tell he was lying.

"And you are here to stay, I hope. I am looking forward to dancing with you at the ball."

"Indeed, you do me honour, Miss Kitty. If you are not already engaged, may I solicit you for the first two dances of the evening?"

Kitty blushed. "Unfortunately, I am already engaged for the first two dances. But other than that my card is clear and I would happily put your name down for another dance."

He bowed and smiled with an appearance of ease that dumbfounded me. He joined us and we set off walking towards the house.

"And was your errand particularly difficult?" I asked pointedly, trying to discompose him.

He looked thoughtful. "Yes, in some ways. But I hope the matter is resolved and will cause no further trouble."

"I expect it is a great secret of state!" Kitty said.

The colonel laughed. "That is it, of course. A great secret on which the security of our nation depends! That is why they entrusted it to me."

Kitty laughed but I refused to be beguiled by his funning. I determined to watch his behaviour with Lizzy closely.

This was to prove difficult, however, because the preparations for the ball began in earnest, now that it was only a few days away. More servants were hired and there were maids and footmen everywhere, removing every speck of dust from every crevice in every statue or ornate picture frame. Urns for flowers were carried from one place to another, chandeliers lowered and cleaned, one jewel at a time. An awning was put up outside the ballroom to provide shelter for overheated dancers, and guests started to appear.

The first arrival of note was the Bingley family, Jane carrying her tiny new-born infant who she seemed to think was a bouncing picture of health, although to me he looked more like a discontented old man. Unlike Lydia, she had also brought two nursery maids and her own personal nurse who helped her with baby. It was very pleasant to see Mr Bingley again: he was always friendly to everyone, simple and unaffected. It was clear to see that he and Jane were very much in love with each other and the best of friends.

Jane begged me to come and sit with her one morning while she fed the baby.

"You will not mind if I nurse little Henry, will you, Mary? It is so agreeable for me to have your company, and things are so busy that we will not have many opportunities to talk. Tell me how your visit is going. You look very well and blooming. I think the air of Derbyshire must agree with you."

"I do not know about that," I replied, trying not to look as the baby suckled her. "It is certainly pleasant to be so much cosseted, and we are very busy all the time, with visits and dances. You heard about our adventure the other night, I know."

"Indeed I did! How terrifying it must have been for you all!"

"I suppose it was, but it was also ridiculous."

"Afterwards, yes, but at the time you must have been frightened."

"I was frightened, but not so very much. The gentlemen looked after us."

"Yes, Elizabeth described your gallant rescuers. How grateful I felt to Signor Moretti, when I heard he had carried you out of the stream! I spoke about it to him at breakfast this morning, I wanted to express my appreciation to him for his efforts."

I frowned. "I wish you had not, Jane. I would prefer not to remember too much, and I am sure it was just as awkward and uncomfortable for Signor Moretti, to be carrying a lady he barely knows in that familiar way. I should think he would not like to be reminded of such an awkward and unwished-for experience."

Jane gave a knowing little smile, which annoyed me very much. "I do not think Signor Moretti minded it one bit," she said. "I think he was delighted to be of service."

I said no more on the subject. It seemed to me that Jane and Elizabeth, now that they were married women, were overly bold when discussing relations between men and women; they insisted on being the chief authorities on the subject, and the opinion of an unmarried sister counted for nothing.

"And what of Mr Speedwell?" Jane asked. "Are you seeing much of him?"

I gasped. "Jane! I wonder why your thoughts should go with such alacrity from Signor Moretti to Mr Speedwell? I hope you have not been listening to Kitty when she says that I am flirting with them?"

"My dear Mary, of course I would never suspect you of mindless flirtation, and although Kitty did say something of the sort, I took that with a pinch of salt. But you do not deny that you and Mr Speedwell went on a long outing together?"

"Why should I deny it? It was an errand of mercy such that any lady should make, in whatever neighbourhood she finds herself. I was most grateful to Mr Speedwell for putting me in the way of being able to do good."

"Yes, that is most admirable, but - he did not invite Kitty."

She took the baby from her breast and laid him upon her shoulder, patting his back. I saw a glimpse of one breast and turned my head away.

"No," I said. "He is not such a fool to ask Kitty on an expedition of that kind. She would not go."

"Perhaps he sees in you a more serious character."

"One who would be a suitable wife for a clergyman?" I cried. "Oh Jane, you are becoming as bad as Mama!"

Jane laughed. "I confess, Mary, I would like to see you and Kitty married. Where there is love in marriage, and children and good health, there is also great happiness."

"We all know that you and Elizabeth are married to the only two good men in the country."

"Why, Mary, how kind of you! I have not heard you speak so warmly before. It does you great credit."

I could think of no reply to that. Fortunately, I was not called upon to speak, as the door opened and Kitty came in followed by another young lady, who I instantly knew to be Georgiana Darcy.

"Mary," cried Kitty, "here is Georgiana come at last! She *would* insist on meeting you straight away."

We curtsied to each other. She was a tall girl, taller than any of the Bennet sisters with dark hair like her brother's and quite a family resemblance to him, though with a more naturally animated countenance. She was not pretty or beautiful, more what people would call a handsome girl, but she was rendered more attractive by an expression of friendliness and anxiety to please, which I saw, in her face. I could not help noticing her dress which, while not ostentatious in any way, showed that it had been made by a modiste of the highest quality, with that simplicity and attention to detail and materials that spoke of great expense.

"Miss Bennet," she said, in a soft, cultured voice, "I am so happy to meet you at last. I have heard so much about you from your sisters."

"And I you," I replied politely. "Did you have a pleasant stay with your aunt at Rosings?"

"Yes I did, but I am so happy to be home. I hope you too are feeling at home at Pemberley."

"Thank you, every attention has been paid to my comfort - how could it be otherwise?"

"And perhaps we might be able to play some music together soon?"

"Perhaps," I said coolly.

She looked a little crestfallen. "You will play at the ball? We always have music there."

"Yes, I will if I am asked. And you?"

She reddened. "Signor Moretti has asked me to play my harp. One of the musicians who will be coming from London plays the flute and we are to play a concerto together."

"How lovely!" Jane said. "We will look forward to hearing you both."

How typical of Jane, always trying to smooth out any difficult situation.

◆

The bustle in Pemberley was very distracting and disturbing, but I was determined to practise as much as I could with the ball now very close. It was fortunate that Georgiana was to play the harp as she did not need to use the pianoforte, but even so, there were servants in and out of the room, fetching and carrying, and it made it difficult to concentrate. Generally I was quite pleased with my progress on the Beethoven sonata, and thought I was sure to carry it off. There were passages that were rather beyond me, but my technique of slowing down for these sections worked well and I felt a quiet confidence, even though Georgiana was to play with the orchestra.

The band members had started to arrive. They were all professional players, friends and colleagues of Signor Moretti, who had been hired for the ball, to accompany the dancing and also to perform. They were being housed in the east wing of Pemberley, which, though extremely luxurious, was separate from the rest of the guests. Even so, the sounds of instruments being played drifted across into the hall, and I occasionally strayed into the east wing to listen more closely. Sometimes I would come across them wandering around the grounds. Once I heard the mournful tones of the bassoon being played in the kitchen garden. When I went to look, I saw the head gardener listening and nodding approvingly.

The number of children in the house was also a distraction. Most of the time they were confined to the nursery, or taken outdoors to walk and play when the weather was fine, but sometimes they escaped and their footsteps could be heard pounding up and down the stairs, accompanied by shouts and squeals. Lydia's children were much more nervous, and much more badly behaved, never listening to any admonishment, crying and whining whenever they wanted anything, or else browbeaten, subdued and silent; whereas Jane's older two, although shy, were friendly and polite once they got over their diffidence.

Sophia, Jane's oldest child, for some reason took a fancy to me. Jane brought her into the room one afternoon when I was practising piano, and the little girl came and stood beside me to watch me play. When I stopped, she reached a tentative hand up to the keys to try for herself. I nodded, and she pressed a key, then looked at me, her face breaking into a smile of pleasure.

Jane said, "If it is not too much interruption for you, Mary, I know Sophy would love to sit on your lap and play with you for a minute or two."

"I am happy to do that," I said. I turned to Sophia and she reached her arms towards me to be picked up. The only child I had ever held was William Darcy, and that had been when he was crying for his mother and struggling in my arms. It was very different to pick up this little girl who was willing to come, and have her sit on my lap, so that my chin just rested on her head. Like Jane she had soft light brown hair, which curled naturally, round her face. It was pleasant to have her there and see her delight in being able to press the keys. After a few moments we played a little duet in which I played a note and she played one in return. Then she took to banging the keys with both hands.

"No, Sophy," Jane called, "not like that. Gently! Do not let her, Mary."

I did not quite know how to stop her so lifted her hands off the keys. She turned to look at me in astonishment. "I will put you down if you do not play nicely," I said. She stared at me for a moment, and I wondered if she was about to start crying. But she put her finger on the keys again, played a note and then turned to me for approval.

"That's better," I said. "Good girl."

From then our relationship was established, and whenever she found me at the piano she would come and sit with me. She could talk, in a strange childish way, and she liked to play with the little cross I wore round my neck, or my newly curled fringe. Her little brother Charles was not so friendly. He would cling to his mother and sometimes reach for the baby as if to hurt it. Jane said, "Poor Charlie! He was the baby himself, and now Henry has taken his place. Never mind, Charlie, Mama and Papa love you, and so does baby Henry, see how he smiles at you!"

Charlie was not impressed by this, which did not surprise me, as baby Henry did not really smile at him, though he did stare fixedly at his brother.

I did not see very much of Georgiana. She and Kitty were very thick together, and went off riding and walking, or could be found talking and sewing in the ladies' sitting-room or in the bedrooms. They would often break off their tête-à-têtes abruptly if I came in, which convinced me that they were talking secrets, although Georgiana always politely began a new topic that included me. Kitty was very possessive of Georgiana however, so these three-way conversations never lasted long. It was not quite as bad as when Kitty and Lydia had been together, because they had always been much more spiteful towards me. I thought Kitty was improved by Georgiana's example.

As it happened, I did not hear Georgiana play the pianoforte until one evening before the ball. Mr Speedwell had come for dinner, wearing a coat of pale green velvet with a gold ribbon edging, and pale yellow pantaloons. I could not tell if he looked ridiculous or simply very fashionable. We were to have dancing - it would be our last chance to practise the waltz before the ball. Signor Moretti was to play the pianoforte and one of the musicians had offered to come too with his violin. However, while the gentlemen were still at table and the ladies had retired, Jane begged Georgiana to play.

"For Mr Darcy tells me you have been learning some of the very latest music that you bought in London."

Georgiana blushed. "I will play it for you if you like, though I have not fully mastered it as I would wish."

She went to the piano and played a piece unlike anything I had ever heard before. It was very beautiful, with a steady left hand accompaniment to an elegant melody in the right hand that became more ornamented as the piece went on. She did not play it perfectly, but she did play it very well, and she conveyed such a mood that a quietness fell on all of us until the last note had died away.

Georgiana nodded and smiled at the applause and praise that followed, and still blushing, started to fold away her music. I went to join her at the keyboard.

"What is that piece?" I asked. "I have never heard anything quite like it."

"It is by John Field, an Irishman. It is only just published, and my brother thought I might enjoy it. But you must have heard that I cannot really play it. I have not shown it to Signor Moretti yet, but I was practising it while at my aunt's."

"You play very well," I said.

She stood up quickly. "Please will you play for us, Miss Bennet. I have not heard you and it would give me so much pleasure."

I did not want to play after Georgiana's performance: for some reason I thought my Clementi or Cimarosa sonatas would sound rather tame and old-fashioned in comparison. I was about to refuse politely, but was spared the trouble by the arrival of the gentlemen.

Nobody wanted tea immediately, so the footmen moved the furniture, and Signor Moretti and his companion went to play. The violin was quickly tuned and the player, a shabbily-dressed man with a shock of black hair and a pitted countenance, began to play. I was surprised that such an unkempt and seedy-looking person could make such a sound, lively and sweet by turns. Signor Moretti joined in with an accompaniment and there seemed to be a duel between them as to who could play the fastest and the most notes. They had no music in front of them and I could not tell if they were making it up as they went along, or playing something they knew well. Instead of beginning to dance, everyone stopped to listen, and burst into laughter and applause when they came to a stop.

"I hope you do not expect us to dance to anything quite so quick!" Lizzy declared.

"I beg your pardon, Mrs Darcy," Signor Moretti said, with mock solemnity. "We shall now play as many waltzes or other dances as you desire."

Mr Speedwell begged me for my hand in the waltz. "For I have not had the pleasure of dancing with you for some time, Miss Bennet. I hope you took no ill from your adventures the other night."

For a moment I was confused and thought he was referring to my frightful experience with Dean Trowbridge: how could he know of that, who could have spoken of it to him? My suspicions instantly alighted on Lizzy, I did not think Signor Moretti was the kind of man to recount such an episode, but Lizzy, I could well imagine Lizzy telling Mr Speedwell perhaps with some pretended motive of doing good, though in reality just being officious and indulging in vulgar gossip.

"Miss Bennet? Are you well?"

"Yes, I am well. I was just wondering who told you of it?"

"Why, Mrs Darcy, and I also heard an account of it from Miss Kitty, and even Mr Darcy's coachman."

I could feel myself reddening and I missed my step. "Oh, *that* adventure! I thought you meant -"

"Something quite different evidently. I gather you have had other adventures that I have not heard about. How very intriguing!"

I did not know where to look. I could almost imagine myself confiding in him, but then could not think why I would be tempted to do such a thing. I did not know whether such a loud and talkative man could be trusted, yet I remembered how understanding he had been at the inn at B__.

"I will not press you to talk of something which has clearly been extremely upsetting to you. But I hope you know that I am yours to command should you ever need a confidant or adviser. I may not be the wisest or most sensible auditor, but you can rely on me for sympathy and handkerchiefs!"

"Th-thank you, Mr Speedwell, you are very kind. I do not think I will - it is in the past now, but thank you for your concern."

"But you were not frightened at being caught in the storm, I gather?"

I was grateful to him for changing the subject. "I was a little, but when I saw Mr Darcy and Signor Moretti fall into the river and then get up exactly where they were rather than being swept away, I realised that it was not as dangerous as it looked. Indeed, it was extremely comical."

He laughed loudly, drawing attention to us. "I imagine it was!"

The dance came to an end and he led me to a seat. "Miss Bennet, may I claim your hand for the first two dances of the Pemberley ball?"

"Thank you, I would be delighted."

"After all, I must show off my star pupil."

"Now you are flattering me again, Mr Speedwell."

"No indeed! You have made such progress. I believe you hardly danced at all before your visit to Pemberley."

"That is true," I replied. "I am usually called upon to accompany the dancers at the piano."

"Well then, I am right: you have had the most to learn and therefore you have come the furthest and it will be a pleasure and an honour to stand up with you."

He left me and I had a few moments to rest and watch the others as the next dance began. Colonel Fitzwilliam stood up with Lizzy, and she looked quite happy and at her ease; but I noticed Darcy leaning against the fireplace watching them with an angry, mistrustful expression. Suddenly Lizzy noticed mid-dance, and I saw the pleasure go out of her face. She stumbled but soon recovered herself, and the colonel glanced across at Darcy in puzzlement to see what had happened. I was not the only person to observe this: Signor Moretti saw it too and although his hands did not falter his eyes went from one to the other with a look of concern on his face.

But then, a much more astonishing event was to take place, that distracted everyone. The butler came in, went up to Mr Darcy and whispered something in his ear. Mr Darcy's expression changed to one of dismay and anger. He looked towards Georgiana briefly, then went up to Lizzy and Colonel Fitzwilliam. They stopped dancing immediately and the three of them began conferring in whispers. Though the others were still dancing, everyone was looking curiously towards them. But without warning, Lydia, who had been lolling on a sofa fanning herself, jumped to her feet with a cry.

"Wickham!"

◆

The music stopped and silence fell in the room. Every eye was turned to the door, where indeed Lydia's husband was standing, having clearly not waited to be formally announced. It was more than three years since I had seen him and he was much changed. Already the ravages of the dissolute life he led were beginning to show in his features. He was thinner than before and somehow not so upstanding. His skin was sallow and his face, which everyone had once thought so agreeable, was now more gaunt and lined, with dark shadows under his oddly blank eyes. He had clearly shaved, but not very well. His clothes, however, were new and well-kept: obviously, like Lydia, he was happy to spend money that he did not have to keep

BECOMING MARY ◆ 121

up appearances. He looked around the gathering with his familiar unapologetic air, believing that if he acted as though nothing was wrong, he could make it so.

Lydia went into his arms.

"Wickham! My darling Wickham! How I have longed to see you!"

He disentangled her arms from around his neck. "Yes, yes, Mrs Wickham, that's quite enough."

"But how are you here? How did you secure your release?"

"Indeed, I do not know," he said. "Some good angel paid off my debts and left me some money beside. What was I to do but come to Pemberley to seek you, my angel!"

Despite his endearments, I did not think he was happy to see Lydia; indeed he was embarrassed by her and kept looking around the company as though seeking someone else to talk to. But everybody else was silent. Darcy was looking thunderous, and though it fell to him to welcome Wickham he said not a word. Finally Lizzy spoke.

"We did not expect to see you here, Mr Wickham."

"No, I did not expect to find myself here, I confess. Yet here I am. I could not leave my family to manage without me."

Kitty muttered in my ear: "His *family* were managing very well as guests at Pemberley! Now they will have to go back with him. Lydia will not like that!"

Lydia was not thinking so far into the future. "Oh Wickham, how lovely, you are here in time for the Pemberley ball, and I will dance with you even though my belly is so big you will barely be able to keep hold of me!" She laughed as though this was a great joke but nobody joined in.

The silence and awkwardness surrounding Wickham's arrival was going on a very long time. It was surely up to Mr Darcy or Elizabeth to welcome him properly, offer him refreshment or invite him to join the dancing, but neither of them made any attempt to do so. I saw a look fly between Elizabeth and Colonel Fitzwilliam, and the colonel ever so slightly shrugged and shook his head. But Georgiana's expression surprised me most: she was pale, her eyes were wide and she looked shocked. The colonel noticed just as I did and moved quietly to stand with her. She seemed to come out of a trance as he stood beside her, and recollect herself. I could not imagine why Georgiana should be so affected by Wickham's arrival: I knew she had more or less grown up with him; perhaps she had had an affection for him herself and did not like to see him married to such a one as Lydia.

Lizzy looked to Mr Darcy but he showed no sign of speaking. At last she went up to Wickham.

"As you see, we are in the middle of dancing. Perhaps you would like to join us? Have you dined?"

"Yes, thank you, I dined at Sheffield, and am now ready to partake of whatever amusements Pemberley has to offer. You look very well, sister."

Lizzy winced at the word sister, but was too polite to say anything. He did have the right to call her that, after all. But the spell was broken; the musicians began to play again. Bingley and Jane came forward to greet Wickham, and Mr Speedwell stepped up to be introduced.

I did not know what to make of it. I had never seen Lizzy and Darcy so discomposed. Clearly they did not want Wickham at Pemberley, and nor did Georgiana. After a few moments I noticed that Georgiana was no longer present, and nor was Colonel Fitzwilliam. Wickham solicited Kitty for a dance, and while they danced, Lizzy spoke urgently to Darcy. He glanced across at Wickham, then nodded, which appeared to content Lizzy as she moved away from him.

I went and stood beside Mr Darcy, thinking there might be something I could say to help matters.

"You are not happy to see Mr Wickham?" was my rather clumsy attempt.

Mr Darcy turned his attention to me with a great effort. "Any relation of my wife is always welcome here," he said, "though he was not expected. He was thought to be still in prison."

He did not mean to confide in me, even though it was obvious to anyone that he was most displeased by Wickham's arrival. I felt the snub extremely and walked away, only to be pulled onto the floor for the next dance by Wickham himself.

"Well, sister, it has been many years since we have met. You are much changed, I should hardly have recognized you. Indeed, I had to ask Kitty who was that charming lady."

"You are very polite, Mr Wickham. Are you always so ready with your compliments?"

The dance separated us at that point so he was not obliged to answer immediately. When we were brought together again, he said, "You believe I offer you mere flattery, but indeed, it is not so, Mary. You have been concealing your true beauty all this time."

Mr Speedwell passed us in the dance and grinned at me. That made me smile and renewed my confidence.

"It is hard to know how much substance there is to your words, Mr Wickham," I said. "Are they as empty as your purse?"

He was not discomposed by my retort, but said, "Now Mary, is that kind, to be throwing a man's errors in his face? Why, the best of us can get into difficulties, and after all, it has not lasted very long, for here I am, liberated from the horrors of York Gaol by the kindness of strangers, and back at Pemberley, the place I most love to call home. How agreeable it is to see my dear wife so indulged and petted as she is here, and no doubt my children too, tasting all the delights of their father's childhood home!"

"As well for them they do not know of their father's disgrace," I said.

"Disgrace, you call it? No! Merely a brief...hiatus, a momentary lapse of means. But I have come about as I always do, and there is enough money for me to invest in my friend Blackstone's business. And then, farewell debts for ever!"

"Even the richest man shall become poor if he do not husband his resources."

"Very true, dear sister, very true. I see you have not lost your turn for moralising. Most apt, most apt indeed."

The ripples caused by Wickham's unexpected arrival at Pemberley were overtaken by the preparations for the ball. At last the day arrived. For me that meant a day of tedium, while we made ourselves ready. Kitty was not quite happy with the fit of my new gown, even though I had stood for hour upon hour while she pinned it and fiddled with it. The sleeves went down to the elbow, and Kitty thought them too loose for my arm. She had made the over dress of the primrose yellow material and had sewn tiny pearls round the bottom of the under dress which was of a paler yellow muslin. My hair had been in curl papers all night, but because it was so straight and lank by nature, Kitty insisted that I leave the curl papers in until the last minute. As there were now so many guests in the building, I did not feel I could practice the pianoforte with hair so clown-like, so was mostly confined to my room. I spent much of the time reading a novel, 'The Monk', which though extremely silly and unlikely, was also strangely enjoyable and made me want to know what happened. I did experience a twinge of guilt, that I had not discovered the Greek primer and begun my studies in earnest.

Judith came to dress my hair in a style called the Antique Roman, copied from a magazine. It meant confining most of my hair at the back of the head, allowing the ringlets to fall from the top knot, and laying a braid of hair around a scarf of the primrose satin. A little sprig of artificial pearls on a pin held it in place at the front, and once it was arranged I was surprised at how modish my appearance was.

There was nothing particularly Antique or Roman about it, however, that I could see. Kitty came in soon after and crowed with delight.

"Mary, you have never looked better in your life, truly you have not!"

Kitty herself looked very pretty in a white striped underdress of satin, with a silver gauze demi-train on top, embroidered with many tiny seed pearls round the neck line. Her hair was curled round her face and fell in studied disorder from a top knot.

"Put your gloves on now, Mary, let me see the whole of it."

I pulled on my long gloves. "I will have to remove them to play the pianoforte," I said.

"Oh, that does not signify. As long as you wear them at other times. Well, your beaux will no doubt have fought a duel over you before the night is over."

"Yes, very amusing, Kitty. And what of your beau? "

Kitty looked coy. "I have not the pleasure of understanding you, Mary."

I said nothing more, aware of the presence of Judith and not wishing to give the servants even more to gossip about. Before I left my room a tiny posy was delivered to me of white and yellow flowers: there was no note with it, so I did not know who had sent it, but though I thought it a mere trifle I was pleased. And it matched my gown.

Kitty and I went down to dine together. All the guests of Pemberley were to dine before the ball, as well as some others who had been invited especially. I saw the Cardings were among their number, but was relieved that Dean Trowbridge was not with them.

"Yes, he had to go back to London rather unexpectedly," I heard Lady Carding saying to Lizzy. Lizzy's face showed nothing but polite interest, though her eyes spoke differently when they met mine.

Frederick Carding went straight to Kitty and engaged her in conversation. I began to think his intentions towards her were serious.

Lydia and Wickham came in together, both dazzling in their ball clothes. Lydia's dress was of turquoise satin, with many flounces around the hem. Her hair was strewn with jewels, and she wore a small black coat draped over the top and caught at the shoulder with a large gold brooch. Wickham was correctly dressed in evening clothes, but perhaps they had been made for him when he was fleshier as they hung off him somewhat.

Elizabeth and Jane both looked very fine, yet without ostentation, Elizabeth in a dress of apple green, Jane in coral pink. Georgiana's dress was ivory silk and she wore only a row of pearls, no doubt genuine, to set it off. I found myself standing next to her while we waited to go into dinner. She did not speak to me, but I thought she seemed very nervous and on edge.

"Are you not well, Miss Darcy?" I asked, although I was sure her complaint was not physical.

"Thank you, Miss Bennet, I am quite well. But I wish you would call me Georgiana, as Kitty does. We are sisters-in-law now."

"Certainly, I would like to. And you must call me Mary. Are you anxious about playing with the orchestra tonight?"

"I am a little, I confess, though in some respects it is easier to play with others, there is less attention paid to oneself."

"Yes, I suppose so. I have never played with anyone else."

She looked astonished. "Never? Oh Miss B - Mary, I sincerely pity you, there is so much enjoyment to be had from playing music with another. But how comes it that you have never played even with your sisters? If I had been fortunate enough to have sisters, I think I would have played with them all day long!"

"That depends on the sisters," I said. I regretted my words as soon as I had uttered them: I knew it was not proper of me to talk so of my sisters, especially now that Lizzy was part of Georgiana's family.

"But were they not musical like you? I know Lizzy can play and sing very well, although she is so modest."

"Our ways did not come much together," I said. "I became accustomed to practising alone."

"I do hope I can persuade you to play something with me while you are here. I have some duets that I long to try. Will you give me the pleasure? After tonight, things will be quieter here, perhaps."

"Thank you, I am sure we will find the time."

Colonel Fitzwilliam came to join us to take Georgiana in to dinner. He took her arm, and I was surprised to see her squeeze his hand and look up into his face with some pain in her own. There was something troubling her very much, I did not doubt, but I could not expect her to confide in me. I knew it was something to do with Wickham, and I was sure that both Lizzy and Colonel Fitzwilliam knew more about it than they were saying.

Part Six: The Ball at Pemberley

◆

I had never been to a ball where I danced so often as at Pemberley. I was far more used to sitting out with the matrons and dowagers, and had been quite content to have it so. I still did not think dancing to be a particularly worthy pastime, but I had come to have a mild enjoyment of it, and it made a difference now that I knew the steps and could retain my dignity. As for Mr Speedwell's talk of *star pupils*, I knew that was his flattery and exaggeration, meant to encourage and tease me in equal measure. I danced the first two with him, and it was very enjoyable to have such a partner, although I was a little overwhelmed by the extravagance of the lapels on his swallowtail coat and his starched neckcloth worn so high that he could barely turn his head. It did not impede his dancing, however, and he was unfailingly merry and a very dainty stepper, if sometimes a trifle over-enthusiastic on the turns. We chatted very easily together, almost like old friends, and indeed he was the first gentleman with whom I had spent so much time. Yet even though he teased me constantly, he was not flirtatious, whatever Lizzy or Jane or Lydia might think.

I sat out the next two and was surprised to see Lizzy sitting out too. Darcy was dancing with another lady that I did not know, and Lizzy's eyes kept following him round the room. She looked unhappy, and though it pained me somewhat, I knew that she deserved it, and would be the better for feeling some remorse. The colonel was dancing with Georgiana, and I thought he was less than his usual cheerful and even-tempered self.

"How do you like the orchestra, Mary?" Lizzy asked me, I presumed by way of making conversation and distracting herself from more painful concerns. "They are certainly the best I have ever heard at Pemberley. And look at Signor Moretti: he is playing the violin now, there is no end to his talents."

"He is certainly very accomplished. I suppose one would need to be versatile to earn a living as a musician."

"He will never be a *very* rich man," Lizzy said thoughtfully, "but I doubt he will ever want for patrons. He is very well thought of in London, both in the musical world and amongst the families whose children he teaches. I wonder if he is still very much mourning his late wife?" she mused. "Certainly there is always an air of sadness about him, but perhaps if he were to marry again he might cheer up."

"I hope he will marry again," I said. "He will get over the loss of his wife all the better. A new interest will distract him."

"Perhaps so."

"And before you say anything, Lizzy, I have no intention of being the person to offer that distraction. In fact, I have no intention of marrying at all, whatever everyone here seems to think. I am not looking for a husband."

Signor Moretti, having left the orchestra to manage without him, approached at this point and asked me to dance, leaving my argument somewhat undermined. For a moment I thought of refusing him, just to convince Lizzy but I decided instantly that that would be unnecessarily cruel to Signor Moretti, who was ignorant of our conversation.

The next dance was a waltz and we acquitted ourselves very well, even managing to maintain a conversation as we went.

"I think Mr Speedwell would be proud of us," I said. "We are both dancing much better, even though you are so much taller than me. He is quite jealous of his prowess as a teacher, you know."

"Perhaps you think all teachers are as jealous of their pupils' accomplishments?"

I thought he was referring to the fact that I had refused lessons from him. I might have ignored it another time, but whether it was the excitement of the ball, the confidence of knowing that I looked better than ever, or the effects of Mr Darcy's punch, I took him up directly.

"Do you think that is why I refused lessons from you?" I said.

"It occurred to me as a possibility."

I laughed derisively. "You think I would refuse your lessons in order to - in order to deny you the gratification of having an apt pupil, such as Mr Speedwell has had?"

"How well you phrase it, Miss Bennet! Yes, I suppose that was a thought that had come to me."

"But that makes me appear to be - like a child, so puffed up in my own conceit and - and egoism, that I would refuse your help simply to spite you! Is that what you think of me?"

He looked at me gravely without responding for a moment, and I gasped, "That *is* what you think of me! You think I cannot bear to take instruction because I am too proud!"

"I think only that you have had to manage for so long without instruction - without help of any kind, that you have to come to rely on your own judgement."

"Well, that is so, I suppose," I said, slightly mollified. "I have been very much alone, and have had to learn everything for myself.

And I do prefer that. I find that people are for ever telling you what to think, what is wrong; other people seem to think that they know everything and are always right about everything, and they do not respect one's opinions or ideas."

"I can understand that would be very irksome. It is not surprising that you have preferred to plough your own furrow."

My heart was beating rather fast now, and I did not think it was the exertion of the dance, more the disturbing nature of my conversation with Signor Moretti. Far from being a suitor for my hand, he had revealed that he thought me conceited and, I suppose, stubborn, too stubborn to take advice from him at any event. Well, I wondered who he thought he was, a catchpenny, paltry music teacher, scraping a living from fiddling away in the orchestra pit, or depending on the goodwill and charity of great families for his bread and butter.

"I think I have offended you, Miss Bennet," he said, as the dance came to an end.

"No, indeed," I responded brightly. "Thank you for the dance."

He bowed politely. "Mine was the pleasure."

There was to be an interlude before refreshments were served, and this was when there was to be some performing. Georgiana's harp was wheeled out and she took her place there. A flautist came out of the orchestra and bowed to her, Signor Moretti took up his fiddle and stood at the front to direct the orchestra and the music began. They played a slow movement of such liquid beauty that within seconds I felt my insides melt: it was Mozart of course, unmistakeably Mozart. No other music could be so utterly tender and poignant, so delicate on the ear yet with such a sense of rightness about every note that it had a strange sort of strength as though it was made of a substance that was at once pliable and unbreakable. I forgot that it was Georgiana Darcy playing; I forgot everything but the sweetness and grace of the music. I was not the only person affected by the glorious sound: all the guests were in a similar trance, such that only certain pieces of music can produce. I turned and looked: there were dazed smiles on people's faces, some had their eyes cast upwards, others stared in concentration at the musicians. When it was over, ending with a tiny trill from the harp, there was a sigh from everyone there, then applause. Georgiana acknowledged it shyly, including the enthusiastic applause that came from the orchestra musicians. I noticed Signor Moretti particularly, nodding and smiling at her.

And then it was my turn. Somebody said my name and I walked up to the pianoforte, which had been carried down to the ballroom earlier and tuned. I had not played in such a big room before, with so much space around me. My music was already on the pianoforte waiting for me; I opened it at the page, looked down at the keys and suddenly felt as though I had never played the piano before in my life. This was not like me, but it was not surprising that I should feel a little nervous in such a place. I must think of nothing now except the music that I was to play: it would be a shock to the listeners after the Mozart; it was much darker, more dramatic, demanding a response of the listener. It was foolish to feel nervous. I fingered the music and in a moment Georgiana was beside me.

"Would you like me to turn the pages?" she whispered. I nodded. She reached across me and turned up the corner of the page. "Any repeats?" I shook my head, not quite trusting myself to speak.

I started to play. The loud first chord sounded satisfying and gave a small shock to the audience I thought. All in all, the slow introduction went well, though Signor Moretti's comments from our lesson rang loud in my ears, and I was conscious of some slight fumbles during the fast scale. However, as I began the allegro section, I started to realise that I had never played the whole movement through from beginning to end, and I did not anticipate how tiring it was for the hands. Nor had I predicted, when it came to the cross-hands section, that I would feel that I had no idea where the keys were, which ones to play, or how to get my arm across and back quickly enough. I slowed down to a speed that I could manage, but then, for some reason, though this had worked perfectly well in private rehearsal, in front of other people it suddenly sounded wrong, infelicitous, and the music no longer made sense. Unfortunately there were a number of such passages where slowing down was necessary, but I did not know what else to do now, and there was nothing for it but to continue to the end.

The music seemed to go on for ever, page after page of awfulness. I started to become aware of the people around me: there was a restlessness among the guests as they listened, and when I looked up to the top of the next page, I caught a glimpse of the members of the orchestra, two of them talking to each other behind their hands, one smiling, the other shaking his head in disbelief. I started to panic. Now I was getting quicker in the passages that were supposed to be slow, simply to get through. The last few bars were torture: the slow chords that were a repeat of the beginning, then the final rushing scale to end with which I knew in advance I would not play correctly, and I did not, though at least the last chord was right.

Of course there was applause, there always was; no party of gentry would ever behave other than politely towards a performer, and I tried to acknowledge it with dignity. I vaguely heard Georgiana whisper a compliment, but then I moved swiftly away to the back of the ballroom and out as quickly as I could.

I found myself under the awning that had been placed over the veranda. There were people there who had wisely chosen to absent themselves from my performance: I saw Kitty and Mr Carding, seated on the wall of the fountain, and standing alone, Colonel Fitzwilliam. I wanted to hide myself away more than anything, so still clutching my music I went onto the lawn and headed down one of the gravelled paths that led through the gardens, hoping to lose myself as quickly as possible. I found a bench in a secluded spot and sank down onto it. Immediately tears burst from my eyes and I sobbed.

Why had I ever thought I could play such a piece? Of course, I realised now, it was much too hard for me, I should never have attempted it. What a disaster! How could this have happened? Had I become so distracted by the hedonistic delights of Pemberley that I had been turned away from more serious purposes? Had my head been so filled by the pleasures of learning to dance, of being dressed up and made to look pretty, by compliments and the unfamiliar attentions of gentlemen? I had never played anything so badly, so ill-prepared in my life.

But then my thoughts and inner ravings ground to a halt: I had to admit to myself that I had often played just that badly, just that ill-prepared. The difference was that I had never known it. For the first time I had truly heard myself as others heard me.

Hearing Georgiana play the harp so sensitively, so aware of what the other musicians were doing, and in such a way as revealed hours of practice, years of trusting herself to the proficiency and knowledge of others in order to learn and improve, had opened my eyes to my own state of impoverished ignorance. It was as though I would rather starve proudly, than eat of a dish that was not of my own making.

Oh god, for how many years had I been thus self-deceiving? Signor Moretti had been absolutely right in what he had said to me while we danced: I would rather disdain help from another than admit my own ignorance, I rejected the truths that people told me, thinking they were simply being unkind and trying to hurt me. Oh, what a bitter, bitter fool I was. He had tried to help me, to drop me a hint, suggesting that I play Haydn instead, but I had brushed him aside.

The tears poured afresh. I was glad of the darkness: I could not bear to see a single person, and I wondered how I was going to get to my bedchamber without meeting anyone.

◆

There were footsteps on the gravel path and murmuring voices. I thought it might be somebody coming to find me and looked hurriedly for somewhere to hide without giving myself away by crunching along the gravel. The low wall I was sitting on served as the edge for a flower bed, but there seemed to be a grassy path behind it so I swung my legs over the wall and jumped down. It was not far, but I must have landed oddly because my ankle twisted under me and I could not help emitting a cry.

"What was that?" said a voice. It was my sister, Elizabeth.

"I did not hear anything."

Colonel Fitzwilliam! This was dreadful! They had come into the gardens for some sort of rendezvous. I prayed that they would not linger near my hiding place, especially as the grass was damp with dew and I could feel the moisture soaking through my dress. I did not want to be such a close witness of their liaison, but the luck was against me and they stopped not a foot from where I had been sitting.

"My dear Rowland," said Lizzy, and it sounded as though she was continuing a conversation, "I know you are very unhappy but I think the time is not yet."

"But we have waited so long, Elizabeth! No, I think I must speak. You know I am not accustomed to deception, and Darcy and I have always been the best of friends -"

Not accustomed to deception! Hardly! I thought.

"Sit down, Rowland, you are agitated and cross and are not thinking properly. I am not comfortable either, though I think it is hardly that. It is about waiting for a propitious moment."

I was so shocked I forgot my own situation for a moment. Oh Lizzy, to what depths have you sunk when you can imagine that there would be a propitious moment for such a revelation?

"Wait, the wall is damp. Here, sit on my coat."

"Thank you."

"I do not understand why you would urge me to such caution. It is hard for a man so much in love as I to wait, I would throw caution to the winds and declare myself!"

"Of course you would, and I do not blame you. But there will be difficulties and the arrival of Lydia and Wickham at Pemberley -"

Further voices were heard in the garden, and then a crunching of footsteps on the gravel as someone walked towards us. Lizzy sighed. "Let us move on. Please be patient, dear cousin, we will prevail."

They moved away, but I dared not get up until whoever was approaching should go past. The footsteps did not go past, but stopped exactly where Lizzy and Colonel Fitzwilliam had stopped. I tried not to breathe, certain that whoever it was would find me. I squeezed myself as small as possible, like a child hiding under the bedclothes from a monster, clutching my music in front of me. The silence and waiting seemed to go on for ever.

Suddenly there was a whoosh and somebody had jumped over the wall, and landed next to me on the grass. I yelped again. It was Mr Speedwell, in full ball dress, creaking slightly with the tightness of the corset he was wearing.

"I'm sorry, Miss Bennet," he whispered, "I did not mean to frighten you."

"Why are you here?" I whispered back.

"I followed you, of course. I saw you leave the ballroom and I thought – I thought you might need a friend."

"I do not want a friend. I want the earth to swallow me up. I can never face anyone ever again."

"Oh, come now, Mary, there's no need for that."

"But I was so very bad!" I whispered, the tears starting to come again. "I was humiliated in front of all those people, in front of all the musicians from London, in front of Georgiana. They are all despising me and laughing at me."

"But when I spoke to your sister she said you played as well as you always did."

I could not stop the tears from flowing now. "But that is why it is so very dreadful. I *did* play as well as I always do, which is to say, execrably badly. Only for some reason I never realised it until tonight. When I heard Georgiana play, I understood what a true musician is like, and I am *not* a true musician! I am a fake, a charlatan, I am entirely hopeless!"

I put my head in my hands and sobbed, but when Mr Speedwell put his arm around me and drew me towards him I pulled away.

"No! Do not be kind to me! I do not deserve it. I am a horrible person, I am not fit for anything, I just want to be left alone."

"Yes, yes, of course you do, and so you shall be, but not just yet. Now stop being so dramatic and come and cry on my shoulder. Isn't that what clergymen are for?"

Indeed it was impossible to resist and Mr Speedwell became the second man within a very short time to receive my tears upon his coat.

After a few minutes my crying abated, and he presented me with a handkerchief.

"I shall have quite a collection of handkerchiefs soon," I said, sniffing loudly in a way that Mama would have thoroughly disapproved.

"I cannot think of a better use for them."

I knew he was laughing at me again but I was too exhausted to take offence. I stared down the garden. In the dark I could make out shadows of hedges and in the distance the black shapes of hills and trees. The dance music was still coming from the open windows of the ballroom, and I felt lonelier than ever.

"I can never face anyone again. Tomorrow I will return to Longbourn."

"Now don't be getting yourself into a stew! I know what you young ladies are like, one little mishap and it is all doom and gloom with you. After all, however badly you did or didn't play, and as you know, I'm no judge, most of the people in there have even less judgement of music than I do."

"But the musicians! They were all laughing at me!"

"And soon they will have all returned to London, never to be seen again. I think the best thing you can do is act as though nothing is wrong and return to the ball - after all, you wouldn't want to disappoint your partners."

"I couldn't go back! Everybody saw me leave!"

"The only people who would have noticed that anything was wrong were those closest to you, your sisters and your friends. And nobody who cares about you would be laughing at you."

"My dress is wet."

"Oh dear! Despite all the instructions of my sisters in the niceties of ladies' dresses, to that I do not have an answer. And it is such a pretty dress too. But there will be someone who can help you with it. Now come, you are going to catch a chill out here without even a shawl to protect you."

He stood up and reached one hand down to me, taking my music from me with the other. There was nothing for it but to take his hand and let him pull me up.

"Shall we vault back over the wall, or shall I pick you up and fling you over?"

I laughed. "I have done enough vaulting for today. I hurt my ankle when I jumped over."

"Then you had better take my arm and we will proceed decorously through the flower bed until we find a path."

We managed not to destroy too many flowers and my ankle did not pain me. But as we moved under the light of one of the flambeaux that illuminated the gardens I inspected my dress and saw that there were indeed two damp patches where I had been kneeling on the dewy grass.

"Oh no!" I said. "My dress is spoiled. I think I had better retire to my room. I cannot go back to the ball like this."

I was relieved; even though Mr Speedwell had lifted my spirits somewhat I did not think I could bear going back, I did not have enough fortitude of mind to present an unconcerned appearance. And a gentleman was no judge of whether a lady looked fit to be seen by company, even a man as familiar with ladies' fashions as Mr Speedwell.

"What if I were to send for your maid?" he asked. "Perhaps you could change into another gown?"

"Oh no! It would be most peculiar - people would notice. Really, Mr Speedwell, I must just go to my room. If you would be so kind as to escort me to the side entrance, then I think I can get upstairs without being seen."

He did not argue any more, but when we reached the side door he took my hand in his and held it. "Will you promise me, Miss Mary Bennet, that you will not lie awake fretting in the way young ladies are prone to do?"

The compassion in his voice very nearly made me start to cry again.

"I will try not to," I said, "but -"

"No buts now."

"Very well, I will do my best."

He squeezed my hand and then raised it to his lips and kissed it.

"Good night then. I shall call tomorrow and see how you do."

"Thank you. You - have been very kind."

I reached my bedchamber without being seen and at first all I could do was sit down on my bed and catch my breath. I did not think I would be able to keep my promise to Mr Speedwell; my mind was too full and showed no sign of being able to be stilled for many hours yet. My eyes rested on the wet patches on my dress. I hoped it was not ruined: Kitty had worked so hard to make it for me, and even I could admit that it became me. I was even a little sorry not to be able to appear properly at the ball, though I could not approve of such vanity in myself. And yet there *was* a pleasure in being sought after, in having gentlemen be kind to one and pay one attention. It made me understand a little more why Lydia was such a determined flirt: it was like a sweet nectar to have that attention, and I could imagine someone without a well-ordered mind wanting more and more of it. But I did have a well-ordered mind, and I would not allow myself to be led down such frivolous paths as Lydia, where only the continual gallantry of innumerable gentlemen could satisfy her.

I could hear the music of the band rising up through the house. They were playing a waltz and I felt tears start to my eyes. I would never waltz again now. Even if the waltz began to be danced in Hertfordshire nobody there ever showed any interest in me or asked me to dance. I looked into my future, living once more at Longbourn, and it suddenly seemed very bleak and empty. I must have become spoiled by the luxuries of Pemberley, and perhaps even led astray from serious pursuits by frivolity and my own hitherto unacknowledged vanity. This was very wrong. I began to think that the humiliation I had suffered at the ball this evening was no more than I deserved. It was a message to me that I had become superficial and overly concerned with worldly triviality. I had allowed myself to be corrupted.

For a moment I felt comforted by this thought; a picture rose in my mind in which I was calm and contented again, studious and concentrated. But there had been another realisation tonight, more painful than anything I had yet experienced: that despite all my studies, despite my best endeavours, I was really not very good. I had not learnt properly.

Now I could not stop from crying again. I felt as though my heart would break. All at once everything that I had believed about myself was a lie. When I compared myself to Georgiana, I realised that I was no musician, but the merest desperate school girl with a bare facility and no depth of learning or understanding at all. Chasms opened before me, chasms impossible to cross, hopelessness and despair. I fell onto my pillow and wept.

◆

I did not remember sleeping that night. I thought I was awake all night, my thoughts and memories turning over and over in my mind, and hearing the guests walk past my room as they made their way to their own chambers after the dancing was over. But when Judith came in to make up the fire I woke with a start, so I must have slept at least some of the night.

Judith heard me stir and came bustling over to the bed.

"Oh Miss, you don't look well. Don't move, I'll fetch you coffee and a roll and some water to wash in. You look worn out."

She opened the curtains and the early morning sun shone silvery through my window.

"I shall get dressed, Judith. I would like to go for a walk before breakfast."

"Very well, miss. I'll lay out your warm dress. For all it's summer, it's fresh out there."

"Oh, have you been out already?"

"Why, of course, Miss! I collected the eggs for cook and some fresh parsley from the garden. It's not my work, but with all these extra mouths I don't begrudge cook a helping hand. I'll get you some water to wash with."

"Thank you, Judith, but I will come back and wash and change later. I would like to go outside quickly before the others are awake. I will ring for you then."

"Very well, miss. And by the way, don't worry about your yellow gown. It didn't stain at all, the laundry maid did a prime job on it." She hurried away in her usual energetic fashion.

There was a shawl carelessly left in the hall and I wrapped it round my shoulders before I went outside. I was glad of it, as the air was cool. I did not know where I was going, I just knew that I had to be outdoors, that I needed the fresh, clean air around me, in hopes that it would clear my head of the chaos that inhabited it still.

There was nobody about except some of the gardeners. They tipped their caps to me but were uninterested: my humiliating exposure of the night before could mean nothing to them. I envied them their humble life, they could not know of my turbulent thoughts. What had they to occupy them but simple physical labour, tending flowers and vegetables, scything the grass for hay and digging the earth? Ah yes, they were fortunate indeed!

I took a path that led into a wood. It was slightly damp underfoot but I was wearing my stout boots and it did not matter if my hem became dirty. Out of the wood I came to a stile; I leant on it and looked across the field. There were more woods beyond, ancient oaks and beech and the sun was glowing palely through the clouds above them. It was a very beautiful prospect and I thought again how fortunate Lizzy was to be able to call such a place home. Inevitably my thoughts then took a sadder direction, and I wondered how she could be so careless as to jeopardise her marriage. I could not understand how she could prefer Colonel Fitzwilliam to Mr Darcy! Colonel Fitzwilliam was merely a pleasant fellow, with a (sadly hypocritical) open manner and countenance, but Darcy! Darcy was a good man, a fine man, so distinguished in manner and bearing, so dutiful to his position, so dignified and yet not so superior as to ignore people of lesser rank or treat them with unbecoming disdain. When I allowed my mind to wander back, it lighted on so many examples of his thoughtfulness and kindness towards me. I could never be sufficiently grateful to him, and it made it all the more incomprehensible that Lizzy should not feel the same. Nor would I ever have suspected that Lizzy could have been so dishonest, so treacherous. She must have changed a great deal. Perhaps being such a rich and important lady now had gone to her head and made her think she had the licence to do anything she wished.

I turned back towards Pemberley feeling somewhat refreshed, and as I came towards the side door, I remembered the little chapel. I thought it might give me peace to sit awhile inside. It was part of the older section of Pemberley, and Mr Darcy had once told me that it was built hundreds of years ago, before the rest of the house, only gradually being incorporated into the building. It was made of an ancient dark stone, built in a simple rectangular shape. As I reached the door, I heard the sound of music within. It was the organ, playing something very slow, with an ancient and mysterious mood to it. I pushed the door carefully so I would not disturb the player and tiptoed in.

It was Signor Moretti, recognisable at once by his tall, narrow frame even though he had his back to me. I sat down quietly, hoping he would play on and not see me. The music suited my sombre reflective mood. It sounded bare – long, plain chords and intertwining melodies. The harmonies were strangely empty compared to music that I was accustomed to, but it suited the little stone chapel. I closed my eyes and let the music fill me.

It cast a spell on me, but I was not so lost to myself that I could not hear what a master of the instrument Signor Moretti was. He moved effortlessly from slow to fast sections, never playing a wrong note, changing the voices on the organ and working the bellows with his feet while still managing to keep the music alive. I felt my heart crack with the pain of it, with the pain of knowing what a proper musician was, and how very far I was from attaining that condition. And the worst, most painful, most humiliating part of it was that I had thought myself so very fine, so very capable, and, most harrowing to admit, so superior to others. Oh, how dreadful it was to see the truth of it!

When the music stopped abruptly I jumped as though being woken suddenly from a deep sleep.

"Miss Bennet!" said Signor Moretti. "I did not hear you come in."

"Oh! No! I - I did not want to disturb you. I was - just listening." I was struggling to regain my composure. I wished I had not stayed and let him see me. "I - I will leave now, I am sorry I interrupted you."

He came swiftly towards me. "You did not interrupt me! I am very glad to see you, and I was sorry that we did not have an opportunity to dance again last night."

He sat beside me, so I could not leave without pushing past him. "You must know -" I began with difficulty, "You must think - oh dear, it is so hard to talk!"

There was a silence while I struggled yet again to gather myself.

"You must think so ill of me!" I burst out, finally.

"I, Miss Bennet? Why should I do so?"

I looked quickly at him. "You heard me play last night. You of all people must know how wretchedly bad it was. I - I did not realise myself until I heard Georgiana play her harp with the orchestra. I - I did not know before then, what it was - you tried to tell me, but I wouldn't listen." I could not speak any more without betraying myself. There was a silence for a few moments.

"I did hear you play, Miss Bennet. You chose a very difficult piece."

I hung my head. He was trying to be kind, to spare me.

"I will not spare you, Miss Bennet."

"Oh."

"You seem to be in the mood for honesty, so I will tell you my thoughts. The Beethoven was too difficult for you and you do not yet have the technique to attempt it. But considering that you are, as you yourself have told me, almost entirely self-taught, you made an ambitious choice of music to perform, and a commendable effort to bring it off."

I drew in a deep breath and let it out again in a sigh. I was taken aback by his plain speaking and did not know whether to be stung by his criticism or pleased by his praise.

"You have a low opinion of me, Signor Moretti."

"On the contrary, Miss Bennet, I am impressed by your dedication to your music and how much you have achieved without the benefit of any guidance."

"But – you still think I was - mistaken to attempt to play that piece?"

He paused. "Do not you think so?"

"I - I suppose so. Yes, yes, I do think so, I was thinking so the moment I started to play, but I thought I must go through with it, it would have been worse to stop in the middle."

He smiled. "You are quite right. Every musician knows that the only parts the audience notice are the beginning and the end, and you played those with great panache."

My feelings burst from me. "Oh, why must people be kind to me! I do not deserve it, and it only makes things worse!"

I laid my head on my arms and lost myself to tears. Signor Moretti said nothing, did nothing; merely he waited until I had stopped. I wiped my face on the borrowed shawl and tried to breathe.

"I beg your pardon," I said, "I do not normally cry so much."

"It is the artist's temperament," Signor Moretti said.

I shook my head. "No. I am no artist. That I know with certainty. I will never play again."

There was a pause. I heard my words ringing through the silence and felt a constriction in my heart. Was that true? Would I really never play again?

"Then you would be making a grave mistake, Miss Bennet."

"But I am so bad, there are so many things I do not understand. It is hopeless, I will never be good enough."

"You can learn. You have made a good start."

"A start? But I am 22 years old! I am too old to learn now."

He smiled. "My wife was a similar age when she started to have singing lessons. Like you, she had some raw talent but was untutored. It was not too late for her."

"But - " I faltered. I dreaded saying this, because I so did not want it to be true. "But perhaps - perhaps I have no talent at all."

"You will never find out unless you allow someone to help you."

This was not the answer I had been hoping for. I wanted him to contradict me outright. "And I suppose you think you are that person?" I retorted, annoyed.

He looked down at his fingers, splayed on the pew in front. "I would be most honoured to be allowed to teach you, but you may wish to find a different master."

I did not know what to say. He disarmed me at every turn. The silence between us lasted some time. Finally he said,

"Have you breakfasted? May I escort you back to the house?"

"Thank you," I answered, and allowed him to lead me to breakfast.

◆

I did not meet anyone else until later in the morning. After breakfast I retired to my bedroom to try to pass the time by reading a book and writing letters. My concentration was sadly awry and I blotted my letter to Maria Lucas shamefully and had to start again with a fresh sheet of paper. It was impossible to write because there was nothing that could be said. I could not describe the ball because I had not been there for most of it, and I could not find words to tell about what had happened to me. It was both too public and too private, a dreadful state of affairs. I saw out the window a number of gentlemen returning from a ride, their boots dusty and their horses puffing. They all looked cheerful and talkative, except Mr Darcy, who rode at the front of the group and did not join in. I saw Mr Bingley trying to attract his attention but without success. Even from this distance, his face looked set and somewhat grim and my sympathies were aroused towards him. He must be meditating on his wrongs, I thought.

Later, Judith told me luncheon was being served, and seemed to expect that I would attend.

"Let me just sort your hair out, Miss, you look like you've been dragged through a hedge backwards."

I sighed, but allowed her to have her way. To present a dishevelled appearance would only draw attention to myself and remind people of last night's disaster. Judith patted my hair in a satisfied way, and then tucked a piece of lace into my bodice.

"There you are, Miss Bennet! That's more fitting for a sister to Mrs Darcy! You look neat as a new pin!"

I thanked her, took a deep breath and went downstairs.

Many of the guests had departed and I was glad of that. But I was not pleased that Lydia and Wickham were seated at the table. Lydia was leaning back in her chair yawning ostentatiously, with one hand on her belly, while Wickham fed her with a tiny silver fork.

"Oh, Mary, is it you? Where have you been? I did not see you at the ball, and there were many charming bachelors I would have introduced you to. Wickham wanted to dance with you himself, did you not, Wickham, but you were nowhere to be found!"

"I did indeed wish to dance with you, Mary, it is always my pleasure to stand up with as many of my fair sisters as my fortitude and my wife will allow."

"Oh Wickham, how can you say so!" Lydia protested, pouting, "You make me quite jealous."

He popped some food into her mouth. "Oh, you think I might run off with your sister Mary, now that she is got so pretty, do you!"

Lydia punched him and choked on her food. "I am sure I do not know *what* you would do, you rogue! Oh Mary, we have had such a dreadful night. No sooner did we go to sleep than that hopeless nursemaid that Lizzy has hired must needs bring Theodosia down to us with some nonsense about her teething, saying that she wouldn't settle. Why should she bring her to me? *I* can never settle her! And poor Wickham had to walk up and down the room with the child crying in his arms till there was no bearing it. And those horrid friends of Lizzy's in the next room kept coming to the door to ask what was the matter and why could we not quiet the child? I said, why don't *you* quiet the child if you know so very much. That soon sent them packing. But I am quite exhausted with all the disturbances. I wonder you did not hear it."

"My room is far away from yours, Lydia."

"Well, that is very fortunate for you. Where did you go, Mary, at the ball last night? I am sure you were not there. Were you?"

"I - I became overheated and had to step outside. Then I felt unwell and retired early."

Lydia nudged Wickham. "Oh, Mary, you devil! I never would have thought it of you! What a story, eh, Wickham? Overheated! Such old hat, Mary. I cannot count the number of times I have become *overheated* in a ballroom and had to step outside."

Wickham pinched her cheek. "Oh you would, wouldn't you, you little coquette. And your poor old husband left to entertain the dowagers."

I said crossly, "I do not know what you are referring to, Lydia."

She gave a tinkling laugh, which grated falsely on my ear. "Oh Mary, such dis - such dis - what is the word I want, Wickham?"

"Disingenuousness, my love."

"Really? How odd! I never said that word in my life before. Well, what I mean to say, Mary, is, which of your beaux accompanied you on your little stroll around the gardens?"

"I do not have any beaux, Lydia. I wish you would not talk so."

This was not a good moment for Mr Speedwell to enter the room. I blushed and started to eat furiously to cover my discomfiture.

Lydia laughed.

"Oh, Mr Speedwell," she cried, "you have quite discomposed my sister! See how she blushes!"

Wickham said in his most drawling tone, "Do you always have this effect on the young ladies of your acquaintance, Speedwell? It must be a prodigious nuisance in your line of work." He paused. "Or perhaps it plays to your advantage? Of course it does! Dash it, why wasn't I a cleric, eh, Mrs Wickham?"

"Because then I should never have seen you in your regimentals, and never have fallen in love with you!" Lydia replied. They began nuzzling in an artificial, exaggerated style and I turned away, not knowing where to look.

Mr Speedwell said calmly without any of his usual affectation, "I was in hopes of finding you here, Miss Bennet. I wanted to take you for a drive. You will be relieved to hear that I have left my curricle at home, and we will proceed sedately in my pony and trap. The day is quite warm now, you need not fear a chill."

I did not fear a chill, but I did not know how to face him again after our encounter of the night before, when he had been so kind and had seen me cry and lose all self-possession. However, a refusal would only cause more comment from Lydia and Wickham, and it seemed simplest to accept with the minimum of fuss.

"Thank you," I said, trying to imitate Mr Speedwell's calm tones. "Let me but fetch a coat and I will come at once."

He bowed and left the room. As the door shut behind him, Lydia burst into peals of laughter. I ran quickly away before she had time to say any more.

Mr Speedwell was chatting animatedly and with surprising familiarity to a groom as I arrived. He helped me up into the trap and we set off at a trot around the gravelled drive. I was not able to begin a conversation, and Mr Speedwell seemed to feel no need to talk at first; I was grateful for the silence. My heart was still very full, as though tears could come at any moment. And Lydia's pert remarks had set my nerves on edge even more, so that I could not be calm.

As we left the gravel drive and turned onto the road that circled the estate, we slowed to a walk and Mr Speedwell said,

"Now, Miss Mary Bennet, would you like to take the reins?"

"Oh! I - I am not very good at driving. I have not been accustomed to."

"I'm sure you would enjoy it, and if anything untoward happens, I will immediately throw myself out of the carriage and run for help."

I braved a look at him: his expression was mischievous and I could tell he was trying to cheer me up.

"Very well," I said, "I *should* like to try. When I drove my sisters when I first came to Pemberley it did not go very well, and I would like to improve."

"Excellent!"

He handed me the reins, and as the pony did not do anything unexpected, indeed it did not change its pace from an active walk, I was soon able to feel quite at ease. It was soothing to sit behind a pony like this, half concentrating but knowing that nothing could go wrong. I started to be aware of the warm breeze that was blowing, of how the leaves moved lightly in the trees, and how very green they were. Gradually my frayed nerves started to settle and I sighed.

"Better?" asked Mr Speedwell.

I smiled at him. "Yes, much better. I think you knew it would make me better."

He smiled. "I admit I hoped so. My sister Eloisa often found a gentle drive an excellent panacea for a disordered mind, as she put it. Not that I mean your mind is disordered, only - only - somewhat - "

"Disordered will do," I said, sadly.

"But I think you are a little recovered since last night?"

"Yes, I am a little." I frowned. "But my mind is still very full, and I do not know what to think of myself."

"Perhaps thinking about someone else might be of help to you. I was in B__ again the other day, visiting the Heelys, and Mrs Heely was asking about you most particularly. You would be doing them a great kindness if you visited them again."

I was surprised. "A kindness? You think they would like to see me again?"

"They have said so, and that is as good an indication as any. I told Mrs Heely that you are a great reader, and she wondered if you would be so good as to help Margaret with her letters sometimes. If you are not *too* appalled at my taste in carriages, I would be happy to escort you there."

I must have dropped my hands in surprise, because the pony broke into a smart trot.

"Oh no!" I cried, remembering my disaster with Lizzy and Kitty. "He is running away!"

"It is perfectly all right," Mr Speedwell said, "He is only trotting. And he is a she, by the way. Her name is Deborah."

"Deborah! That is a very curious name for a horse!"

Mr Speedwell laughed. "Why so? What should she be called?"

I had no answer to that. "Is she named after Deborah in the old testament?"

He laughed. "No indeed, though it would suit her very well, as she must always be in charge. She was named after her own mother, and her grandmother before that."

"She seems to be trotting rather fast, Mr Speedwell."

"I assure you there is no need to worry unless she breaks into a canter. And you may have noticed that your sister calls me Arthur."

"Oh!"

"Do you think you might be able to do the same?"

"I - I'm not sure. Isn't it too - familiar?"

"Well, I must say, Mary," he laughed, "if that's too familiar, what do you call crying into a man's shoulder?"

I blushed. "I wish you had not mentioned that. I regret it."

"I on the other hand, do *not* regret it. Nor should you. It was quite the right place for you to cry."

I was vexed. "I am not a child, Mr Speedwell!"

"I am not a child, *Arthur*."

That made me laugh. "And you called me Mary."

"I did, and I would like to go on doing so, unless you object *very* strongly?"

I thought about it for a moment. I probably ought to object, but I did not really know. No man had ever wanted to use my Christian name, or asked that I use his. I suspected that it might be improper, and I thought he was teasing me.

"I hope you are not flirting with me, Mr Speedwell?"

He gave one of his booming shouts of laughter, flung an arm round my shoulder and gave me a tight squeeze. "Oh Mary," he cried, releasing me, "you are so delightfully frank. If it will reassure you, I am not flirting with you."

"Well - I am glad of that," I gasped, recovering my breath. "I do not know - I am not accustomed to it, and I do not know how to go on. When Lydia flirts, all rational conversation goes out the window and she becomes excessively silly." I thought for a moment. "Actually, she is always excessively silly, but she is silly *and* vulgar when she is flirting." I turned to look at him. "I do not wish to be either of those things. I enjoy our conversations, and I would not like them to degenerate into nonsense. Oh! I think the pony, I think *Deborah*, really is beginning to run away now."

He laughed again as he took the reins.

"I knew you would be a tonic the day I met you!" he cried. "*How* my sister would love to meet you, I am sure you would be such friends. She is always telling me how to behave too. Goodness, how I do miss her! Shall we strike a bargain? I promise at least to attempt to observe the social niceties, and if I prove myself not to be a complete ass, we shall be Mary and Arthur to each other!"

"Very well, I cannot see the harm in that."

"And shall we go to B__ soon?"

The pony was slowing to a trot.

"I should be very pleased to do so."

Part Seven: The Fall

◆

The day or two after the ball were not like any I had known before at Pemberley, or indeed anywhere, at any time. I kept thinking I might be sickening for something; my head stung and tingled around my ears. I wondered if something might be wrong with my eyesight, because everything I looked at was different: it may have been the changing season and the summer light, but the world seemed vivid and somehow shining. Things took on a strange particularity: a tree or a vase would loom at me, come forward and demand my attention. It was most odd. I spent some time in the library, leafing through books and trying to find a description of this peculiar phenomenon, but I found nothing.

Mr Speedwell – Arthur – was true to his promise, and we returned to visit the Heelys. Mrs Heely was indeed pleased to see me again, and Margaret and little Samuel frisked about me as though I were a long-lost relative returned. I could not help but be touched by their welcome; I sat quietly with them, poring over an alphabet while Mr Speedwell performed some errands in the town, and enjoyed myself very much. They begged me to return as soon as may be, and I thought it might be a pleasant thing to do: my feelings of shame receded somewhat when I was there, and the bright, eager eyes of the children charmed me.

There were still guests staying in the house, friends of Lizzy and Darcy who had come for the ball and were remaining: there were many visitors too, and I tried to avoid them as much as possible, by keeping to my room or running away and hiding if I encountered people around the house.

As I passed along the upstairs hallway towards my bedroom I saw coming towards me a party of gentlemen and recognised some of the musicians who had come from London. My heart sank: of all people, I did not want to face them. Whatever Mr Speedwell said, the musicians were sure to remember my disgrace. I saw my opportunity to escape by going through a door into the back stairs that led down to the kitchens and up to the servants' quarters.

The stairwell was lit from above by a skylight, and I stood by the door I had just entered, waiting for my heart beat to slow down, and to be sure that the musicians had passed. As their voices grew louder I thought for a moment with dread that they might enter into these very stairs: after all, they were not proper guests, and so might be considered to be servants, but their voices grew fainter as they passed. I stayed where I was, feeling suddenly foolish: what if somebody saw me emerge from the servants' stairs? They would think it most peculiar, and I did not know how I would explain it.

I became aware of voices from further down the stairs, and I froze. There was a man's voice and a woman's, and I listened intently. There were no footsteps on the wooden treads so it seemed that they were not coming closer. The woman gave a squeal and made my heart start to thud again: what could be going on? Cautiously, I peered down the stairwell. Just below me I saw them: the man was clearly a gentleman, dressed in morning clothes, and he was pressed up against one of the maids who had her back to the wall. I did not recognise the maid, she was a lady's maid who must have come with one of the guests, but with a shock I saw that the gentleman who was importuning her was none other than my brother-in-law Wickham. I could not help myself: I gasped in shock and outrage. Wickham looked up straight into my face, and next thing I knew he had bounded up the stairs towards me. The maid vanished.

"My dear sister!" he said, showing no sign of shame or consternation, "what an unexpected place to see you! I did not know that you frequented the servants' quarters!"

"I do not!" I spluttered. "I was -" but I did not know how to continue.

Wickham interrupted. "But of course! My dear wife told me that you have been flirting with the music teacher! I commend you, sister, but I think you will find him with your rival, Georgiana Darcy, rather than here."

"How can you talk about your *dear wife* when you are - behaving like - like - "

"Behaving like a *gentleman*, Mary?"

"No! You are no gentleman, Wickham! How can you betray your wife and your marriage vows, and with a servant! How unhappy Lydia will be when she hears of this!"

I turned to go, but Wickham stood by the door.

"But why should Lydia hear of this, sister? It is such a commonplace, you know, why would you want to distress her by telling her of it?"

"It is better that she should know the truth! She has been sadly deceived in you, Wickham, you, the father of her children!"

He laughed. "The father of her children? Well, well, very possibly, one or two of them at all events!"

"No! How can you say so?"

"Very easily, my dear, I assure you. Good god, Mary, you cannot be so virtuously innocent as you pretend to be."

"It is no pretence, I assure you. Do not assume that everyone is as licentious as you are."

He smiled. "We are all human, Mary, even you. We all have our animal passions."

"But it is our duty to control the base passions, to act with propriety and Christian restraint. That is why God ordained the institution of marriage, as well you know. You took your vows!"

"Oh Mary, Mary, if only we could all show such virtue as you. Not everyone is as blessed with such iron self-control."

"No!" I retorted, "It is not a blessing, it is a matter of will and determination. It is everyone's duty to fight against such feelings!"

"You surprise me, sister! I did not know such a battle raged inside your bosom."

That was not what I meant at all. "I - I am not talking of myself, I am not prey to such things. I am talking about you and the wrong you have done your wife. I can see that you think this is a matter for amusement, and only the shame of confession will change you. I am sorry to cause my sister pain, but I am willing to bear the burden of being the carrier of ill tidings for the sake of truth, and to help you on the path of righteousness. Now, please excuse me."

Wickham did not appear at all perturbed by my threat, but nor did he step out of my way. Instead with a sudden movement his arms were around me, he pulled me against him and kissed me extremely forcefully on my lips. A squeal escaped me which was disconcertingly similar to the sound I had heard from the maid previously. He lifted his head away but did not release his tight hold on me.

"Let me go at once!" I said. He looked down into my face with a glint in his eye.

"Oh sister! So - *disingenuous*! Come now, what could be more pleasant and friendly than a little affection between brother and sister!"

I tried in vain to pull away. "That is pure hypocrisy. I do not feel any affection towards you, *brother*, and you have never shown any towards me!"

"Not hitherto I admit, but then, you have been disguising your attractions all this time. You will never be as pretty as your sisters, or as much of a handful as my lovely Mrs Wickham, but as they have all been saying, you are much improved of late, and believe me, my dear, nothing presents so much of a challenge to a fellow such as me, as a prim and proper bluestocking such as yourself. When you start at such a height, the fall is so very glorious!"

I struggled again but his hold only tightened and my arms were crushed against his chest.

"I do not intend to fall anywhere, Mr Wickham," I said, my breath coming rather fast.

"Believe me, you ladies never do intend it, but you always fall in the end."

I was shocked and angry, but for a moment I thought of my sister Lizzy and felt suddenly sad: was he right? Were there no virtuous women? Or men? Had Lydia really had children with other men? It was a terrible thought; I could not believe it, even of Lydia.

"Now come, Mary, let me kiss you again. It was not so very bad, was it?"

The realisation flashed through my mind that in some circumstances it might not be so very bad to be kissed. But not by my sister's husband.

"Mr Wickham," I said, trying to be calm and dignified, "I do not understand the relations between my sister and you. Nor do I wish to. Please release me at once or I shall be obliged to summon assistance."

This made him laugh. "And how do you intend to do that? Do you really wish the servants, or worse still, the Pemberley family to know that you have been kissing your brother-in-law?"

"I have not been kissing you! *You* have been kissing *me*!"

He considered that for a moment. "It's a moot point, but either way, I don't think you would appreciate the gossip, not such a good Christian lady as you are."

"And you would not mind the gossip, I suppose?"

"Oh Mary, my reputation is sullied beyond repair long since. There is nothing I can do now to make it worse. Or better for that matter," he added thoughtfully.

"You would redeem yourself with me if you let me go."

"What, and have you run off to my wife with your sordid tales?"

I looked at him through narrowed eyes, trying to read his expression. It did occur to me that it was extremely odd to be having this conversation with our bodies pressed tightly together on the servants' stairs.

"If I was to undertake to say nothing of what happened here today, will you let me go without further ado?" I asked.

"What, Mary, you would sacrifice your moral principles to escape a difficult situation? You disappoint me." He looked over my head, seemingly lost in thought. "A man of sense and propriety would jump at your generous offer, but as you know very well, I have neither sense *nor* propriety, so -" And with that he bent his head and kissed me again with equal force, pressing his lips against mine so hard that my mouth was forced open. I tried to pull away, but he held my head, and to my horror I felt his tongue enter my mouth. I heard the same feeble squealing sound that I had made before emanating from my throat as I tried to push him away.

"Come, come, Mary," he whispered, "why not simply yield to me? This could be so very pleasant." He began to drop kisses on my shoulders, and suddenly a strange sensation coursed down the centre of my body and made me gasp.

"That's better!" Wickham said. "I knew you would not resist for ever. Nobody ever has you know. Confess, you are starting to enjoy yourself!"

"You are mistaken, Mr Wickham, now let me go!" And I pushed him as hard as I could. He released me very sharply with some surprise, and unfortunately I fell backwards and tumbled down the stairs.

◆

"Good god, Mary!"

I was lying in a heap, half way down the stairs, I did not know which way was up and which was down. All was confusion. Wickham was beside me in a flash, lifting my head.

"Are you hurt?" he asked, his voice full of concern.

"I don't know," I said. "Can you help me up?"

"Ho, is anyone about?" Wickham called.

I vaguely heard a door opening, and the voice of Mr Darcy's butler calling up the stairs.

"What's amiss, Sir?"

"It is Miss Bennet, she has taken a fall down the stairs. Here, help me lift her."

I protested. "No, please, if I could but sit up, I will be quite well in a moment."

Wickham supported me and I sat up. The butler was standing below looking at me curiously.

"What was Miss doing on the servants' stair?" he asked.

"Never mind that, man. Go and get water, or better still, brandy."

"Please do not trouble," I said quickly. "Help me stand, Wickham."

I managed to stand but my legs were sadly shaky.

"Are you hurt, Mary?"

"I don't think so. Perhaps you could call Judith to me," I said to the butler.

"Here, lean on my arm, sister, I will help you to your chamber."

What a different Wickham to a few moments ago! He was filled with remorse and concern; I did not fear him now.

"Why must you needs be so violent?" he said, when the butler had gone. "I would not have harmed you, now look what you have done?"

"Do not speak of it again. You behaved most improperly."

"But I have never been able to resist the temptation of mischief! And it was so very wrong to kiss my wife's sister, that it was bound to happen." I could hear the laugh returned to his voice. I should have known his contrition would not last long.

"No, it was not bound to happen!" I said crossly. "You must learn restraint!"

"Oh, Mary, I am past reforming I'm afraid."

"Nobody is past reforming. If you would but attend church and read improving texts you would gradually come to a better state."

We were back in the main house.

"That is all very well, Mary, but I like the state I am in. And you did not dislike it yourself so very much."

I felt myself blush and knew that Wickham saw it. Fortunately I saw Lizzy and Darcy coming towards us down the hall. Wickham leaned into my ear. "I have done a great kindness to your future husband at any rate," he whispered.

I wanted to retort but Lizzy and Darcy were upon us.

"Mary!" Lizzy cried, "What has happened?"

"Your sister went into the servants' stairs in error and took a tumble," Wickham said smoothly. "By chance I was passing and heard her cry out."

"How fortuitous," Darcy said, his voice flat and unfriendly. "Are you hurt, Mary?"

"No, I am well, only a little shaken."

"Come," said Lizzy, "I will take you to your room. You must lie on your bed and your maid will bring you a tisane."

Wickham handed me over to her and we went back to my chamber. Lizzy made a fuss over me, rang for Judith and then sat beside me on the bed.

"Mary, what happened? Why were you on the back stairs?"

Her sympathetic voice was too much. "Do not question me, Lizzy. It is more of my foolishness and I have had so many blows to my pride that I do not think I can bear any more."

Lizzy held my hand. "Oh Mary, what do you mean? What has been happening?"

"The ball!" I said. "Surely you must know -!"

"Did something happen at the ball?"

I was astonished. "You are hoaxing me. You must have seen, have heard -!"

Lizzy shook her head. "I am sorry, Mary, but I was very much occupied with my guests and making sure that all ran smoothly. I am afraid I had no energy to spare to notice you. Did you not enjoy yourself? Was somebody unkind to you?"

"No, not that!" I bit my lip. I was going to have to tell her and I did not want to recount the sorry tale aloud. "My playing! Did you not hear my playing?"

She looked puzzled. "Yes, I heard you play. I noticed nothing amiss."

"That is worse than ever! Could you not hear -? You play yourself, Lizzy, and you are used to hearing Georgiana and all the finest musicians of the district - could you not hear how dreadfully badly I played?"

She spoke without thinking. "But it was no worse than usual!" She snapped her hand over her mouth. "Oh, I am sorry, Mary, that was unkind. I did not mean -"

I interrupted her. "Yes, you did, and that is what makes it all so very dreadful. You have always thought I play badly, but you have never said. Or perhaps you did try to tell me, but I refused to hear." I covered my face with my hands. "Why did nobody ever stop me? Why did you all let me humiliate myself time and time again?"

"Dear Mary, it is not as bad as that!" She put her arms around me. I heard Judith come in but I did not look up. Lizzy spoke to her.

"Please ask Mrs Bingley to come here. And then bring a chamomile tea for Miss Bennet."

"Oh no, not Jane too!" I said when Judith had gone. "Must everyone know of my disgrace?"

"Jane will restore your mind much better than I can, you know she will, Mary. I - I cannot stay now." She looked towards the window and I could see her face was troubled. "I was about to speak with Mr Darcy about - about a matter of importance when we came across you and Wickham just now. I must go after him." She turned back and smiled at me. "You would not credit how hard it is to have time alone with one's husband. It is no small matter being master of Pemberley, Darcy is always so busy, especially of late. And then I have been much occupied with our guests."

"You do right to talk to him," I said earnestly. "Go at once, Lizzy, do not delay."

She looked at me in surprise. "Why Mary, you are so serious!"

"I was never more serious in my life," I said, looking intently into her eyes. "There is nothing so important as complete candour between a husband and wife. Remember your wedding vows, the dreadful day of judgement when the secrets of all hearts shall be disclosed? You - you would not want to wait until the day of judgement!"

Lizzy gave a puzzled laugh and I clutched her hand. "This is not the time for laughing. I know it all, I have seen -"

She started. "You know? How can you know?"

"I could not help it. I was not spying, but I did notice."

"Good gracious, Mary, what have you seen?"

I shook my head. "I do not wish to say it aloud, but let it be understood between us that - you must tell Mr Darcy. I have noticed his coldness towards you, I - I am sure he knows also." I suddenly felt a great perturbation as I thought of the anonymous letter I had written to him: it was a feeling of guilt, but I did not know if the guilt was because of having written the letter, or because I was not telling Lizzy that I had done it. It was not important: what was important was that she should come to her senses and save her marriage if she could.

I saw that she was flushed and I thought there were tears standing in her eyes ready to be shed but they dried away. She squeezed my hand.

"Well, Mary, I do not think Darcy knows anything about it just yet, and I would ask you not to speak of it to anyone. As you can understand, such a matter is of great delicacy to the people concerned."

I shook my head sorrowfully. "I never thought to hear you speak so, Elizabeth."

She was about to reply when the door opened and Jane came in, so all private conversation between us was at an end.

Lizzy and Jane spoke together quietly at the door, and then Lizzy left and Jane came to me.

"Poor Mary, you have had a fall, how shocked you must be! But Lizzy tells me you are not hurt, so that relieves my mind greatly. And I am happy to hear that Wickham was so gentlemanly and attended to you so well."

"Gentlemanly? Not he!"

I was about to tell Jane everything that had passed between Wickham and me, when I found I could not speak.

"What do you mean, Mary?" Jane asked.

"I - I was thinking of his being in debtors' prison," I stammered lamely, wondering at myself for lying so easily. "*That* is not how a gentleman should behave!"

"I am surprised at you, Mary!" Jane said in her gentle way. "Not everyone is capable or practical with money, and it is unbecoming of you to judge our brother-in-law too harshly without understanding the full particulars of the case."

I blushed fiercely. I did not like to be reprimanded for being harsh, and it was unjust to be taken to task myself and not be able to tell Jane of Wickham's wrongdoing. Jane saw my discomfiture. "I do not mean to be severe on you in my turn, Mary, only as a Christian it is forgiveness and understanding that must be your aspiration."

Oh, I could hardly bear it! I wanted so much to tell her what kind of a man Wickham really was - even worse than we had ever known him to be - but I felt as though a spell had been cast on me, as if in a fairy tale, and I could not speak. I did not know what force was preventing me from telling my sister about Wickham. I knew she would not tell Lydia, so I did not think it was from *that* fear.

No, it was a fear of what she would think of me!

This was most strange! I had not *asked* Wickham to kiss me; I had not expected it in the least. And yet somehow I felt as though I was to blame, as though *I* was the one at fault, not him! It made no sense at all and contradicted the facts of the matter. *He* was in the wrong, *he* had been kissing the maid, *he* had kissed me even though I had struggled to escape, and yet *I* felt ashamed! I frowned in concentration to unravel the mystery, and Jane sensed my preoccupation and left me in silence.

In my mind I went over what had happened moment by moment, and I remembered Wickham's whispered words when he insisted that I was enjoying being kissed. My face went hot with shame because in that moment I realised he was right; there had been a response in me which could only be considered to be enjoyment. This was entirely dreadful. Now I remembered there had been a strange tingling sensation inside me, even though at the same time I was disgusted and morally outraged. What kind of creature was I becoming? Was I as debauched and depraved as Lydia?

Jane was regarding me with curiosity.

"Jane!" I began, hardly knowing what I was going to ask her. "When you and Mr Bingley - when you were first married - oh, this is impossible!"

"What is it, Mary? If you have a question, I will try to answer it as best I can. It is - it is quite usual for unmarried girls to have questions to ask of married ladies, especially if -"

"Especially if what?" I asked warily.

"Especially if they are considering matrimony themselves. And who better to ask than your own sister?"

"I wish everyone would not think I was considering matrimony all the time! Cannot a woman talk to a man without everyone accusing her of flirting or trying to catch a husband?"

"*You* may not be on the catch for a husband, Mary, but that does not mean that the gentlemen concerned are not looking for a wife."

I pursed my lips. "I am sure I know nothing of that. But Jane, what I wanted to ask, what I do not understand, when - when you and Mr Bingley -" My mind froze at this point in my sentence: I knew the words, they were there in the marriage service for all to hear, the actions themselves were there on the farm for all to see, but I could no sooner utter them than I could stand on my head.

◆

Jane was waiting patiently for me to speak, but I shook my head, unable to form the words.

"Shall I try and answer what I think you want to know?" Jane asked. I nodded, still mute with embarrassment.

"I think you are asking about the relations between a man and a woman in marriage, the physical relations?"

I nodded again.

"And you are wondering what it was like for me when I was first married to Mr Bingley?"

"Yes. Did you - like it?"

Jane stared off into the distance. "I did like it. I do like it. It was strange and perhaps uncomfortable at first, but when a man and a woman love each other and wish to devote their lives to each other, then any difficulties can be overcome with time and patience."

"But if - if one were to feel a feeling - *not* within marriage - then, is that not wrong, would not that mean that one was no better than a wanton, than a woman of ill repute?"

Jane smiled. "I do not think a woman can help her emotions, Mary. It is how she acts that is important. Unmarried women can feel a wish, a wish for something which morality forbids, but feelings can be regulated, and - and a desire for physical relations is not necessarily the best guide as to whether a man would make a suitable husband."

"Oh no, indeed," I replied, revolted at the thought of Wickham as a husband. I did find myself musing on the two men whom everyone considered to be my suitors, however. The fancy passed through my mind of what it would be like if either one of them behaved towards me as Wickham had done. They had both held me in their arms, I had cried on both of them, been carried by Signor Moretti. I tried to imagine them kissing me, holding me tightly; would I feel that same disturbance, the fluttering and agitation, with either of them? I could not be sure. I could not help smiling to myself at the thought of it: how different it all was from my ordinary life at Longbourn! It was as though I had entered another world. I could not imagine telling Mama of all that had been going on.

I looked up at Jane and she was watching me with an expression of tender concern.

I smiled. "I was just thinking of Mama. It is perhaps as well she is not here."

This made Jane laugh. "Indeed! This is not a conversation for her."

I paused. "Lizzy said I should not look to Mama and Papa as the only guide to how a marriage can be."

"Did she? Yes, I know why Lizzy would say that. It is true they are not always good companions; they - they do not bring out the *best* in each other."

"And you and Mr Bingley do?"

"I believe we do. We are certainly very happy together, and we both dote on our children. Which reminds me, I wanted to ask you, if you would like to come up to the nursery when you are better. Sophia often speaks of you, and I know you did some teaching with the family you visited, and I thought you might like to help Sophy learn her letters too. She is just beginning to play with the bricks with letters on and to try and draw and write, and you have such a way with her, that I thought you might be the very person to help her. I would do it myself but little Henry needs me so much at the moment that I cannot concentrate for long enough."

"I did not realise I had a way with her," I said slowly. "I did do some letters with the Heely family in B____ who Mr Speedwell introduced me to. I will try and help Sophia too. She is a dear child, Jane. She is very different from Lydia's children."

Jane frowned. "Lydia's children have not had an easy time while Wickham has been in prison. We must make allowances. I am sure they will settle down now that things are better for Lydia and Wickham."

I should have remembered that Jane would never criticise anyone.

"I will leave you to rest now, dear Mary, and to recover from your misadventure. You will be well enough for dinner, I hope."

"I - I do not know. I may eat in my room tonight." In fact I was rather hungry, but I did not think I could face Wickham again so soon. Or Lydia.

Jane left me and I lay on my bed. I felt so dishonoured, both by what had happened and by my need to lie about it to my sisters. But I also knew from previous experiences at Longbourn that the longer I stayed away the more fuss and notice would be taken, and questions asked, and no doubt teasing and poking fun from Lydia and Kitty. Though perhaps not Kitty so much any more.

I rested for half an hour and then called Judith to help me dress for dinner. I decided I should like to look as nice as possible, so that Wickham should not think I was distressed or even bothered in any way by his behaviour. I did not have a new dress to wear, but I allowed Judith to do my hair in a different way, pushed up at the back of my head and with a length of silk tied around. It made me look different and more grown up, I thought. There was a silk shawl too which Lizzy had lent me and that completed my outfit. I would have wished for some jewellery but I had only my small silver cross so that would have to suffice.

There were a great many people gathered in the hall waiting for dinner to be announced. I saw all my sisters and their husbands, Mr Speedwell, Signor Moretti, one or two of the musicians, Georgiana, Colonel Fitzwilliam, Squire Carding and his wife and son, and other guests from the ball that I did not know. Nobody noticed me come down the stairs so I was able to mingle unobtrusively with the crowd. I kept away from Wickham and Lydia and was pleased when I found myself next to Mr Darcy.

"I hope you are quite recovered, Mary," he said, in his serious way.

"Yes, I am, thank you. A short rest was all that was required."

"You were fortunate not to have sustained an injury."

"I was. I still cannot understand how I escaped unharmed."

"An injury? What's this?" It was Mr Speedwell, who must have been close by.

"Mary fell on the stairs earlier today."

"But I am quite unhurt, I assure you," I said, not wanting the dreaded fuss to begin.

"You certainly *look* very well," Mr Speedwell said. "How becoming your hair is in that style!"

I was flustered and glanced at Mr Darcy. I did not like Mr Speedwell to be talking like this to me in front of Mr Darcy. For some reason I did not wish to draw Mr Darcy's attention to myself. But I need not have worried: Mr Darcy was staring across the room to where Elizabeth and Colonel Fitzwilliam were deep in conversation. The colonel had his head bent towards Lizzy, the better to catch her quiet comments, and she was talking quickly with an intent expression on her face. I saw the colonel shake his head and Lizzy put her hand on his arm. I glanced at Darcy's face. He had flushed and his mouth was grim, his eyes unblinking. I could not bear to see such a look on his face and turned swiftly away, catching Mr Speedwell's eye. Mr Speedwell had observed it all and he looked both puzzled and concerned.

"Come, Mary," he said, "I will take you into dinner tonight." He led me away on his arm and Mr Darcy did not even appear to notice our departure. It was not time to go in yet so we stood by one of the large windows that looked out onto the driveway.

Signor Moretti approached us and stood beside me, staring out at the terrace. He and Speedwell bowed to each other, and there was such a look of mock solemnity on Mr Speedwell's face, that I could not help laughing. He started laughing too, with his embarrassing braying sound, and even Signor Moretti smiled. The noise attracted the attention of Squire Carding, who was standing nearby. He leaned over and pinched my cheek.

"Well now, that's what I like, young people laughing together! If I could see half as much animation in that block of a son of mine, I should be quite content, eh, my dear?" And he pinched my cheek again. I tried not to wince and pull away as I thought it would not be polite.

"Well, Speedwell," the Squire went on, "my friend the Dean was very taken with our little Miss here on his last visit. Very taken, he was."

I turned my head away and caught Signor Moretti's eye. His expression reassured me that he would say nothing of my misadventures.

"Oh, which Dean was that?" asked Mr Speedwell.

"Trowbridge, of course. Very old friend of mine. Do you know him?"

"I have met him in London. He is a Dean at St Paul's cathedral, I believe."

I was stunned by Mr Speedwell's altered manner. His face was genuinely serious now, such as I had never before witnessed, and I thought he did not like Dean Trowbridge, for his voice was cold. Squire Carding was oblivious to any change of mood. "Aye, that's the fellow. A very good man, does excellent work amongst the - well, enough said about that, eh? Eh?" And he nudged Mr Speedwell in the ribs.

Mr Speedwell's face was blank and the Squire, receiving no response, drifted away.

"You do not like the Dean?"

"I do not," said Mr Speedwell, still curt and frowning. "He is a pious hypocrite, Mary, and I do not like to think that your paths have crossed."

"I think you are right. I was - I was mistaken in him. He was not what he seemed."

"Certainly not! It vexes me that you came in his way. You could have come to harm, especially if he took a fancy to you, as the squire said."

I felt my cheeks flaming with embarrassment, and was relieved when Signor Moretti spoke.

"Fortunately, Mrs Darcy and I were able to intervene before any harm had befallen Miss Bennet."

"I am glad to hear it," Mr Speedwell replied, still unusually grave.

I looked away in embarrassment, just as Wickham glanced toward me; he bowed, managing to make his expression both sarcastic and provoking.

Signor Moretti and Mr Speedwell saw it too: they had a habit of noticing things, it seemed.

"Wickham is very particular in his attention to you tonight, Mary," Mr Speedwell said.

I flushed. "He - he rescued me when I fell on the stairs. That is what he is acknowledging."

"You fell on the stairs?" Signor Moretti asked.

"Please do not speak of it any more!" I said. "It was nothing, I am quite well."

Mr Speedwell ignored my plea. "Wickham rescued you? How very romantic of him!"

"It was not romantic at all, I assure you. Let us not talk of it."

He raised his eyebrows, quizzing me. "My dear Mary, you intrigue me! I am now convinced that you have had an adventure, which you are very anxious to conceal."

I realised I had fallen into a trap. "Not at all. Falling down the stairs was a small adventure if you could call it that, but there was nothing else to speak of."

"Mary, you are blushing!"

I pressed my hand to my cheek. "Indeed I am not, why should you think I have anything to blush for?"

"Simply because as a brother of many sisters, I pride myself on my perceptive ability, and your face is a tolerable reflection of your mood; and although I do not know your brother-in-law well, I know his type, and I can well imagine how he might take advantage of a young lady taking a tumble."

This at least I could answer truthfully. "He did not take advantage of me falling. He was very considerate and a perfect gentleman."

"I am glad to hear that," Signor Moretti said.

Mr Speedwell added, "But there is something you are not telling us, and I will get it out of you."

I was beginning to feel annoyed. "If you are so sure that I am concealing something, why would you persist in trying to uncover it? Do you never think that perhaps your levity is misplaced?"

Mr Speedwell tried to look repentant but I could see that he was not in earnest.

"You are severe on me, Mary. Very well, I will try to be serious."

"But Miss Bennet," said Signor Moretti, "you will not deny that there has also been a misadventure of some kind with your brother-in-law as well as with the dean. Will you not tell us what has happened?"

I was mortified and my eyes filled. "I wish you will not speak of it. You yourself know that I am not accustomed to men - I have not been used to receive attention from any gentleman in the past, and I have not previously considered that there are situations in which – well, in short, I have learned my lesson, I think."

"Poor Mary!" Mr Speedwell said warmly. "You are having some trying times. But tell me, how can it be that this is new to you? You speak as though no man has ever been interested in you before you came to Pemberley!"

"It is true! My sisters are much prettier and livelier than I am and the gentlemen of our acquaintance generally ignore me."

"What nonsense! You cannot expect me to believe such a thing! Why, I had to fight off all the young bucks at Amberfield the other day, just to get one country dance with you!"

"It is true, however. Nobody solicits me to dance where I am known in Meryton. Usually I sit with my mother and bear her company."

"You danced at the Cardings," said Signor Moretti.

"But that was most unusual, and it is only since I came to Pemberley that I have been dancing."

Mr Speedwell nodded conspiratorially. "I begin to understand! So when Wickham or the Dean tries to kiss you, you are taken quite by surprise."

I gasped. "How did you know? *How did you know*?"

There was a silence. He looked at me solemnly. "I did not know - I only suspected, but you have confirmed my belief."

I hung my head. "It was bad enough that Signor Moretti should witness my stupidity, but now you both know."

"Not stupidity, Mary, of course not," said Mr Speedwell.

"It is as I told you," Signor Moretti said, "you have been rather sheltered from the world, and have had to learn its ways swiftly and in a shocking manner."

"What did Wickham do?" Mr Speedwell asked.

I could not meet his eye, and my voice came out small and weak in the sound I hated. "I saw him kissing one of the maids. Then he kissed me, I think to stop me telling my sister. He thought I would be too ashamed to make it public, and he was right."

While I was talking, I had noticed Signor Moretti's face turn first pale, then red. "In the absence of any other protector," he said, "I will go now and speak directly to Wickham. The man is a blackguard, and his actions should not go unchallenged." His voice was angry and hard, and he marched across the room, his fists clenched.

"Goodness!" exclaimed Mr Speedwell. "What has come over him? What is he going to do?"

"Please!" I begged. "Do not let him cause a fuss!"

"Oh, good gracious!" said Mr Speedwell. "But what can I do? These Italians are so violent, once their blood is up -!"

"He is going to fight him!" I cried. "Do not allow it, Mr Speedwell! He would be ruined if he did such an insane thing!"

Mr Speedwell stammered, "I - I - good lord, what to do, what to do?"

He fidgeted uncertainly, then trotted across the room after Signor Moretti, who was talking angrily to Wickham. Wickham's expression was calmly sarcastic as usual, while Signor Moretti's whole body was becoming more and more tense. I watched in horror. It was all too dreadful, Signor Moretti moved closer to Wickham, till they were almost nose to nose, any moment now Wickham must react and they would fight. I could hardly bear to watch. I was about to cry out, stop, stop, when Mr Speedwell pushed between them, swung his fist and punched Wickham on the chin.

◆

Wickham fell backwards, taking a vase and a small occasional table down with him. I think I screamed: I know I heard a scream, but it might have been Lydia. There was suddenly a great commotion in the room. Wickham was prostrate on the floor as though dead, Lydia had swooned into the arms of Colonel Fitzwilliam, and Darcy and Elizabeth had taken an arm each of Mr Speedwell and pulled him away from Wickham. The whole company moved towards the scene, forming what seemed like an enormous crowd.

I remained where I was, unable to move, my hands pressed convulsively to my cheeks. I was relieved that nobody was paying attention to me, and I hoped that they would not connect what Mr Speedwell had just done with the fact that he had been talking to me moments before. Signor Moretti was standing to one side, a look of bewilderment on his face. Fortunately all eyes were still on the mêlée gathered round Mr Speedwell and the Wickhams and this gave me a moment to recover myself. I came forward to join the crowd, to avoid attracting attention to myself. I was standing next to Kitty as she craned to see Wickham. She was laughing in a nervous, over-excited way.

"What do you think could have come over Mr Speedwell?" she said.

"I can't imagine," I replied, lying yet again without hesitation.

"He simply hit Wickham out of the blue, without any warning at all. What could be the matter? I would never have thought he would have it in him, such a foppish man as he is. And in the church, as well! It is so unlike him."

"Yes," I said woodenly, "most unlike him."

Kitty gripped my arm. "Perhaps Wickham insulted him, or cheated him at cards? What do you think?"

"Nothing Wickham does could surprise me."

Colonel Fitzwilliam deposited Lydia on a sofa, where she lay moaning. A maid arrived with some smelling salts, and for a moment I thought Lydia was exactly like Mama when she was in one of her agitated states. I saw Darcy take Mr Speedwell aside for a private conversation. Mr Speedwell was very flushed, and was nursing his left hand. Wickham was helped to his feet and sat down next to Lydia on the sofa, looking extremely dazed.

"Oh, my poor Wickham!" Lydia cried. "What monstrous treatment! And from a man of the church! You will have to call him out for this, Wickham! You know you will."

I gasped in horror at the thought, and Signor Moretti glanced at me with a look of alarm on his face. I thought he was still as confused and horrified as I was. Luckily, Wickham showed as much distaste for a duel as I felt.

"No, no, my dear, this is all some misunderstanding," he said. "I do not fight duels over misunderstandings. I am sure it can be cleared up, but not tonight, please, not tonight. I will go to my room. I find I am quite overcome." He turned to a servant. "Please have a light supper brought to me in my chamber."

"I will come with you," said Lydia, "I am sure I will have one of my spasms. I will not be surprised if it brings the baby on, a woman in my condition should not have to tolerate such shocks. Kitty, help me."

Kitty went forward rather unwillingly, and lent Lydia her arm.

With the departure of the Wickhams from the scene, the crowd dispersed. I overheard whispers and saw heads shaken in consternation. Mr Darcy and Mr Speedwell had left the room without me noticing. I found Signor Moretti standing beside me.

"Miss Bennet, you look shocked. Come and sit down."

He led me to the sofa where Lydia had been lying and sat beside me.

"I *was* shocked," I said. "I never thought Mr Speedwell would do such a thing."

"No, nor did I. I was – I might have done the same myself in a moment or two." He looked at me intently. "What do you think made Speedwell intervene in such a manner?"

I could feel my face reddening but tried to hold his gaze. "You will have to ask him yourself," I said. "I could not answer you."

It was true – I did not really understand it. I knew that both men had become angry on my behalf, but I had never expected them to act in such a way. I had expected Mr Speedwell to pour oil on troubled waters, to come between Wickham and Moretti in a calm and pacific manner, but perhaps it had been too late for that, and he had acted on instinct and stopped Signor Moretti from fighting in the only possible way he could.

I sighed deeply.

"Oh, dear!" I said. I had almost forgotten Signor Moretti was sitting beside me.

"Miss Bennet? What is it that is troubling you?"

I shook my head. "Too many things to enumerate. I am very confused, Signor Moretti. I sometimes think I do not understand anything."

He gave his melancholy smile. "I often feel just so, Miss Bennet. But see, it is time to eat. Shall we go in?"

I sat next to Signor Moretti. He barely spoke to me, but was quietly attentive to my needs, passing condiments and calling the footman to fill my glass. His anger from before seemed to have vanished. It gave time for my mind to settle, and gradually I was able to look about me and observe the company. The table was much quieter and more polite without Wickham and Lydia, and people were talking to their neighbours in the conventional way. I did not hear anyone mention Mr Speedwell's violent act. He himself was not at the meal: I thought he must have gone home. Darcy had come late to the table with a flushed countenance: I could not miss Lizzy's look at him of silent entreaty, nor his quick, stern shake of the head. Both Darcy and Lizzy were subdued during the meal, I thought, though both were punctilious and gracious hosts, and nobody who did not know them very well would have noticed anything amiss. But when their faces were in repose Darcy looked remote and grave, and Lizzy had a bewildered frown, which I had never seen before. Again I felt a pang of guilt for writing that letter, but I quickly took myself to task over the feeling: it was not I who was in the wrong, but the malefactors themselves. Lizzy had only herself to blame if Darcy was angry with her; she should have known better than to treat her marriage so casually. She should have thought of the consequences of her actions before she encouraged the attentions of Mr Darcy's own cousin.

The colonel also looked sombre. He was sitting next to Georgiana, and they talked privately and quietly often through the meal. They too were not quite themselves, and I wondered how what Mr Speedwell had done could have such an effect on everyone.

I fell into an abstraction, thinking of all the ways in which my behaviour had fallen below the standards I had set for myself, the standards which I knew were correct. I had lied, I had kissed a man, no, two men, well, they had kissed me, but I could not deny that in Wickham's case there had been some reciprocation on my part; in my piano playing I had been a victim of my own vanity and ignorance, two vices which I had always found particularly opprobrious.

It was painful to think that I had been guilty of such breaches of morality and proper conduct: I who had always prided myself on my superior righteousness and my deep study of all the instructive texts. How my sisters would gloat if they knew! Perhaps not Jane and

Elizabeth, but certainly my two younger sisters! They had always despised me anyway - how much more would they despise me now that I deserved it?

By the time dessert came I had formed a resolution. There was so much that I could not change, but one thing I might do.

"Signor Moretti," I began with difficulty, "you - you tried before to help me with my piano playing. I think I was not very receptive, but -" My throat was tight as I spoke and I dreaded that I would start crying again. "I *would* like you to help me, to try and teach me. If you would be so kind."

Signor Moretti turned to look at me. I noticed again how soulful and unfathomable his eyes were. "I said I would be honoured, and I meant it."

"Then would you - could we - might I ask you to -?"

I appeared to be unable to finish my sentence but he stepped in. "You would like to have some lessons after all?"

"Yes!" I gasped. "If you would be so good!"

"Of course. That is why I am here at Pemberley."

"Then could we start tomorrow?"

He smiled, not his melancholy smile but something else, which lit up his face, and I found myself smiling back at him.

"Tomorrow it is. After breakfast?"

I nodded, strangely relieved and even elated. My mood was so much improved that even listening to Georgiana Darcy play and sing after the meal did not aggravate me. I was more concerned with remembering the events of the day.

When I stood up to go to bed, Mr Darcy followed me out of the drawing room, and called me to wait. I stood at the bottom of the stair with my candle and he came up to me.

"Mary, I wish to speak with you for a moment. Will you step into the library?"

I sat in one of the leather wing chairs and Mr Darcy sat opposite me. I waited anxiously, not knowing what he would say and dreading anything that came to my mind.

"This is a rather delicate matter, Mary, and I do not wish to make precipitate assumptions." He paused and I held my breath, while my heart beat in my ears. "You saw what happened tonight with Mr Speedwell and Mr Wickham?" I nodded. Relief made me feel quite faint: I thought he had been going to speak about the anonymous letter. "Mary, I have to ask you this, even though it may seem meddlesome and even indecorous. Did something happen between you and Mr Wickham?"

I stared at him. "Did Mr Speedwell say so?" I asked.

"No, Mr Speedwell told me nothing. I am acting on my own suspicions. You will forgive me if I am mistaken."

"No indeed, I cannot - there is nothing to tell. Is - is Mr Speedwell gone away?"

Darcy looked solemn. "He returned to the parsonage. Naturally he could not continue here, having assaulted my brother-in-law."

I gulped. "No, of course not. I see that."

"My loyalty must be at all times to my family, but within my family you can be assured that my loyalty is to you before Mr Wickham. I would wish -" he hesitated, searching for words, "I would wish to extend my protection to any of my wife's sisters as necessary, and I would greatly dislike that any ill should befall you while you are here at Pemberley."

"You are very kind, Mr Darcy. Indeed, I have no complaints to make." He was looking at me most intently in a way that made me feel extremely awkward. I had the felicitous notion to change the subject. "On another matter, I wanted to tell you that I have decided to - to make use of Signor Moretti after all, and have asked him to teach me on the pianoforte, starting tomorrow."

Mr Darcy reached towards me and took my hand. "I am so very glad, Mary. Elizabeth will be delighted too, I know. I am sure you will not regret your decision."

I could not speak. To have Mr Darcy holding my hand so was too overwhelming and I could find no words. I was relieved when he released me and we stood and bade each other goodnight.

Part Eight: The Lesson

◆

I was very nervous about my first piano lesson. I could hardly eat the sumptuous breakfast that Pemberley's kitchens provided for us, and I was glad that only Kitty and I were at the table. Kitty was peevish and cross, a discontented expression on her face as she drooped over her plate. We hardly spoke at first, but then I became anxious that she might start to question me about last night, so I decided to question her instead.

"You look unhappy, Kitty," I said.

Kitty lifted her head and stared at me in silent astonishment.

"What?" I said. "Why do you look at me so?"

She gave her contemptuous snort. "I am just surprised that you notice how I am feeling. You have never done so before."

I was about to give a hot denial, when a moment's reflection made me realise that she was speaking the truth. I did not normally have any interest in Kitty's emotions, just as she had none in mine.

"Well," I said hesitantly, "I am noticing now. Is - is something troubling you?"

To my surprise, she blushed, and I thought her eyes started to shine with tears. "It is nothing you would understand, Mary," she said petulantly.

I felt my hackles rising again, but I was determined not to react to her attacks. If there was one thing I could understand, it was that unhappiness could often provoke a person to be bad-tempered and repudiating.

"I - I would *try* to understand, Kitty, if you would honour me with your confidence."

She looked at me with a derisive disbelief in her face that hurt my feelings very much. I wanted to try again but needed a moment to recover myself.

At last I said, "I know we are not very accustomed to - to sharing our troubles, but perhaps we might become so? After all, our other sisters all have their husbands now and cannot have time to be our intimates in the way they might have been once."

Kitty's expression became suspicious. "Why should you want to know what I am thinking all of a sudden, Mary? Why should you be so curious?"

"It is not *idle* curiosity, I assure you. It is very simple: I saw that you looked sad and I thought you might like to speak to somebody." I looked away, humiliated. "I did not mean to intrude, Kitty."

"No, you do not intrude, it is just that I have not been used to that kind of attention from you. I could not help wondering why you would take such a sudden interest. But I see you are trying to be kind."

I stared at my plate. "And I am not generally very kind, I suppose."

"No, you are not!" she retorted. I would rather have wished her to contradict me than to agree with such alacrity. There was a silence for a moment or two, then she seemed to relent. "But I am not very kind to you either."

We sat without speaking, both toying with our food but not eating it. We had never had such a conversation in our lives before, and it appeared that neither of us knew what to do next.

Kitty made a decision. "Well, I will tell you. I am not enjoying my visit to Pemberley as much as before. There is something amiss with Georgiana: she has been used to confide in me, but I know she has some secret which she is not telling me. Then, Lydia is so much changed since she married and had children, she is so selfish and so full of her own importance I hardly know her."

"I do not think she is so very different. She was always so to me when we lived at Longbourn."

"But not to me!" burst out Kitty. "We were used to do everything together, but now she thinks she is too fine for anyone. And I do not like how she treats her children! She does not care for them at all."

"Jane says we must make allowances, that Wickham being in prison was very difficult for Lydia."

"Jane always thinks we must make allowances! I am tired of making allowances! Lydia does not make allowances for anyone. It is all Lydia, Lydia, Lydia, that is all she cares about, with a little tiny concern for Wickham, but only as it affects her own comfort! I hate her!"

"Kitty, no! You must not speak so of your own sister! We have a Christian duty to forgive, especially our own family members!"

"Ha! *You* have never been forgiving of Lydia! You have always judged her more than anyone! Why do you tell *me* I must forgive and be a Christian, when *your* idea of being a Christian is to moralise over everybody and think yourself so superior?"

I was about to say something sharp and cutting about when a person is actually righteous, that it was then allowable to judge and condemn the behaviour of others, when it came clearly to me that I could no longer consider myself righteous. I was not as bad as Lydia, but I had started to know that there were aspects of me that did not match with the standards expected of a good person, a good daughter, sister or friend.

"You are quite correct, Kitty," I said slowly, and with some difficulty. "I have been quick to judge in the past, I am trying to rectify the fault if I can."

"Well, bless me! I never thought I would hear such a confession from *your* lips, Mary! And I cannot even tell Lydia any more!"

"I am *trying* to be a better person, Kitty! Can you not afford me some small dispensation?"

Kitty laughed - not her disdainful snort but something friendlier and more spontaneous. "Very well, Mary, I will give you credit for trying! However imperfect your success! You cannot change overnight, you know."

I sighed. "I know that all too well. But Kitty, is that all that is on your mind? There is not anything else?"

She looked at me consideringly for a long moment, then at the door, then back to me. "Can you keep a confidence in your new character?"

"Of course I can!" I said. "At least, I believe I can. At least, I know no reason why I should not be able to. Certainly I will try," I amended, rather feebly.

Kitty shook her head. "Do not let me down, Mary." She leant across the table to me and whispered, "I have reason to think that Mr Carding has taken quite a fancy to me."

"Oh! Why do you think so?"

"Well - you really can keep a secret, can't you, Mary?"

I nodded.

"I have been thinking so for some time, ever since the party we went to at the Cardings, remember? When we got stuck in the river on the way home?"

"What happened?"

"Oh, nothing *happened*. Not *then*. But we did dance together and talk together and he did look at me in such a way. And then at the ball here we danced together often again. Did you not see?"

"I did not - notice. I was - preoccupied."

"And we went outside together onto the veranda to cool down."

"What did he say to you then?"

She frowned. "He did not precisely *say* anything. He does not speak very much, you know, at least only about horses and shooting and farming and such like. On those topics he is very eloquent. But a woman does not always need words. If you are wise, you can tell much by observation!"

"And what did you observe, Kitty?" I was starting to feel a little anxious for Kitty. I thought she might be supposing too much.

"He was practically shaking with nerves, so I took him for a walk into the knot garden."

"And then what?"

Kitty looked anxiously at the door again. "Promise you won't say anything, Mary?"

"I promise!"

"Then I asked him if he wanted to kiss me!"

"You asked him! And did he? Want to?"

"Well - he did not say so, but he did kiss me straight away, so I had my answer. You do not think I was too forward, do you, Mary?"

I did not reply. I *did* think she had been too forward, but I felt so muddled in my head about what was right and what was wrong in these matters that I did not know what to say.

"What did he think of you saying that?" I asked instead. "Did he seem surprised?"

"I think he was relieved. He has certainly kissed me again at every opportunity since."

"Kitty!" I could not help it, I was shocked.

"Well, it is not so very bad. It is just a kiss after all."

"But what are his intentions towards you? Do you think he wishes to marry you?"

"I do not know. Perhaps. Perhaps if he does not yet wish to marry me, he will soon. I do not think he has ever kissed a girl before."

"How can you tell?"

"Because – oh, never mind. But at least I am sure he likes me now. I was not absolutely sure before."

"But do you like him, Kitty?"

She considered the question. "I like him well enough. I think if we were to marry we would have a comfortable home and would do very nicely together. He would be a kind husband I think, as long as he could do the things he enjoys unhindered. I am sure I would be able to manage him."

"Manage him? Is - is that what one does with husbands?"

Kitty looked at me as though I were stupid. "Of course!"

I passed in review my sisters' marriages, and that of my parents. I did not see much evidence of managing going on. If that was what was happening, they either did it very ill as in my mother's case, or it was so disguised and subtle that neither I nor the husbands would have any idea that they were being managed. I tried to conceive of myself managing a man: I soon realised that I would have no idea what that would entail, yet Kitty somehow knew as if by nature.

"How does one *manage* a husband, Kitty?" I asked.

"Oh, you know, Mary! You keep them content so that they give you what you want."

"But how do you know what will keep them content?"

I almost added, how do you know what you want, but that seemed to be a question with no answer, or no answer that could be found in this conversation.

Kitty laughed. "You are such an innocent, Mary! Men have their needs, they need to be able to pursue their interests like hunting and farming, they need to be well fed, they need an heir usually, and they need their - well, their appetites to be satisfied. If a wife is clever she can provide all these things, and keep her husband happy so that she can have what she wishes - new clothes or furnishings, or trips to London."

"What makes you think you will be able to get what you want from Mr Carding?"

"I do not think he is a clever man," she mused. "He already minds me when I tell him what I think he should do. He is crying out for guidance."

"You are very sure of yourself, Kitty. I do not know how you can be so sure."

Kitty shrugged. "I do not know things from books or music, but by some means or other I know Frederick."

I was silent. It appeared that she did know Frederick Carding, in a confident way that I could not imagine knowing any man.

"And you have power over him!" I said suddenly, surprising myself with the thought.

She smiled. "I suppose I do. And now that he has kissed me, I have the power to refuse him and drive him wild with longing!"

"Kitty, be careful what you are about! He may become too wild."

"Oh, sensible Mary! I do not fear it. It is as I said, he is easy to manage."

Our conversation gave me much to think about as I went to the drawing room to meet Signor Moretti. I was surprised to know about this aspect of Kitty, and I was still absorbing the strangeness of our having such an intimate conversation at all. Kitty and I had more or less hated each other our entire lives, and when we were thrown more together after our sisters had married and gone away, although there was some improvement in our relations, nobody could say that we were close or confiding or even took pleasure in each other's company. It might be too much to say that there had been pleasure in our breakfast discussion, but it was certainly a new departure, and it made me think that it would be possible for something to be better between us. But Kitty had led me this way before, and always there had been a return to her sarcastic and derogatory remarks. I shook my head. It was better not to set too much store by one conversation.

◆

When I entered the drawing room, Signor Moretti was seated at the piano. There was no music on the stand in front of him but he was playing something from memory. It was similar to the music I had heard him play in the little church - interweaving lines of melody so close with each other that my ear did not know which line to follow. I stood in the doorway and waited for him to notice me, which he did after a few moments.

"Miss Bennet!" He stopped abruptly and stood up.

"What was that you were playing?" I asked. "Who wrote it?"

"Nobody. I did - at least, it is not written down, I was merely improvising."

"Improvising? You were making it up as you went along? But how could you do that? It was so - so intricate. There were so many voices! How could you make them all fit together?"

He smiled and shrugged. "I have always done it since I first learned to play. One gets better at it over the years, and these days it is a form of reverie for me."

I approached the piano. "I cannot play by ear at all," I said. "That is, I have never tried, but I do not think I could."

"I am sure you could. You can try it now."

I was dismayed. This was going to be just as humiliating as I had dreaded. Signor Moretti must have read the fear in my expression, because he said,

"You do not have to. Perhaps we should start with something that is less novel to you."

I shook my head. "No, I - I would like to try." I regretted the words as soon as I had said them, but there was a momentum in me over which my usual caution had no power, this strange new Mary who was insisting on trying to do things differently.

Signor Moretti gestured me to sit down at the keyboard.

"Do you know Baa Baa Black Sheep?" he asked.

"The nursery rhyme? Yes."

"Why don't you try and play it? Start on middle C."

Quailing inwardly I put my right thumb on middle C and started to fumble my way through the tune. I discovered that I had no idea what distance away the next note was likely to be, though I could tell if the melody went up or down. When I reached the end, Signor Moretti did not speak, but merely nodded.

"Now add a bass line," he said.

Again the voice in my head was saying no, it was not possible, I could not do it, but I was resolved to try and ignore it and carry on.

"It need not be complicated," he said, anticipating my question, "single notes will do very well."

I started with C in both hands. It was very difficult, because I had not properly mastered the melody yet; and there were strange mewing and grunting sounds, which after a few moments I realised were coming from me as I struggled to find the notes. To reach the end was a great relief: I sighed. "I am afraid I am not very good at this," I said. "I do not think I have a talent for it."

Signor Moretti was grave. "I know you have a talent for application, and with practice you will improve. To master any skill requires hard work over a period of time."

I nodded, blushing. I knew he was right, and that I must not be discouraged. I was surprised at how painful it was to have a witness to my struggles. I did not like it. I preferred to work in private, and then astound people with my performance. I felt ashamed at how bad I was.

"I will try to work," I said, "but it might be hopeless, and then I will have wasted my time in practising."

"No practice is ever wasted," he said firmly, "and you cannot know if it is hopeless until you have tried."

"But I have tried!" I burst out. "I have been practising the piano since I was a little girl."

"Yes, you have, and you have done very well. But when you decided to have lessons with me, it was because you realised that you had done as much as you could on your own. I know that you believe that you should be entirely self-sufficient, but that is not possible in the world of music. It is like being an apprentice to a weaver or a clockmaker: yes, there is much that the diligent student can encompass alone, but there is special knowledge which is passed from master to pupil. I did not teach myself, I have had many teachers who have shared their wisdom with me."

I nodded. I knew he was right. But I hated to admit another person into my world. I did not like to be told what to do, or to be criticised. I did not like another person to know that something was difficult for me: there had been too many times in my life when my sisters had mocked me and insulted me: they would leap on any sign of weakness with the alacrity of an owl onto a dormouse. I had striven to make myself above criticism so that they should never be able to find a chink through which to attack me. But those days were gone. Since I was at Pemberley, it had come over me gradually, and then with unmistakable force at the fateful ball, that I had many weaknesses and many flaws.

I tried again. "I would like you to help me, Signor Moretti, even though it is at the same time very difficult for me to allow you to."

He smiled at me. "Thank you, Miss Bennet. I understand. Perhaps we could start now by thinking about the shape of your hand on the keyboard."

Although it lasted for only an hour, I was strangely exhausted by my lesson. I was not accustomed to such concentrated attention from another person, and it was difficult to take in all that Signor Moretti had explained to me or shown me. Every time he gave me an instruction I wanted to sneer or reject it or defend myself from the implied criticism, and it was very tiring to have to overcome this urge time and time again.

I lay on my bed for a while to reflect on the lesson and to recover myself somewhat. It was Signor Moretti's kindness that astonished me as much as anything. He was so patient with my mistakes and my struggles, and when I did say something snappish he took no notice and did not seem to wish to retaliate or take offence. It made me think about Mama, how impatient she was, how distracted, how caught up in her ailments and her worries about the future. I had no memory of her spending time quietly with me or trying to teach me: in fact, my older sisters had been more attentive and helpful. It was Jane who had taught me to read, and there had been times when Lizzy had tried to help me with my music, deciphering a difficult passage. Such things seemed to come easily to Lizzy and only came to me with great labour and perseverance. This thought made me sad: to admit to myself that my sister had greater innate ability than I did, while all our lives I had done my best to despise her for her frivolity and lack of application. The truth was she did not need to apply herself as I did, for these things came naturally to her.

My father had never been interested in me either. In later years I had given up on the hope of it, but sometimes I still felt the pain of his rejection and mockery.

I did not like being so disloyal towards my parents: I had always held by the commandment to honour my father and mother, and never questioned their actions or utterances. But my time at Pemberley had changed me, and I was starting to see things differently. It made me feel very alone, with all that I had taken for granted my entire life melting away. How was I now to decide on anything? How was I to know what was right and wrong, when there was nobody about me who I could look up to or who could act as my moral compass? Perhaps there was only Jane who was without fault, without blemish or weakness. She had never shown anything but goodness and kindness all her life.

Thinking of Jane reminded me of our conversation from the day before, that she had asked me to teach my niece. I resolved to do so that very day. Accordingly I went up to the nursery after the midday meal. I could hear the noise as I walked along the passage to the nursery. There was the sound of at least one baby crying, a raised voice of a nurse, some repeated banging noises. I could not imagine what scene would meet my eye.

My entry caused the noise to stop abruptly, as all the children turned to the door to look at me. Even the baby, Lydia's youngest, stopped crying for a moment. One of the nursemaids was holding her: the child's face was red and wet with crying, and the nursemaid's cap was askew with hair escaping from under it as though it had been mauled by the infant. Standing frozen to the spot, a large stick in his hand, was Horatio, Lydia's eldest child. He looked as though he was about to use the stick to hit little Charles Bingley on the head, but another maid saw it at the same time as I did, and stepped in quickly to remove the stick. Horatio immediately started to wail loudly, and both his sisters joined in. Charles Bingley's lip started to quiver, and I saw Sophia Bingley go to him and hold his hand protectively. William Darcy was sitting on the rocking horse and doing his best to ignore the commotion. It made me think of drawings of scenes from Bedlam.

The tableau broke up swiftly, as the children realised in unison that I was not one of their mothers, and their disappointment became vocal. Theodosia started to roar and fling herself about in the nurse's arms, Horatio and Philomela both cried even louder, followed immediately by Charles and then William.

"Perhaps I should fetch Mrs Bingley and Mrs Wickham?" I said. "I will take Sophia with me to find her mother, if she will come."

Sophia was willing to accompany me, and we set off hand in hand through the halls of Pemberley.

◆

Jane was in Lizzy's parlour, embroidering a dress for baby Henry, while he slept in a basket on the floor beside her. Sophia immediately ran into her mother's arms and Jane held her for a few moments on her lap. I stood in the doorway and looked on, finding myself prey to many emotions and noting an ache in my chest as I watched mother and daughter so close and caressing with each other.

Eventually Jane looked up. "Am I wanted in the nursery, Mary?"

"Yes, the nursemaids are distressed and I said I would fetch you and Lydia. When Lydia's children began to cry, then Charles cried also."

"Oh dear! I will go at once. Will you - would you be so good as to watch Henry for a few minutes? He is very full of milk and will not wake up for some time."

"I? But I do not know - I do not know how to look after a baby!"

"Sophia will help you," Jane said. "And Sophy, your embroidery is in my sewing box there. Aunt Mary will help you with it, and I will return soon. Be a good girl."

"But - I am not very good at embroidery!" I protested.

"Neither is Sophy!" Jane whispered in my ear as she passed.

I sat on the small sofa and looked at the baby. He was very pale, and fast asleep. There was something intent about his face, as though sleep was an extremely serious task that required great concentration. I prayed inwardly that he would not wake up. In my mind's eye was the image of the nursemaid with Lydia's screaming infant in her arms, and I did not want such an experience for myself.

Meanwhile Sophy had found her scrap of linen which she proudly showed me. It had a few rough stitches of various colours in no particular order, and I felt relieved that even my poor skills would be adequate to help her.

We got on quite happily for some minutes: very little was required of me, except to rethread Sophy's needle and occasionally say something in praise of her work. Inevitably, the baby started to stir and I began to wish for Jane to return. I watched him anxiously, as he shuffled about under his many coverings and his face crumpled up as though in pain.

"Oh!" I said. "He does not look happy."

Sophy peered into the basket calmly. "He's waking up."

I stared at him, willing him to stay asleep, or for Jane to come back, but he continued wriggling, and then let out a great cry, which disturbed him even more. His eyes opened, blinking and unseeing and gradually focussing as he realised that he was awake. His mouth opened again into a large square and he started to cry.

Sophy tugged at my sleeve. "Pick him up," she said. I waited for a few moments to see if the crying would stop, but it only increased in intensity. I was going to have to pick him up.

With great trepidation, I peeled back the layers of cloths and blankets. He started to flail his limbs and his peculiar bowed legs kicked out from under his nightdress. I did not know how to pick up a baby, but I slid my hands under him and scooped him up. His head flopped alarmingly and I quickly caught it with one hand and put him on my lap. This did not stop his crying, and his face was getting redder so in desperation I raised him to lie against my shoulder and patted his back as I had seen Jane do. Miraculously this worked and his sobs abated. I did not dare stop patting, and I wondered how long I must do this, and what I would try next if he started to cry again. But nothing happened, and gradually I realised that he had stopped moving about and had become strangely heavy.

"He's asleep now," Sophy said helpfully. Then she asked, "Where's your baby?"

"I do not have a baby," I said.

Sophy nodded and cast another large stitch. "Aunt Lizzy has a baby. William is my cousin."

"Yes," I answered, "and Horatio and Theodosia and Philomela," I added, endeavouring to be fair to Lydia.

"Horatio hit me," Sophy said.

"Did he? That was - very naughty of him."

"It hurt my arm. But I hit him back."

"Oh!" I did not know how to reply to that; I supposed I should reprimand Sophy but I did not think it was my place, and I found that I did not want to be stern with her. I had never had a child like me before and I did not want to ruin it. And now I had Henry too, who was quite content to sleep on my shoulder. It was most odd to have this miniature person reposing there in so trusting a fashion. I could feel his chest moving as he breathed, small hot breaths next to my ear.

When Jane entered a minute or two later I was almost sorry. She had Charles by the hand and they came quietly into the room.

"Oh Mary, you look very peaceful there. He woke then?"

"He cried," Sophy said.

"He is very happy now on his Aunt Mary's shoulder!" Jane exclaimed. "Will you keep him a little longer, Mary? He might wake if I move him, and I would love him to have his sleep out."

"I will hold him with pleasure, but should I not fetch Lydia to the nursery?"

"No need. I sent one of the footmen to rouse her."

I spent the next hour very happily with Jane and her children. Jane's sewing basket contained many treasures to amuse the children, little picture books, tiny wooden farm animals and a kaleidoscope, which even I enjoyed looking through. There was a kind of balm being with Jane: she was always so patient and knew what the children needed even before they did. Even after Henry woke up and began suckling, she still attended to the other two. I did not know how she could be so unruffled and at ease. She even managed to have a conversation with me, though slightly broken up.

Our peaceful time was not destined to last. The door burst open and Lydia stormed in, dragging Horatio by the hand. She was wearing a nightdress with some sort of diaphanous coat over the top. Her hair was flying around her face and her cheeks were patchy red.

"Jane! I am at my wit's end with this boy! He is impossible! He is so naughty and disobedient; I do not know what I am supposed to do with him! He is a devil!"

Horatio looked like anything but a devil. His head was bowed, his thumb in his mouth, and his eyes hollow. "He is just like his father but worse in every respect! You must help me, Jane. They keep calling me up to the nursery, but *I* cannot manage him, why do they think I can? I am worn out with carrying this child in my belly, and I have my hands full with Wickham who can only lie abed and moan in agony!" Lydia noticed me and turned her fury on me. "And you may stare, Miss Mary Bennet, do not think I am not fully aware of your little ploys! It was you who put Speedwell up to punching my Wickham; I know it very well, stirring things up with your lies! Well, Mary, if you think that will answer, you are quite wrong. You may try your little games, but I have been about the world now, and you cannot deceive me."

My jaw dropped. I did not know what to say. Fortunately, Jane intervened.

"Lydia, you are frightening the children with all your shouting. Leave Horatio with us for a while and go back to Wickham. It is nearly time for nursery supper. We will take him upstairs with the others shortly."

"Thank you, Jane. You are so much more homely than me; you are more cut out for looking after children. I wish I could leave the children with you forever! And now I am to have another one! Lord!"

"You know you do not mean that, I know you love your children," Jane said gently, "and things will improve now that Wickham is out of debt."

"I should like to see him out of *bed!*" Lydia retorted, and flounced out of the room.

There was a silence. Horatio stood where Lydia had left him, his face blank.

"Come, Horry," Jane said, "come and play with Charlie."

Horatio stared at her stupidly, but the words must have penetrated his mind, because he sat on the floor with Charlie and started listlessly fingering the wooden farm animals with one hand, while continuing to suck the thumb of the other.

"Is he quite -?" I whispered to Jane. "He seems so..."

Jane shook her head. "He is not a very happy little boy. I wish I could - oh well, it is not to be. But Mary, what does Lydia mean about Mr Speedwell? Is there some truth in what she says? Did Mr Speedwell punch Wickham on your behalf?"

How I longed to confide in Jane, even to ask her advice, but I could not, *could not*, tell her about what had happened with Wickham. It was too disgraceful, and the repercussions of telling Mr Speedwell had already been too extreme. If I told Jane, she might tell Lizzy who would tell Mr Darcy: he would discover that I had lied to him, and then he might fight Wickham or throw him out of the house, it would be my fault, Mama would hear of the rift in the family and would blame me terribly and there would be no end to her reproaches. No, I must keep silence, but it was very difficult.

"I cannot discuss it, Jane. I - I would like to confide in you, but I cannot."

"Then I will ask no more. But you know I will be happy to listen to you at any time."

I bowed my head. "Thank you."

◆

The guests had left except for the Bingleys and the Wickhams, Colonel Fitzwilliam and Signor Moretti. Some of the musicians still lingered. I did not know if it was our reduced company that was responsible, but I thought that Elizabeth was in low spirits. She had rarely been seen out of her room before ten o'clock since I had first come to Pemberley, which was unlike her: at Longbourn she was always up early, always going for walks and spurring the rest of us on to greater activity. To be sure, she had much more to occupy her as lady of an estate such as Pemberley: but now that the ball was over, there was something of a lull in her duties, and when I had overheard her giving instructions to Mrs Reynolds, she was just as likely to let Mrs Reynolds decide matters. Mrs Reynolds did not mind, indeed, she was quite solicitous of Lizzy and once I even saw her pat Lizzy's hand, which shocked me greatly. I did not know how Lizzy could maintain her authority if she allowed such impropriety from a servant.

I still did not know how matters stood between Lizzy and Mr Darcy. One afternoon I was out walking around the grounds with Jane and Lizzy, Sophy and William. I was occupied with Sophy watching a bee take nectar from a flower, and did not realise that Mr Darcy had approached until I heard William cry, "Papa!" and set off running down the path. Mr Darcy swept the boy up and smiled when William curled his arms around his father's neck. I had never seen Mr Darcy look so happy and carefree, but when I glanced at Lizzy I could see that she was frowning slightly and that a wave passed over her face that looked like sorrow. She quickly composed her features into her habitual friendly openness, but I thought Darcy had seen it and he frowned in response before he too resumed his expression.

I felt an unaccustomed twinge in my stomach. Hitherto, when I saw Lizzy looking unhappy or guilty I had been pleased: she had done wrong, and wrongdoers should feel guilty for their sins. But something was starting to make me uncomfortable. It was when I thought about how Mr Wickham had kissed me, and how I had decided not to tell Lydia or Mr Darcy because I had thought it would cause trouble. And I had been right not to, as the result of telling Mr Speedwell too clearly showed. But this set me to a moral puzzle: why was it then right to tell Mr Darcy about my suspicions of Elizabeth and Colonel Fitzwilliam? It was quite clear to me that I *had* caused trouble between the Darcys - and at the time that was exactly what I had intended - but only for the highest moral purpose of putting an end to my sister's depravity.

Lizzy and Jane were talking to Mr Darcy but I hardly heard them, my mind was too full. Sophy was still chattering to me - she had found some ants now, but I was only responding perfunctorily to her. Fortunately she did not mind, and crouching down with her meant that I could be unobserved by the others while I tried to puzzle my way through the confusion.

A shocking thought occurred to me: what if Lizzy had been a victim of Colonel Fitzwilliam's unwanted intentions, just as I had with Wickham? Then what a wrong would I have done my sister! I passed my mind back over the various scenes I had witnessed: no, Lizzy had been equally eager to whisper to the colonel, and there had been no sign of discomfort or anxiety between them. And that of course made it all the more reprehensible in my eyes. Lizzy had become like all the great aristocratic ladies of whom one heard gossip and rumour - profligate of her virtue, careless with her marriage - and her marriage to Mr Darcy, who was no doubt the finest man ever to have come in our way, and a very great personage in the county besides. What she had done was very wrong, and I was the only person able to bring her to account.

I knew I had done right: any person of ordinary Christian morality would agree with me. And yet this feeling in the pit of my stomach would not go away. I did not think I had got to the core of it: there was something else exercising my mind, a tiny distant sound that could drive one mad until the source of it was discovered, like a mouse scratching away behind the wainscot.

My absorption was such that it was not until Sophy tugged my sleeve that I realised that Mr Darcy was speaking to me.

"I beg your pardon!" I said, standing up. "I did not hear you."

He looked at me somewhat quizzically. "I have had a letter from Mr Speedwell," he said.

I flushed, though trying to appear unconcerned. "Oh! Is - is he well? We have not seen him for some days."

"Yes, he is quite well." We began to walk, my sisters going on ahead with the children, and Mr Darcy and I walking together. "He writes - in part to apologise for his assault on Mr Wickham, but also because he believes he is in disgrace with you, and would like to rectify matters if possible."

I looked down. I did not know what to say at first. "Why should he think he is in disgrace with me?" I asked.

"He did not say."

There was a pause, and I felt some pressure to tell Mr Darcy the answer to my own question, which I knew very well, and which I was sure Mr Darcy knew that I knew very well. Instead I asked, "Will he be returning to Pemberley?"

"He cannot come here while Mr Wickham is visiting us, that would be quite wrong, but I count Mr Speedwell very much my friend, and in due course he will be welcome here as our guest once more."

"So he is not in disgrace with you?" I asked anxiously, venturing to look up at his face.

"No indeed!" For a moment I thought I saw a glimmer of what might in a lesser man be considered a mischievous grin. "Mr Speedwell did what I am not able to do myself."

"Oh!"

"Mr Speedwell also asks my permission to take you on another trip to B__. He says that Mrs Heely's child Margaret is eager for you to return. She and her little brother often speak of you, and wish to see you again, I believe to have another spelling lesson."

I pondered for a moment and then decided to speak as frankly as I could. "After what happened between Mr Speedwell and Mr Wickham, do you think it would be wise for me to - to take this trip?"

Mr Darcy frowned. "You are concerned whether there will be some particularity, some cause for speculation or gossip in you going to B__ with Mr Speedwell?"

"Yes."

"Your sister and I know that your behaviour is at all times above reproach. While you are our guest here, Mary, you are safe from the calumnies and scandal-mongering of the ignorant and vulgar."

There was a heated edge to his voice, and I knew that he was thinking angrily of the anonymous letter I had written. Oh, how dreadful it would be if he ever discovered that it had come from me! Even though what I had told him was the truth, he would forever class me as a gossip, a talebearer, the worst kind of busybody. I had known when I wrote it that such letters were the province of the ignorant and vulgar, I had even tried to disguise my writing so that it should be thought to come from an uneducated person. In my heart, I knew it was beneath me. If I had had any courage or honour, I would have spoken to him directly, or at least to my sister, to warn her or allow her to explain herself. How I wished the letter unwritten, unsent! I could imagine the look on Mr Darcy's face if he should find out the source of the letter: the disdain, the contempt, and at last, the turning away, never to look on me with kindness or friendship again.

I wanted to run up to my room and hide myself, but I knew I must gather my wits and present a good countenance to Mr Darcy. He must not suspect.

"If you think there will be no impropriety, I would like to go back to the Heelys. I have become interested in them, and I enjoyed helping them, even though it was only in a small way."

"Very well. A groom or maid will travel with you of course. Elizabeth will see to that. Meanwhile, I shall write to Mr Speedwell and tell him your decision. After that, he may write to you in person to make the arrangements, although you will of course show Elizabeth your correspondence with him."

"Oh, of course, though there would be nothing - I am sure that he is not -"

To my relief, Elizabeth and Jane had slowed down to join us, so I had no need to explain more.

◆

I was still shaken when I went for my piano lesson with Signor Moretti. I had had two or three lessons since the ball at Pemberley and had practised conscientiously between each one. Signor Moretti had given me scales and arpeggios to work on, which I resented very much, as I would have liked to work on some actual music, but I was trying to be humble and allow him to be in charge of the lessons, instead of assuming that my way of doing things was the best way. After all, me teaching myself had not yielded particularly satisfactory results, as the disaster of the Pemberley ball had demonstrated to me.

Signor Moretti was waiting for me in the music room. I could hear him playing as I approached, it was something glittering and fast, cascades of notes tumbling over each other at great speed. He stopped as I entered, stood up and bowed to me. His hair had flopped over his face. I thought he should have it cut more like Mr Darcy, then he would not look so rough and distracted. Still, if one did not compare him too closely with Mr Darcy, I could see why Kitty thought him a well-looking man, though her idea that his gloomy air was mysterious and romantic I thought nonsensical.

"Good day, Miss Bennet," he said quietly, looking intently at me in that way he had as though he was examining my mind for flaws and weaknesses, just as a horse trader would check over a potential purchase for lameness or spavins or a bad nature. I did not like the way he was able to peer inside and know what I was thinking or feeling, sometimes better than I did myself. Annoyingly, I felt my face grow hot as I tried to return his stare calmly.

"Good day, Signor Moretti. I am sorry to interrupt your playing. Pray continue."

He looked searchingly at me again. "If you wish."

He sat down again and started to play. I came and stood behind him, to follow the music and also to watch his hands on the keyboard. There was something enthralling about the sight of his fingers flying effortlessly across the keys, and I soon gave up following the printed page, until he nodded at me to turn, which I did awkwardly and in a rush. I was stricken by the thought that I would never be able to play with such speed and dexterity. I wondered if it might be because his hands were so much bigger than mine and could cover more keys at once, but I knew it could not be so, as Georgiana's hands were small and she could play much more nimbly than I. Signor Moretti's hands were so different: his fingers were long with pronounced knuckles, and as he played I noticed how the bones moved under the skin. It seemed that the more I looked, the more I saw. I saw how his hand attached to his wrist, how the skin pulled as he played. I saw the cuff of his shirt and noticed that it was slightly frayed in one place, that there were dark hairs on his wrist, coarse and wiry. My gaze travelled along his arm, to his shoulder, his collar where his over-long hair rested, to the angle of his cheekbone and the darker, grey-blue skin of his chin.

Suddenly, for no reason at all, the memory of Wickham kissing me flooded into my head; it felt as though a fist clutched my entrails in the pit of my stomach and a wave of heat passed over me. I must have taken an involuntary step back because Signor Moretti ceased playing abruptly and turned to look at me questioningly. I prayed he could have no idea of my thoughts.

"I have played long enough," he said.

"No, no! I did not mean to interrupt you! Pray do not stop! I was enjoying listening to you. It was only -" I stopped short. I had started a sentence that was impossible to finish. I had almost blurted out that I had been examining his hands, his body, his face, that I had become distracted from the music by the thought of that shameful kiss with my brother-in-law, unwanted and yet so tenacious in my memory. Signor Moretti was looking at me, waiting for me to finish. I shook my head to clear it. He stood up and gestured to me to sit.

"Are you quite well, Miss Bennet?" he asked me.

"Yes, I am well, thank you," I said quickly. "Let us begin."

"Very well. Please play your right hand scales."

I began to play but my hand was awkward and tremulous. I fumbled my way through the first two or three before he stopped me.

"I see you have been studying hard," he said. "Your memory is good, but you are tense and anxious today."

I blushed. "I am all thumbs." He did not reply immediately and I glanced back towards him to see him deep in thought.

"Miss Bennet, if it will not embarrass you, may I place my hands on your shoulders while you play?"

I caught my breath. "What? Why - why would you do that?"

Inside I was thinking, oh no, he has read my mind. He knows I have been thinking about being kissed by Wickham, he knows I have been looking at his hands and his collar and his shoulder. Perhaps he thinks I want - but I could not even finish the thought in my own mind, it whirled away.

His voice cut into my startled thoughts. He said, "I do not mean to discommode you, but I think it might help you, if you will allow me?"

"Very well," I said, my voice coming out small and weak, the tone I most hated to hear from myself.

He stood immediately behind me and placed his hands on my shoulders and I tried not to flinch away from the unaccustomed touch.

"Start to play, Miss Bennet, and concentrate on my hands. You will begin to understand what I am trying to help you with."

There was no need for the instruction as it was impossible to think of anything else but the pressure of his hands on my shoulders. I felt the heat of them through my dress, and it was as though my entire self was concentrated on this one part of my body. I had no idea what my own hands were doing: evidently I was playing the scales in a passable way, because he made no comment about them.

"Can you understand what I am trying to do, Miss Bennet?"

"I - um...I am not sure. "

"When you begin to play, your shoulders rise, and the tension communicates itself to your hands."

"Oh! I did not realise!"

His hands were still on my shoulders as we spoke, and I was making every attempt to concentrate on his words, and to behave as though I was unaffected by this proximity. But I was sure he must feel my heart beating, as it was making my entire body shake.

"Shall I try again?" I said. "I will see if I can pay more attention to what you describe."

I started to play and this time I did notice my shoulders rise up and made an effort to keep them relaxed. Signor Moretti kept his hands in place and I managed to keep going and my agitation stilled somewhat. But I could not stop being aware of the strange sensation of what was happening. When eventually he took his hands away, I felt the imprint of them for some time.

I was pleased when Signor Moretti said I could start to work on the lower part of a duet to play with Georgiana. At last he considered I was doing well enough to learn some music, and I was quietly excited at the thought of playing with Georgiana.

"Do you think I can really play well enough?" I asked.

He smiled. "Do not you?"

"I hope I can. I confess I am not as confident as I was before the ball." I reddened. "You saw how I was after that."

"I did. I hope over time you will feel it less."

I stared down at my hands. "I am sure I will never forget. It was the most dreadful night of my life." I turned my head to look up at him. "You were so kind to me that morning after the ball. I never thanked you."

He returned my gaze steadily. "Kind? I did not think you had found me so. I thought rather that I had been too outspoken and perhaps overly severe."

"Perhaps you were somewhat blunt, and I admit that at the time it took me aback. You did not compliment me, or reassure me when I was castigating myself. But you said nothing but what was true, and what I knew in my heart to be true." I hesitated. I was saying too much, but I was determined to express my gratitude to him, even at the cost of embarrassment to myself. "Your words steadied me. I needed help to face the truth, and if you had not said what you did, it might have been impossible for me to benefit from your lessons, which I have been enjoying very much."

"You are very generous, Miss Bennet."

I started to feel sad and low. "Perhaps if more people had spoken to me thus in the past, I would not have fallen into such error. But then, I cannot say with honesty that they have not, only that in earlier days I would not listen to them."

Signor Moretti sat beside me on the piano stool and took my hand. "I think you distress yourself unduly, Miss Bennet. You do not give yourself credit for your struggles, and your single-mindedness."

I shook my head. "Thank you for trying to make me feel better. I appreciate your efforts. But I must take responsibility if - if I am to change my life for the better."

There was a silence for a moment or two, and for some reason we both looked down at our hands, his lightly holding mine. He kissed my hand swiftly, released me and then stood up quickly. I felt extremely shy, and I thought he was embarrassed too. He bowed and left the room.

That night, before I fell asleep, I remembered the sensation of his hands on my shoulders. I was sure he had meant nothing by it except as an aid to teaching, but it was not nothing to me. It had had a powerful effect on me, especially followed as it was by our conversation, and then his kissing my hand. I wondered what his feelings were towards me. He was unfailingly kind, and showed his concern for my happiness and also for my character. He was inclined to help me with my music and to stop me falling into despondency, either in regretting the past or despairing of the future. I thought he was a warm and good man, and he seemed like an honourable man, but still, I did not know what to make of him.

Unbidden, the memory returned to me of when he had carried me in his arms. In my mind's eye, I was back there again, only this time I reached up my hand and rested it on his cheek.

I turned over, infuriated with myself. The best thing to do was to put these thoughts out of my mind and go to sleep. Unfortunately this proved to be impossible and the images repeated in my head for many hours of the night.

Part Nine: The Eavesdropping

◆

The next day Jane, Kitty and I were sitting in Lizzy's parlour. This was the room we always ended up in, perhaps because it made us feel at home, being in size and appearance most like the parlour at Longbourn where we would sit together when we were girls. Kitty was sewing, I was reading and Jane was writing to our mother.

"Would you like me to send any messages to Mama?" Jane asked us.

"No, thank you, Jane," I said, "I wrote to her two days ago and have nothing more to say."

Kitty laughed loudly. "Have you told her about your adventures yet, Mary?"

"What adventures can you possibly mean?"

Kitty shook her head and gave a knowing smile. "Everyone knows that Mr Speedwell is planning to propose to you when you drive out to B__ with him."

I nearly laughed with relief. Of all the things she could have come out with, this was of least concern to me. "You are quite mistaken, Kitty. And I cannot imagine what you mean by *everyone*! Have you been gossiping about me again? I do not expect any better from *you* but I do not think anyone here would join you, except perhaps Lydia."

Kitty was not at all put out by my reprimand.

"I do not think anybody here will have been *gossiping* about you, Mary," Jane said, "but it may be that your family has shown a natural interest in your affairs and your future."

"You are not writing about me to Mama, I hope, Jane?"

"Nothing of moment. Certainly nothing about Mr Speedwell."

"Or Signor Moretti?" Kitty asked provokingly.

"Why should she write about Signor Moretti?" I said, irritated to find myself blushing. "At least, why should you think of his name in connection with Mr Speedwell? Surely you do not think *he* has an interest in me too? Really, Kitty, in your mind I am turned into some kind of flirtatious hussy with a string of beaux!"

"Well, you do spend hours alone with him each day."

"Having piano lessons! That is all! It is quite innocent, I assure you." I was nettled and added, "Anyway, I do not think a jobbing musician is quite the suitor that our parents would have in mind for me."

"I think they would be grateful if any man would take you off their hands!"

"Kitty!" Jane said. "That is spiteful."

Kitty had the grace to look abashed. Jane was the only person who could ever instil any sense of shame or wrongdoing in Kitty, particularly where I was concerned.

"I do not know why you should be so superior about Signor Moretti, Mary," Kitty went on. "He is a very handsome man, and makes a good living through his music. He is welcome in all the best houses in London."

"Yes, but he is little more than a servant. That hardly recommends him as an eligible husband."

Jane said, "He is more than a servant here at Pemberley. Lizzy and Mr Darcy count him as their friend."

I was beginning to feel uncomfortable with this conversation. I hardly knew what I was saying. The memory of our last lesson and my subsequent thoughts were fresh in my mind. "Of course, *they* can be friends where they choose. The Darcys of Pemberley are so respected that they do not have to protect their position in a way that others might do."

"But why do you worry about position? If I loved a man, I should be happy to share his life, however humble," said Kitty. "And he is very attentive to you, Mary. You should not be so quick to dismiss him."

"He is not attentive, nor do I dismiss him!" I cried. "He is my teacher, and has been very – helpful to me, and kind. I am grateful for that, and I - I respect him as a musician, and of course for his goodness and patience. But it is no more than that, and I wish you would not keep supposing that there is something between us. Why, Mr Speedwell is more of a friend to me than Signor Moretti, if you must suppose things!"

Kitty smirked, but Jane's expression was thoughtful. "Love - the love that might lead to marriage - does not always arise from friendship. They are different emotions. I believe it is possible to be friends with a man, even an eligible man, without wishing for anything more. But sometimes a woman's feelings can surprise her."

I did not really understand what she was saying. It made sense in a way, in that I did feel friendship towards Mr Speedwell and yet never thought that I might wish to be married to him. But I did not understand what the other feelings were that she was describing. Was she talking about romantic love, the silly ideas of silly young females in melodramatic novels, where impossibly handsome and heroic men seemed to embody every good quality and were there to be worshipped and adored, and then to be married and lived with happily ever after? And what *was* happily ever after anyway? Was that what Jane was living? I thought she was happy, but there was nothing heroic about Bingley, and nothing romantic or extraordinary about her life. I knew she and Bingley loved each other, and loved their children. Did she think that Signor Moretti could be to me what Bingley was to her? I could not believe so.

For a moment I allowed myself to imagine being married to Signor Moretti, imagined having children with him, imagined sharing his life in London, though I knew nothing about the life of a musician. I remembered the heat of his hands on my shoulders, even imagined being kissed by him. I frowned and shook myself. These were pointless imaginings. Signor Moretti did not have feelings of that nature for me, nor I for him. If I indulged these thoughts any further I would become embarrassed to be with him, and that would destroy my lessons.

I stood up. "I do not like to discuss these things. I shall go to the library and read for a while."

Kitty laughed. "You always run away, Mary. You can't run away for ever."

I ignored her comment and went down to the library. It was empty, exuding calm and peacefulness. I wandered amongst the shelves for a while, and then found the novel that Mr Speedwell had recommended to me, The Italian. I thought if anyone were to see me reading it, they would perhaps think with Kitty that I did have some kind of romantic attachment to Signor Moretti. Well, I would not be self-conscious and deny myself the pleasure of reading a book that Mr Speedwell had suggested because it might set frivolous tongues like Kitty's wagging. I picked up the book and took it to an embrasure where I could read by the light from the window and be comfortable on the cushions in the window seat.

I realised quickly that it was going to be an extremely silly book, by the glowing descriptions of the beauty of the heroine. Why could not a heroine be plain for once? And of course, her admirer was a scion of a wealthy family. It was always so in these stories, one would think that somebody might come up with a different scheme for a change! Still, I read on, and had to admit that it was quite engaging. I was struck by the author's opinion of how Ellena, the impoverished beauty, was ashamed that she had to work for a living, and was described as too young and weak of character to 'glory in the dignity of virtuous independence'. Was that what Kitty had meant when she chastised me for setting store by Signor Moretti's profession? That I was subject to 'narrow prejudices', or at least, too irresolute to stand up for more important values?

The truth was, that I did not know what I thought. I returned to my book and was becoming comfortably immersed in it when I heard the door of the library open and close.

A voice said, "We may be uninterrupted here for a few moments at least, Elizabeth."

It was Mr Darcy and my sister. She said, "What do you wish to talk about?"

I knew I should quickly reveal my presence in the window seat, but something in the tone of Lizzy's voice affected me and I could not move. She did not sound quite herself, her voice was almost tremulous. This was so unlike her that I felt both terrified of discovery, and frozen with an intense curiosity.

Mr Darcy's reply was warm and urgent. "My darling, I do not mean to alarm you! Come, sit here. It is only that there is a matter to discuss which I would like to resolve immediately."

"Yes?"

"I -" he hesitated, "I do not mean to pain you, Eliza, but I have received some bills today, which normally would have come to you. They are very respectfully worded, but they were sent to you before and I wonder that you have not paid them."

There was a long silence. Mr Darcy went on:

"Well, Lizzy? I had thought that the pin money I gave you each quarter was sufficient to your needs, but if it is not, you surely know that you have only to tell me. I do not want you to do without anything, but at the same time I would prefer you not to build up debts." Lizzy still did not speak and after a few moments Darcy continued, his voice gentle and low so that I struggled to make out the words. "Lizzy, I hardly know - is there something troubling you? It is not like you to be silent, or to keep anything from me if it is distressing you. Are you well? It is not -? You are not worried about - ?"

"No, no, not at all. It is not that, if anything it is easier than before. It is - there *is* something - but it is not for me to - I cannot -" Her voice caught. I held my breath and a feeling of absolute horror overwhelmed me. Was she going to tell him about herself and Colonel Fitzwilliam?

She collected herself and continued. "I can explain about the money. I wanted to talk to you about it, but I have been so busy with all our guests, that somehow it kept going out of my mind, and just recently I have not felt - I have not felt that you and I-"

There was a sound of movement and muffled speaking. I thought they kissed and I hid my face in my hands. I wished I had disclosed my presence immediately. It was too late now and I could not bear the thought of them discovering me.

"I know you have been very much occupied with your sisters," Darcy said after a while, "and when I saw that the bills were from various dressmakers and haberdashers, I thought that with your usual generosity you had been providing for them. But still, the amounts are paltry and should have been well within your allowance."

"Yes, I know."

There was another pause that felt to me to last for an hour. Finally Mr Darcy spoke and his voice had a colder edge.

"Elizabeth, I must ask you to tell me the truth."

I waited, my whole body tense with dread.

"Oh, my love," Elizabeth cried, "I have done very wrong!" She burst into tears and there was more muffled murmuring.

"There can be nothing so wrong between us that total frankness cannot dispel," Mr Darcy said, "I am sure of that."

My heart was pounding in my breast so that I thought I should burst. She was going to tell him about Colonel Fitzwilliam, unaware that he already knew. Mr Darcy's optimism that this could be repaired seemed to me hopelessly misplaced. What a disaster was about to unfold, and I was to witness it! I wished I could be anywhere else. I even looked desperately at the window to see if I could open it quietly and jump out; I could not bear to hear what was about to be said.

◆

There was knock on the door and it opened immediately.

"I beg your pardon, Mr Darcy, sir, but there's been an accident."

I expelled my breath in a long sigh. Thank heavens, an interruption.

"An accident? What has happened, Thomas?"

"It's Mr Blakely, sir. He's fallen from a roof and looks to have broke his leg. He's been taken up on a stretcher into Westcott farmhouse, but Mrs Blakely thought you should be told. I'm sorry to interrupt."

"You were quite right, Thomas," Lizzy said. I thought I heard relief in her voice.

"Yes, indeed, I shall come at once. Thomas, will you go down to the stables and ask for a horse to be made ready for me?"

I heard the door close, and guessed Thomas was gone.

"I must go," Mr Darcy said.

"Of course you must! We will talk later, it is not - it is not so very urgent."

There was another pause. When he spoke, Mr Darcy's voice was cold again. "I must have truth between us, Elizabeth. Whatever you have done, we must be open with one another."

Elizabeth made a sound which chilled me, a sort of sob or gulp, like nothing I had ever heard from her. "I am sorry," she whispered.

Darcy left the room without speaking. There was a deadly silence. Please go, I silently begged my sister. Please put an end to this torture and leave the room. On and on the silence went. Then there was another terrible sob from Elizabeth, and she went out, closing the door behind her. A series of shivers ran over my body as I released the tension I had been holding. I had pins and needles in my foot, and my neck and head were aching. I felt horribly disturbed and upset, it was as though a catastrophe was looming and I wished more than anything that I had never written that anonymous letter to Mr Darcy. Surely it would have been better that he continued to be deceived than that his love for Elizabeth was destroyed, better even that my sister should continue in her debauchery and sin than that they should live their lives out together in mistrust and betrayal. For Mr Darcy would never forgive Elizabeth for this: he was too open and honest himself, it was clear to me that he abhorred deception or meanness or pettiness, he was all generosity and kindness and integrity; yet I could hear the anger in his voice at his suspicion of what Lizzy was doing.

I knew it was Lizzy's fault really, but I could not bear the thought that I was responsible for destroying my sister's marriage. If only I had never seen her and the colonel together, and if only I had not written that letter! I could not imagine a world with Lizzy and Mr Darcy out of harmony with each other.

But I did wonder why, for someone who valued truth and openness as much as he did, he had not gone straight to Lizzy with my letter and confronted her with it immediately. Now they both had secrets from each other and it was all my doing.

The next day I had a letter from Mr Speedwell, begging me to accompany him to the Heelys. I dutifully showed it to Elizabeth, and she told me to take Judith, as she had relatives in the town, and could visit them while we were at the Heelys. I was glad to have an opportunity to be away from Pemberley. I was confused and sad; a change of scene would no doubt do me good.

Mr Speedwell arrived at the appointed time, wearing yet another many-caped driving coat, a beaver hat and highly polished boots, driving his blue chaise and his greys again. Judith and I went in the carriage with him, along with a large basket of provisions from Pemberley's kitchen. We talked of ordinary things while Judith was with us, but as soon as we had dropped her at her aunt's house on the outskirts of B__, I turned to him.

"I did not think you would have punched Wickham, you know. You are a clergyman, and I expected you to intervene and be conciliatory, to quieten the situation, not to commit violence!"

"Alas, I have disappointed you again! To be honest, Mary, I did not know what to do, and in the heat of the moment I acted on impulse." He smiled ruefully, and looked at his left hand, which was still scabbed and bruised. "Yet I confess I am unrepentant. I am not a fighting man, as no doubt you could guess from my laughable attempt at a left hook, but if ever a man deserved to be punched, that man was George Wickham. You cannot disagree with *that*."

"No, I suppose not. But many people now suspect that it was for my benefit. People are gossiping about us, and assuming all sorts of things, and that I thoroughly dislike."

"They must have something to gossip about, life would be so dull else."

"Even Mr Darcy has asked me if I have any complaint against Wickham."

"And did you confide in him?"

"No! It would have given rise to exactly the kind of situation that I wish to avoid. How I wish you had not done it!"

"But how could I ignore such a heart-felt plea? It was not only to rescue you, it was to rescue Moretti, as you begged me to!"

"I did not beg!"

"You did beg, Mary. You knew at once that if Moretti had fought with Wickham, which I have no doubt Wickham was trying to provoke, it would have been much worse for Moretti than for me. And at least now they are gossiping about you and me, rather than you and Moretti."

I reddened. "I do not wish people to gossip about me at all! There is no substance to their conjectures."

"Is that so? Methinks the lady doth protest too much!"

"You will not be serious about it, will you, even though Mr Darcy has forbidden you the house?"

"Now that I do regret. I am so terrifically bored without my visits to Pemberley. You cannot imagine how lonely it is, rattling around in that rectory of mine, going for solitary rides across the countryside. I suppose I should think myself lucky that I am allowed to take you for a drive."

"How happy I am to be of service. I should hate to think of you being *bored*."

"Oh ho, the lady has claws! Are you very angry with me for behaving so abominably?"

"No, no, I understand that you did your best. It is only mortifying to be the cause of speculation. My sisters' greatest pleasure is to imagine that there are weddings to plan for."

He took my hand to help me down from the carriage. "Weddings, Mary? Not yours and mine, surely?"

I blushed. "Yes, ours and..." But I stopped myself.

"Ours, and...?"

"Oh, it is all nonsense. Never mind! Will I meet Mrs Heely's husband today?"

"Neat change of subject, Mary. Very well, I will take the hint. No, you will not meet Mr Heely. He has gone away to look for work in another town, as the employers here have blacklisted him for drunkenness and general misbehaviour. It is probably a good thing for the family to be rid of him, but they are desperately short of money. I think Mrs Heely would go to the mill herself but Sam is too young, and Meg not old enough to mind him. I believe they are taking in washing."

The door of the house was open, and we went in to find the family at work washing clothes over a large tin bath. Mrs Heely looked up.

"Eh, it's you is it, lass? And Mr S! Well, the children will be glad of a rest from this work. Come on, the pair of you!"

The children rushed forward to look in the basket, and immediately found the slates and chalks that I had secreted there.

"Look, Mam, look what's she brought us!"

"Mrs Darcy has sent some food," I said a little anxiously, remembering Mrs Heely's pride.

"There now, I'd say you shouldn't have, but I can't turn anything away just now, with Mr Heely gone off for goodness knows how long." She was delighted with the contents of the basket, including a large soap, which she immediately applied to some of the dirty clothes.

Mr Speedwell left us alone to visit another family, and I found myself chatting easily with Mrs Heely while the children played with

AMY STREET

their slates with great concentration. I even told her about the disaster of the Pemberley ball, and the difficulty of subjecting myself to lessons with Signor Moretti. She was pushing clothes through a mangle by this time, and she nodded and shook her head sympathetically.

"You don't half take things to heart, Miss Mary."

"Do you think I am indulging in self-pity?"

"Now, I didn't say that, but you're making a right mountain out of a molehill. You may have learning, but my goodness, you lack for common sense!"

"I am afraid you are right. I am – too easily wounded perhaps, and sometimes, sometimes I do give too much consequence to trivial matters, and do not realise that my troubles are not so very great, not compared to – other people."

"Oh, don't you be starting to feel sorry for *me*, young lady. Money is all very well, but there, it's not everything in life, and I wouldn't trade places with you for anything."

I did not wholly believe her, but it would have offended her to say it, so I did not.

The morning sped by, and all too soon it was time to return to Pemberley. As we approached the house, I said to Mr Speedwell,

"When will I see you again? How long will Mr Darcy forbid you the house?"

"I do not know," he said. "Meanwhile, do your best to ignore the chatterboxes and their mischief-making. I will write again soon, begging permission to take you to the Heelys. You are quite a fixture there now, you know."

I felt refreshed by my trip to B____, but I was aware of an oppression of spirits on my return to Pemberley, as I mused on all that I had witnessed, all the secrets to which I was now privy. I went to the music room, thinking some contemplative piano playing might soothe me, but when I opened the door saw Georgiana seated at the piano. Colonel Fitzwilliam was on one of the small sofas, looking towards her, as though waiting to be entertained by some music. He stood up quickly as I came in. His smile was warm, open and friendly. I hardly knew how to meet his eye.

"Please join us," he said. "Georgiana was about to sing a song that she has been learning. I am sure she would like you to hear it too."

"Please do, Mary," Georgiana said. "I would so value your opinion."

It was not quite what I was looking for but I sat on an armchair and listened.

Georgiana played and sang extremely well. Her voice was lovely, clear and warm and without artifice. She sang very true to the note. It was not a song I had ever heard before, it did not sound particularly difficult to execute, yet her natural musicianship shone through. I turned to look at Colonel Fitzwilliam and saw him staring at Georgiana with a happy expression on his face, as though lost in a pleasant dream, as I had often seen men do when listening to pretty ladies perform. She looked up, caught his eye and blushed. He smiled in return. I looked again. Was I becoming mistrustful of everybody, or was there a more than ordinary interest in his eye when he looked at Georgiana? I began to watch them closely.

The colonel's expression I suppose could have been likened to a man in love, but it was also quite consistent with an indulgent older relative enjoying beautiful music. Nor could I be sure of Georgiana's feelings. True, she had blushed and looked away when she caught Colonel Fitzwilliam's eye, but she was shy by nature and had often turned away from another's regard in just that way. Yet he was her cousin: why should she be shy with her cousin, unless it betokened something other than cousinly emotions in her breast?

"What did you think, Mary?" Georgiana asked.

"What? I beg your pardon, I - I was lost in the music. It - it was very lovely, Georgiana, you play and sing so well."

"Does she not!" the colonel said, getting up abruptly and joining her at the keyboard. "I could listen to you sing for ever, Georgie."

Georgiana looked at her hands shyly. "You flatter me too much. Mary, won't you come and play with me? Signor Moretti said he had given you the Mozart duet to look at, I should love to try it with you."

"Oh! I have not had much time to look at it! If you do not mind all the mistakes -!"

"Of course not! I make mistakes too, sight-reading is difficult for me. And you," she added, turning to Colonel Fitzwilliam, "you must leave us alone. We cannot sight-read while you are listening."

He gave her a glinting smile, which again I could not interpret. "I am at your command, Miss Darcy." She laughed as he executed an exaggerated military bow, even clicking his heels. Georgiana watched him as he walked out of the room.

There was a moment's silence. I decided to take a risk. If Georgiana really did have feelings for the colonel, then it was incumbent on me to find them out, and save her from heartbreak.

"Your cousin is a very charming man," I said.

She turned towards me quickly. "He *is* charming! Yet it is not a superficial quality, he is truly a good man."

I was not so sure of that, but I did not have enough evidence yet to the contrary. At least, I knew he was not a good man, because a good man would not have come between Mr Darcy and my sister, but I did not know if he was as bad a man as I suspected.

"You are fortunate to have a relative who is so fond of you. Our cousin, Mr Collins, is also a good man, a very religious man, but - well, I do not know how much he actually likes us. But of course you know Mr Collins, he has a living near your aunt's house at Rosings."

"Yes, I do know him. And I have come to know Mrs Collins too, whom I like very much. Her daughter is a charming child, though not always in the best of health." She smiled. "It seems we share our cousins now, perhaps they are *cousins-in-law* or some such! Is there such a thing?"

I laughed. "I do not know! But our cousin was a stranger to us until a few years ago: you, on the other hand, have known Colonel Fitzwilliam all your life. In a sense you have had two older brothers."

"Oh, no! Rowland is not like a brother at all! That is, he was appointed my guardian when our parents died, but - no, he is not like a brother."

Her face took on rather a wistful expression and my heart fell. Whatever his feelings towards her, it looked as though there was something more on her side. This was worse and worse! Colonel Fitzwilliam was deceiving both Lizzy and Georgiana, each thought she was the woman of his choice, both were in love with him! How despicable! He was proving himself to be the most complete ruffian! This could only end in heartbreak. And poor Mr Darcy! What would be his sentiments when he discovered what his own cousin and friend had been doing – toying with the affections of both his wife and sister? I could not believe it, it was more shocking than anything I had ever encountered.

"Mary, what are you thinking of?" Georgiana asked in a merry voice. "You have quite a frown on your brow!"

I could not answer her honestly. "I do not know what I was thinking of. Shall we play?"

After all, we did not make such a bad job of it. Georgiana was the better player by far, but I had seen the music before, so between us we stumbled through and landed breathlessly but at least simultaneously on the final chord. We burst out laughing and started to speak, when we were interrupted.

"Bravo, ladies! What a sound! What a sight!"

It was Mr Wickham. Neither of us had noticed him come into the room, and we both jumped to our feet. He was dressed in breeches and a shirt, but no neckcloth of any kind, and instead of a jacket he wore a rusty and frayed robe in velvet. He was unshaven and looked thoroughly disreputable, like a man who had been up all night drinking and gambling. If Mr Speedwell's blow had marked him, his face was healed now, and he was grinning at us and quite in possession of himself.

I could not say the same for Georgiana or me. We stood side by side as though frozen into statues. Georgiana's hand crept into mine and squeezed it tight. At first I thought she was trying to reassure me, and that she must know what had happened between Wickham and me, but I glanced quickly at her face and she looked white and tense. There was some distress on her own account associated with Wickham.

"Please, ladies, do not let me interrupt. I came to this room for the very purpose of soothing the savage beast with some music - or is it the savage breast? Either will do, for I am greatly in need of being soothed, and I cannot imagine anything more delightful than to be entertained by such fair performers as yourselves."

"Mr Wickham -" I began, but he held up his hand to stop me.

"I pray you, no false modesty. Let it suffice that it will give me pleasure and comfort to hear you, and to have the honour of two such lovely creatures playing together will be a rare treat indeed. You would not deprive an invalid surely."

"You do not look so very ill!" I retorted.

He sank onto the sofa recently vacated by the colonel, his hand draped across his brow.

"Sister Mary! Your heartlessness does you no credit! Especially as you yourself were the cause of my injury."

I blushed hotly. "I did not hit you!"

"Oh, Mary, Mary, do I need to spell it out? I am sure Georgie would love to hear all the details of our sad little story."

"Do not call me by that name!" Georgiana whispered, gripping my hand convulsively. I looked at her in surprise: I had never heard such forcefulness in her voice. What could be the matter with her? Something was troubling her dreadfully, her face was pale with two spots of high colour on her cheeks, and her eyes were wide and staring at Wickham with a mixture of fear and hatred. Her hand in mine was trembling.

My only thought was that Georgiana must not be forced by good manners to perform for Wickham; she was in no state to play or sing. I did not know what relations were between them, only that it was very disturbing to Georgiana and somehow I must get her out of the room as tactfully as possible, and make everything seem normal.

"Georgiana," I began, somewhat breathlessly, not sure how the sentence was going to end, "I wonder - I am sure that Jane and Kitty would love to hear us play our new duet." I pressed her hand as I spoke, hoping she would understand what I was doing. Of course nobody would want to hear us but it was all I could think of in that moment. "I believe they are presently in Lizzy's parlour. Perhaps you could go and ask them to join us and we could have some refreshments also? It must be time for tea."

She stared at me blankly for a moment; I stared back at her willing her to understand. Finally she spoke.

"Oh! Yes, yes, of course! Of course it would be lovely to have your sisters to hear. And tea! Yes, tea!"

Another surreptitious squeeze of my fingers and she practically ran from the room. This left me with a problem: I was now alone with Mr Wickham.

◆

Wickham clapped his hands deliberately. "Oh, bravo, Mary, bravo indeed! What a performance! I could almost forgo the pleasure of hearing you play after that effort. To get Georgiana to leave the room without a hint of anything awkward or untoward, nothing needing to be said outright, what an achievement! I would not have thought you could manage it, you who always speak so plainly."

He was sitting at his ease, with his arm along the back of the sofa.

"Why must you always be so sneering?" I snapped. "Does it give you pleasure to torment people?"

He made a face of fake penitence. "I confess it does, especially young ladies. They become so delightfully animated, you see. Just as you are now. And how well it suits you, dear sister!"

I snorted in a way that made me sound just like Kitty.

"Does that kind of flattery generally succeed with the ladies of your acquaintance?"

Wickham laughed. "Mary! I swear I could come to love you as much as I love my sister Elizabeth! I did not know you were capable of such penetrating sarcasm."

I felt myself flushing, more with anger than embarrassment.

"You are utterly disgraceful!" I said. "Have you no shame or remorse about what you did, that you can talk to me in such a way?"

"I confess my only regret is that I have not had the opportunity to kiss you again. But that can soon be remedied." To my alarm he was on his feet and coming towards me. "We must be quick though," he said. "Your protectors will be here in a moment."

I moved away from him, keeping the piano between us, my heart thudding. There was a very determined and wicked expression on his face.

"Mr Wickham," I said desperately, "you cannot mean to be so foolish as to do such a thing. When my sisters arrive, we should both be disgraced."

He laughed, circling closer towards me round the piano. "My dear Mary, I have no character to lose as you know, so that argument is wasted on me."

"Can you not think of my character then?" I said desperately, keeping a distance between us.

"You can always say I forced you. I'm sure you will be believed."

I was round the piano now and made a dash for the door, any attempts at keeping up an appearance of normality abandoned. Wickham anticipated me, caught my arm, and pulled me swiftly against him, pressing his lips to mine with great force. I pushed against him with no effect except to make him hold me tighter. He stopped but did not release me, pinioning my arms with one of his, and using his free hand to push the hair away from my face.

"Such pink cheeks, Mary, such glowing eyes!" he said. "One might be persuaded that you were enjoying my attentions."

I struggled again but it was hopeless, I had no strength at all compared to him.

"Now what if I was your combative clerical friend?" he said, planting light kisses on my face as he spoke. "You would not be trying to get away from me then, I think."

The feel of his lips so gentle on my face was distracting me. "You are quite mistaken," I said. "You have forced your attentions on me, and I would not welcome that from any man. How can you behave like this? You are married to my sister!"

His lips were on mine again, so he virtually whispered into my mouth, "I really do not understand it at all." In a swift and practised move, he sat down on the sofa, pulling me onto his lap, his hand behind my head keeping our lips locked together. He pushed against my mouth, trying to open it with his. I became really alarmed. The door opened, I gave a muffled shriek and Wickham released me, though without any great urgency. I put my hand to my mouth: it was not my sisters at the door, come to rescue me, but Signor Moretti.

He looked at me in surprise; he had seen me on Wickham's lap. God knows what he thought. "I beg your pardon," he said coldly, bowed and withdrew, closing the door behind him.

"No!" I called, but it was too late, he was gone.

I turned to Wickham in a fury and before I knew what I was doing I slapped his face.

"Now look what you have done!" I cried. "You horrid man! He will think - oh never mind!"

Wickham was nursing his cheek. "You *would* choose to hit the same side as Speedwell," he said in a voice of exaggerated woe.

"I hope it hurt!" I had to go immediately after Signor Moretti and explain to him. Seeing me on Wickham's lap, he must have thought I was a willing participant, and I could not bear the idea that he believed *that* of me. But before I could pursue him, the door opened again, and this time it was Jane and Kitty, with Georgiana, and behind them Thomas the footman bearing a tray of refreshments. Various polite commonplaces passed between Jane and Wickham but I was hardly aware of what was said. In my mind's eye I was following Signor Moretti's progress through the house, wondering where he would go, what thoughts he would be having. I stood irresolute: it was dreadful to think he had misunderstood the situation. Surely he could not believe that I had chosen to sit on Wickham's lap?

Georgiana came to me and squeezed my arm.

"Thank you," she whispered. "You saved me from an unpleasant ordeal. I would not have liked to play for Wickham. I hope he did not annoy you."

I looked at her blankly for a moment. The idea of playing piano for Wickham was so barely annoying to me compared with what had just happened that I did not know how to speak.

"Oh no," I said finally, whispering like her, "there was no difficulty." Unfortunately, I caught Wickham's eye at this point and he winked at me. I did not think that anyone else noticed.

We had hardly sat down when the door opened and Lydia came in, her expression one of great fury. Like Wickham she was wearing a robe over her clothes: the robe itself was grubby and creased, the dress of yellow crepe looked as though it had been pulled from the bottom of a trunk and dragged over her head with no care either for the dress, or for her hair which was loose about her shoulders. Her pregnant stomach looked bigger than ever and she rested her hands on it as though it was a shelf built for that purpose. The only thing that made this new arrival bearable was the look of consternation on

Wickham's face, rapidly covered up with his more usual smile of false amiability.

"So there you are!" Lydia said to Wickham, ignoring the rest of us. "And how long were you going to leave me alone without a soul within earshot nor a servant to be had?" She turned to Georgiana who seemed to represent the household for her present purpose. "Are all the servants on holiday? Can nobody be found to look after a sick woman and her unborn child? And me the sister-in-law of Mr Darcy too! Or is this more of your Darcy snobbery, the Darcy revenge against the Wickhams?"

"My dear - " Mr Wickham interrupted faintly.

Georgiana paled but spoke resolutely. "No, indeed, Mrs Wickham, there is no such revenge. I am sorry you have been so neglected, and I know my brother and sister will be most sorry too. Thomas," she addressed the footman who stood frozen with the tea tray in his hands, "please ask Mrs Reynolds to attend Mrs Wickham in her room." He almost scuttled out in his relief. "Mrs Wickham, and Mr Wickham too, you must tell Mrs Reynolds whatever you need and she will see to it that you are provided for. Now please, won't you sit down and join us?"

"Yes, do sit down, Lydia," Jane said gently, "you must be quite worn out with the baby due so soon."

Lydia was a little mollified, but shot a look at Wickham. "Thank you, Jane! It seems that *some* people have no care for anyone but themselves, *some* people do not understand what it is like to carry a child for month after month and then go through all that giving birth when the pain is so bad you think you might die. Oh no, they think their work is done after one quick -"

"Lydia! Please!" Jane interrupted. Wickham covered his face with an elegant hand, although I could see he was laughing. "Come and sit down and calm yourself," Jane insisted. "It is not good for you or the baby to be so upset."

Lydia sat next to Jane and burst into tears, flinging herself into Jane's arms. "How can I not be upset?" she stormed. "I did not want another baby. I have quite enough on my hands with the other two..."

"Three," Kitty said. "You have three children."

"Well, it is too many."

"I think you know by now how babies are made, my sweet," murmured Wickham, emerging briefly. Jane lifted her eyebrows towards him and he hid his face again.

"Never mind, Lydia," Jane said, patting her shoulder, "these last weeks are always dreadfully long. I quite thought I should go mad waiting for Henry to be born, I thought he would never come."

"It is all very well for you, Jane," Lydia went on, "you have a rich husband, you are not always contriving and wondering where the next meal will be coming from."

"Or the next dress," said Kitty.

I turned on Kitty. "That is not helpful, Kitty."

She gasped. "Ha! *That* from you, Mary! It was you who was always moralising about Lydia's debts."

"*Yes*, Mary," Lydia said, "you are so quick to moralise at me. *You* have never had my troubles, you are not even married, you do not know what it is like to be married to a gambler and a reprobate, to a man who cannot keep a job and pays you no attention and flirts with every lady he meets -"

"You should have thought of all that when you eloped with him," I retorted, "instead of bringing the family into disgrace because you could not control your base impulses and would rather ally yourself to a man whom everyone knew was of a bad character."

"They did not know!" Lydia shouted. "You were all in love with him, you were all jealous because I was the one he liked best, because you were too ugly for any man to even look at you!"

"I would not want a man to look at me if it led me into situations like that."

"You are just jealous, Mary, because no man has ever wanted to *kiss* you, let alone elope with you."

I thought I would burst with the effort of keeping back a full description of Wickham's behaviour towards me.

"I am *not* jealous of *you*, of all people, Lydia. Nobody would want your life, you say so yourself. You are the one complaining about the man you have married."

"Well...well...well - nothing could be worse than being a spinster all your life and living at home with Mama until you get old and being despised by everyone and being plain and having no bosom and thinking yourself so very superior when everyone is laughing at you behind your back."

"Really, Lydia," Jane said, "I know you are upset, but there is no need to be cruel to your sister. Of course we all feel for you in your situation, but you know there is nothing to be done except endure it and hope for happier times."

Lydia wailed. "I do not *want* to endure it! I do not *want* this baby! I do not *want* to be poor!" She sobbed afresh into Jane's shoulder.

Wickham rose, "I think I will just - "

"Don't you dare leave this room, George Wickham!" Lydia said.

"But I am sure you could tear my character to shreds much more happily if I were not present!"

"Your presence hasn't precisely impeded her so far," Kitty said.

"No, no, I will go. Your sisters can attend to you much better than I."

He left the room at speed.

Lydia continued sobbing, but her heart was not in it now that Wickham had gone. Kitty broke the moment by starting to pour the tea.

"We might as well drink it before it gets cold," she said.

♦

It was torment to sit with my sisters and Georgiana sipping tea and trying to help Jane bring Lydia to a more rational condition. Lydia made me so cross with her barbs and attacks that I wanted to tell her exactly what kind of man she had married in order to get revenge. The urgency to seek out Signor Moretti became unbearable. I had to find him. I had to explain, I had to make sure that he understood what he had seen, what it meant. Surely he could not imagine, after everything he had heard, that I would have welcomed Wickham's advances! But to find me sitting upon Wickham's knee! How equivocal it must have appeared!

I barely heard Jane offering me another cup of tea. "I beg your pardon!" I said. "No, I thank you, I must go - go to my room and write a letter."

Lydia stood up. "Will you escort me, Mary? I do not feel able to walk so far unaided."

I was surprised and annoyed at the delay but there was nothing for it but to agree. Lydia took my arm and we left the room together.

"Oh sister, you cannot imagine how I suffer! Why must we women go through such tribulations!"

I did not know what to say. "It is the woman's lot, I suppose."

Lydia huffed. "I might have known you would have said something sermonising and pitiless! *You* will never be married so you do not have to worry."

I tried to ignore her jibe. "I do not mean to be hard-hearted, Lydia," I said, "I suppose I am only thinking that it cannot be helped and must be endured, as Jane said."

She was slightly pacified. "Be thankful that you will never have to endure it, Mary. Marriage is all very well and I do love my dear Wickham, but I did not know there would be so many babies all the time. I will tell Wickham after this one that there will be no more, he must stop it happening."

I frowned. "But how can he do that?"

"Oh, I will tell him he must take his pleasures elsewhere, that is how everyone does it."

"Lydia! You cannot mean that! You - you would not want your husband to commit adultery! That is a sin!"

"You are such an innocent, Mary! Do you not realise -" she broke off and stopped where she was and gave a gasp.

"What is it, Lydia?"

She paused, waiting. "No, it is nothing. I thought for a moment it might be beginning."

"The baby?"

"Of course the baby! But I am sure it is not time yet. At least, I do not think it is. To tell the truth I do not know when I started increasing this time, but I am sure it cannot be time yet."

We continued to walk with maddening slowness to her chamber, but halfway up the stairs, she stopped again and doubled over.

"Oh, my goodness!" she exclaimed. "I do think -" but she was unable to finish her sentence and gave a horrible groan, squeezing my arm with shocking force.

"Lydia!" I cried.

The sound of my voice must have carried through the stairwell, because Mrs Reynolds appeared at the top of the stairs, her arms full of linen. In a moment the linen was put aside and she was with us, taking Lydia's other arm.

"There, there, Mrs Wickham!" she said. "I was just on my way to attend to you. Now, don't you fret. We'll get you to your chamber and have the doctor to you in no time. Have you just started?"

"Yes, just," Lydia said, able to talk now, "but it is not like before, it is too fast this time, it was not so quick before."

There was a note of panic in her voice, and Mrs Reynolds kept talking to her gently as we escorted her up the stairs. We made very slow progress, as every few minutes Lydia doubled over and began groaning and clutching her belly. Mrs Reynolds spoke soothingly to her throughout these episodes, rubbing her back, while I stood uselessly by, having all sensation driven from my arm by Lydia's fierce grip.

"We'll take you to your chamber for now, Mrs Wickham, and no doubt Miss Bennet here will stay with you till the physician comes. You don't mind, do you, Miss Bennet?"

I did mind, very much, and I did not think Lydia would want me with her. "Perhaps Kitty..." I murmured, but Lydia gripped my arm again and gave a great howl, which seemed to mean that I was not to leave her.

Even as we went along the hall to Lydia's bedroom with her leaning heavily upon me, I was looking out for Signor Moretti, although there was no reason why he should be in this part of the house. I did not want to stay with Lydia: I was impatient to find Signor Moretti and I had never been with a woman at her lying-in and I did not know what to do or what to expect. Also Wickham might be in her chamber and that would be extremely awkward if I was expected to remain there with both of them. However, the room was empty and Lydia staggered to the bed and crawled on to it, remaining in an ungainly position on her hands and knees as another spasm shook her. Her groaning was hideous to hear.

"I'll leave you with Mrs Wickham for a moment, Miss," Mrs Reynolds said, "and I'll send a maid up to you."

"Brandy!" Lydia gasped, "bring me brandy! I must have something to take this pain away! Ohhh!"

Mrs Reynolds must have seen my expression because she whispered to me, "Do not upset yourself, Miss Bennet, ladies often become a little deranged at these times. I will send Mrs Deakins - she's the laundry-woman but she knows what to do better than anyone when there's a baby coming. And no need for brandy."

"Are you sure?" I whispered in return. "She is in such pain, surely - "

"The doctor will sort all that out. But - I do think this one might be here quickly. It's often the way when it's a later baby."

Lydia gave another unearthly bellow. I could just make out the name of Wickham and some dreadful expletive that I would not even have expected from a stable hand.

Mrs Reynolds shook her head smiling, and left me alone. Lydia was still on all fours on the bed, her head hanging down and sweat on her face. I found a towel and wet it in the basin to mop her brow. At last she lay on her back and let me dab her.

"This baby - I did not want another baby, I do not even like babies, and now it is coming so fast, oh, good lord -" There was another spasm which went on for ever. I was relieved to hear a knock on the door. Mrs Deakins appeared, a rather squat and ugly woman of middle years but with an air of calm certainty. She nodded to me, but I was soon pushed out the way and I was happy to let her take over. I hovered by the bed.

"No need for you to stay, Miss," Mrs Deakins said, sensing my uncertainty, "I'm going to have a look at Mrs Wickham now, see where that baby is, so -"

I took her meaning and left the room hurriedly, a dreadful cry from Lydia following me on my flight.

◆

I wanted to go straight away to find Signor Moretti, but the thought came to me that my sisters might not know what was happening to Lydia. Accordingly I went back to the music room where I had left Jane, Kitty and Georgiana.

"How is Lydia?" Jane asked me.

"That is what I came here to tell you," I said, "she has gone into labour! While we were walking to her room she started her pains and Mrs Reynolds has sent a woman to her and they think the baby might come quickly."

Jane and Kitty stood up as one and without another word ran from the room. I turned to Georgiana, to take my leave of her, but she impulsively took my hand and led me to the sofa.

"I am glad we are alone, Mary, I want to talk to you - and to thank you for rescuing me before."

"Oh! I - I did not - that is - I knew you were troubled by Wickham's presence but I did not understand why." Inwardly my heart was sinking. Was I never to get to Signor Moretti? He would be thinking all manner of mistaken thoughts about me.

She took my hand and pressed it fervently. "That makes your action doubly kind and thoughtful. But - can it be that you really did not know about my - dealings - with Mr Wickham?"

I shook my head. "I confess I did wonder, having seen you together, but I did not feel it was my place to ask."

"That is like your consideration, dear Mary. I think until I had come to know you I would not have been able to tell you about my past, but now that you have shown such thoughtfulness and discretion towards me, I feel I would like to give you my confidence."

"You honour me," I said. "I would endeavour to be worthy of your trust." I sounded stilted even to my own ears, but I did not know how else to express it. Although it was flattering that Georgiana wished to talk to me, I was also impatient to be seeking Signor Moretti. One thing after another was interfering with my quest! Georgiana did not sense my restlessness and began talking.

"When I was a girl, George - Mr Wickham - was like a brother to me, you know. He grew up here and was a pet of my father's and a companion to my own brother. He was -" she paused and her eyes seemed to turn inward to some landscape of memory. "He was, as you can no doubt imagine, extremely attractive and exciting to a young and strictly raised girl, he had a streak of daredevilry quite lacking in the Darcy family. At the time, I thought he offered me freedom - he looked on me as the young woman I wished to consider myself, rather than as a silly and innocent girl who did not understand the ways of the world, as my brother insisted I was!" She smiled ruefully. "It is painful to remember one's past follies, is it not?"

"Indeed it is!" I replied, looking longingly towards the door.

"I am sure you do not have any such painful memories as I do, Mary! You who have led such an exemplary life, so devoted and conscientious as you have always been."

She looked at me with such trust and expectation that I could do nothing but shake my head.

"You are so modest, Mary!"

"We all have regrets," I said.

"But I know you cannot regret as much as I. You have not heard the full extent of my rashness and self-deception. When I was 15, Mr Wickham left Pemberley. At the time I did not know why he had gone, only that I missed him terribly. My brother suspected that I was suffering, and in order to distract me, he arranged for me to go to the seaside with a respectable lady. As it turned out, she was not so respectable! Nor did I like her over much. I was so happy when Wickham appeared at Ramsgate to entertain me. I did not think there was anything wrong in being alone so much with one who had grown up in my own home, and I very much enjoyed his attentions and his flirting. If I had been a little less innocent of the ways of the world, I might have wondered why Mrs Younge was such a negligent chaperone. But I was infatuated." She blushed. "You will not tell, Mary. I have never told anyone this, not even my brother or Eliza, but Wickham kissed me when we were private together. At the time it made me feel like the most sophisticated and desirable female in all creation!"

I blushed myself at this point, and hoped Georgiana would not notice. I was certainly not ready to be as confiding as she was.

"I finally came to my senses when he began to talk of elopement. It startled me out of the dream I had been in and suddenly I knew what we were doing was wrong, underhand and deceitful. I thought of my brother's feelings if I were to run away and I became anxious. Wickham tried to persuade me, but I could not be comforted. Even his most tender kisses could not reassure me." She stopped speaking abruptly and examined my face. "You look distressed, Mary. I am sorry, I do not mean to shock you. I know Wickham is your brother-in-law now and perhaps you are offended."

"No, no! You do not shock me precisely, at least not on account of my sister Lydia. It is Wickham's audacity that is surprising. Why would he think that he could seduce the sister of so notable a person as Mr Darcy?"

Georgiana shook her head. "He *is* very audacious, and as I am sure you know, profligate with money. My fantasy was most truly shattered when I realised that it was my inheritance that interested him far more than my person."

"Then that makes it even harder to understand why he should have become entangled with my sister. He must have known she had no fortune."

"Wickham has always been impulsive by nature, and not one to consider the consequences of his actions. I imagine - at least, I do not mean to disparage Mrs Wickham - but I imagine that he took an opportunity that presented itself."

"A willing female," I mused.

"Yes, and Lizzy told me that he never intended to marry her. If it had not been for the intervention of my brother I do not think he would have."

"Your brother? How is that?"

"Oh!" Georgiana cried. "I thought you must know by now. I did not realise it was still meant to be a secret."

"Can you mean that Mr Darcy *paid* Wickham to marry Lydia?"

She nodded, studying my features. "He did it for love of Elizabeth. He did not wish Lizzy to suffer and he felt he was to blame for not warning people of Wickham's character. He was trying to protect me from the consequences of my foolishness."

"How like Mr Darcy!" I exclaimed. "Your brother is quite the kindest and most generous man I have ever encountered."

"Thank you, Mary," Georgiana said, squeezing my hand. "I count myself so fortunate to have him as a brother, and now that I have you and your sisters also, my family is complete."

"But how did you recover after you discovered Wickham's true character?" I asked.

"I think if it was not for Signor Moretti it would have been much harder."

"Signor Moretti?" My heart gave a lurch in my chest. "Did you - did you have feelings for him too?"

"Oh no, no, no! Not at all! His wife had died, and he was so sad. Yet he helped me so much by making me immerse myself in music. He said music and study would sustain me through a difficult time."

I thought for a moment. "Perhaps it sustained him too at that time, when he needed something else to think about apart from the loss of his wife."

"I think you are right, Mary. We were two heartbroken people and it was fortuitous that we could offer each other something that we both needed. Of course I do not compare my loss to his. Mine was a silly schoolgirl passion, he lost the love of his life."

I could not help wondering what Georgiana had come to mean to Signor Moretti at that time. It would not surprise me if their mutual suffering had brought them close together, and perhaps Signor Moretti felt more for Georgiana than she knew. She was so kind, so sweet, so genuinely musical; well educated, refined in her manner yet always natural and never condescending or superior. Add to that list that she was handsome and wealthy and it would only be surprising were he *not* to have fallen in love with her. No doubt she had been loveliness and understanding itself as he grieved for his wife.

I felt a hollowness open up in me: Georgiana was everything I was not; where she shone, I was dull; what she had in abundance I lacked completely. My eyes clouded with tears, I could not help myself.

Georgiana was quick to notice. "My dear Mary! Whatever is the matter?"

I shook my head.

"I have been boring on about my own concerns with never a thought for your feelings, and here you are with your sister in her confinement, and your gallant rescue of me from the toils of Mr Wickham! And my careless revelation about the circumstances behind your sister's marriage!" She squeezed my hands. "How inconsiderate of me, when I am sure you need to reflect on what has been happening."

"It is not that, Georgiana," I said, with some difficulty, "though all that you mentioned has affected me, I own. It is just - sometimes when I compare myself to you, I despair of myself."

"Oh, Mary, no!"

"It is true, you are so good, so kind, so talented. It is no wonder that you were able to help Signor Moretti through his grief."

"But Mary, you also are good and kind and clever. How can you talk so?"

"You do not really know me, Georgiana. I am not a nice person like you, at least it does not come naturally to me."

"That is not so, Mary! When you rescued me so nobly just now! I did not have to explain anything, you sensed my distress and acted upon it like the thoughtful and sensitive person that you are. And I have seen you with other people, with your little niece. You are too severe on yourself."

"But I have been so *envious* of you, Georgiana!" I burst out.

Georgiana's expression was sombre. "I am sorry you have felt so, Mary. I am - I know I am very fortunate, but it is only fortune, I did nothing to deserve my lot in life."

"I know, I know, but I have been so ignorant and foolish and naive - and now..."

She waited expectantly for me to continue.

"Something happened, Georgiana," I began, "something - oh, I cannot bear this. I must find Signor Moretti! Excuse me!"

I ran from the room.

◆

I did not know where to look for Signor Moretti. I tried first the little chapel where I had heard him play the organ, but it was empty and silent. The hour was quite advanced and it would soon be time to dress for dinner, but I needed to talk to him before seeing him in public. I could not bear the thought that he was imagining me to be a wanton, an adulteress, or even that he might think I was actually in love with Wickham. For some reason, that would be worst of all.

I tried all the principal public rooms of the house, thinking that he might be there. Some were occupied by members of the household or servants, but I did not speak or tell them my business. I did not think I could explain.

Signor Moretti was nowhere to be found. I decided that I would have to seek him out in his room. I supposed it was improper, but considering what I had been through with Wickham, it did not seem important.

I had to pass my sister Lydia's room on my way to the east wing where the musicians stayed. A horrifying wail emanated from behind the door, followed by sobbing. I ran quickly away. I did not want to think about what was happening in that room, or what the outcome might be. So far, my sisters had given birth without incident, but I knew well that anything could happen, even with a fourth baby. I wished Lydia well in my mind as I flitted past.

As I entered the east wing, I realised that I had no idea which might be Signor Moretti's room. There was a passage with a number of doors leading off it. I heard the sound of a violin coming from one of the rooms. I knocked at the door, and it was answered by the black-haired violinist from the orchestra. He looked astonished.

"I beg your pardon," I said, trying to sound as if this visit was the merest commonplace, "I am looking for Signor Moretti. Do you know which is his chamber?"

Silently he pointed with his bow at a door on the opposite side of the hall. I thanked him and waited until he had gone back inside and the violin had started again before I knocked on the door he had indicated.

"Come in!" said Signor Moretti. I opened the door tentatively and stood in the doorway. He was sitting at a desk in the window writing something, and stood up when he saw me. He was dressed in breeches, shirt and stockings, without shoes or coat. His hair was rather disordered; it reminded me of the engraving of Beethoven from the front of the sonata book. His expression on seeing me was just as astonished as the violinist's, but there was something else in his features, a fixed look that did not bode well for me.

"I beg your pardon, Miss Bennet, I thought you were the maid with my clean collars."

"Um, no, I am not."

"I can see that."

This seemed to end the conversation for the moment.

I stood irresolute in the doorway. Signor Moretti looked at me and I at him. This lasted for a very long time. I suddenly became aware of silence: the violin practice had ceased. This decided me and I stepped into the room and closed the door behind me.

"Signor Moretti -" I began, and then stopped. Here I was again, putting myself in a position of having to start an impossible topic of conversation.

"Signor Moretti - I do not know - whatever you think - I cannot explain - no, I can explain - you see -" I stopped. "Oh lord, this is quite hopeless!"

There was something of a pause.

"Why are you here, Miss Bennet?" Signor Moretti asked.

"Because I need to explain, of course!"

"I do not see why."

"But you *must* see why! Of course I have to explain, I cannot have you thinking -"

"Thinking what?"

"Thinking - well, I do not know what you are thinking. What are you thinking?"

"About what?"

"About - about - about what you saw!"

"Did I see anything?"

"Of course you did! Oh, why are you being like this? This is difficult enough, you know it is, and yet you are being utterly obtuse and unhelpful."

His voice was expressionless. "But Miss Bennet, I saw nothing that is of my concern. You are an adult woman, you are quite in charge of your own - self, your own wishes."

I wanted to stamp my foot with frustration. "But don't you see - that is exactly what I am *not!* You thought - you think - that I was..." Embarrassment overtook me for a moment and I put my hand to my face.

There was another heavy silence in which the loudest noise appeared to be my heart beating. Finally Signor Moretti spoke in brisker tones.

"Very well, Miss Bennet, let us not mince matters. I interrupted you just now when you were kissing Mr Wickham. Is this what you wished to *explain* to me?"

"Yes! Because I was *not* kissing Mr Wickham - "

"I beg your pardon, it looked very much as though you were."

"Yes, yes, I know. But you see, Wickham - oh, where do I begin? I told you what happened before. I thought you understood that it was not my doing. Wickham - you know what kind of man Wickham is. He - he is not a *good* man."

"No - but he is a very handsome one."

I looked at him in horror. "You really do believe it of me, don't you, that I would voluntarily kiss my brother-in-law, my sister's husband! That I lied to you when I told you what happened before! You truly think that is the sort of woman I am!"

He looked away for a moment. "Miss Bennet, I have spent many years in the houses of the wealthy. There is nothing I would not believe."

Hot, angry tears started to my eyes. "You would place me with women of that sort? I thought you knew me better than that."

He hesitated and his face looked pained. "But what am I to think of such a sight? I did think I knew you better than that, but I must believe the evidence of my eyes."

"You *do* know me better than that!" I cried. "I would never kiss Wickham, I would never kiss *anyone*, but particularly not a married man, particularly not my own brother-in-law!" I realised I was stumbling into a morass of complications about who I might or might not kiss and changed tack. "Wickham - Wickham importuned me. He has no serious intent, he is making mischief, he thought -" I blushed hotly. "He thought it would be amusing to - to conquer me, because I am, well, because I am straight-laced. I tried to get away from him, in fact, I - I slapped his face."

He made a sound that was like a laugh. "How very resourceful of you," he said.

I peered at him to try and understand his tone. "Are you mocking me?"

"Um - yes."

"Well, that is not very kind of you."

He started towards me when there was a knock on the door. We both froze.

"Sir, it's Daisy with your collars!" came a voice from outside.

"Good god! What shall I do?" I whispered wildly. "I must not be seen here!"

"No, a woman with your reputation -" he whispered back.

"Do not joke at such a time!"

"Quickly, then, under the bed!"

"What? No!"

"You have not a moment to lose! Please wait," he called to the maid. I ran to the closet, pulled it open and stepped in, finding myself amongst some coats and shirts. I pulled the door behind me and tried to hold my breath, which was difficult as terror made it come so fast.

"I'll put them in the closet, sir," said the maid.

"No!" Moretti almost shouted. "Uh, if you please, lay them out on the bed, I will - I will choose which one to wear."

"Very good, sir."

I heard the bedroom door open and shut, and then Moretti opened the closet door and reached his hand toward me to help me out.

"She could have discovered me!" I said, still whispering.

"I told you to go under the bed," he responded.

"This is so undignified! I wish I had never come here!"

"But why did you come here, Miss Bennet? I do not understand why you should care what I think of you. I am only a music teacher."

He was still holding my hand and I wrenched it away furiously. "I do not like *any* person to have a false conception of me. In any case, why do you talk in that foolish manner, as if there was such a gulf between us? I am only Mary Bennet of Longbourn, you need not be so humble."

"But you are also the sister to Mr and Mrs Darcy of Pemberley. Perhaps you do not realise that your position in society has changed accordingly?"

"Only by association," I replied. "My portion that I will inherit from my father has not changed, the circumstances of my birth have not changed. And I myself in essence am much as I ever was."

"Truly?"

"Of course. I - I think I know myself a little better. In some respects, I wish I had changed in essence. I might like myself better if I had."

"You are very stern."

I shook my head. "You do not know what I deserve."

"Are you speaking of Mr Wickham?"

"No, for that was not my doing. There are other things, things I can never tell a soul. Well, you would dislike me even more if I told you."

"Dislike you? Now who is talking foolishly?"

I looked up at him. He was regarding me in his usual steady way. Our look held and neither of us looked away. My breath grew short. I could not read his expression but there was something in his eyes that seemed to bore into me and without thought or volition I reached my hands up and pulled his head down towards mine. Instantly our lips were together and we were kissing each other.

Part Ten: The Kiss

♦

Kissing Signor Moretti was quite unlike kissing Wickham. His lips felt firm and soft at once, he was insistent but I did not feel afraid. It was like the sensation of being stung by nettles, only pleasurable. And in one sense Wickham had done me a service, because he had taught me the difference between a kiss with a man for whom there were warm feelings, and that where I felt only fear and disgust. Mostly fear and disgust.

At last we drew apart, although I stayed within the circle of his arms. We were both breathing fast and Signor Moretti had a flush on each cheekbone. I imagined my own face was red, as I certainly felt extremely hot.

"I beg your pardon, Miss Bennet." He was about to loosen his hold on me, but I held him fast.

"Why do you apologise?"

"It is wrong of me to take advantage of you. I have no right. You have already suffered at the hands of Wickham -"

I was shocked and angry. "How can you - how can you compare that with what happened with Wickham? Did you think -?" I became embarrassed at the words I was about to utter, but forced myself to go on, "Did you think that I did not wish to kiss you?"

"I barely know. You are very excited and upset, perhaps you will think better of it in a few moments."

"You think I do not know my own mind?"

"It is easy to get overtaken by the heat of the moment."

I looked up into his face but I could not read his expression. A horrible suspicion dawned on me.

"Perhaps," I said slowly, "perhaps it is you who have been overtaken by the heat of the moment, perhaps it is you who regrets what just happened."

He was silent for a moment, and then another moment. I stood away from him with a jolt.

"Indeed, Miss Bennet -"

"Oh, do not *spare* me!" I said angrily. "You have always been mercilessly honest with me, for god's sake do not trifle with me now. I see what you are trying to say. You are trying to tell me that I have been mistaken in your feelings for me. I thought you felt something for me, I thought this feeling was mutual."

"Miss Bennet, I am - I *must* be mindful of our situation, of the difference in rank, of my status at Pemberley halfway between guest and servant, of your presence here in my bedchamber -"

"But why should any of that matter to you if you returned my regard?" I was almost shouting now; I barely knew where my words were coming from, but as I spoke them I knew they were right. I had made a terrible error of judgement. "If you felt as I do, such considerations would mean as little to you as they do to me. But clearly you do not. And now I am utterly shamed!" I felt tears start to my eyes. "Good god, you must think me as bad as Wickham, forcing my unwanted attentions on you! My trip to Pemberley has been salutary indeed! It has been one horrible mortification after another, self-deception after self-deception. But this! This is the worst of them all!"

"Miss Bennet! Mary! Please listen to me!"

He grasped my shoulders but I shook myself free.

"Why should I listen to you when all I hear from you is lectures and humiliation? I am leaving now and I never wish to speak of this again! I trust you to be a gentleman and tell no-one."

He was angry now. "Of course I will tell no-one! But why do you not give me a chance to explain?"

The tears were flowing down my cheeks, and I wiped them away with my bare arm. "Nothing good can come of this now," I said. "Explanation would be pointless. You do not return my feelings and nothing else matters."

Before he could say another word, I ran from the room. As soon as I opened the door, I nearly collided with the black-haired violinist who looked at me with great astonishment. There was nothing I could say to him so I pushed past him and ran for my bedchamber.

I hoped not to meet anyone on the way, but this hope was vain as there were many people rushing up and down the halls: servants bursting out of the servants' door, laden with linen and buckets of water; Jane and Bingley deep in conversation in a window embrasure; Colonel Fitzwilliam, Kitty, Mrs Reynolds; one of the nursery maids pulling a stubborn and resistant Horatio by the hand towards the nursery stairs. From further away I heard more of Lydia's dreadful cries and groans. As I passed her room she gave out a low moan that went on and on: it was followed by a piercing scream, Wickham's name, and then with horrifying clarity the words, "I am going to push! I have to push!"

I ran on. What a horror was childbirth! I thanked god I would never have to go through such pain and indignity. For a moment I had allowed myself the fantasy that I - even I, Miss Mary Bennet, confirmed spinster - might some day be married and a mother - but that was over, and hearing Lydia, thinking of her marriage to Wickham, I could only be grateful that sanity was restored to me.

I reached the sanctuary of my room, and flung myself on the bed with relief. Never had solitude been so welcome! At last, to be able to shut my door to the chaos that was overrunning the house! Yes, I could shut all of it out; Lydia's screams, Moretti's rejection, children and warring couples, the vision of the gore and horror that was taking place as Lydia gave birth to another unwanted child, danger and pain and blood, heartbreak and sadness and disappointment. All of it, shut out, kept out, away. No more Wickham and his betrayals and predations; no more clever, lovely Georgiana and her sad story and her exquisite piano playing and the years of attention lavished upon her; no more Elizabeth and her hypocrisy, no more Kitty and her changeable nature, no more Jane even, with everything so good and right in her eyes. What madness had possessed me to venture into their world? It was not my world, it had never been my world, there was no place for me in it. My place was at Longbourn and locked into myself. The only person I could trust was myself.

I had been gripped in a kind of madness at Pemberley. For the first time in my life I had ventured into the world, in the belief that there could be something for me, some possibility of - what? love? pleasure? friendship? Instead, I had met hurt and betrayal, humiliation and hypocrisy. From Wickham came nothing but a malevolent lust; Moretti had no feelings for me except as a pupil, as the sister of Mrs Darcy, and of course as an object of pity. I was not so blind that I did not realise how much he pitied me.

It was no wonder that I had lived a solitary life if this was what awaited me in the world. Well, I would retreat once more. As soon as may be, I would beg Lizzy for a carriage to send me back to Longbourn. I was sure Mama would be glad of my company, no doubt she would need my help as she looked after Aunt Philips. Kitty need not cut her visit short, and anyway, I knew she would be happy to have Georgiana to herself.

I heard the distant sound of a gong. It was time to dress for dinner. I was shocked to be reminded that the ordinary life of Pemberley was still carrying on, even while Lydia laboured. I did not wish to see anyone but there was a knock at the door and Judith came in, a dress over her arm, followed by Jane.

"Oh Mary!" Jane's face was streaked with tears, and a dreadful thought assailed me.

"Lydia? Is she -?"

"She is well, Mary, she is well. She is delivered of twins, Mary! Twins! Our little sister to have five children, all well and safe! It is too much!"

She threw her arms around me and sobbed.

"Yes, Ma'am," said Judith, "Twin boys too! What a fine addition to the family! But they are sending for a wet nurse as poor Mrs Wickham is much too exhausted to feed them."

"Twin boys!" I gasped. "How will she manage? She cannot keep count of the children she has already!"

Jane laughed through her tears. "She will have help, Lizzy and I will see to it, she will not be left friendless and helpless. Oh Mary, they are so small, so very small, you cannot believe that such tiny creatures can live, yet they do, they are both crying lustily."

"And how is Lydia?" I asked.

"She is well, very tired, very bruised."

"Has Wickham seen his sons?"

"I believe he has ridden out somewhere. Lydia says he is always thus when she gives birth."

"A birth is no place for a gentleman," Judith said as she laid out my clean linen.

"I will leave you to dress, Mary, I must send an express to our dear mother. She will be so happy to hear the news, and to know that Lydia has given birth with all her sisters around her. No doubt she will want to visit as soon as possible."

A visit from our mother! That would not suit me at all! I could not then go to Longbourn if Mama came to Pemberley.

◆

At dinner that night, we drank a toast to the Wickhams and their new arrivals. Wickham had come late to the table, looking unkempt and smelling strongly of drink. He replied to Mr Darcy's toast in slurring, self-pitying tones:

"I thank you all for your kind wishes. It makes me truly happy that my sons should be born in the very house in which I was raised. I only hope that they will not be ejected as brutally as I was."

I was sitting next to Elizabeth, and I heard her give a quiet and angry sigh. I did not blame her, knowing what I now knew about Wickham's behaviour towards Georgiana, and how much Darcy had given him to make him marry Lydia. I dearly wanted to say something cutting to Wickham and I could see from Lizzy's tight lips that she was having to stop herself doing the same. It was not right that he should be allowed to cast aspersions on Mr Darcy, when it was his own wrongdoing that had led to his estrangement from the family. Briefly, I caught Georgiana's eye, and she shook her head at me in a tiny movement, so I realised I would just have to endure Wickham's hypocrisy, as would we all.

Mr Darcy looked particularly grim. I saw his eyes stray from his wife to Colonel Fitzwilliam and I thought he must be sad and angry at how they had betrayed him. No doubt Wickham's thoughtless, selfish words had reminded Mr Darcy of the bad character that was not only in Lydia, but also in his own wife, Elizabeth. I felt for him extremely, and felt even angrier towards Lizzy.

"We will of course be happy for Lydia to remain here while she recovers from her confinement," Lizzy said calmly. "Have you decided on names for the babies?" she asked, clearly thinking it wise to change the subject.

"When we thought we were only having one child, we had decided to call him Bennet, after my father-in-law. But now there are two, my dear wife has honoured me by suggesting that the other be called George after his own father." He bowed his head modestly.

Kitty, who was sitting on my other side, whispered to me, "He assumes he is the father!"

I gasped and whispered back, "Kitty! Hush! You should not!"

Kitty's reply was to snigger quietly.

Signor Moretti was sitting opposite me on Lizzy's other side, but I did not want to meet his eye. When I did, he looked even more sombre than usual, and he avoided my gaze as well. For one moment our eyes did meet, and I tried to read his expression, but could not. I did not know what to make of him. If he had been made unhappy by our conversation earlier, then I was almost glad; but why should he be unhappy, if he did not care for me at all? I did not understand him. At that moment, I hated him.

When the ladies retired from the table, I found that I felt rather lacklustre and depressed. I thought Lizzy was also low in spirits, but none of us were particularly animated.

Jane said, "I feel quite exhausted after the anxieties and emotions of the day! Do not you, Lizzy?"

Lizzy did not answer, she was deep in thought.

"Eliza? Did you hear me?"

"I beg your pardon, Jane, my mind is so full. Yes, I do feel strangely exhausted. Of course, one should be happy that Lydia is safely delivered of her twins but I suppose that I cannot help wishing that she was married to a better man! Every child she has binds her closer to Wickham! I know I am being fanciful – she could not part from him with or without children – but that she and they should be dependent on such a man!"

Jane reached across and squeezed Lizzy's hand. "I know, Lizzy, it is not what we would wish. Charles and I have been discussing an idea, we plan to ask the Wickhams if Horatio would like to come and live with us. If not him, then Philomela. We are agreed that there are too many for Lydia to look after."

Kitty looked up from a piece of lace that she was mending. "Would you do that, Jane? That is very kind of you, I'm sure, but Lydia's children are so naughty. Horatio hits the others and cannot be controlled. Do you really want him in your family? What about Sophy? I am sure she would not like it."

"I know Horatio can be a little wild," Jane replied, "but I do not believe he is past saving. If he were to have somewhere fixed, and then a decent education, I am sure he would learn to be a good boy and to make something of his life."

Kitty looked doubtful. "I think you should not be too hasty. I have never seen a child like that, so passive one moment, so vicious the next."

"No, not vicious!" cried Jane. "You cannot call a child of that age vicious! He is merely to a certain extent unsettled, and needing a firm and consistent hand."

"Yes, to give him a good slap!" retorted Kitty. "Oh Jane, he is not a nice child. He will cause chaos in your nursery, as he has done here."

"He has been very troublesome, you know, Jane," Lizzy said. "I have had to hire another nursery maid to tend to him and no other."

"All the more reason for him to be taken off Lydia and Wickham's hands and looked after with the care and love he needs."

"You have great faith in the power of love," I said.

"I believe I do. I know how powerful the love of parents and family can be."

"But not everyone is as fortunate or as lovable as you, Jane!" Lizzy said. "You and Bingley are both so good and kind, it concerns me that you would take on a child who does not have a good nature. Your happy family might be destroyed."

"No, Lizzy, you are too pessimistic! You are thinking that love is weak."

I was shocked to see Lizzy's eyes become wet with tears. "I do not know if love is weak or strong," she said. "I do not know how long it lasts."

We all looked at her in shock.

BECOMING MARY • 221

"I am thinking of Lydia and Wickham," she said quickly, recovering herself. "Lydia loved Wickham when they were first married, but does she love him still?"

We were all silent. I knew Elizabeth was not thinking of the Wickhams, but of herself and Mr Darcy. I wondered if she was contemplating her own fickle emotions, that could allow her to succumb to the attentions of another man only three years after her marriage; or was she thinking of Mr Darcy's coolness towards her since he had received my anonymous letter? If so, she must know in her heart that she did not deserve that he continued to love her.

"I do not think Lydia ever loved Wickham," Kitty said. "She had a fancy for him because he was the handsomest man in the regiment, and because he liked her. She always liked anyone who likes her, she does so still."

"You are very severe on your sister, Kitty," Jane said.

"I know her better than you," Kitty replied. "The other reason she ran off with Wickham was because he preferred you at the time, Lizzy. She was determined to best you, she told me so herself."

"You cannot take seriously such idle remarks as that!" Jane said. "I believe that Lydia and Wickham did care for each other, however unconventional their liaison was at first, and I believe they still do."

I shook my head. "He does not care for her, that I know."

Kitty looked up at me sharply. "How can you know such a thing, Mary? Do you believe Lydia when she says he is a philanderer? I think she is merely excusing her own behaviour by blaming him."

"I think he is a man of no character," I said. I paused. I was perilously close to telling them what Wickham had done to me. "I saw him kissing a maid once."

Kitty laughed, and I saw a look of relief on Georgiana's face. Georgiana must have been dreading that I would betray her confidence. She did not know that I was in more danger of betraying my own stupidity.

"Kissing a maid?" Kitty snorted. "I would not put it past him to try and kiss one of us!"

A heat rose up my neck; I hoped that Kitty did not notice, but of course she did.

"Ha, Mary! You cannot tell me he kissed you? That would be so amusing!"

"Of course not!"

"Why do you blush so, then?"

"Because - because I feel ashamed for him at the very idea that he would betray his wife with one of her own sisters! And of you, for thinking such a thing!"

Jane had been ignoring my exchange with Kitty, and I saw that she had taken Elizabeth's hand.

"But Lizzy, these sad thoughts of yours, this sense of despair, this is not like you. Is something else troubling you?"

"I do not know, Jane, it is nothing I am sure, just sometimes..." Lizzy's voice trailed off.

Jane patted her hand reassuringly. "I remember feeling much as you do when I was first expecting little Charlie. I think many women feel rather low during the early months, and you have not been well either, you know you have not. That will sap anyone's spirits."

Lizzy looked away, her face still troubled. "I am sure you are right, Jane, I am sure it is only that."

"Lizzy!" I cried. "Are you going to have a child?"

Kitty rolled her eyes. "Did you not know? Really, Mary, sometimes you are so blind! How could you not know? The whole household knows, Mrs Reynolds knows, even the laundry-woman knows! You knew, did you not, Georgiana?"

"Yes, I guessed, and I asked Elizabeth if it were so."

"I – I did not realise!" I stammered.

My mind was galloping like a runaway horse: Lizzy with child! This was terrible news. Now Lizzy's debauchery had gone too far: she was carrying Colonel Fitzwilliam's child! No wonder she was feeling depressed; she must still be capable of some feeling of shame. And did she mean to pass it off as Mr Darcy's own? To what depths she had sunk!

This was terribly wrong, this must not be! Didn't Mr Darcy have any idea of the deception that was about to be perpetrated on him?

Kitty was looking at me strangely. "Are you not happy for Lizzy, Mary? You are not going to be disapproving just because you are the last to know, surely?"

I tried to recover my composure. "Of course I am happy for you, Eliza, only I am surprised, and now I feel silly because I did not realise."

Lizzy smiled at me. "I should have told you directly, Mary. I suppose I thought one of the others would have said something to you."

"Does Mr Darcy know?" I asked.

I thought Lizzy looked sad again. "Yes, of course he knows, and has been particularly solicitous of my comfort." Her words sounded hollow, and I thought she was covering up their estrangement so that none of us would suspect the reason.

◆

When the gentlemen came in to join us that evening, thankfully without Wickham who had gone off to bed, exhausted by the events of the day, I did not know where to concentrate my attention. I wanted to watch Darcy, and Colonel Fitzwilliam, to see what I could make of their behaviour, to see how much they each knew of what was going on with Elizabeth, but I was also distracted by the presence of Signor Moretti. I was aware of him wherever he was in the room, whatever he was doing, however much I tried not to think about him; I could only hold the book in front of me and occasionally turn a page. My head was so full and every few minutes, whenever I tried to think about the terrible web that my sister had woven around herself, I felt palpitations in my chest and could hardly breathe.

Signor Moretti was sitting with Georgiana and after a brief discussion they went to the piano, where, after a short hunt for some music, he started to play and she to sing. They were not performing, but were quietly trying out some songs for their own pleasure, stopping at intervals to go over a tricky passage or to discuss something. All my animosity towards Georgiana returned: as usual, she was the favoured one, she put herself forward to perform and Moretti chose her to accompany. It was all very well for him to talk about me working to become a musician, but he never encouraged me, and clearly he would always prefer Georgiana to me.

Not that Signor Moretti could ever aspire to the hand of such a one as Georgiana, she was destined for a much greater match, but no doubt he was still somewhat in love with her, after they had cheered each other up from their grief and melancholy.

I must have been staring at him without realising, because suddenly he looked up from the keyboard and our eyes met. Immediately a blush spread itself over my face, and he raised his eyebrows in a question. I looked away. My humiliation was complete.

What on earth had possessed me to behave in such a forward and wanton manner with this man who clearly cared nothing for me? I must have been out of my senses, driven to be unlike myself by the pressure of Wickham's attentions, and the delusion and fantasies that I had allowed to exist since I had come to Pemberley. I had simply forgotten who and what I was: in terms of my person and my talents, I was no match for Signor Moretti – he had shown he did not admire me as a woman, and I was shocked at myself that I had ever allowed myself to think that he might; but in terms of family and social standing, was he a match for me? Even if he had liked me, would Mama and Papa have given permission for such a match?

I started to feel extremely low. I did not see why I should be always at the bottom of the heap, always the despised and rejected and lonely one. I looked across the room at Elizabeth and saw that she was talking privately to Colonel Fitzwilliam. Occasionally, as I watched, I would see them glance up from their conversation, either at Georgiana or Mr Darcy. Mr Darcy did not notice: he was innocently playing at whist with Kitty and the Bingleys. I thought, why should Lizzy have so much and yet treat what she had so carelessly? She was not content with one man, but must have two. It had always been thus, always she thought she could have who she wanted and not care who she might wound in the process. I remembered when Mr Collins had solicited her hand in marriage and she had turned him down: well, she was fortunate that Mr Darcy liked her so much, she might easily have been left on the shelf to turn into a spinster by such profligacy. And now it seemed even the great Mr Darcy was not enough for my sister, she must needs find herself another beau, and one who was so close to her husband! And such carelessness, to allow herself to become pregnant by another man! I had not expected it of Elizabeth. In Lydia's case it would not surprise me if Kitty's conjectures were correct, and Wickham was not the father of all her children, but I confess Lizzy had surprised me, I did not think she would be so abandoned to all propriety as to force a bastard on her husband.

Everyone in the room was ignoring me: I was able to feign reading my book while observing the pantomime that went on around me. I watched as Colonel Fitzwilliam squeezed Lizzy's hand, and then went over to the card table. He stood behind Darcy, and at a suitable point in the game as the last trick was played, leant over Darcy and whispered in his ear. Darcy nodded and stood up.

"Please excuse me from the game," he said. "Fitzwilliam and I have some business to discuss."

"Oh, no!" Kitty cried. "I am sure we will defeat the Bingleys in the next round. If only I would get better cards! Just one more game, Mr Darcy, please?"

He turned towards me. "Mary, will you take my place so that the game can continue, or are you too immersed in your reading?"

I hardly knew how to reply, I was so surprised at being addressed. "N-no, I thank you," I managed to say. "I do not enjoy cards very much."

"Oh, Mary!" Kitty said, "who cares what you enjoy? We need a fourth if Mr Darcy must go! I would like it much better if Georgiana played, but as you see she is busy."

Elizabeth came forward. "I will play if you wish, Kitty."

"Yes, yes, you play, Lizzy, that will do very well. Mary can stay with her nose stuck in her book."

I refused to let Kitty's words sting me. I told myself that she was beneath my notice and I would not let her rile me. Instead I turned to watch Darcy and Fitzwilliam leave together. I did not doubt that there was to be a reckoning between them but I could hardly imagine what the conversation would be. Did the Colonel intend to confess that he had cuckolded his cousin? Did he mean to ask Mr Darcy to relinquish his claim on his wife, to divorce her? Or perhaps Colonel Fitzwilliam realised that his affair had been discovered, and was intending to put a stop to it, and to inform Darcy of this, perhaps as a way of making amends between them and preserving the Darcys' marriage, rather than trying to end it?

Whatever was to be the conversation, I was astonished to see Elizabeth so calm and collected as she was, coolly playing at cards as though nothing was the matter. I turned my attention to Georgiana and Signor Moretti. The music had faltered briefly when Darcy and Fitzwilliam left the room and now I saw Georgiana looking intently towards Elizabeth. After a moment Elizabeth became aware of it, and nodded slightly towards her sister-in-law. Instantly Georgiana's face was suffused with such a blush that I thought tears might have started to her eyes. She stopped singing abruptly, and after a quiet conversation with Signor Moretti, bid us all good night and left the room. It was all very mysterious. I had no idea what troubled Georgiana.

Now there was nothing for Signor Moretti to do but to come and sit with me, as I was the only person unattended.

He took a seat beside me on the sofa. I continued reading my book.

"What is it you read, Miss Bennet?" he asked me after a while.

"I doubt it would interest you," I said.

"But why would I ask if I were not interested?"

"How should I know? I do not know what you think about anything."

"No, and I wish to remedy that," he said quietly.

He leaned towards me and I shifted away. "Well, *I* do not wish to know what you are thinking. You have made it clear enough and there can be nothing more to be said on the matter."

"You are mistaken, Miss Bennet, there can be a great deal more to say on the matter. You left me too abruptly this afternoon, and I did not have time to talk with you properly and answer your concerns."

"That is just as well," I said, "as I no longer have any concerns."

I turned back to my book, hoping that he would leave me alone. Instead he said in a much louder voice: "Shall we play the duet you have been practising with Georgiana? I'm sure your sisters and Mr Bingley would like to hear how you have been getting on."

Mr Bingley overheard, as no doubt he was meant to. "Oh, do please play for us, Mary! What a capital idea. I have not heard you play since the night of the ball."

Mr Bingley meant well, but his comment brought up painful memories for me. The familiar heat crept into my cheeks.

"I'm sure you do not wish to hear me, perhaps Signor Moretti could entertain us?"

"Oh, go on, Mary!" snapped Kitty. "Don't pretend to be modest all of a sudden, it doesn't become you. And if you keep refusing, everyone will start to try and persuade you, and then they won't concentrate on the game."

Lizzy laughed. "How can you resist such a charmingly-worded request, Mary! Really, Kitty, must you be so ill-humoured? Mary, please do play your duet for us. It is so pleasant to have music while one plays cards, and we have not heard the duet."

I sighed. "Very well, though I cannot play it."

Kitty could not resist crowing at my expense once more. "That is the first time I have ever heard you admit it!"

◆

I did not like to be sitting beside Signor Moretti at the pianoforte. He, of course, was entirely at his ease, finding the music, moving the long stool so that we could sit side by side. I realised it would be one of those occasions when to make any kind of fuss or commotion would only make the situation worse, so I resolved to be completely calm. However, it was not easy to be calm once we were so close together. It was impossible to ignore the warmth of his body, impossible to forget what had happened between us earlier that very day. I wanted to run out of the room, but I would endure anything rather than provoke the caustic observations of my younger sister.

"Shall I count us in?" he asked quietly. I nodded, barely paying attention to his words. I placed my hands on the keys, and hoped that some strength or automatic function would get me through these next moments.

"I think the key you want is B flat."

I looked at my hands; they were nowhere near the right place.

"I can't do this," I whispered.

"Yes, you can. We must now."

"Why did you make me play? It is cruel. I cannot concentrate, I am too unhappy."

"One, two, three, four..."

We started to play. By a miracle, my practice and my sessions with Georgiana had paid off, and my hands seemed to know what they were doing, more or less. I did not think it mattered if I made mistakes, as everyone was used to hearing me play badly anyway.

"Miss Bennet, you must let me explain," Moretti whispered under cover of the music. I immediately made a hideous error and had to stop for a moment. He pointed to the music to show me where we would start again.

"Do not talk to me while we play!" I whispered fiercely. "It is not fair."

"I must. You shall listen to me, I want you to understand. Do you not see, that while I am a teacher in this house, I cannot pursue courtships with members of my employer's family?"

"You are assuming that I wish you to 'pursue a *courtship*' as you put it. You need not worry about that, I have no interest in any courtships at all."

There was a pause in the conversation while we continued to stumble through the music. When Signor Moretti whispered to me again it was clipped and harsh.

"Perhaps it is Mr Speedwell whose courtship is of interest to you?"

I stopped playing again.

"For goodness' sake, Mary, at least try and keep going no matter how many wrong notes you play," Kitty cried. "It is so irksome to have you stopping and starting all the time."

I began to make a retort and rise to my feet, when Signor Moretti's hand closed on top of mine. "Let us continue," he said.

I sat down again, my hand burning from his touch. The imperative to observe the proprieties was torture. I wanted nothing more than to run away to the sanctuary of my bedroom, to calm my overheated mind of all the thoughts that were scurrying around it.

"Please do not talk to me, Signor Moretti," I said. "As you know I am not really adept enough at this piece to be able to talk while I play. You are humiliating me and annoying my sister."

"Very well, Miss Bennet, but I must and will find a time to explain myself to you."

"I do not want your explanations!" I hissed. "How often must I repeat that?" And without waiting for an answer I began to play at random. There was nothing for him to do but join in with me and we managed to get to the end of the piece without more mishap.

"Very nicely played, Mary!" Mr Bingley called from the card table.

"Indeed it was!" Jane said. "Your lessons and practice have made such a difference."

I stood up and replied with what I hoped was a good grace, though I had very little idea of what I said as I was too upset. I had to leave the room; I had to get away from Signor Moretti. Once again he was causing me an unwelcome disturbance, and I knew my best hope was to get as far away from him as possible.

"Are you going to bed already?" Elizabeth asked me.

"Yes," I said, "it has been a very tiring day. I am not accustomed to so much excitement. Good night, everyone."

The next morning I was resolved. I would ask Mr Darcy to provide me with a carriage, or at least lend me a maid as an escort, and I would leave Pemberley. I could not bear to see Signor Moretti each day like this and pretend that nothing had happened between us, it was too humiliating.

But before I could ask Mr Darcy for the carriage, I would have to speak to him about Elizabeth and tell him what I knew. Now that I knew she was carrying Colonel Fitzwilliam's child, my duty had become even clearer to me. It was not fair that Mr Darcy should go through life blind to his wife's infidelity with his own cousin. It was terrible to think that I must be the instrument that ended his marriage but I knew it was the right thing to do, even though it involved the lifelong shame of my own sister.

Accordingly I went to try and find him.

I went first to the library and found Elizabeth there, reading a novel. She looked up on hearing me enter.

"Do not run away, Mary! How are you this morning?"

"I am well thank you, Eliza." I could not help speaking somewhat coldly to her. "I am looking for Mr Darcy to solicit a carriage or an escort so that I can go back to Longbourn."

She looked at me curiously. "You wish to return to Longbourn?"

"I do. I think I have trespassed on your hospitality long enough."

"My dear Mary, it is no trespass, as you surely know! What is the matter? Has something happened to make you unhappy? I know Kitty and Lydia can be unkind, but surely you would not cut your visit short for that?"

"No indeed, Lizzy, it is just...I believe it is time for me to return to my proper place, which is at Mama's side. I...I do not think that the life at Pemberley...in short, it is better for me to be at home now."

Lizzy jumped up from her seat and took my hands. "Mary, I must understand. Something is behind this. I do no mean to pry, but perhaps I can help."

I pulled my hands away. "Really, no, Lizzy. It is as I have said. I am not designed...it is not my way...I am better off at home."

"But what about your lessons? You were doing so well! Signor Moretti will be here another month, and you have made him so happy with your progress."

"I? I do not think so! Anyway, he will soon find other consolations, I am sure, and will forget about me when he returns to London. Now please, Elizabeth, do you know where Mr Darcy is to be found?"

"Mary, is there something between you and Signor Moretti? I have wondered...there is something in the way he looks at you..."

"*Please*, Lizzy, do not assume that everyone is always flirting and falling in love. I am not like the rest of you, I do not hold myself so cheap -" I broke off; I found I did not wish to bring the subject up to Elizabeth: I could not bear it if she lied to me directly. "It is simply as I have said. I did not intend to stay here even this long."

"But Mama has no expectation of you returning so soon. I think she hoped you would stay here till she can visit herself, then you can travel back with her after she has seen Lydia and the babies."

"I do not care to."

"Well, I am sorry for it, Mary. I had hoped you would be happy here at Pemberley, and I am sorry if there is anything amiss."

"I do not mean to be ungrateful, Lizzy. I am sure you and Mr Darcy have been as hospitable as anyone could be. But it does not suit me to be with so many people all the time. I am accustomed to our quiet life at Longbourn with Kitty and my parents. I have a great need of solitude and time for reflection."

Lizzy shook her head, bemused. "I do understand, Mary, but as you can see there is plenty of opportunity for reflection and quiet reading. You could come to the library as I do."

I did not want to have this conversation, I had made up my mind, and I did not like Elizabeth to be pressing me.

"Where can I find Mr Darcy?"

"You will not be persuaded?"

"I will not."

"Very well. But have you told Mama your intentions? She may even now be on her way to Pemberley."

"I wrote to her, but I have not heard. If she is not at home, our father will be there surely."

Lizzy smiled. "I am sure he will have to come to Pemberley to escort Mama, as little as he is interested in Lydia's new babies. I doubt he could remember the names of her other children. I doubt Lydia herself remembers their names sometimes!"

Knowing what I knew about Lizzy and her relations with Colonel Fitzwilliam, I was shocked to hear her joking so calmly about babies. Surely she must be experiencing some guilt, some remorse for her predicament? However, this was not the time to discuss it. It was more important for me to arrange my departure from Pemberley.

I said, "Lizzy, will you provide me with an escort, perhaps one of the maids?"

"Of course, Mary, and I think you may find Mr Darcy in his bookroom this morning, although he is much engaged on estate business."

Her face took on the anxious, bewildered look that I had noticed before when she thought of her husband, but I ignored it and went in search of him.

Part Eleven: The Arrival

◆

I was determined to speak to Mr Darcy though I was quailing inside. My trepidation only increased as I neared the bookroom, but there I came across various men, some farmers by their dress, others men of business, all waiting to see Mr Darcy. I remembered that his steward had broken his leg, and it occurred to me that this would mean Mr Darcy was busier than ever. I could not interrupt him now.

As I walked back to my own bedroom, trying to adopt a nonchalant air, I heard a commotion arising from the main entrance hall of the house. I went to the top of the stairs to look down. There was a bustle of servants, footmen and maids starting to come up the stairs with trunks and bandboxes. I heard a familiar voice:

"Oh, dear Wickham, take me to my darling Lydia at once! I cannot wait to see her. To think that my girl should have had twins, and her own mama not there to help her and give her support! Was she properly looked after, Wickham? I do not trust these northern people to know how to look after her properly; she should have been at home with her Mama! Why did you not bring her into Hertfordshire?"

I did not hear Wickham's reply, but was surprised to hear another masculine voice instead: it was my father! How had my mother prevailed upon him to leave his library and his solitude, and travel with her to Pemberley? I suppose she could not undertake the journey alone, and so he must come. How would he bear it? I ran downstairs to greet my parents. Wickham was standing with them, looking rather sheepish, still in his louche dressing-gown, but there were as yet no other family members.

"Mama!"

She looked up in surprise from directing a maid to fetch Lizzy, and stared at me.

"Well, well, Mary, this is very pleasant, is it not? We shall be all together again, just as it should be. Come child, come and greet your mama and let me look at you."

I went forward to embrace her. She held me at arm's length.

"You look very well, Mary. Is this a new gown? It becomes you well."

"It is one of Kitty's that she altered for me, Mama."

"Did she indeed? She has done a splendid job, you look quite changed. I think you are a little plumper too. You do not have that meagre, scrawny appearance that you are wont to. You must have been spending more time out of doors."

"I suppose so, to some degree. I am not too fat?"

"Of course not, child! I am only pleased to see you looking more comely. Jane said the air of Pemberley was suiting you."

I was aware of Wickham shifting slightly just out of my sight.

"As to that, Mama, I was hoping to return to Longbourn as soon as may be."

"No indeed, Mary, for there is nobody there. It is too early for our summer visit, but Lizzy knew we would want to see you all and Lydia's new babies. We shall not be here for long, you will just have to return with us."

"But my Aunt Philips! Perhaps I could stay with her in Meryton?"

She shook her head impatiently. "Don't be nonsensical! She is too unwell to support a visitor. Why would you want to leave Pemberley, where you have every advantage, and your sisters all about you?"

She had a certain knowing expression on her face, and I realised that one of my sisters had been gossiping to her about my marriage prospects. My heart sank.

My father reached towards me and took my hand. "You look very well, Mary. Do not trouble yourself, we will all return to Longbourn soon enough."

I sighed and was about to speak to him, when I saw his eyes stray over my shoulder and his expression lit up. I turned. Lizzy was coming downstairs. She went straight to our father and they embraced.

"Lizzy!" Mama cried. "Take me to Lydia at once. I must see her, I have been so worried about her."

"She is resting just at present, Mama. Would you like to settle yourselves first and have some tea? Then I am sure Lydia will be ready to receive you."

Mama was about to protest, but just then Mr Darcy appeared, and she was too much in awe of him to say any more. Mr Darcy greeted her politely, and my father with real affection. Lizzy led my mother upstairs, Mr Darcy and my father followed, and I went quickly to the music room so as not to be left alone with Wickham.

I sat down at the pianoforte and started to play absently. For once nobody came in to interrupt me. I tried some scales and arpeggios. The memory of Signor Moretti's hands on my shoulders came flooding back to me; inevitably this led my mind to the terrible scene in his bedchamber when I had wantonly kissed him and he had rejected me. There was a terrible aching in my chest and I knew that

I might easily begin to cry. I wished more than anything that there was someone I could turn to, someone who could offer me some comfort.

I left the music room and went out into the grounds. It was strange how much I needed to be alone, and yet how much I needed someone to talk to. I cast around in my mind – I thought of the chapel, of how I had gone there the day after the ball and spoken with Signor Moretti, how kind he had been, how honest. I thought he was a truly good man, and I realised that he did care something about me in his way, but not in the way I had thought. I could not think why I had ever imagined that he might: I was not pretty, I was small, pinched, narrow in form, and in my mind also I was ungenerous and dull. I had no wit or conversation. Why would Signor Moretti, or any man, pay me attention, except to torment me like Wickham, or to abuse me like the Dean?

I passed a certain bench, and remembered the night of the ball, how I had run out here and cried in the gardens. Mr Speedwell had found me. He had been kind to me; he had been a true friend. I would see him soon, no doubt, and perhaps I might find a way of confiding in him to relieve my mind. I had never felt so lonely.

Later in the afternoon, there was tea served in Elizabeth's parlour, and Mama joined Kitty, Jane and me. Mama was ecstatic: she had seen the babies, she had seen Lydia.

"And I already love those dear boys as much as any of my grandchildren." She was holding Jane's little Henry at the time; he had finished feeding and seemed to be in a state of drunken bliss. "But my poor Lydia! How will she manage? And Wickham just released from prison, and so keen to be setting up in business, but without any funds! Jane, could not Mr Bingley help? Lydia is *his* sister too now."

"Mama, you should not ask Jane!" Kitty said. "Mr Bingley has often lent money to the Wickhams, and has never received a penny of it back."

"Do not distress yourself on our account, Kitty. Charles and I have not expected – that is, we know, that when circumstances allow, Wickham will pay us back. And Mama, you must know that we have offered to have Horatio, to bring up as our own."

"Well, I am sure that is very kind of you, Jane, but can Lydia spare him? You know how she dotes on her children."

Kitty snorted.

"Of course she does," Jane said quickly, "and we hope that she will want the best for them."

"I do not think she could bear to be parted from dear little Horry. You had much better give Wickham the money he needs to set up in business."

"But Wickham cannot be trusted, Mama!" I said. "He is always in debt, always having to be rescued by my sisters and their husbands. Why should Jane throw good money after bad?"

"I don't need your opinion, Mary, and as an unmarried girl you are hardly fit to pronounce on your sister's affairs. I see what has happened to you since you have been out from under my eye, you have become quite puffed up in your own consequence."

"Indeed, Mama, I have not!" I began, but she interrupted me.

"These suitors of yours must have gone to your head. I want no more of it, Mary."

"Mama," Kitty said, "Mary is only saying what we all know to be true. Wickham has not been a good husband to Lydia."

"He is better than no husband at all!" my mother replied, silencing both Kitty and myself.

Part Twelve: The Announcement

◆

I would have thought that the presence of two new guests, particularly my talkative mother, would have livened up the conversation at the dinner table, but the air was full of tension, and a subdued atmosphere prevailed. I was acutely aware of Signor Moretti. I wished he would leave Pemberley, or that I could leave. The frustrations of my dependent state as an unwed daughter had never been more painful.

Georgiana was sitting beside Signor Moretti: she too looked pale and tense, as did Mr Darcy. Mr Darcy's mouth was tight and thin, and although he conversed politely when the occasion demanded it, in repose his expression became preoccupied with unhappy thoughts. I followed his gaze as he glanced every so often at Lizzy, at Colonel Fitzwilliam and at Georgiana: there was concern and speculation there, but all overtopped with a brooding unhappiness. Lizzy and the Colonel avoided each other's eyes, and their expressions bespoke their guilt.

There were times when my mother's constant conversation made me want to scream with impatience. She chattered on about Lydia, about the children, about the furnishings of Pemberley. She made comments under her breath about the lack of generosity shown by the Darcys and Bingleys towards the Wickhams, she even complained again about the terms of the entail which meant that my cousin Collins and his wife would inherit Longbourn at my father's death. In the past I would have listened calmly, but now I found myself disagreeing inwardly with her and being embarrassed by her at the same time.

At long last the meal came to an end and the ladies retired, my mother still talking as we moved out of the dining room. I was the last, and saw Darcy and Colonel Fitzwilliam leave the dining room and go into the library. My heart started to beat rather fast: Darcy must be going to have it out with the Colonel! I dreaded to think what the outcome might be. When the gentlemen came to join us, both parties looked perfectly calm, even smiling, but I was then astonished to see Colonel Fitzwilliam walk boldly across the room to Georgiana and take her hand. Georgiana stood up, her face suffused with pink and a tremulous smile on her lips.

"My friends," said the Colonel in a loud voice, "I would like to share some momentous news with you. At least," he added, looking tenderly at Georgiana, "it is momentous to me. My cousin, Fitzwilliam Darcy has today given me permission to marry his sister, thus making me the happiest man on earth."

There was a silence and then a murmur of congratulations. I was aghast; my mouth dropped open in shock.

The Colonel continued: "This will be of no surprise to many of you, as I am sure my feelings for Georgiana have been all too obvious, try as I might to hide them. I have quite understood that Darcy wished us to wait until I had received my full discharge from the army, and also to give Georgiana time to be sure of her own mind. My feelings – have never been in doubt. I have been Georgiana's guardian since the tragically early death of her parents, I have watched her grow from a little girl into the lovely woman that we know today, and I feel more privileged and honoured than I can say, that she has not only consented to marry me, but that she is quite insistent that she returns my regard."

"Well, that is very charming I am sure," my mother said, with a hint of bitterness in her tone. "Of course, if certain other people had not been so squeamish about marrying their cousin, then the entail of Longbourn might have stayed in the Bennet family where it belongs. But hey ho, it is all water under the bridge now. I'm sure I hope you will be very happy."

Lizzy jumped quickly to her feet and embraced both the Colonel and Georgiana. "My dears, I am so very, very happy for you both, and for us too." Darcy too stood up, shook Fitzwilliam's hand and embraced his sister.

"I cannot think of a better husband for you, Georgie," he said quietly. He released her and reached over for Elizabeth's hand. One by one all the company gave their congratulations and good wishes. Georgiana took it all with grace, despite her shyness.

Only I was frozen to my seat. I knew I should stand up, and add my congratulations to the throng, but I could not.

For a moment I did not hear Kitty's voice: she was standing beside me and had clearly been speaking for some time.

"Mary! What is the matter? You look so shocked. Did you not know, had you not seen that there was an understanding between Georgiana and the colonel?"

"No! No, I did not see it. They – they were very discreet, were they not?"

Kitty laughed. "Oh yes, they were discreet, but anyone who had eyes in their head could have seen what a preference they had for one another."

BECOMING MARY • 237

"As relatives only, I thought. Just as cousins!" Then I did remember certain meaningful looks that had passed between them, and the thought I had had only the other day that perhaps Fitzwilliam might be deceiving Georgiana as well as Elizabeth. Now I hardly knew what to think.

"You are so innocent, Mary! You cannot tell the difference between cousinly love and romantic love."

"No – no, I suppose I cannot. But – but why was it so secret?"

"Oh as to that," Kitty said knowingly, "Lizzy was worried that Darcy might not approve."

"*Lizzy* was worried?"

"Oh yes! She was always saying to the colonel that he should wait, not declare himself, not rush Georgie. Of course she was quite mistaken – Georgiana has been in love with him for such a long time, and so I would have told Lizzy if she had asked me. But she was always saying, wait, wait till Mr Darcy is in the right humour, wait till he is not so engaged, wait till you have got your furlough. I cannot imagine why she was so worried, you can see that Mr Darcy is very happy about it, and Colonel Fitzwilliam need not have been so anxious."

I did not know what to think. Kitty's story threw the events of the past weeks into a completely different light. According to what she was saying, Lizzy and Colonel Fitzwilliam were not trying to hide their own affair at all! All the conspiring I had witnessed, all Lizzy's injunctions to the Colonel to wait, their fear of Mr Darcy: it was not to conceal a shameful secret, but to promote and protect the romance between Colonel Fitzwilliam and Georgiana! I dropped my head on my hand. My brain was like mud.

"I suppose," I said haltingly, a glimmer of light appearing in the dim murk of my mind, "I suppose that Lizzy must often have had to reassure the colonel, must have had many private conferences with him to keep his spirits up?"

"I think she did," said Kitty. "I know he was often quite despondent, but you know what Lizzy is like, she is very encouraging, and she would not let him give up. Georgiana told me all about it this morning."

Of course, of course! It all made sense. Lizzy had been exhorting Colonel Fitzwilliam to remain steadfast, to keep hoping. Everything I had overheard was explained and justified by this version of events. How could I have thought otherwise? I must have been completely mad! I had been in the grip of an obsession, of a fabricated story born out of the dark sordidness of my own imagination, with no basis in reality whatsoever. If only I had stopped and considered, stopped for even one moment, surely I would have realised that my misgivings could not possibly be founded on truth.

And based on these hare-brained suspicions, I had poisoned the mind of Mr Darcy against his wife – my own sister, and his cousin with my dreadful anonymous letter.

I stood up abruptly.

"I am very tired, Kitty. I think I will go to bed early tonight. I will just creep quietly away, do not say anything or make a fuss, I do not wish to distract from the attention to Georgiana and the colonel."

Kitty looked at me strangely but said nothing. I left the room as quietly as I could.

◆

Oh god, oh god, what had I done? Even if all was now understood between Darcy and Elizabeth, it might be that they would never trust each other again. There was no doubt that Darcy had been influenced by my note, that he had suspected some secret on her part, and Elizabeth now knew that Darcy's trust *could* be shaken. She would be hurt and insulted that he could ever doubt her so. Something had crept into their marriage that had no right to be there like a worm in an apple: it was my own evil, unkind, suspicious mind. I had poisoned them, and I would live with the regret for the rest of my life. I was utterly undone. I must leave Pemberley and leave at once. I could not face anyone ever again. I would be disgraced in my family, and if there was any justice, I would be cast off and spurned for ever.

I threw myself onto my bed and lay staring at the ceiling. I was the lowest creature on the earth, I was not worthy to live, and if I had been carried off by a seizure or a long, lingering and agonising illness, it would be no more than I deserved. I was not fit for human company, and I must take myself away and never more be among anyone who had ever known me.

I heard voices outside my room and froze in silence. Faint lights swept under my door and disappeared: it was people going to their bedrooms, saying goodnight, talking quietly. Briefly, I distinguished my mother's voice, then Kitty's. I could imagine their scathing denunciatory comments when they heard what I had done. It was not to be borne! Yet I knew I deserved every word of censure that had ever been directed at me. I could not face them; I could not face any of them. And they must never see me again.

I think I slept, fully dressed on top of my bed, for I became aware that there was a pale, grey light in the sky. It was just dawn, perhaps five of the clock. I sat up and rubbed my eyes. The servants would be stirring soon. I had no time to waste. I splashed my face with the water from my basin, and looked at myself in the glass. My eyes were hollow with lack of sleep, my hair was hideously dishevelled and I was pale as I had ever been. I was still wearing my evening gown: that would not do, so I changed quickly into one of my older frocks that would be suitable for walking. I made a bundle inside a shawl of a few necessary items and clothes, tidied my hair as best I could and slowly unlocked my door.

All was quiet in the house. I went to the servant's stair, ran swiftly down and made my way to the side entrance. I heard nothing and saw nobody, even as I ran through the gardens. Once again I cursed the enormous grounds of Pemberley, and this made me remember when I had driven round the grounds with Lizzy and Kitty and had fallen out with them, walked back and met Mr Speedwell. I thought about what a good friend he had been to me and how he would despise me now.

When I finally reached the public road, I was already weary, with aching feet and a blister forming on my left heel. I did not know where to go; it did not matter, but I had to go somewhere, and I had to find a way to support myself. I had very little money in my purse, enough for two or three days lodging perhaps. I barely cared what happened to me, I wished I could die in a ditch and never be heard of again. But that could not be; even in my distracted state I knew that I had to find a way to live.

I took the northward direction, with a vague idea of getting to a place as far away from Hertfordshire as possible, and was greatly relieved when a cart came trundling slowly up the road, driven by a stolid-looking man in working clothes, with a number of barrels in the back of the cart. He stared at me, more with idle curiosity than insolence, and I took my courage in my hands and asked him if I might have a ride.

"I can pay you something," I added.

He shrugged and pulled up so that I could scramble aboard.

"How far are you going?" I asked.

"Just to B__. Delivering beer."

B__? This was providential. Of all the places, B__ offered work – and anonymity. There was the new mill there, shops, schools: surely one of them would have employment for me. And best of all, I knew the Heely family, and Mrs Heely might be able to guide me until I established myself.

The pony's pace was slow, and we were overtaken by a number of swifter carts and coaches. Every time one of them approached us, I became rigid with fear that I was being followed. I tried to think

when I would be missed. I had left no note, no-one had seen me
leave.

I wondered whether anyone would miss me at all. Did my
presence make any difference to anyone? It was a sobering thought: I
was not necessary to anyone's well-being, to anyone's comfort, to
anyone's amusement. Tears lodged in my throat and I swallowed
fiercely. I would not succumb to self-pity. This was nothing more
than I deserved, and I would face my future alone.

After perhaps two hours, we came over the brow of the hill which
gave us a view of B__. There were people walking towards the town,
carrying bundles, leading horses and cows, one woman with a
chicken tucked under her arm. I looked about me, hoping I would
recognise the street where the Heelys lived. I did not see it, but when
we pulled up at the inn, I realised it was the same inn where I had
had lunch with Mr Speedwell and I thought I could remember how to
find the Heelys from here. I gave some coins to the carter; he barely
looked at them but nodded his thanks, and I stepped down quickly
and walked confidently towards the Heelys'.

I was proud of myself when I found the house straight away: it
was as neat and poor-looking as ever, and I knocked anxiously. Mrs
Heely herself came to the door and was astonished at the sight of me.

"Miss Mary! What brings you here? You're not expected!"
Despite her words, her manner was friendly and she stood aside for
me to enter. Meg was there, and little Samuel, hiding behind their
mother's skirts until they saw who it was. Meg came forward to
throw her arms around me and for a moment I clung to her, then, to
my shame, burst into tears.

Mrs Heely looked at me shrewdly. "Now then, lass, come and sit
down here, I'm just lighting a fire. For all it's summer, it's always
cold in here. I'll boil up a kettle and we'll have a drink and then we'll
see."

"I am sorry to intrude, Mrs Heely, but – but I have left home, and
must find work, and I did not know where to go, and the carter was
coming here, so I came. I am sorry, I will not be a burden to you, but
I hoped you could direct me and tell me what to do."

She pulled up the stool for me and I buried my head in her skirt,
weeping uncontrollably, while she patted me and murmured
soothing words. When I had somewhat recovered and looked up,
Meg and Samuel had gone and we were alone.

"I've sent them on an errand so we can have a talk. Now, what
can have happened to make you up and leave all your folks? You're
not carrying, are you?"

"Carrying?"

She laughed. "Carrying a baby, you daft girl. That's the only reason I know for a girl to run away."

"A baby? No, no! Nothing of that nature."

"What is it? Broken heart? That music master you're so keen on?"

"The music master? No, it is not that, not really, but - how – how could you know? I have never mentioned him, never given a hint -"

"That's what you think. Them's who have ears to hear -"

I should have realised. Just because *my* eyes were blind and *my* ears made of cloth, it did not follow that everyone else was as dull as I.

"That is not why I have left, though I am – it is – I misunderstood – I thought – well, he does not care for me, and that is that. It has been a lesson to me, which I hope I will profit from in the future. But there is another matter, and I have done very wrong. I can never face my family again, and when they realise what I have done, *they* will never want to see me again either."

"Goodness me, child, what are you talking about? If I know you, you're making something out of nothing, and it's nowhere near as bad as you think."

I shook my head. "I know I am prone to exaggerate, but if you knew what I had done this time, you would agree with me."

There was a moment's silence.

"Well? Are you going to tell me?"

"I cannot. It is too dreadful, and it does not concern only me." I glanced up at her face to see her frowning thoughtfully, and I said quickly, "It is not that I do not trust you, Mrs Heely, for I do know that I can trust you of all people. But I must not speak of it ever again. It is best for everyone concerned if it is forgotten. I wish to make a new life with new people, and to put the past behind me. My family will not miss me, and – I am sure I will make new friends eventually."

"Very well, if that's the way you want it. And of course I'll help you, though I'm not sure what work you're fit to do. You've never worked in your life, I don't know how you'd manage, but we'll think of something, don't you worry."

I squeezed her hand. "Thank you, Mrs Heely, you are so much kinder to me than I deserve."

"That's enough of that. You and I have been getting on well, and my Meg has got fond of you. And I don't turn away a lass in trouble, whatever grand house she comes from. Now, you'd better stop here for a few days while we look about us."

"Here? Really? Do you have room for me? I do have some money, I can pay my way, I would not be a burden to you, I will help you do whatever you need me to do, only – only I think I should not be seen in case someone recognises me or comes looking for me."

"Don't fuss over the details. You can sleep in the bed with Meg, and we'll make Sam and Joe as comfortable as anything on a mat on the floor. As to your money, well, I'd like to say keep it for yourself, but I can't afford to feed you and that's that. And as to helping me with the chores, of course you will, and you can make a start now and finish sweeping this floor."

I was so grateful to her that I embraced her, and set to immediately to sweep the floor. I did not do a very good job, because when Meg and Samuel returned, Meg picked up the brush and went over it again.

◆

I enjoyed the rest of the day with the Heelys though it felt somewhat as though we were playing a game. I was a visitor, and could never truly be part of their world; it was more like being on holiday, despite having to do more domestic work than I had ever been called on to do in my life. Joseph came home from school and he and the others immediately went out to play. Mrs Heely and I began to prepare food for an evening meal. There was not very much to do, as there was no meat, just some bread, some dripping to melt, and some carrots to wash and chop.

After supper, as it was dark, and we were all tired, Mrs Heely suggested that we went to bed. The little truckle bed that I was to share with Meg was little indeed, even for two such small people as we were, but we pressed in together, and at least it was soon very warm. Mrs Heely left a tallow candle for us, and Meg and I whispered together as its light gradually faded. The boys fell asleep quickly despite being on the floor, and Meg fell asleep in my arms. Sleep did not come easily to me, however; my mind was too full.

I could not help but wonder what was going on at Pemberley. Surely they would have missed me by now! I began to feel a little guilty and anxious: perhaps I should have left a note, so at least they would know that I was safe. They might be scouring the grounds by this time, there might be search parties ranging over the county, the parish constables alerted to try and find me. My mother would be in hysterics, and it would fall on Jane to comfort and manage her. Poor Jane! She had enough to do without having to look after Mama as well. Kitty would just be irritated. If Elizabeth and Darcy had come to the obvious conclusion about the anonymous letter, they would know why I had left, and I thought they might be secretly, vengefully pleased that I was gone, that I was to suffer, alone and friendless.

But then an image of Lizzy came to my mind, her concern for me, her thoughtfulness in engaging Signor Moretti to teach me, her humour and kindness, and I wondered how I could suspect her of such base and petty wishes towards me. Darcy too had shown nothing but kindness. Remorse overwhelmed me. How could I have done what I did, sent that dreadful letter, harboured such suspicions?

Meg twitched and moaned slightly, and I held my breath lest she wake, but she settled quickly back to sleep. I closed my eyes, hoping that I too might get some rest, but there was still too much to think about. Of course my family would not let me slide into oblivion: even Lydia, whose wanton behaviour in running off with Wickham was known to everyone, had been sought out and taken back into the family she had wronged so badly. Of course they would be worried about me. How could I have been so thoughtless as to run away without a word?

Oh god, what had I done? I had made things worse, not better. It struck me with blinding force that I must return the very next day, to confess to Elizabeth and Darcy and beg their forgiveness. Whatever happened, I would be returning to my old life at Longbourn with Mama and Papa and Kitty, but at least I could clear up any confusion that might have arisen between Lizzy and Darcy first.

Facing my family was one ordeal, facing Signor Moretti quite another. I wished I could stop myself thinking about him: even though I knew that he had no feelings for me, it did not enable me to put him out of my mind. I knew the sensible thing would be to forget all that had passed between us, and think of him merely as an acquaintance, a friend of the Darcys, my music teacher, but my feelings could not be controlled. I could not help but remember how we had kissed, how he had held me in his arms, and weakling that I was, I could not stop myself longing for him to do it again. The realisation that it would never be made a pain in my chest, and I supposed that this was what it meant to have a broken heart. I felt like a silly girl from a melodrama or a romance: I had always despised such characters, thought them ridiculous and exaggerated, but now I was finding that I too could be just as silly, just as prey to extremes of feeling.

Tears coursed down my face. I would have liked to sob out loud, but I had to control myself so as not to disturb the children. Meg turned, in her sleep perhaps, and put her arms around my neck. This made me cry even harder, and at last she woke up, and stroked my hair, soothing me as though she were much older and wiser than I. So we drifted off to sleep.

It was not a comfortable night, and I felt stiff and tired and sad in the morning, but I would not dream of complaining, and tried to be as helpful as I could, stirring the porridge while helping Samuel to dress, and hearing Joseph recite a psalm. Joseph soon ran off to school, and Meg and I helped Mrs Heely to start to clean the house. Despite the early hour there was a knock at the door. Mrs Heely looked intently at me.

"Expecting anyone, Mary?"

"No!"

"I think you are. Get the door, Meg."

"Who is it? Did you send for someone?"

The door opened, and it was a great relief to see the familiar and comforting figure of Mr Speedwell.

"Mary! I came as soon as I heard from Mrs Heely that you were here! What has happened? What has led you to run away? I thought I'd dealt with that cad Wickham, but if he's been bothering you again -"

"No, it isn't that," I said, "it is something quite different." I was conscious that my appearance was wild: my hair was still loose, my gown was grimy and creased, and I had no shoes on.

"Can you tell me?"

Mrs Heely took the children and went out, leaving me alone with Mr Speedwell.

"I would *like* to tell you, but -" I hesitated, "I do not want to lose your friendship."

He came towards me and took my hands. "Mary! I hope you know me better than that. Is it something very dreadful? Have you stolen the silver epergne from Pemberley and sold it to a tinker?"

"You are teasing me again! It is no laughing matter, it truly is dreadful, and I will deserve to be despised by everyone for it."

He frowned. "This sounds very serious!" He led me to the bench and we sat down.

"It is serious! It is the worst thing I have ever done, and I should not have run away, because I have made it all worse and caused everyone worry."

"I may set your mind at ease on that count, for when I received Mrs Heely's message, I sent word to Mrs Darcy at once."

I was a little comforted. "Will you escort me back to Pemberley? I have to explain, even though it will mean my banishment for ever. This deed of mine – I must go back and I must tell everything to my sister and Mr Darcy before it is too late. I may have done irreparable harm by my stupidity and spite!"

Mr Speedwell squeezed my hands. "Mary, Mary! Such drama! I am sure you cannot have done so."

"Oh, Arthur, you have been such a good friend to me, but you do not know me, and when I tell you what I have done, you will no longer *want* to know me. I do not want to know myself; I do not want to *be* myself. When you discover what I have done - when everyone knows, I will be cast out, and rightly so, and so you must not say anything until you know the whole painful truth."

He pressed my hand hard. "Mary, I cannot believe that you have done anything that would warrant you being cast out."

"I have! I have!" I cried. "Oh, they will behave properly, I have no doubt, and I will not be thrown into the street to fend for myself. Merely my life will return to how it was before I ever came to Pemberley, but in their hearts they will not forgive me, and they should not. I have done such wrong."

"Will you at least tell me what has happened, what this dreadful deed is?"

"I – will tell you. Perhaps I could tell you as we drive back to Pemberley. At least, have you a gig here or some other sort of conveyance?"

"Of course, I brought Deborah and the trap and I should be glad to escort you. Shall we set off at once?"

He left me to finish dressing, and went to fetch the trap from the inn. Mrs Heely came in as I was fastening my shoe.

"There now, lass, you know you're doing the right thing going back, don't you?"

"Yes, I must. Thank you for your hospitality, Mrs Heely, you have been a true friend to me."

She hugged me, dabbed my face with a handkerchief and murmured there, there as I cried again and hugged the children goodbye.

"We'll be happy to see you again any time, Miss Mary. You've come on a treat since I've known you, and I hope you'll keep up your visits."

"Oh I shall, I shall! That is – if my sister does not immediately send me home to Hertfordshire in disgrace."

"We'll see, but that don't sound like the Mrs Darcy I've heard tell on."

Part Thirteen: The Confession

◆

Mr Speedwell drove at a sedate pace. I felt both impatience and a dread of arrival, willing him to speed up, and at the same time wanting him to turn around and drive back to B___. It was another glorious morning. Never had the Derbyshire scene looked more beautiful to me, when I knew I was seeing it all for the last time, that I would soon be leaving these spectacular hills and valleys and moors, never to return.

Mr Speedwell turned to look at me and smiled sympathetically.

"Well, Mary?"

I looked into his funny, friendly, ugly, kindly face, and thought that I might never look on it again, at least not as a friend. "You hear confession, don't you?" I said.

"I do, but this is not confession. If, however, you are wondering if I can keep a secret, of course I can. Many sisterly secrets have been poured into my ears, and we are as good as brother and sister now, aren't we? So I think I can be trusted."

I took a deep breath and spoke in a rush. "I have destroyed the marriage of Mr and Mrs Darcy!"

"Mary, no! How can you say so? If ever there were two people who loved each other and will love each for ever, it is your sister Elizabeth and Mr Darcy. They could not be more devoted."

"I know, I know! They were! But you have observed, I know you have, the cold looks he has given her. *I* have done this; *I* have poisoned his ears with lies. At least, I did not know they were lies, but I have filled his head with slander and untruth about Lizzy, and now he does not love her any longer, and their lives are ruined and it is all my doing."

"But Mary," Mr Speedwell said, "if you were genuinely mistaken about these lies, then of course that will be understood. If someone has misled you, it is not your fault."

"No! No! I was not misled! Nobody lied to me; it was my own imagination, my own black and distrustful mind that invented it all. And now my poor sister will never be happy again! And she is expecting another child!"

"Oh dear, this is certainly all very terrible. But I know Darcy, have known him for years, and a fairer-minded man does not exist. He will not blame you for your errors, and he will certainly be reconciled with Mrs Darcy, if indeed they *have* become seriously estranged, which I beg leave to doubt."

I shook my head. "I know you are trying to comfort me, but it has gone too far for forgiveness – and anyway, I do not wish to be forgiven. I do not deserve to be. I only hope they can find a way to recover, so that the damage I have done can be repaired."

He took my hand and held it. "Well, Mary, I think you may be proved wrong, and you will find that these misunderstandings can be cleared up by such rational people as your sister and brother. Meanwhile, if they do cast you off and you need shelter, I have been told that old Mr Jackson's grandson who works the bellows on a Sunday no longer wishes to do so, so there is a vacancy there for a strong young person such as yourself."

I smiled at his attempt to cheer me up. "You are such a good friend, Arthur," I said. "I envy your sisters that they had such a brother as you. If you never see me again after this day, please accept this avowal of my gratitude and affection to you."

"Never see you again? What nonsense! I intend to marry you one day."

I gasped in shock. "What? No! You do not mean it." I was about to add – I am in love with someone else, but the words caught in my throat.

He burst out laughing. "Oh lord, that's not what I was supposed to say! What I meant was, when you get married, I intend to be the parson who conducts the service. Good god, Mary, I hope you didn't think – well, I'm extremely fond of you and all that, but -"

I laughed at his discomfiture, and for a few minutes I felt lightened and distracted from what was to come.

"I do not wish to marry you either, Arthur. I – I am extremely fond of you too, but I think – not in the marrying way, as far as I understand it."

"No, no, of course not! We're the best of good friends, you're like a little sister to me! And you know, I'm not the marrying kind and that's all there is to it. Everyone knows that about me. But I mean it, if you're in trouble, you can count on me, I won't let you fall."

I leaned against his shoulder. "You are so kind! If – if I were in love with you, and if you were the marrying kind, then – well, anyhow, I'm not and you're not so that's that. But thank you again and again for your kindness. I won't tell you any more about what I've done, because you know the nature of it. I will never forget you."

"Silly girl, you won't have the opportunity."

We were turning into the gates of Pemberley, and I was overcome with a wave of feelings: fear, dread, shame, sadness, regret, self-loathing – all jostled within me. Conversation was at an end, and I watched the horse's ears flick away the flies, and waited for the view of the house as we rounded the corner towards the stables. I would have liked to change my dress before facing Mr Darcy, but the danger of meeting someone, or even of having to explain the situation to my maid, dissuaded me. A groom was sent to ask Mr Darcy to meet me at the library. Mr Speedwell escorted me there.

"Please leave me now," I said. "Thank you for everything, but I would like to face Mr Darcy alone."

He bent over my hand. "As you wish. Only don't go and condemn yourself to perdition. Let Darcy be the judge."

The library was empty when I went in. The sun was coming in through the casement, lighting up the dust in the air and causing the oak shelves to gleam. Sadness overtook me as I thought that I would never come here again, and even while I had been at Pemberley I had not used the library as much as I had intended. Well, there would be plenty of time now for me to make good the deficits in my education, and I intended to immerse myself in scholarship from now on. It would be preferable to my mother's reproaches, and my father's contempt.

I wandered round the shelves, trailing my hand along the leather spines of books warmed by the sun, enjoying the texture of the leather binding under my fingers, and the slight indentation where the titles were embossed in gold. The sound of the door opening made me jump, and I turned to see Mr Darcy come in.

"I am so glad to see you safe, Mary. You should not have run away and worried us all like that."

"I am sorry," I stammered, "I was not thinking, I acted on the impulse of the moment, and I did not realise until last night that of course you would have been worried."

"Did something happen to make you so unhappy?" Mr Darcy asked, his face very serious.

"No, no, it is not that. Nothing has happened. But I must speak with you on a matter of great importance."

"Shall we sit down?" said Mr Darcy.

Acting on a barely thought impulse, I said breathlessly, "I would like Signor Moretti to join us."

"Of course. I will ring, and perhaps some refreshments could be brought. You look a little – travel-weary."

A servant came, and a few moments later returned with a tray of green tea and bread and butter. He had just left the library when Signor Moretti came in. He started when he saw me, probably because I looked like a ghoul, and also because of the horrid nature of our last exchange playing duets.

"Pray be seated, Moretti," said Mr Darcy. "Mary has something she wishes to say, and she begged your presence here."

The three of us sat around a small table, Mr Darcy opposite Signor Moretti and me.

"I have to confess something," I said. "I have done very wrong, and I think I may have caused - I do not know what I may have caused, but if I have, I want to put it right."

I took a breath. I saw Mr Darcy's eyes narrow suddenly. He knows, I thought.

I blurted out, "It was I who wrote that anonymous letter to you, Mr Darcy!"

He stared at me intently. "You, Mary?" he said. I nodded, quailing inwardly and thinking that if ever there was a time for the earth to open and swallow me up, this was it.

"Let me hear this story from its beginning, Mary. How came you to do such a thing?"

I shook my head. I could feel the betraying tears forming as a lump in my throat but I was determined to tell my story, however badly and haltingly. "It was a dreadful, dreadful error. I was utterly mistaken, but I did not know what to think." I reddened. "I am so sorry, but when I saw Lizzy with Colonel Fitzwilliam, I thought - I thought -"

I watched his countenance as he digested what I was saying and tried to make sense of it. "You thought, in fact, that Elizabeth was - romantically involved with Colonel Fitzwilliam?"

I nodded and said desperately, "I did not understand, I saw her so - so secret with him, and so warm, and I knew nothing of his attachment to Georgiana! I did not know what to think!"

Mr Darcy looked steadily at me. "You thought Elizabeth would betray me."

"I - I did. I was stupid, I was suspicious, I could not imagine any other interpretation of what I saw, what I heard! I thought you should be suspicious also. I – I did not want you to be deceived."

"Mary, why did not you come to me and tell me directly? Or go to Elizabeth and ask her? She is no dissembler, you know her better than that."

"Of course I know that! But I could not speak of it, it was so very dreadful, I did not know what words I could use, how to describe it."

"I think in your heart of hearts you knew that you were in error, that your suspicions could not possibly be well-founded, and that is why you would not talk to us. If you had, you must have realised at once that you were completely mistaken."

"I do not understand what came over me!"

"It was the height of foolishness, Mary, it was reprehensible. Such sentiments are quite beneath you."

For a moment or two I could not speak. His reprimand was no more than I deserved, but it weighed very heavily upon me.

"Mr Darcy," I said at last, "I do beg your forgiveness though I quite understand if you feel you never wish to speak to me again. I have misled you, accused Elizabeth, I have destroyed your marriage!"

Mr Darcy spoke sternly. "Mary, it is as much of a sin to magnify this, as it would be to understate the matter. Neither you, nor anyone else, has the power to destroy my marriage." He stood up. "I admonish you not to speak of this to anyone. Your absence was explained to the household as a putrid cold which kept you to your room, and, out of consideration for Lydia and her twins, we said that you decided to remain in solitude, and not pass on the infection. Only the three of us in this room, Mr Speedwell and Mrs Reynolds know what has happened, and none of us will speak of it. But I believe you must not remain at Pemberley any longer."

Even though this was the outcome I had expected, it was a dreadful blow.

"But – where shall I go?" I asked. "There is nobody at Longbourn."

"Your parents are to return there tomorrow. Your mother has received a letter from your Aunt Philips, saying that she is in great distress and begging your mother to return as soon as may be, so of course your father is to accompany her on the journey."

And I was to be sent back with them in disgrace! Well, no doubt it was fitting and I deserved no less.

"I will leave you now, Mary. I am grateful to you for your honesty."

He left the room. Signor Moretti stood up. I could not look at him. I felt nothing, just a great emptiness. I could not imagine what he must have thought during my confession, and I did not want to know. We stayed as we were for some moments, Signor Moretti hovering above me, while I stared at the table in front of me. He made a sound as though to speak. Quickly I spoke first:

"Do not stay with me. There is nothing to say between us now. You have seen everything, you have heard everything." He did not speak, and I could not bear the silence. "Thank you for coming to hear me, Signor Moretti. I - I am glad you heard what I said to Mr Darcy, now there is nothing you do not know about me. Since we are about to part for ever, it does not really matter. There is nothing to hide, you know the worst."

Again he moved as if to speak, but I did not want to hear, and I curtsied and ran out of the room.

♦

My mother was not pleased to be taking me back to Longbourn.

"For I must say, Mary, I did hope that you might look about you for a husband while you were at Pemberley. It was such an opportunity for you, and I am disappointed that I must take you back to Longbourn still a spinster. That rector of Kympton would have done very nicely for you, but you did not make a push to attract him, and Lizzy said he showed great friendliness towards you. But you never do make the most of your chances, and I quite despair of you. Though I will admit you are looking better than before. I am glad you have let Kitty dress you, for she always had a way with a needle, and you are certainly not so plain as I have been used to think you. So perhaps there will be someone in Longbourn who we have not considered before. I did wonder about young Ashton, but then he is not at all bookish and would no doubt think you too much of a blue-stocking for his taste. I am sorry you did not ride more while you had the chance at Pemberley."

"Mama, I wish you will not trouble yourself on my behalf. I do not intend to be married."

"What nonsense! Every woman must intend to be married! What, would you end your days a spinster like Miss Hastings with her poultices and her potions?"

"The wearing of poultices is not an inevitable result of spinsterhood," my father said.

"If it isn't the poultices, it will be the vapours or consumption or some such thing, you can be sure of that."

"I believe there are also many married women who suffer from the vapours, are there not?" Papa said.

"I am quite content to stay with you and Papa and be of service to you both. You will need me as you get older."

"It is unwise to remind your mother that she will one day get older."

Mama ignored him. "It is my dearest wish that my daughters should all be married with households of their own. What if Mary were to stay with us unmarried? What would become of her when you die, Mr Bennet, and those Collinses come and take over the house? They will turn her out onto the street. She *must* marry and so must Kitty. I am sure Kitty will find someone, she is so practical. But you will not make the effort, Mary! Do you not understand what a dreadful fate awaits you? To be mocked and derided by the neighbourhood? And then what of me? What will people think of me with a great grown-up daughter still on my hands? They shall think I am a poor kind of mother if I cannot get my daughter married."

"But Mama! Think of Jane and Lizzy! They are both well married, everyone must envy and admire you for that!"

"Oh, you do not understand! To have Lady Lucas crowing over me now that Maria is engaged, even if it is to that good-for-nothing boy of the Summertons with his ginger hair and his limp. And I cannot be forever taking you to parties and assemblies, I am past the age for gallivanting, and my joints plague me so. But nobody cares for my sufferings."

"I do, Mama! And that is why I want to stay with you, so that I might take care of you."

"I'm not in my grave yet, child! I did not say I want to sit at home stitching night after night like some ancient crone, but I cannot be expected to wear myself to shreds if you will not make the effort!"

I sank back against the cushions. There was nothing I could say. We drove in silence for some time: I looked covertly at my mother's face, and there was an expression of dissatisfaction on it. After perhaps half an hour, my father surprised me by addressing me directly.

"You are not so insipid as you were before, Mary. The air of Pemberley has agreed with you."

I was taken aback. My father had never said a kind or complimentary thing to me in my life before that I could remember.

He continued: "But then, it is the first time you have ever been away from Longbourn, and no doubt it has done you good to see something of the world. I gather you have been visiting the poor or some such?"

"I did go to the manufacturing town at B___ and Mr Speedwell introduced me to a family there."

My mother's attention was caught. "What, they let you go visiting in one of those nasty hovels? That was not very responsible of Darcy. You might have picked up all manner of illnesses from such people!"

"Truly they were not – dirty people, Mama. Mrs Heely keeps a very clean house. She is a most sensible, practical woman. And I am sure Mr Speedwell would not have taken me if there was any danger."

"Well, I do not trust these Derbyshire paupers. I hope you did not take any refreshment from them, Mary. That would be quite fatal, you know."

"Really, Mama, I think I may be trusted to use my judgement in such a case. After all, you yourself have taken me into poor homes before. I thought you would be pleased to know that I was doing good."

"Do not be contradicting me, Mary. I know better than you on these matters. A chit of a girl like you, indeed, to be thinking you are doing good! You do not know what you are talking about, and anyway, these people never show any gratitude, it is a waste of time and money trying to help them. Half the time they fritter it all away or spend money on drink while their children go hungry."

"Mrs Heely was not like that, Mama. Truly, she was a good woman who cared greatly for her children and was trying to get them educated."

"Trying to better herself no doubt!" my mother said contemptuously. "I wish you would not meddle in matters you do not understand, Mary."

"But I did understand, Mama. We became in some sort, friends. I came to know her quite well, and I respected her. She was very kind to me."

"Kind to you? What nonsense! As if a person of that order can be kind to a person of your order, the sister of Mr Darcy no less, as she knew very well. I suppose she was out for what she could get."

I felt tears pricking in my eyes. "No indeed, Mama, she did not want charity. She asked me to help her little girl learn her letters."

"And what good would that do? A child who will spend her life working in a manufactory and then doubtless marry and produce hundreds of children she cannot feed? What good are letters in that situation?"

"I – I do not know," I said.

The conversation was at an end, but my father, who I had thought asleep, murmured, "*Much* less insipid, Mary!"

No more was said: my father resolutely shut his eyes and my mother genuinely fell asleep and began to snore. I was left with my thoughts and reflections and they were not happy. I had never felt so low. Everything was ruined, and it was all my own doing. I was disgraced with Lizzy and Mr Darcy, and Signor Moretti despised me, now that he knew my true character. There was no reason for me to be on this earth. I closed my eyes and gave myself up to despair.

◆

It was very odd to be back at Longbourn. All the rooms seemed smaller, grey and drab, ill-lit and dusty. It was familiar and strange at once, as though seen in a dream.

I went to my room: once it had been a refuge, a place to hide when the racket of family life became too much. The furniture was still draped in holland covers and I walked around touching each object, trying to remember my old life. I felt as though I were a ghost.

Was I the same person who had gone to Pemberley all those months ago? I looked the same – more or less – even though everyone said I had changed for the better. To me I was no different: a person of no account, lacking charm or interest. I stared at my face in the mirror. My face returned the gaze, questioning.

Where did I belong? This bedroom, this house, this village: was this my home? It did not feel as it had before I went to Pemberley. But Pemberley was not my home either, even though I had never felt more alive than when I was there. I felt a pang of longing as I thought of it, as I remembered the creeping warmth that had started to melt me during my time there. I had had a chance to be happy, and I had destroyed it. I could never go back, even if I wanted to.

A knock on my door broke into my reverie. It was Hill, looking reassuringly the same.

"Miss Mary, there's tea in the drawing room now. I'll unpack and get your room ready for you."

I thanked her and went downstairs, back into the routine of life at Longbourn that was so familiar to me, and yet felt so empty.

Over the days that followed, my spirits were extremely low, as I went over and over the events of the past months in my mind. Sometimes, alone in my room, I wept with frustration and regret. My parents returned to their former habits and lives just as they had before, my father in his library, my mother bustling about the house appearing to be extremely busy yet in reality the servants doing everything. She took me with her on a visit to Aunt Philips, which I did not enjoy. Aunt Philips was still in black, and she burst into tears immediately on seeing my mother and me. She even flung her arms around me and sobbed on my neck.

"Oh, my poor niece! How you must be feeling this! Your dear uncle taken away from us so soon."

I did not know how to reply as I was not feeling anything. I hardly knew my Uncle Philips: he had never taken an interest in any of his Longbourn nieces; nor did he take much part in my aunt's social gatherings as he did not play at cards or have any taste for idle conversation of the type that prevailed on these occasions.

"I am so sorry, Aunt," I said awkwardly.

Eventually her tears subsided and we sat down to tea.

"So you have been to Pemberley, Mary!" my aunt said brightly. "You must tell me all about it! How did you go on in such grand company? Did you make any conquests?"

My mother spoke before I could answer.

"She? Oh no, sister, with every opportunity before her she comes home a spinster still. I despair, truly I do."

"She blushes!" crowed my Aunt Philips. "There is something she has not told you, the minx!"

"Indeed, there is not!" I said. "I had – I had a most pleasant visit at Pemberley, every consideration was made for my comfort, but I was not seeking a husband."

My mother rolled her eyes. "You see what I have to endure? Do they think eligible men will just fall into their laps? There she is, at one of the finest houses in the land and I know for a fact that the rector of the parish was showing a great interest in her, taking her about to visit the poor, and you don't have to tell me about what *that* means, but no, she comes home unmarried still."

"Visiting the poor?" said my aunt. "Well! We do indeed know what that means. I have seen many a marriage built on such a ruse."

"It was no ruse!" I protested faintly. "I was interested in the family, and I wanted – I wanted to do good. And he - he is not the marrying kind."

"Oh, pooh! What do you know about who is the marrying kind? Of course he is the marrying kind and if you had only made a push to attract him you would have found it to be so."

"But he told me so himself, Mama!" I was betrayed into saying.

"He *told you so himself?* Good god, Mary, what have you been doing? To be so unbecomingly forward as to have such a conversation with a man? Have you no sense?"

"No decorum!" my aunt added.

I flushed. "Was it so very bad? I did not think so. We were friends, I think."

"Friends! As if a single man could ever be friends with a young woman!" My mother shook her head at me.

"And why you would want to be friends with such a man is beyond *my* comprehension," my aunt said, "when he was so violent towards our poor dear Wickham!"

"And all for a misunderstanding, or so Mr Darcy told me," my mother said. "But for my part I think there is some jealousy there. After all, that man had the living that should have been Wickham's, you know, and I would not be surprised if there had been words between them, because of course Wickham is not one to take his fate lying down, especially not with dear Lydia about to be delivered of her twins. Twins, dear sister, twins! Such lovely, healthy boys. Lydia was made to be a mother!"

The conversation turned to the story of the birth of the twins, which my mother described, in full detail. I had no part to play in this subject so was able to recover myself. At least my mother's vigilant gaze had not alighted on Signor Moretti. In that instance, I knew I would betray myself much more seriously than I had in our discussion of Mr Speedwell. I realised that I had entered into a reverie about Signor Moretti, and had to call myself severely to task. There was no point thinking about him, there could be nothing between us. I then continued to dwell on various memories, of his kindness, his interest and even his kiss, until a pain in my heart reminded me again that I must not allow myself to think so.

While I was in the depths of these struggles within myself, I realised that my mother and aunt had turned their attention to me once more.

"That settles it!" my mother was saying, "I have allowed Mary far too much freedom to indulge her ridiculous bluestocking tendencies. It is no wonder she does not know how to go on in society. She must learn!"

"It is not too late," said Aunt Philips.

"It is too late for Pemberley, however. And what opportunities she will have in Meryton I barely know. I suppose the Draycott boy might do, although his constitution is very weak."

"And pimples, sister! We cannot like a young man with pimples."

"Please do not make matches for me, Mama. I would rather not -"

"No! If it was left to you, you would sit in your room and read all day long, for no purpose whatever!"

My aunt trilled with laughter. "Or, no doubt, run off with the music master or some such!"

But this was too serious a subject for my mother to laugh at. Fortunately for me, the notion that I should have an interest in a music master was so remote, that neither woman paid me any attention at this point.

"We shall have to bring you out, Mary," said Aunt Philips. "It will give me something to occupy myself and take my mind off my troubles and the loss of my dear Mr Philips."

"Yes, indeed," Mama replied, "you must not lose all pleasure in life, Mr Philips would not have wanted it so. Perhaps a small card party at Longbourn would be permissible. And if there was to be dancing, you need not dance."

"And I could play for the dancing!" I said.

"Of course you could not!" my mother said. "This hiding behind the pianoforte cannot continue. We will hire musicians and you will dance. I know very well that you have been dancing while at Pemberley so no more stories about not being able to. I have told you time and time again, you will not meet a husband at the piano."

♦

The idea of a party to be held at Longbourn became my mother's main preoccupation. My father retired more and more to his library or his grounds, preparing for the autumn shooting, he said. I wished I could retire too, but there was no such escape for me. I received the full force of my mother's attention, something I had managed to avoid most of my life. It was not the attention that I might have allowed myself to wish for: there was no softness in it, no enjoyment for either of us, and everything about me met with my mother's disapproval. My hair was so fine that it could not hold any style that she tried; my figure was inadequate, scrawny and lacking in womanly attributes; my teeth it seemed were passable, and she did not quite despair of my skin, insisting that I maintain its whiteness by remaining incarcerated in the house all through the warm weather and applying a number of creams, potions and purées of fruit.

"To think that a daughter of mine should be so plain and lacking in vivacity!" she cried, two or three times a day.

The only relief came when she saw me in the dresses that Kitty had fashioned for me at Pemberley, when she pronounced that I might not utterly disgrace her after all, and that if we put a scarf of matching material round my head it might disguise the worst defects of my hair.

I had tried to protest about the party early in the proceedings, but I quickly realised that it was useless. My mother was determined, and I saw that it did provide a distraction for her and for aunt Philips which was a relief from their grieving, so I tried to submit with a good grace, but it was not easy. I would never be the daughter she wished me to be: I was too stupid, too plain, too awkward. I could neither cheer nor amuse her. She had no interest in music, only enough to be well aware how poor were my abilities, and she became irritated by my attempts to carry on the work I had done with Signor Moretti.

However, this was the one aspect of the party that I was desperate to claim for myself. I knew that I and other young ladies would be called upon to perform, and I was determined that this time I would not disgrace myself. Although I would never see Signor Moretti again, I wanted to play a piece that he would approve of, to show him, even if only in my imagination, that I had not been too conceited or too foolish to learn from him.

My practising infuriated my mother. She would call from the other room for me to stop, or at least play something with a tune and not all those tiresome scales. I explained that I was trying to improve, but her response to that was scathing: "You will never attract a husband while you play that dreadful stuff, Mary. If only you could sing! But you had better not try, last time I heard you I thought one of the horses had got into the house." I had not thought I was as bad as that, but after that I never sang if she was at home. Instead I concentrated on the Haydn sonata that Signor Moretti had recommended me to play instead of the Beethoven. I often felt sad as I played it, when I remembered our lessons, but I thought that perhaps if I persevered, the feelings would lessen over time, and at least I might have the satisfaction of playing something well.

I did wonder why my mother was so set on giving this party, as it caused her so much aggravation. The engagement of Maria Lucas was another source of pain: that Lady Lucas should have fired Maria off while Mrs Bennet still had two daughters unmarried was a disgrace.

"To think how that woman will triumph over me!" she cried at breakfast one day. "I have a good mind not to invite her to the party. It is so typical of her to poach the only half-way decent young man in Hertfordshire for her daughter. Well, I wish she may not regret her bargain! Old Mr Summerton is well-known for being the meanest man in the district! And the young man has gone quite the other way and spends money on whatever takes his fancy with no thought for the expense. I notice he bought a new pair for his curricle only a month ago. No doubt his father had cooked the old carriage horse in one of those nasty gristly stews he serves. If Maria does not end up in the poor-house, I shall be very much surprised. I suppose I shall have to invite the Summertons too, now that they are to be related to the Lucases. Oh, what a trial you are to me, Mary!"

"I am sorry, Mama, that you should go to such trouble for me. If you would rather not give a party -"

"After all the effort I've made? You ungrateful child! You have no sympathy at all, no consideration for my nerves. If only Jane was here, she understood my feelings; she would be such a comfort to me. And you are so ignorant, Mary, I have to think of everything."

"I am trying to learn, Mama. I am sorry."

"But you do not learn fast enough! Kitty could always assist me in all the arrangements, and my darling Lydia!"

My father had been ignoring the conversation as he read his letters, but now he looked up.

"You do not say how Lydia would be of use," he commented.

Even my mother could not miss the sarcasm in his tone.

"Oh, you have never appreciated Lydia! Such sweetness as she has, such vitality!"

"I fear you are right. Her silliness has blotted out her other qualities."

My mother refused to respond.

"But your wish is to be granted in some form," my father continued. "Your daughter Elizabeth has written to me, and she and Darcy will be passing through Hertfordshire on their way to Kent. They will bring Kitty home with them, and they will stay a night or two at the White Hart in Meryton."

My mother was thunderstruck, fortunately for me, as I knew my face must have showed my dismay and shame at the thought of seeing the Darcys again. "That man comes here?" she said. "Well, he will not soil himself by staying at Longbourn, I see. I suppose we are not good enough for them now."

I could not help defending Mr Darcy. "Mama, they would not wish to give you the trouble when they know you are preparing for the party."

"Do not spoil your mother's enjoyment, Mary, by suggesting that the Darcys have good intentions. What pleasure would there be in that for her?"

Mama's attention was now elsewhere. "Well, I hope they will stay for the party! That will show the Lucases a thing or two with their Summertons! To have Mr Darcy at the party will make them feel very shabby."

"There is a letter here for you, Mary, from your sister."

"From Elizabeth? To me?"

"Are you so surprised?" he asked me.

"I – I did not expect to hear from her. I do not know what she can have to say."

"Well, pass it to me, child!" said my mother. "Do not be so slow about everything! You are driving me into my grave with your lingering."

I hoped that Elizabeth would know that my mother was bound to read any letter that came into the house, and not write anything private in it. I was terribly afraid: if she should reveal either deliberately or casually anything of my dealings with Mr Darcy, or my running away, or even god forbid some mention of Signor Moretti, I did not know how I would command myself.

"Let me see," Mama said. "Her writing does not improve then. I can barely read this scrawl. Take it, Mary, and read it aloud."

I cleared the lump from my throat. The letter was innocuous enough. "'I hope this letter finds you quite recovered from your journey, my dear Mary. You will have heard from Papa that Darcy and I are to travel to London, and break our journey in Hertfordshire in time for your party. We will be staying at the White Hart, and we would like it very much if you were to take tea with us on Tuesday next, the day after your party. We will send a carriage for you at 3 o'clock. Your loving sister, Elizabeth.'"

"So, they invite you to tea do they. That is very condescending of them, I'm sure. A very kind attention after all their goodness to you at Pemberley. I do not know what you do to deserve it."

"No, nor do I," I said.

Part Fourteen: The Party

◆

We did not see the Darcys when they left Kitty with us. Kitty told us that Elizabeth was rather tired from the journey and that they had gone straight to the White Hart so that she could rest.

Kitty said, "Come and help me unpack, Mary."

I was surprised to be asked but went with her. She threw herself onto her bed, and made no effort to unpack at all.

"I think I may die of boredom now I am returned to Longbourn!" she said. "This house is so small and dull after Pemberley. Do you not find it so?"

"I did when I first returned but I am used to it now. And I have been busy. I did not realise how onerous it is to prepare for a party."

"Oh, this party to find you a husband! I suppose I will have to look about me also. Mr Carding will forget me if I am not in front of him. There must be tolerable men enough in the district for us both. I did see a handsome fellow on our journey when we stopped at Oxford, and he looked at me very much when we were sitting at the inn there, but we were not introduced so it came to nothing. He had nice curly hair, and a very fine figure. Apart from that the journey was dull as anything. Lizzy was not feeling quite well so Darcy had to attend to her the whole time and Signor Moretti had nothing to say for himself at all."

"Signor Moretti! He was with you?"

Kitty looked at me enquiringly. "Yes, the Darcys are taking him back to London. He is staying with them at the White Hart." A look of mischievous understanding came into her face: "I see! There *was* something between you! I knew it! Perhaps *that* is why he came to Meryton, so that he could pay his addresses to you!"

"No indeed, Kitty, there is nothing, was nothing."

"Don't lie, Mary, your face betrays you. Oh, I see it all now, all those hours spent together at the pianoforte! Well, well, you are such a dark horse. But Mama would never allow you to marry a music master."

"Marriage is not in question, Kitty, truly! I did – *like* Signor Moretti, he was very kind to me at Pemberley, and of course, I would be happy to see him again. But there was nothing of that nature between us, it was purely a matter of teacher and pupil."

I could see from Kitty's expression that she did not believe me. She continued: "Of course, if you do not *take* at your party on Monday – which you probably won't, as you are not very good at parties and flirting and meeting new people, although I will say that your dancing has improved - well, Mama might be so desperate that she would have to give her consent, and Papa wouldn't care one way or another who you marry, as long as he is not inconvenienced by it. I think it would be a very good match. Moretti is very handsome, he likes music and so do you, and he is not precisely poor even though he is not a member of the gentry. He could teach you to play better too!"

Kitty seemed to think that this was a very amusing notion, and went into peals of laughter. I tried to protest once more that there was nothing between Signor Moretti and me, but she only laughed all the harder.

Despite her endless teasing, I was glad that Kitty had arrived in time for the party. I had grown used to her ways of improving my appearance, and far preferred her ministrations to those of my mother. By the time she had finished with my hair and my sleeves and lent me her own pearl choker (artificial pearls, of course), I looked presentable enough even for Mama. We went down to the drawing room, where Mama was overseeing the final arrangements.

"I do not believe Mr Darcy will have any cause to complain," she said. "I have been down to the kitchen and everything is just as it should be. He will find that the beef is as tender and delicious as anything served at Pemberley, I am quite sure." She looked up at Kitty and me, and almost smiled. "You look very well, Mary, and you, Kitty. I need not feel any shame for my daughters tonight. But do raise your head, Mary, and for goodness' sake, Kitty, try not to giggle in that affected way of yours. Now come and look at the table, both of you."

All the best glassware and napery was on display, and it did indeed look very fine. The Darcys were to join us for dinner before most of the guests arrived, and a few friends had been invited to meet them. I was dreading seeing Mr Darcy again: our last meeting was seared on my memory and still caused me to wake up in the night, sweating and shaking.

Mama was counting the places, and muttering to herself about who was to sit where.

"Though why Elizabeth must needs bring that music teacher, I cannot for the life of me imagine," she said.

I gasped, and Kitty's elbow jabbed hard into my ribs.

"Let him sit next to Mary, Mama," she said, with false affability. "They can talk of music and you need not entertain him."

I looked fiercely at Kitty, but she only smiled.

"That will do very well," my mother said, as the bell clanged and the first guests arrived.

It was fortunate for me that the Lucases, the Summertons, and Aunt Philips had come before the Darcys arrived with Signor Moretti. I had installed myself on an out of the way sofa, and was talking to Maria, although I had been listening for the sound of a carriage and barely attending to her. I had perforce to look up when they came in, but only briefly met Signor Moretti's eye, before turning my attention to my sister and brother. Lizzy looked extremely well. There was a noticeable change to her figure now that the baby had grown larger, but she was as pretty as ever. I could hardly look at Darcy, but when I shook his hand, I risked a glance at his face, which, though serious was not angry. I hardly dared hope that I might be forgiven. He and Lizzy were soon surrounded by the other guests, and I saw with relief that my father took Signor Moretti to one side and was soon conversing quietly with him by the fireplace.

Nobody could have any idea of the tumult of feelings and memories that I was experiencing. It was so very painful to be in the room with the three people who knew the worst of what I had done, for I did not doubt that Darcy had informed Elizabeth of the full extent of my crimes against her. I was deeply ashamed; my folly and stupidity came rushing back into my mind with a terrible vividness, and I did not know how I would get through the evening and do all that my mother expected of me. When Signor Moretti approached me to lead me into dinner, I could barely speak. My mouth was dry and my legs felt weak.

At least he did not try to talk to me, but merely drew my arm through his and led me to the table. I did not know whether he meant to be kind or whether he simply could not bring himself to say anything to me, but either way I was grateful for the time to restore my composure. It was not until after the pigeons had been removed with some glazed carrots that I was able to talk, and then it was a bland question about his journey.

He answered that he was grateful to be able to come through Hertfordshire on his way to London, in the comfort of the Darcys' travelling carriage. "I have never visited this part of the world before, and was glad to be able to do so."

"Do you like the countryside here?" I asked.

"I have not yet seen it. Darcy has promised to take me about tomorrow if the weather is fine."

"How pleasant," I said, sounding stupid even to my own ears.

There was a longish silence.

"It was kind of your parents to allow me to come to this party in your honour."

"Yes. It is my first such party," I said, "and hopefully my last."

He looked at me quickly, but I stared resolutely at the table, though this was not necessarily the best idea, as my eye fell on his hands, and this brought back more disturbing memories.

"You do not like such parties?" he asked

"I am not fitted for such things," I mumbled. "I do not have the way of it."

He did not contradict me. After a pause he said,

"Will you play?"

"It is likely. Though there are musicians come from Hertford to accompany the dancing. My mother does not wish me to sit at the piano all evening."

He nodded. "I understand she wishes you to meet young men of your own class."

I did not reply to this. The gulf between us felt more insurmountable than ever. We fell into silence and Sir William Lucas, who was sitting on my other side, claimed my attention.

I did not have an opportunity to dance with Signor Moretti, as my mother had made sure that my hand was claimed by the various eligible men of the neighbourhood, young and old. But when I sat at the piano to play, he was at my side.

"Would you like me to turn for you?" he asked.

I blushed. "I have memorised the piece. It is - " I hesitated, "it is the Haydn Sonata you showed me at Pemberley."

His eyes widened and he made a movement towards me.

"Miss Bennet! Mary, I - "

I did not know what he would have said, because one of the young ladies came over to ask me if I could accompany her afterwards in some songs. Signor Moretti moved away.

◆

I began playing. Simply knowing that Signor Moretti was in the room strengthened my resolve and I found myself remembering many of the things he had said to me. My fingers did not fail me, and although at times I stumbled, and my hands occasionally felt as though they belonged to someone else, I played to the end of the movement without more than one or two wrong notes. There was enthusiastic applause as I finished, and I thought it was perhaps more genuine than on other occasions. My father approached the piano.

"You are much improved, child. Your lessons have done you good."

"Thank you, Papa. Miss Astley has requested me to accompany her in a song now."

"Very well, you may do so. You know, you will never equal your sisters Darcy and Bingley for charm and grace, but yes, much improved, Mary, much improved."

It was not the most fulsome of compliments, but coming from my father it was more than I had ever received before and I was conscious of it. I wanted to speak to Signor Moretti, and I hoped that he would have something to say to me, that he would know how I had taken his teaching to heart, but Miss Astley was placing her music before me and whispering nervously about repeats and tempo and I could do nothing about it.

After we had finished the song, and she had obliged the company with a second, which I played rather too fast, I went around the room looking for Signor Moretti.

Kitty saw what I was about.

"He has gone, Mary. He stayed to hear you, but then he left while Lucy Astley was singing. Lord, I wish *I* could have done so! Thank goodness the musicians are getting ready and we can dance again!"

A wave of disappointment hit me, hollowing out my stomach, and making me want to cry aloud, but the fiddles were striking up, and Maria Lucas's brother was before me, requesting the pleasure of the next two dances. I would have liked to refuse, but saw my mother's eyes upon me; there was nothing for it but to comply. At least she could not accuse me of not trying.

Later, when the musicians started a waltz, I was astonished to find Mr Darcy beside me, begging me for the honour of this dance. I barely had time to nod before he had taken my hand and we were turning about the room.

"But Eliza -" I said. "Does she not wish to waltz?"

"She cannot abide the turns at present, so you must recompense me, Mary! After all our lessons at Pemberley, I believe we shall show them the way at Longbourn!"

He was trying to put me at ease and I smiled dutifully, though I still felt all the pain of our last meeting at Pemberley. After a moment or two I realised that there was only one other couple dancing, Kitty, with a young man whose name I did not remember.

"Mr Darcy," I said, "you must know that you are infamous in Hertfordshire for your dislike of dancing. Everyone will wonder at you."

"It is possible for a person to change," he said quietly. "Do not you agree, Mary?"

I nodded, unable to speak. He must mean me; he must mean that he knew how much I regretted what I had done.

As though in confirmation of my thought, he said: "And Elizabeth expects you at the White Hart tomorrow afternoon. She wishes to speak privately to you. You will come?"

"Yes, of course." I was relieved to hear that she would be alone.

The dance came to an end, and we all applauded the musicians. The guests left and I retired to my room to reflect on the events of the evening. I was not to be left alone, as Kitty soon came in, carrying a pile of rags.

"Oh no, Kitty!"

"Yes, Mary, you must have your hair done again. You know if it is left it will be lank and straight tomorrow, and you are going to meet Lizzy at the White Hart, and no doubt Signor Moretti will be there, so you must look your best."

"He will not be there, Mr Darcy said Lizzy would see me alone."

"We shall see, we shall see. Now sit at the mirror."

There was nothing for it but to obey and I went to bed that night with my face stretched around my head and irritating little pulls where the rags were too tight. I did not dare interfere, however.

Next day, Kitty was determined to dress me.

"After all, this may be your only chance," she said. "You must look your best."

She had found a spencer of Jane's that had been left behind, and she changed the buttons on it and added some braid around the collar. She even sewed some buckles onto my shoes, and made a lace flower to pin into the small bun at the back of my hair. When I entered the White Hart, I was still as terrified as I had been of what the afternoon would bring, but feeling as though at least I looked passably well. More than my improved appearance, I felt gratitude to Kitty for her attentions to me, and that warmed me.

I was shown to a small parlour on the first floor, and there after a few moments Lizzy came to greet me, quite alone. There was nothing in her face to cause me anxiety: indeed, she was smiling and her eyes were bright with laughter. I was so relieved to see her alone that I returned her embrace with unusual ardour.

"Well, Mary, how lovely to see you again. You look very fine – oh, was that not Jane's jacket at one time? I detect Kitty's hand in the decoration of it – but you are pale! Are you well?"

"Yes, I am well. You look very well too, Lizzy. The party did not tire you too much?"

"Not I! Now, come and sit down and I will pour some tea while you tell me how you have been since you left Pemberley."

We sat, and Elizabeth looked at me expectantly. I stared stupidly at the tea tray.

"Lizzy," I blurted out, "why have you invited me here today so particularly? What is it you wish to discuss with me?"

"Quite a number of things, Mary. But I see you cannot be calm and chat about ordinary things until we have spoken of the reasons I wanted to see you without Mama." She poured us both tea. I was afraid to lift my cup and saucer as my hands might shake.

"Is Mr Darcy to join us?" I asked. I could not bring myself to mention Signor Moretti.

"No, he is out riding at the moment with Signor Moretti, showing him the country. I wanted to see you alone. You must know that Darcy told me about his conversation with you on the day before you left Pemberley for Longbourn."

I nodded.

"He told me that you had sent him an anonymous letter and that you had made various accusations about my dealings with Colonel Fitzwilliam."

I nodded again, unable to speak.

"You understand now that those suspicions were groundless, that my private discussions with the colonel were concerning his aspirations to Georgiana's hand?"

"Yes, yes, I know," I said, stammering as the words began to pour out of me. "Lizzy, I am sorry, I do not know how I could have been so foolish, so *base*, to think such things of you, and after all your kindness to me at Pemberley. You would never lie to Mr Darcy, I know that, I realise you love each other too much. I think I did not understand that, I *could* not understand it, all I could see was deception and intrigue and faithlessness and secrets. Of course you would not have secrets from Mr Darcy!"

Lizzy reached out her hand to me. "But I did have secrets from Mr Darcy, Mary, and I think you deserve to know. About the *nature* of the secrets you were wholly wrong, but I *was* deceiving him, and actually I am grateful to you, because your actions forced me to talk to him about those secrets and to return to a state of openness and trust once more. However mistaken you were in your suspicions, and wrong in your actions, much good has come from it."

"Good?" I cried. "How can there be good?"

Lizzy smiled. "I will tell you. I had two secrets from Mr Darcy, and both had come about because I had allowed myself to fall into a state of mind where I could no longer see clearly the man I had married. The first you know – Colonel Fitzwilliam fell in love with Georgiana and had reason to think his feelings were returned. He was afraid that Darcy would see him as a fortune hunter, and he could not bring himself to ask Darcy's permission to apply for Georgiana's hand for fear of refusal. I was advising him to wait his moment."

"Oh, Lizzy, I thought he was wanting to run away with *you!* What a dreadful misunderstanding!"

She laughed. "Indeed it was! But if I had trusted to Mr Darcy's sense of fairness and judgement of character, none of this would have happened. I ought to have encouraged Rowland to approach Darcy and be open with him from the first, instead of waiting for *the right time*, the propitious moment. *I* am as much at fault as you, Mary."

"No, no! You meant it for the best, whereas I, I meant nothing but mischief and self-righteousness. If only I had spoken to you!"

Lizzy smiled. "Yes, it would have helped if you had, and if only *I* had spoken to Mr Darcy!"

"And - they are to marry! They seemed to be very much in love."

I remembered with a sudden rush of shame, how I had observed them together and suspected the colonel of seducing *both* Elizabeth and Georgiana. I said nothing of this to Lizzy; I could not bear to be even more humiliated.

"Yes, they are to marry, but it is not known yet beyond our party at Pemberley. Darcy and I are going to Rosings after we have stayed in London to break the news to Lady Catherine ourselves."

"Oh Lizzy, must you? She was so unkind to you, she does not deserve such consideration."

"As to that, well, she is an elderly lady and Darcy's aunt. However misguided, she does care for the family and the family name, and it will be a shock and a disappointment to her that yet another Darcy is marrying into a lower stratum of society! After all, a younger son, even the younger son of an earl, is not sufficiently grand to satisfy *her* ambitions."

"She cannot *still* resent you," I said, "when she knows how happy Mr Darcy is, and you have even borne him a healthy son to carry on the family name!"

"Oh, I think she can bear a grievance for her life long with no let up of energy! She has great fortitude of mind, as she would tell you herself."

This made me laugh, and for a moment my own troubles were forgotten.

Elizabeth went on. "But there is another matter, Mary, and I suppose it links somewhat to Lady Catherine's belief that Darcy has married beneath him. I kept another secret from Darcy."

I had a flash of memory. "Is it to do with money?"

Lizzy looked at me in astonishment. "How did you know that?"

I blushed. "I'm afraid I was concealed in the library one day and overheard a conversation between you and Mr Darcy about money, something to do with you overspending your pin money."

Now Lizzy blushed. "Yes, that was not a good day. Again, if only I had not allowed myself to be beset by stupid worries, I would not have misjudged my husband." She became thoughtful. "You know, I think somewhere in my mind, Lady Catherine's prejudice towards me had had an effect. Without really knowing that I did so, I was worried that Darcy might share some part of that prejudice. I could not but be aware of how painful it had been for him to become, so to speak, the brother of Mr Wickham, whose dealings with Georgiana I think you now know. He had thought himself free of Wickham, so then to be tied once more to him by the indelible bonds of family, I felt must be a grief to him."

I nodded. "Yes, I understand. Georgiana told me what happened between them."

"She was very grateful to you for how you protected her from him, even before you knew her story. She has spoken of it a number of times. I was so proud of you when she told me of your consideration."

I shook my head, blushing. Nobody had ever said they were proud of me before.

"But what of the money?" I asked, eager both to change the subject and to hear the story.

"Do you remember when Wickham arrived at Pemberley unannounced?"

"Indeed I do! That was when I first noticed how he caused Georgiana such discomfiture."

"Well, up to that time he had been in prison for debt, owing something like £500. By careful management of the money Darcy gives me, I was able to pay off his debt and secure his release. Much as I dislike the way Lydia and Wickham live their lives, I could not stand by and let her and her children suffer so, especially when she was soon to deliver another child, or children as it turned out. And there was more to it than that: I felt ashamed for our family and I could not bear the disgrace it brought to the Darcys to be linked with such ignominy, and I felt for the distress of our mother. I knew she could never be at peace while Lydia was living in such difficult circumstances."

"Oh!" A thought had occurred to me. "Did Colonel Fitzwilliam discharge the debt for you?"

"Yes, he did. I thought, foolishly, that all could be managed without Mr Darcy having to be troubled by it. I think that of all the things I have done, my lack of trust in him in this matter has wounded him most."

Elizabeth's expression clouded.

"Oh, Lizzy, no! He cannot - you did not - you meant it for the best!"

"I did, but I was mistaken. His resentment of Wickham would never be such as to allow Lydia and her children to suffer. They are, after all, innocent in the matter."

"The children are," I said scornfully, "but not Lydia. She is as spendthrift and careless as Wickham. They will never amend their way of life, Lizzy."

"No, most likely not. But we must hope that this new venture may succeed. Darcy invited Mr Blackstone to Pemberley for a visit and found him a most sensible and prudent man. I think Darcy intends to keep a close eye on the business, and perhaps even invest in it himself."

"Well, that is most generous of him."

"Generous, yes, but not foolhardy. And so, Mary, you are now in full possession of the facts, and perhaps you may forgive yourself for some of your actions, knowing that you are not the only Bennet sister capable of making errors of judgement."

"Your errors do not compare to mine, Lizzy. You meant well and I simply deceived myself that I was doing good and promoting morality, because I could not allow you to be happy. You see? I am a truly dreadful person."

Lizzy came and sat beside me on the small sofa and put her arm around me.

"We are none of us without fault, Mary, and it is admirable in you that you have acknowledged your mistakes. You are quite changed, you know."

I shook my head but could not speak. Lizzy poured me a fresh cup of tea.

"And now, Mary, what of Signor Moretti?"

◆

"Signor Moretti?"

Elizabeth smiled knowingly. "Yes, sister, Signor Moretti. He will be returning soon from his ride, and I know he would like to speak with you."

"Oh Lizzy, no! I cannot bear it! He knows everything about me; he was there when I told Mr Darcy what I had done. He despises me, I know he does, and Lizzy – Lizzy, you do not know the worst! I kissed him!"

She stared at me in silence for a moment, and then burst out laughing.

"It is no laughing matter, Lizzy! I behaved disgracefully. I went to his room, I was *in his room*, and I threw myself at him."

"No wonder he is so eager to see you again! I am sure he is not in the habit of having young ladies throw themselves at him. But tell me more, Mary!"

"I cannot, Lizzy, it is all too dreadful. You see, I had to explain something to him, he saw - something. I did not want him to be thinking that - well, I ran to find him and he was in his room, and then – then, I do not know how it happened, I did not plan it, I did not even know that I wanted to. So you see, I cannot speak to him, I would not know what to say, and Lizzy, I dread what he might say to me."

"I do not think you need to dread what he has to say to you, Mary. He seems to me to be a man deeply in love."

My hands flew to my face. "No! He cannot be! You cannot know that!"

"Perhaps you might allow that I know something more of these matters than you, Mary. I think he wishes to pay his addresses to you."

"Oh Lizzy, I could not marry him. He knows – he knows everything about me, all the abominable things I did, and not only that -" I stopped myself quickly.

"What, Mary? Did something happen at Pemberley? Darcy noticed something, and I have long had an inkling that you had a secret of some sort, something perhaps to do with Wickham?"

She saw me blush and went on. "I suspected something when Mr Speedwell behaved so out of character and hit Wickham. Will you not tell me, Mary dear? Please believe me that you will not shock me."

"I suppose nothing Wickham does can surprise anyone now," I said bitterly, "He might be expected to sink to any depths." I thought for a moment or two, then resolved to speak. "Do you remember when I fell downstairs? It *was* because of Wickham – I saw him on the servants' stairs, he was kissing a housemaid, and I was so angry with him, I said I would tell Lydia. The maid ran away, and Wickham – he kissed me, Lizzy. I could not get away. He said he would tell people that *I* had kissed *him*, I did not know what to do, I was so ashamed."

Her face betrayed nothing but compassion, no judgement, no mockery. "Oh, poor Mary! What a tangle! And you did not tell me! I wish you had: nobody would have believed Wickham over you! I would have sent him away, and I know Darcy would too."

"I did not want to cause trouble. I was mortified when Mr Speedwell guessed that something had happened."

Lizzy started laughing. "I do not mean to make light of it, Mary, but when I think back to that moment when Mr Speedwell hit Wickham, I cannot help laughing. Nothing so fantastic or hilarious has ever happened at Pemberley before. It was almost funnier than when Darcy and Signor Moretti fell in the stream during the storm."

Lizzy's laughter infected me, and suddenly I could see how funny it was, that Mr Speedwell, a peaceful man of the church and a polished member of society, should out of the blue punch a man in the face, causing consternation to everyone gathered there, including Lydia's case of hysterics. We collapsed into laughing.

"But Lizzy," I said eventually, "the thing is, Wickham did it again – when I rescued Georgiana as she called it. I was left alone with him, he cornered me, and then Signor Moretti came in and saw, and he thought, he thought *that* of me!"

"Oh no, Mary, I am sure he did not. More likely he was too jealous to see clearly at all."

"Jealous? You cannot mean it! He was – he was *disgusted* by me. And then I went and kissed *him!* He must have thought I was the very worst kind of woman, no better than Lydia!"

"I am sure he did not think so, dearest Mary," Lizzy said, laughing again. "He is a man of the world, you know, he is accustomed to moving in all the first circles, *and* in the world of the theatre."

"Yes, and both those parts of society are full of wanton women. And now he will think I am just one of them, and not only that, that I am a coward, a sneak, and a slanderer."

The window to the parlour where we sat was open, and there was all at once a commotion outside of horses, grooms, and then distinctly, the voice of Mr Darcy.

"They are back!" I whispered. "They are back! He must not find me here. Is there another door? Where can I hide myself?"

Lizzy took my hands. "Be calm, do be calm, dear Mary! I will stay with you, we will talk like rational people and all will be well. Now compose yourself."

"Please, Lizzy, no, I do not wish to meet him! I cannot!"

But it was too late. There was nothing for it, no escape. I had to go through with it. I took a deep breath hoping to still the rapid beating of my heart. Lizzy rang the bell, and the door was opened by a maid. Behind her came Mr Darcy and Signor Moretti. We stood up and I managed an awkward, curtsey. The maid was instructed to bring tea and cold drinks, and the gentlemen came and sat opposite us on the two easy chairs.

"How nice to see you again, Mary," Mr Darcy said. "I trust you have experienced no ill effects from your exertions last night?"

I nodded, unable to speak. Without looking I could tell that Signor Moretti's eyes were upon me.

"Did you have a pleasant ride?" Elizabeth asked. "I shall be very disappointed if you do not tell me that the Hertfordshire scene is as fine as any in England, Signor Moretti."

"I am obviously loth to disappoint you, Mrs Darcy, but how am I to say so without insulting the country at Derbyshire?"

"Very true," Lizzy replied, "you cannot possibly return a satisfactory answer. Where did you ride?" she asked her husband.

"I took Moretti past Longbourn and almost to Netherfield. After that we went to admire the view from Oakham Mount, and had a decentish gallop across the commons above Sir William Lucas's land. I say 'decentish' but I have never ridden such a dreadful animal in my life and hope never to do so again! Moretti fared no better."

"Indeed," said Signor Moretti, "it was not a comfortable ride, but it is pleasant to be riding out in open country, and I will have few opportunities for any such rides when I return to London. The opera season is about to begin at the King's."

I had recovered sufficient composure during this conversation to speak. "Will you be conducting many operas this year?" I asked, daring to meet his eyes at last.

"Yes I will, Miss Bennet. I am engaged for the whole season. Our first performance will be Orfeo, and rehearsals have already begun. Perhaps you might come to London and see it?"

"I do not think Mama would allow it. I am – I am much needed here at Longbourn," I stammered, embarrassment overcoming me.

Elizabeth rose. "Darcy, would you be so kind as to accompany me to my room? I fear I am more fatigued than I knew, and I would be glad of a rest before supper."

Mr Darcy stood up at once. "Of course! Here, take my arm."

I looked meaningly at Elizabeth: what was she doing? She had promised she would stay with me. She did not meet my eye, but I was convinced that I saw an expression of mischief on her face. There was nothing I could do to stop her. The Darcys left the room.

Signor Moretti had stood up politely as the Darcys left. Then he turned, irresolute, and I thought he was wondering whether to sit beside me on the small sofa. I stared at my feet and sat on my hands to stop them shaking.

"So," he said, and I noticed his voice was not so gravely in his command as usual, "did you enjoy your party last night, Miss Bennet?"

"Um yes, I think so."

There was a long and agonising silence.

"You did not stay for long," I said at last.

"No. But I heard you perform. You played very well."

I blushed. "I – I had been practising it very slowly as you advised, only Mama does not like it when I repeat the same thing too many times, so I have to wait till she is out of the house which is difficult as she wants me to go about with her, to meet people and develop company manners, which she says I have not, which I know is true, I do not know how to go on at all. Um..."

I ran out of things to say, but it did not signify, because Signor Moretti crossed the room, and all in a moment was sitting beside me and had taken my hands. I could not speak for shock, but gaped at him, and tried half-heartedly to pull my hands away. He would not release me, however. Instead he reached around me and pulled me against him. Then he kissed me, his lips pressed very firmly onto mine, his hand cradling my head. I made some sort of squeak of protest, but it was neither very loud nor very earnest and it had no effect at all, mainly because I had thrown my arms around his neck and was returning his kiss with ardour. I did not stop until I needed to breathe.

Part Fifteen: The Proposal

◆

We looked into each other's eyes. Both of us were breathing fast; my own face was hot and flushed; Signor Moretti's rather pale. He spoke first.

"Mary, please marry me and come and live with me in London."

I pulled away from him with a start. "You cannot mean it," I said. "You cannot truly want me."

He looked at me seriously. "I am not in the habit of proposing marriage to ladies I do not wish to marry."

"Now you are making fun of me! I do not mean to doubt you, but you *know* me, you *know* what a horrible person I am, how stupid, how vain, how unkind, you know what I did, the letter I wrote to Mr Darcy. I *wanted* you to know, I wanted you to know the truth, and not be deceived by – by – by passion, by that kiss in your room."

"But I wasn't deceived by that kiss, it only confirmed what I was already feeling." He took my hand again but I snatched it away, stood up and began pacing the room.

"But Signor Moretti -"

"Antonio -"

"No - no, I can never call you that. Signor Moretti, you – you have been married, you were married to another musician like yourself, a woman of real talent, and no doubt she was beautiful and charming too. How can you now think you could be content with me? I am no musician, as you know yourself. I am not pretty, I have no address, I have no figure, I certainly have no fortune. You could marry a wealthy woman, she could be your patroness, and help you make your mark in the world."

He laughed. "But Mary, I have no need of a wealthy patroness. If my circumstances concern you, or you think your parents might be concerned for you, I can assure you that I am perfectly well-to-do, with more work than I can manage and a small house in a pleasant though unfashionable part of London. As for making my mark in the world, I flatter myself that I *am* making my mark, and doing work that I enjoy and have a talent for, and am getting well paid for. I am no virtuoso, nor a great composer, but I am much in demand as teacher, pianoforte player in the opera orchestras and conductor at the opera."

"Oh! But what of your family? What would they think?"

"When they know how happy you make me they will be happy for me. They will be pleased that I have found someone to love again at last."

"Oh no no no!" I said, bursting into tears. "How can you love such a person as I am?"

He got up and crossed the room, taking me into his arms again. "It's not easy to explain these things but I will try. I am not blind, but although I saw all your pride and self-righteousness, I also saw your regret, I saw how you changed. Last night, when you played the Haydn, and played it so well, I could see how much work you had done, how you had abandoned all stubbornness and allowed yourself to learn from me in our lessons. I think it was those things – watching the ice that encased you begin to melt, seeing you start to blossom and take pleasure in life, seeing you change from a – a – shrivelled waif, pinched and starved of affection, to the vital, feeling woman that I hold now in my arms. It – it moved me, and I found myself drawn towards you more and more. Now please stop crying and try to believe that I mean what I say, and there is no difficulty to overcome on my side. If you return my affection, that is -"

"I do, I do," I cried, holding him close to me and surreptitiously wiping my tears on his lapel. He immediately bent his head and kissed me again.

"Well then, since you *do* return my affection, will you marry me?"

"I do not know what my parents will say."

"No, they may think a mere musician is not fit to marry their daughter. Specially since your mother has gathered all the most eligible young men of the country to present themselves for your inspection."

"Fortunately, none of them were at all interested in me."

He laughed, then said more seriously, "You have not answered my question yet, Mary."

"I would be the most dreadful wife, you know."

He pulled me closer. "I do not think it." He reached down to kiss me again but I stopped him.

"I do not know if I can be married," I whispered. "I do not know how to do it."

"You would learn. If we love each other -"

"You must be mad."

"No, Mary, I am not mad. Nor will I go mad if you refuse me, but I will be deeply disappointed."

I was overcome with agitation. "I do not know! I do not know! I am afraid, afraid that I would spoil everything, that you might love me now but it would fade and then we would be stuck with one another and become bitter and cruel to each other."

"That could happen, I suppose. It is a risk to throw in our lot with each other. Marriage is always a risk, more for you than for me."

"What do you mean?"

"I was thinking of childbirth. If we were to have children – well, think of what happened to Isabella – there are many dangers."

"Good god, the thought of being a mother! I cannot even imagine being a *wife!*"

"I wish you would *try* to imagine it. I can certainly imagine being your husband."

We were silent for a few minutes. I was lost in thought, trying to understand my heart. I knew I loved him - at least, I thought that was what the feeling was. I did not have anything to compare it with: I had never been in love before, never even really looked at a man as a man, except I suppose my sisters' husbands, but only because their marriages forced the thought into my consciousness. And yet here I was, in the crook of his arm, leaning against him, feeling comfortable and strangely at home.

But how could I trust my own judgement? I was so wrong about everything, perhaps this feeling was simply another of my delusions, another false belief in something that I wanted to be true. I tried to imagine being married to Signor Moretti. I had a picture in my head of his house; it might be pleasant and welcoming, but there would be servants to manage, I would have to order food for our dinner, tell the housekeeper to air the sheets. I would have to have dresses made for me and choose what fabrics and trimmings to have. So many things I would have to decide for myself that I had never given a thought to. And children! I did not know how to look after a child! True, I had had some success with Jane's daughter Sophia, and with Meg Heely, but an infant was a different matter. Then I remembered how little Henry Bingley had cried and cried, and how eventually I had comforted him. Could I do that, again and again? Could I be calm like Jane, playful like Lizzy? I did not think so. At least I would not be like Lydia, of that I was sure.

And then there was the making of the babies. Of course I knew how that happened, I was no ignorant schoolgirl, but could I, *Mary Bennet*, actually do such a thing? I remembered Wickham kissing me, his wicked tongue and his roving hands; I remembered my shameful feelings, half pleasure, half disgust, the strange excitement that rushed through my body despite my horror and fear, how I had been compelled by some inner dynamism to go to Signor Moretti's room, to kiss him. I looked at Signor Moretti. Would we sleep in the same bed? What would he think when he saw my puny body without even the poor disguises of my wardrobe? I knew he wanted me *now*: I did not have to be Kitty to sense his warmth for me. But would he want me when he saw me? Would he go on wanting me once he had me, when the novelty wore off?

He returned my gaze. "What is it, Mary? What are you thinking?"

I blushed hotly. "Nothing particular."

"Cannot you tell me?"

I shook my head vigorously. "Not possibly."

He laughed. "It must be something very particular, if you are so adamant that it cannot be spoken."

"Yes it is, *extremely* particular. Do not question me, please. Signor Moretti, I keep saying this, but it is true: I do not know what I think or feel, or how to act. I think I must speak to my parents. I need time."

He took both my hands in his and held them tightly. "I can give you time to think. But tomorrow I must return to London, as I am wanted at rehearsals."

"I will be able to answer you then. I am sorry to be so – so prevaricating. I had better call for the carriage," I said. He rang for the servant and gave the necessary instructions while I tied the strings of my bonnet. We stood apart now, and I turned away as the treacherous tears started to fall yet again. The servant returned to announce that the carriage awaited me, and we walked downstairs together. Signor Moretti handed me in and stood with his hand on the door.

"I hope to hear from you soon, Mary. And do not cry. Please do not cry."

◆

As soon as I reached home, I ran up to my room and disobeyed Signor Moretti by crying my eyes out for a good half hour. My curls, my lovely dress, were all forgotten as I lay in a heap on my bed. I was sitting up and mopping my eyes when Kitty burst in without knocking.

"Mary! Why did you not tell me you were home? When I have been waiting to hear this last hour! Well? What happened? Did he propose?"

I nodded. Kitty sat beside me and embraced me, something she had never done before.

"You goose! Did you say yes?"

"No!" I wailed. "I did not know what to say. I said I would think about it."

"Oh, Mary! You really are a goose! There is nothing to think about. He wants you, and you have a chance of escape."

"But what about Mama! How would she manage without me? She would not let me marry a man of his standing!"

"I should think she would be relieved to see you married to anyone. You must marry, you cannot remain a spinster. And you do like him, don't you? You know you do."

"Yes, yes, I do, but - oh I don't know, Kitty. I think I am not meant to be married. I would not know how to go on!"

"Oh, nonsense! You would soon learn. Anyone can keep house, it is not difficult. Just think, to be free, to have your own home, not to be at Mama's beck and call. And I am sure Signor Moretti would not object to your playing the piano all the hours there are. Why would you hesitate? You are hardly likely to receive another offer, despite Mama's efforts with this party."

"I know, I know! Oh Kitty! How would I live? I do not know anyone in London, what should I do all day?"

"Why, much as you do here, dawdle around the house, go for walks, play the piano, and on top of that, deal with the servants and the shopping. Signor Moretti is not rich so you will have to do more housework than you are used to. And you could take pupils you know, now that you have been teaching Sophy. And no doubt he has friends and family, you would be for ever meeting musicians, and going to soirées, and family gatherings: these Italians always have hundreds of brothers and sisters."

"I do not know. He has never mentioned them. You see? I know nothing about him!"

Kitty scoffed. "You know he is a nice man who loves you and wishes to marry you. What else do you need? Darcy and Elizabeth like him, he has been Georgie's teacher all this time, he must be a decent man otherwise it would be known by now."

"I suppose you are right. But Kitty, I should be frightened to run a house. And what of – well, you know, marital relations?"

"If Lydia can work that out, you can. Any animal can do it, just follow his lead."

I looked at her in astonishment. "How do you *know* things like that, Kitty? You haven't...?

"No, of course I haven't. You only have to keep your eyes and ears open to pick up any amount of knowledge and tips. And Lydia will say anything, she is so immodest. You would scarcely believe what she has told me."

"Oh, Kitty!"

"Never mind oh Kitty. How would it be, if once you are returned from your bridal trip, I come and stay with you for a few weeks? I will be able to see the sights and join in the London season to some degree, though I am sure Signor Moretti does not exactly move in the highest levels of society, and I could help you set up house and deal with servants and all that sort of thing? It would suit me very well to come and stay in London, and I could be of great assistance to you in all these matters and keep you company while your husband was at work."

"My husband! How strange that sounds!"

Kitty laughed. "It does sound strange! How can it be that you of all people have caught a husband before me? I am sure nobody would have predicted it."

"No, indeed! But I have not finally decided, and I would need Mama's permission."

"If Papa gives his permission, you have no need of Mama."

"But I could not marry without her blessing."

"Then let us go find her now."

"I had better speak to her alone, I think. Oh Kitty, am I really going to do this?"

"Yes, of course you are! Why would you not? Since the party Mama will see that her schemes are quite hopeless, and she will be grateful that you are to marry somebody, even if it is only Georgiana Darcy's music teacher."

"He is not just a music teacher to fine ladies, you know. He is much in demand at the Opera."

This made Kitty laugh. "Well, well, sister dear, I believe you *are* rather in love with our Italian friend. You sound quite hot in his defence."

My interview with Mama did not go well. She was in her bedroom with every undergarment that she owned laid out on the bed. Hill was with her and they were trying to decide which pieces could be saved or mended or altered for other purposes.

"What is it, Mary? Can you not see I am busy?"

"I need to talk to you alone."

"Oh, what now? Off you go, Hill, I shall call you in a moment or two."

Hill left, and I sat down on the bed.

"Not there, child! Now look what you have done, I shall have to start again. Oh, you are vexing!"

This was not a promising start.

"Mama, I have met someone."

"What? Don't be ridiculous! Who is it?"

"It is Signor Moretti, who came to the party last night. He taught Georgiana Darcy, and me." Her face was a mask of shock but I stumbled on. "Mama, he – he loves me and he wishes to marry me."

"Loves you? I should think he does not! A music master? A child of mine to marry a music master? I can well believe he says he loves you, what nonsense! He is aiming far above his station if he thinks he can wed a Bennet of Longbourn! What can you be thinking of? Oh, I shall have hysterics if you mention another word of this ever again! After all my efforts, she thinks she can marry a music master!"

"Mama, please, he is - Mr Darcy holds him in very high esteem, he counts him as a friend."

"Mr Darcy can be friends where he chooses and nobody think any the worse of him, but you to be the wife, the wife of a *music* master. It is unthinkable. You will sink so low nobody will recognise you."

"Lower than Lydia and Wickham?" I said before I could help myself.

"Do not mention your dear sister's name! Oh, my nerves, my nerves, my tic is returning, just when I was starting to feel better." She rang the bell. "Go to your room, Mary, and never speak of this again. Impossible, ridiculous girl!"

I fled.

When I told Kitty of what had happened, she was not cast down.

"You must tell Signor Moretti to go to Papa directly," she said. "Papa will do anything for peace, so he will not refuse his permission. And you are of age, so it doesn't signify anyway. Write to Signor Moretti at the White Hart and ask him to call tomorrow."

"He is returning to London tomorrow, it will be too late."

"Then write to him today! He must come at once!"

I did as she said, and before very long we were rewarded by the sound of carriage wheels outside the house. It was the Darcys' travelling carriage and I was astonished to see both Darcys as well as Signor Moretti climb out and come to the front door. Kitty nodded with satisfaction.

"Mama is still in awe of Mr Darcy and she will not go her length if he is here."

We went downstairs to greet them. Lizzy came straight to me and took my hands, her eyes alight with pleasure. She embraced me, and over her shoulder I saw Signor Moretti. His smile was reassuring.

Lizzy led me into the drawing room.

"Mary, Moretti has told us everything, and he is to ask our father's permission to wed you. But Darcy and I will go first and talk to Papa. Even though you are of age, it would be best if all is done properly, and Darcy and I believe that if we vouch for Signor Moretti, Papa will not refuse his consent."

"I spoke to Mama," I whispered, "she was like to fall into a fit!"

Lizzy laughed. "Never mind, she will come round when our father consents. She will be so happy to have you married, and when she realises you are not to be a pauper, that will give relief to her mind."

◆

Darcy beckoned to Elizabeth, and she followed him to the library, leaving me with Signor Moretti and Kitty. Kitty simpered, but Signor Moretti and I were both too embarrassed, and too nervous of the forthcoming interview with my father, to be able to speak at all.

It felt like an age, but was only ten minutes by the clock, until Elizabeth and Mr Darcy returned. Mr Darcy nodded to Signor Moretti, and showed him the way to the library. I looked a question at Lizzy. She nodded.

"All is well, Mary, Papa had no objections, once we told him of Signor Moretti's character, and his circumstances in life. In a moment, you must go in to him, and I will go and speak to Mama. Where is she?"

"Laid down upon her bed, of course!" said Kitty scornfully. "She is utterly prostrated and has a headache and I know not how many spasms."

"She will soon be on her feet again," Lizzy said. "I will invite her and Aunt Philips to Pemberley for a long visit this summer. Lydia will be staying for a while, and they can come and worship the babies to their hearts' content." She smiled. "Pemberley is a large house, after all."

She went away just as Signor Moretti came back.

"Your father wishes to speak to you in the library, Mary," he said. He squeezed my hand as I passed him.

My father was standing by his desk, a small glass of wine in his hand. I looked at him fearfully but his expression was benign.

"Well, Mary, it appears I am to drink your health. You have inconvenienced me extremely, for now who is to look after your mother and keep her company? I was quite reliant on you to remain a spinster for the rest of your life. Still, there is nothing for it, we shall have to invite my sister Philips to come and live with us."

"I am sorry, Papa," I stuttered.

"Oh, do not fret, child, I am teasing you. You have done very well for yourself. I did notice quite a change come over you after your time at Pemberley this spring, but I had no notion you were courting the music master! You have hidden depths, Mary."

I did not know how to reply, but my father was quite happy to talk at length.

"Of course I have given my permission," he said. "He seems a very pleasant fellow, and the recommendation of the Darcys is not to be taken lightly. I wondered at the improvement in your playing last night, but now all has been made clear. Well, well, come and embrace me. I shall look forward to giving you away as soon as it can be arranged. But you will not be rich like your sisters, you know."

"I know. I do not consider it."

"You will, believe me. We shall just have to hope that he becomes director of the Opera or some such. And you will do me a great kindness if you take your sister Kitty with you to London. I cannot have her drooping about the house and nagging me for entertainment. I'm sure you will be able to find a juggler or a chimney sweep amongst your husband's acquaintance for Kitty to marry."

I did not think my mother's change of heart would be so easily accomplished, despite Lizzy's sanguine assurances. However, I had reckoned without the authority of Mr Darcy, and also how much it meant to her to have a daughter married. She came downstairs for tea and there was nothing remaining of the fury I had seen earlier.

"My dear, dear Mary, you clever little thing," she cried, flinging her arms about me, "And you, sir," she turned to Signor Moretti, offering him her hand. "Oh! How very tall you are! I did not realise you were so tall."

"There is no accounting for it," he said. "My parents are both of rather small stature, but my brothers and sisters and I are all tall. I think it must be the air of England that agrees with us."

My mother laughed. "I should think it is so much better than the air of Italy."

"I could not say; I have never been to Italy."

"Never been? But how can this be?"

"I was born in London, and have never had cause to travel. I would like to go one day."

"Sit beside me and let me become more acquainted with you. My daughter Darcy tells me you are known to Lord Cottrell. I knew him many years ago when he was a mere Mr Gilbert and there was no thought of him coming into the title. I expect he is very grand nowadays."

I saw Signor Moretti raise his eyebrows at Lizzy, before obeying my mother's command and sitting next to her. "I am fortunate enough to count Lord Cottrell amongst my patrons. He is a great enthusiast of the opera and a fine singer himself."

Kitty and I sat in the window seat.

"I am so *happy* for you, Mary. He is so handsome and kind and hard-working, how fortunate you are!"

"Dear Kitty!"

She laughed. "I can tell you are in love, for you never would have said Dear Kitty before!" She whispered in my ear: "He has won Mama over. I cannot think what Lizzy said to persuade her!"

"Nor I!"

Lizzy came over to us.

"Content, Mary?"

"I – I think so. I think so indeed."

She took my hand. "He is a good and kind man, and it is my belief you will be very happy together. You will always be welcome to visit us at Pemberley, you know."

"Thank you, Lizzy. And thank you for all your care of me. If you had not had the idea to ask Signor Moretti to teach me, then none of this would have happened."

She laughed. "Yes, I will take all the credit with pleasure. And now, Kitty, it is your turn. You cannot stay at Longbourn for ever you know."

"Certainly not!"

"I did think young Mr Carding was growing rather particular in his attentions."

Kitty made a face. "Yes, he was, but I do not think I wish to marry him. I would have to live with his parents and that I could not abide. No, I have made a plan. I am to go to London with Mary! I will keep house for her and show her how to go on so that she does not end up in the poor house, and I am sure I will meet an eligible man somehow or other. For with all my sisters *and* Georgiana married, I *must* get myself a husband as soon as possible!"

THE END

Acknowledgements

The author would like to acknowledge her debt of gratitude to the following:

Jane Austen, particularly for *Pride and Prejudice, Emma* and *Northanger Abbey*.

Mrs. Gaskell, for *North and South*.

Charlotte Brontë, for *Jane Eyre*.

Georgette Heyer, for everything.

Random people on the internet who have done all the research already.

History, for taking liberties with it to suit the needs of the plot.

The ladies of Eek, my writing group – Karin Dixon Wilkins, Constance Fleuriot and Hazel Grian – who have been unfailingly supportive, insightful, and have just been there.

My daughter Molly Jamieson, whose idea it was in the first place, and for her fantastic editing and writing tips.

My bloke, for lovely dinners, tolerance – and the rest.

And my mother, to whom this book is lovingly dedicated.

I hope you enjoyed *Becoming Mary*. Why not leave a review at your favourite retailer such as Amazon US or Amazon UK!

I welcome contact from readers. At my website you can contact me, read my blog, and find me on social networking:

https://amystreetauthor.wordpress.com/

- Amy Street

Made in the USA
Middletown, DE
16 February 2018